FIRS✝
BLOOD

SUSAN SIZEMORE

ERIN McCARTHY

CHRIS MARIE GREEN

MELJEAN BROOK

B
BERKLEY BOOKS, NEW YORK

THE BERKLEY PUBLISHING GROUP
Published by the Penguin Group
Penguin Group (USA) Inc.
375 Hudson Street, New York, New York 10014, USA
Penguin Group (Canada), 90 Eglinton Avenue East, Suite 700, Toronto, Ontario M4P 2Y3, Canada
(a division of Pearson Penguin Canada Inc.)
Penguin Books Ltd., 80 Strand, London WC2R 0RL, England
Penguin Group Ireland, 25 St. Stephen's Green, Dublin 2, Ireland (a division of Penguin Books Ltd.)
Penguin Group (Australia), 250 Camberwell Road, Camberwell, Victoria 3124, Australia
(a division of Pearson Australia Group Pty. Ltd.)
Penguin Books India Pvt. Ltd., 11 Community Centre, Panchsheel Park, New Delhi—110 017, India
Penguin Group (NZ), 67 Apollo Drive, Rosedale, North Shore 0632, New Zealand
(a division of Pearson New Zealand Ltd.)
Penguin Books (South Africa) (Pty.) Ltd., 24 Sturdee Avenue, Rosebank, Johannesburg 2196,
South Africa

Penguin Books Ltd., Registered Offices: 80 Strand, London WC2R 0RL, England

This is a work of fiction. Names, characters, places, and incidents either are the product of the authors' imagination or are used fictitiously, and any resemblance to actual persons, living or dead, business establishments, events, or locales is entirely coincidental. The publisher does not have any control over and does not assume any responsibility for author or third-party websites or their content.

FIRST BLOOD

A Berkley Book / published by arrangement with the authors

PRINTING HISTORY
Berkley edition / August 2008

ISBN: 978-0-425-22400-7

BERKLEY®
Berkley Books are published by The Berkley Publishing Group,
a division of Penguin Group (USA) Inc.,
375 Hudson Street, New York, New York 10014.
BERKLEY® is a registered trademark of Penguin Group (USA) Inc.
The "B" design is a trademark belonging to Penguin Group (USA) Inc.

PRINTED IN THE UNITED STATES OF AMERICA

10 9 8 7 6 5 4 3 2 1

CONTENTS

Cave Canem

✝

SUSAN SIZEMORE

*This is for all those people who've e-mailed me asking,
"When's the next Laws of the Blood book out?"* . . .

Oпe

This is the tradition concerning hellhounds:
Survive a year and the beast is yours.

"YOU MUST PROTECT MY BABY." SYRILLA PUT HER hand on her swollen belly, and grimaced. "The babies. There's more than one, I'm certain."

"It is not possible for the child to be mine," Corvei said to his former lover. "You know that."

He'd been surprised to find her waiting for him in the small garden of his villa when he stepped outside to take the evening air. Not so long ago finding her there was what he expected every night but the three around the full moon. Their passion had cooled when his own existence changed, but he still looked upon her as a friend.

"The last time we met was at a feast here five months hence," he reminded her. He remembered the night well, and how Syrilla had paid more attention to the newly acquired war dog he'd showed off to his guests than she had to any human at the banquet. "You came with your husband that evening, and left with him. I know very well that nothing happened between us that night. Nor could anything have come of it if there had. You know what I am."

Her eyes burned with feverish anguish. "And you know what I am."

She glanced away. Everything about her spoke of guilt, and dread. The hand clutching her belly was pale with tension. She had grown thin but for the roundness of her abdomen. Her beautiful full lips were pressed tightly into a thin line, as though she was holding back a secret she could hardly bear.

He was certain her attitude was not because she had betrayed her husband with yet another man. She could easily make Patrius believe any child she bore belonged to him. No, this fear was for something far more serious than infidelity, nothing to do with the life she lived as a Roman matron. It was something from her other life, one he knew far less about than the daylight face she turned to the world.

Corvei went to her and took her hands in his, though even with his strength it took an effort to pry the one protecting the babe away from her belly. Her skin felt dry and feverish. He drew her to sit next to him on the bench near the fountain. The spraying water cooled the evening breeze that touched them. They gazed together into the fountain pool.

"Tell me," he said after they had sat silently for some time.

"It is hard to speak of, even to you."

"You had best find the words if I am to be of help."

A sideways glance showed him that she was crying. This was the most shocking sight of all, for Syrilla had always been so strong, so confident in her place and in her power. He would never forget the alabaster serenity of her expression the first time he had seen her. How she sat in the stands and watched a beast hunt in the arena with her hands folded in her lap, not joining in the howling enthusiasm of the crowd. He'd never taken notice of any of the spectators until the day he saw her. His gaze kept going back to the woman above him even though he knew distraction could bring him death. His main battle ended up just below where she sat. It was as though he'd made the kill for her alone and she leaned forward to intensely watch. She'd been close enough for a spray of blood to splash across the front of her silk gown when his spear took the giant wolf he'd been stalking. She hadn't flinched when the wolf leapt toward her. Nor did she take any notice of the gore that stained her clothes. She had smiled and nodded, like a goddess accepting the sacrifice he presented.

He'd found out her name and sent her the tanned wolf skin and a length of dearly bought silk. She'd come to his bed, for it was easy for a wealthy woman to bribe her way into the locked cell of even the lowliest and roughest gladiator.

It was only much later, after he was granted not only freedom but a totally new life that he discovered the wolf he had killed was her own brother. Her only comment had been, "He should not have gotten caught."

Werewolves were pitiless when one of the pack failed them. Syrilla's brother had been a casualty of a feud with a dark wizard. His own kindred had sent him to die when the wizard trapped him in his wolf form.

Corvei began to have an inkling of why she was afraid now. "What have you done against the pack?"

She turned her head away and mumbled, "I don't understand myself." She rubbed her belly as she spoke. "The call to mate that night was something I couldn't fight. I barely remember it." She swept a hand around the garden. "But it happened here. This is where the heat took me, and where—"

"This is something to do with your child, then?"

"Children. Pups." She spit the second word. "I hate what crawls inside me—but I love them, too."

She was not one to love easily. He'd never heard that word from her in all the years he'd known her, living and dead, as lover and then as friend.

She grasped his hand so tightly the bones would have broken if he was not what he was. "This is your responsibility, too," she said. A snarl escaped her throat. "You and that cursed beautiful war hound of yours."

What she meant came to him then, shocking him too much for words. She had not mated with one of his guests, but . . .

"Uhh . . ."

Revulsion roiled through him though he'd thought he'd seen and done every dark thing imaginable, even more as a gladiator than as a vampire.

He recalled how proudly he'd showed the dog off at the feast. He called it Beast, and it was as square-built and hard-muscled as any gladiator, with a huge, heavy jaw and sleek black fur that gleamed in the torchlight. He'd acquired the dog to guard his crypt through the hours of daylight, a trustworthy companion since he wanted no mortal slaves.

"A beautiful animal," Syrilla said. "Animal." The word was as bitter as poison from her mouth.

Corvei made himself look into her eyes. He would not normally have been able to look into her soul, but all her guards were down. Or perhaps she was acting, because of course she was attempting to manipulate him. He didn't mind that. One always had to play to win, and the stakes were always life and death, even the times when they didn't seem to be. Syrilla was a high-born Roman matron as well as a werewolf, both those birthrights sent the will for power and dominance flowing through her veins.

Her fear was real, even if she used it as a weapon. He saw it in her eyes, felt it in her mind and heart and soul. It truly was a mother's fear for her unborn babe. Babes.

"Pups," he said. He might have thrown back his head and laughed had the truth not been so horrible. "You mated with my war hound?" he shouted. "It's a dog's get in your belly?"

She shuddered, and made a shushing gesture. She stood, suddenly as stately as the Chief Vestal. "Protect my offspring. I require this of you. You know my own kind will destroy them as an abomination if they discover them."

And perhaps the werewolves would be right. "They'll destroy you as well if they find out."

"I'll take care of myself. You take care of my babes. Hide them. Keep them safe. This I require of you."

He stood as well. "You're calling in your debt, then?"

"I am."

Syrilla had saved his life while in her wolf form in his mortal days, when he'd been on a dangerous errand for the vampire woman who turned him. He had sworn to repay her, and now was the time. He also supposed he bore some responsibility for her offspring, since what had sired them belonged to him.

"What am I supposed to do with a litter of puppies?" he demanded.

She didn't answer. He thought for a long time, coming to only one conclusion. Finally, he gave her what she wanted. "I'll keep my vow to you. I'll protect your children."

I have to talk to Valentia, he thought.

Two

"And so began the race of hellhounds," Dan Conover murmured as though he was ending a fairy tale.

As the vivid memory faded Dan realized his eyes were closed. He felt like he'd been sleeping, although it was the middle of the night. He looked up at what few stars he could see in the sky over Phoenix from his backyard and wondered why he could still smell the night-blooming flowers in his Roman garden. Some of those flowers no longer existed in this modern world. He took a few deep breaths. Yes, there were definitely aromas swirling on the breeze that didn't belong in this cool desert air.

And the sky didn't look right, either.

It took him a few more seconds to recognize that he was looking at the night with human vision. Usually looking at things from a human perspective was a conscious decision, not something that was automatic upon waking. And he had been asleep, hadn't he?

Asleep, or something more complicated?

He couldn't remember how long it had been since he'd sat down on the bench on the patio at the back of the modest adobe house. When existence depended on knowing every second between sundown and sunrise you didn't lose track of time after a couple thousand years of practice.

"Magic."

Strong enough magic that it took him several more minutes to shake off the pleasant lethargy holding him in place.

When he could move, worry and anger propelled him into the house and straight to the back bedroom where Baby was kenneled with her three puppies. Only one pair of red eyes glowed out of the dark at him when he opened the door. When he flipped on the light, Baby yawned. She should have growled at anyone approaching her young, even him, but she only gave a placid whine as he peered into the birthing box. At five weeks the pups were outgrowing the confines of the box, but Baby liked curling up with her offspring there and who was he to argue with the wisdom of a hellhound mother?

Even though the scars healed quickly on both of them when they had the occasional confrontation. It took a firm hand to raise a hellhound, but he'd been doing it for a long time.

She'd had three pups in this litter. After gazing at him for a moment, Baby turned her head and began to lick the one that slept closely tucked beside her.

"One."

When the word came out, Dan blinked. He didn't know how long he'd been standing over the hellhounds. At first, he didn't even know what the word meant. The magic was stronger here than anywhere else in the house. So strong that it was like a hood pulled over his head, like bindings on his limbs. The numbness pressed on him, making him not even want to breathe.

Then he remembered that he was a vampire, he didn't need to breathe. Magic kept him alive, not air or food or water. Though all were pleasant, he didn't need them. He needed magic. He controlled magic.

"It does not control me."

He spoke the words in the Nabatean language of his birth land, not the Latin of the place where he had fought and died, been reborn and then remade, or the English he thought and spoke in this era. Only words that came to him with his mother's milk were enough to break him free. It was the language in which the spell had been cast and controlling the language controlled the magic.

The fog around his senses was banished as soon as the words were spoken.

Baby began to bark. He knelt beside her and put out a hand to soothe her. Her frantic worry flowed into him at the touch.

There was only one pup in the bed with her.

Two of her babies were gone!

"Son of a bitch!" he shouted, rising to his feet.

Only then did he see the pile of gold coins left in the dog bed. He scooped up one and swore again. Who the hell knew what these meant to him? Who the hell among the living dead knew that he was Nabatean?

"Valentine," he said.

THE warning came to Tess Sirella in her sleep as a dream filled with lightning and shadows, but changed to the scent of wet dog when she woke. She wrinkled her sensitive nose, then sneezed. The bedside clock told her it was 3:18 in the morning, but she knew there'd be no getting back to sleep. She supposed she should be wracked with guilt for the longing to turn over and ignore the alarm, but duty was too bred into her bones.

"Why me?" she grumbled as she got up.

No trouble had stirred for decades, and even though family was always on guard she resented that a demon was playing games on her watch. It was frustrating that she didn't recognize the spell simply by sensing the warning. Now she was going to have to do research. Not to mention call in sick or take vacation time to hunt down and destroy whatever evil was afoot.

"If demons lived normal lives, they wouldn't have the time to pull any of this magic crap."

Then people like her wouldn't have to clean up after them and everyone could get on with messing up the world in the usual mortal ways. A lot of magic didn't affect mortals anyway, but she already knew this spell wouldn't be that sort. There were things that could be created and summoned that found mortals mighty tasty. Heck, she didn't mind the occasional human nosh herself under the right circumstances, and she was one of the good guys.

"I like to think of myself as a sheepdog in wolves' clothing. Who talks to herself," Tess added. It wasn't good for werewolves to be alone too much. Okay, the world was about to be confronted with some sort of demonic disaster but at least she'd have fulfilled her obligation to guardian duty once she'd saved the day and she could hand over the position to the next generation, which happened to be her anime-addicted fourteen-year-old nephew.

She stripped off her pink-flowered pajamas and then went

naked into the closet she'd converted into a workroom. It took a few minutes to light all the candles and set up the psychic barrier she needed to maintain her shielding. Then she settled down cross-legged on the bare wooden floor and prepared to do absolutely nothing for as long as it took.

Ritual magic was actually rather tedious. A lot of it consisted of sitting around waiting for the cosmic phone to be picked up by some other entity along the line. The vampires had fancier names for it, but she wasn't a vampire and—

All her senses tingled, including some she'd rather didn't when she was naked and alone.

Ah-ha! So there was a vampire involved.

Vampires smelled bad and tasted worse, but they always made you think of sex. They could also always be counted on whenever trouble popped up for her pack. It was vampires that had started the trouble in the first place. Well, to be fair, vampires had gotten unwittingly involved in a demon's scheme and the problem hadn't been resolved for nearly two thousand years. It was the vampires' fault, of course. The moment they got involved in anything, it got complicated. They couldn't just deal with life and death and black and white. Oh, no, things had shades of gray for them, not just gray, but an entire spectrum of colors and emotions that werewolves didn't want or need. It was probably because the strigoi started out as humans to begin with and brought all that mortal baggage with them when they stepped over into the supernatural world.

Tess realized she'd let resentment of being woken lead her off on a very humanlike, distracted tangent. She smiled. "Ah, but the machinations of magic are varied and subtle—even for a werewolf well-trained in the arcane . . . and stuff like that."

She laughed, and suddenly knew what the psychic alarm was trying to tell her, besides that there were demons scheming, monsters on the loose, and mortals in danger. The magical wards that twisted and turned like invisible smoke around Syrilla's Litter had picked up some useful data for her. She had a clue that the most emotional vampire of them all was at the heart of it.

She laughed again as she rose to her feet. It was bravado to cover a shudder of fear, knowing she had to confront Valentine.

THREE

KRAAS COULDN'T KEEP FROM WAITING FOR THE
police to arrive, though it took longer than he expected. Nothing happened with the instant efficiency the way the magic
box showed police investigations. But since he wanted to
know what they had to say at this first of what would be many
such events, he lingered.

Hunting humans was always fun, and it was especially so
at the moment, when his weapon of choice was a puppy. The
victims had come into the park after it closed as Kraas had
watched them do before. He'd loosed the hellhound and it
had trotted forward into the mortals' midst. The youths saw
the pretty black dog and immediately surrounded it. Whether
they meant to pet it or take their bats to it didn't matter because the hellhound struck first. Kraas snatched up the hound
and ran before the boys' screams died away.

With the little one safely hidden away, Kraas returned and
climbed the tree. He felt safe to indulge himself for a little
while. Tonight's work had been spectacular for the young
hound and the demon was full of pride and anticipation.

Kraas breathed deeply, enjoying the stink of oozing guts
mingled with the scent of blood on the warm evening breeze.
Flies circled and settled on the four corpses on the park's
baseball field. They were waiting for the officer by the fence
to stop vomiting so they could settle there as well.

Such a beautiful sight, Kraas thought. Such a beautiful
night.

"Four bodies," one of the detectives said. "What caused this
much damage?"

A technician looked up from where she squatted, her face a
stark white circle in the glare of the field's spotlights. "Squir-
rels?" she suggested. When the detective glared she pointed at
the wound she'd been examining. "Look at those bite marks.
They're from something small."

"Rabid raccoons?" someone else spoke up.

"Come on!" the detective barked. "No more jokes. These people were murdered!"

"Don't jump to conclusions," the tech advised. She went back to her examination.

The irritated detective looked like he wanted to pace, but he stayed perfectly still. He didn't want to contaminate the crime scene, Kraas supposed.

What a fine puzzle he'd set for them. It didn't matter for him, of course, except as entertainment. Feeding his hell-hound on soul-sucking death was what mattered. The mortals would suffer many such losses before his little darling was ready for the greatest hunt. The hound would grow strong and powerful on the blood and souls of many mortals before it could be loosed on vampires, then the vampires that preyed on vampires. And finally—

"Valentine." Kraas breathed the name almost reverently, though in truth it was a curse.

Someday soon the hellhound would make a sacrifice of the old bitch herself. Only when the great kill was made could the work truly begin.

†ESS saw the news about the killings on a podcast in the back of a shuttle on her way to the airport. She stared at the small iPhone screen, silently mouthing obscenities, mundane and magical, as she could do nothing to show her outrage in such a public place. As it was, the other passengers in the van gave her strange looks.

Putting down a hellhound was not as easy as it sounded—come to think of it, it didn't sound easy—and this one was already feeding.

The killings stank of ritual magic and human sacrifice. Maybe the vampires had finally realized the true purpose of hellhounds and were putting their pets to work. The murders had been in Santa Barbara and reinforced her belief that the Los Angeles–based Valentine was involved.

"But why?" she whispered. She fought off the urge to howl with impatience. She had a three-hour flight ahead of her before she could even begin to find answers. She had to conserve her energy until then.

* * *

"I'm going to be out of town for a while," Dan told Olympias, the supervisor of all the other Enforcers in the country. She even lived in Washington, D.C.

"Are you asking permission?" the rich female voice on the end of the phone line asked. "Or do you want a favor?"

"Perceptive, aren't you?" he replied.

"I know how hard it is to find a pet sitter. You could use a vacation. How many years has it been since you left Tucson?"

"As the Law in these parts—"

He was interrupted by her laughter. "You have the best-behaved nests and strigs on the continent. Anyone who breeds hellhounds for a hobby would."

Bringing up the hellhounds was the opening he needed. "I'm looking for a dog sitter. That's the favor you suspected I called about. No one is better with hellhounds than you are. I could really use your help."

"Pouring the flattery on a little thick, aren't you, Gladiator?"

Dan wondered if she was reminding him that she'd once been a queen and he'd been a lowly slave. But he couldn't take offense, not when the word could as easily be a nickname here in the twenty-first century.

"Are you being over-sensitive?" she asked when he didn't answer immediately.

He used the tone of guilt in her voice. "I'd appreciate your help. Baby has a pup. When's the last time you saw a hellhound pup?"

"Not since Bitch was little."

"That was at least five hundred years ago." Bitch was Olympias's pet.

Across the miles he heard a sigh that was both longing and exasperation. "I need to get Bitch out of Washington to avoid some werewolves that will be in town for the Save the Earth rally," she said. "But the plan was to head for Las Vegas."

"It's more peaceful here," he said. "And there's a puppy." No Enforcer was soft-hearted, not when they ate the hearts of other vampires for snacks, but everyone had soft spots that could be manipulated. Like him, Olympias's was for dogs.

"I love puppies."

"I know."

"And we could use some private time," she said.

He didn't ask who *we* were, though it was likely she had a new mortal companion. "I promise that you won't be disturbed, with the house all to yourself. Bring Bitch and come for a visit. How soon can you be here?" he added.

"My car's already packed." She sighed. "Okay, Las Vegas can wait. Put Baby under a sleep spell I can break and leave a key in the mailbox."

"I'll do that," he answered. "Thanks."

Dan hung up before Olympias could change her mind.

FOUR

"WE NEED TO TALK."

"Damn," Valentine said. She was more annoyed with herself than with the person standing on the balcony behind her.

She knew she was distracted, and the hotel was full of vampires, which certainly messed with a girl's brainwaves, but she should have sensed his approach. Of course, she hadn't been aware of him since the companion connection had been severed between them several years before. She didn't miss the time when such awareness had been a constant ache. She'd missed him.

"I'm busy, Yevgeny."

"How busy can you be when you've been staring into space for the last hour?"

He'd lived in the States for going on sixty years, yet his voice still held a hint of Russian accent. She still found the sound hot. "Damn," she muttered again.

She'd actually been staring at the lights of the Las Vegas strip far below her penthouse suite. He came closer and put his hands on her shoulders. She automatically leaned back against his wide chest. She was small and he was very large, but somehow it had always been a remarkably good fit.

"I'm pining," she told him, "and brooding."

"You don't have a Russian soul, brooding doesn't suit you."

He was right. He generally was. She'd missed that, too.

"You feel different," she said after a few minutes.

"I am a vampire now," he answered.

Of course. She'd refused to turn him, so he'd gotten someone else to do it. She didn't know why that should leave her feeling betrayed, or why the differences disturbed her. His body temperature was lower than a mortal's. Not by much, but enough to notice. His heart beat, but at a much slower rate than before. Blood flowed, but it was different blood now than when he'd been—well, alive—though he wasn't actually dead.

"I liked you better as a mortal, Yevgeny."

Maybe that was the reason she'd kept him on far longer than was good for him. Maybe that was why she'd refused to change him. Maybe her excuses about not wanting to make any more monsters were just ways of pretending she had noble intentions.

"You just don't like change," he said. "You are remarkably, happily, set in your ways. You'll like me better when you get used to me."

No one had ever known her so well. "I won't."

He pressed her a little closer. "No one sulks as well as you do. Brooding no, sulking yes."

"That's not exactly a compliment."

"It's time for honesty between us at last."

She continued looking at the city despite the temptation to break his grip and whirl to face him. She didn't want to look at him. Even now that they were no longer connected, she feared seeing her beautiful blond giant might stir the old desire. Not possible, but old habits were hard to break.

"I never lied to you," she said.

Fingers began to massage her tense shoulders. "Perhaps not, but you must own to other—abuses."

Okay, so she'd kidnapped him away from the family and country he loved and made him her sex slave for fifty-plus years. She shrugged under his hands. "Yeah, well . . ."

"I'm ready to forgive you," he added.

In other words, he needed something. She sighed. "How did you find me?"

"Jebel Haven's a friend of mine. In a recent e-mail, he mentioned having adventures with you."

Pain shot through her at hearing Haven's name, but she managed not to flinch. Her fingers curled around the balcony railing, but the hotel had been built by vampires and the metal didn't crush. "What's a nice man like you doing hanging out with a mortal vampire hunter like Haven?"

"He's not a bad guy, as long as you don't turn your back on him. What have *you* been doing with Haven?"

Lady, but there were a lot of layers in that question! "Making mistakes," she answered.

"I've heard rumors of dragons," he said.

"That would make a great title for something." Once a writer, always a writer, she supposed. "And it was only one dragon."

"I heard that you and Haven saved Las Vegas from the dragon."

"Haven did the work."

"And that you gave him your blood to save his life."

Longing twisted her, mind, body, and soul. Her blood was in Haven, but where was he? She'd given him her soul and Haven had rejected it.

"He's mine now!" Tears blurred all the pretty lights below. She let out a feral growl. "The ungrateful bastard ran off with his girlfriend."

"What would a nice lady like you do with a man like Haven? Is his blood in you?" he asked after she was silent for a while. "It isn't, is it? You don't love him."

"Instinct says he's mine," she answered. "Instinct is all I have to go on."

He laughed. "You've ignored instinct before."

She finally turned to face him, though she regretted it when she saw the bitterness twisting his handsome face. "I was trying to help you."

"By driving me crazy?"

"It was a mistake to refuse to help you turn. I admit it. Maybe saving Haven was a mistake, too, but—"

"Doing the wrong thing for the right reasons again?" He suddenly smiled. "At least you always try. That's why I love you."

It sounded good, and brought them back to why he was here. "What do you want? You didn't come here to *talk*. You need my help."

Yevgeny stepped back. "You know how Daniel Conover will give away the animals he breeds but he won't sell them? How he treats them better than most strigoi do their mortal companions?"

"Dan has good reasons for that. Besides, those creatures are smarter and more valuable than most companions."

Yevgeny, who'd been her companion far longer than any other, carefully refrained from the angry reply she saw in his eyes. "But companions are much easier to housebreak."

"And how would you know—" She shook her head in disbelief. "Oh, no, tell me you don't have one of those monsters? You're too young to deal with a hellhound. Dan wouldn't give you one."

"Of course not," Yevgeny answered. Before she could sigh in relief, he added, "I stole it from him."

"He's going to kill you. And I'm not going to protect you."

"I'm not asking you to. That's not why I'm here. I took the puppy knowing that the law states that if you can keep one for a year it belongs to you. I made the decision going into it that I could elude Conover for a year."

"That's not a law, it's a tradition. Dan doesn't have to stop hunting you for the theft if he doesn't want to."

"It wasn't theft. I left him a generous payment for the puppy."

"You could have just put your name on the waiting list."

"I'm a strig, he'd never consider giving a hellhound to a vampire that lives outside the Laws of the Blood. Even if he would put me on his list of potential owners it would be a while before he considered me old enough to deal with one of his darlings." Yevgeny laughed. "I was not prepared to wait until hell freezes over. Sebastian's birthday is coming up soon."

"Oh, good Goddess! You want a hellhound for a *child*? You're not trying to kill him again are you?"

He drew himself up to his full height. "I have sworn to protect Sebastian Avella with my life."

Now didn't that sound just like Yevgeny? He was an absolutely brilliant sorcerer and had decided to use ritual magic to turn himself into a vampire when she refused to do the deed for him. He'd kidnapped young Sebastian, a *dhamphir*—the unlawful offspring of a vampire and a Romany woman—to sacrifice in the spell. Only at the last moment he'd come to his senses and been unable to murder a child, even one that was genetically programmed to grow up and become a vampire hunter.

"Of course you'd appoint yourself the kid's guardian angel of death to assuage your guilt."

"It's the least I can do."

"He's a menace to our kind, and now you want to give him a hellhound?"

"He wants a puppy for his birthday."

She didn't understand it, but then, she'd never had children as a mortal, whereas Yevgeny had been a loving father. And she'd taken him away from being able to raise his children to serve her insatiable sexual needs. Damn, those had been fun years! So of course now he was about to play on her guilt over her own misdeeds to draw her into this birthday present scheme.

"The kid's already a spoiled brat," she pointed out. "If he wants a dog let his parents get him a rottweiler."

"A hellhound will help keep him safe." He looked a bit sheepish. "At least it will when it's properly socialized."

Valentine crossed her arms under her ample breasts. "That's what you came here for? To get me to help you with dog training?"

Yevgeny smiled. "Well, Cesar Millan isn't available."

She had no idea what that meant. "Why do you think I can be of any help?"

"Because back when Conover called himself Corvei you helped him raise the first litter of hellhounds."

The problem with having lived with Yevgeny for so long was that there was very little about her she hadn't told him. "We shared too much," she complained. "Strigoi shouldn't be so damn—domestic."

He took her hands. "Come with me."

She pulled them away. "I'm busy!"

"Waiting for a man who doesn't want to come back to you?"

"It doesn't matter what he—" She managed to stop herself as she remembered who she was talking to.

He had no qualms about using her hesitation. "Haven doesn't really matter to you or you'd be searching for him yourself instead of sending someone to look for him. Put your time to use and come with me."

The sight of Yevgeny was seductive; his voice was seductive. His needing her was the most seductive of all, even if it was only to help housetrain one of Corvei's nasty little pets. She'd thought she'd put Yevgeny out of her mind as she had every other companion that had gone into the night as a strigoi, but she'd missed him far more than any of the others. She just hadn't realized it until now.

Maybe she could spend a little bit of time with him. It would give her something to do while waiting for Haven's return. "You always could divert me," she admitted. "All right. Fine. I'll help. But if Corvei shows up to kill you to get his puppy back, I will not get in his way."

Five

"You are the most beautiful woman I have ever seen," Corvei blurted out to the woman who'd entered his cell.

Dark curls swirled down her back and over her rich, round breasts. Her skin truly was alabaster pale, and her eyes huge and black, her mouth full and lush. Her garments were of Seresian silk, bright red embroidered in gold. The cloth was so fine and thin it revealed more than it hid of her firm, perfect body.

She smiled, bringing light into the dark world. "Women come to you often and you service them." She stepped close to him and spoke in a whisper. "I hear even a werewolf bitch takes you into her bed. That's a rare honor for a mortal. So I've come to have a look." She put cool hands on his shoulders and he felt her drawing the heat from his body. She looked into his eyes, and he could not look away. "You are special," she said after a long time. "I am Valentia."

He put his hands where her narrow waist flared into her rounded hips, taking his warmth back from her. "What are you?" he asked.

"I'm not looking for a new lover," she said. "What I'm looking for is an apprentice. But you'll do for both. If you are truly interested in destroying Rome," she added. "And if you want it."

She was asking rather than ordering him. No one had done that for a long time. More important, he *knew* that her hatred of the empire matched his own. She wanted his help. How could he deny her anything?

Dan relished the memory of their first meeting as well as the thought of seeing Valentine again, even if he didn't completely trust her and hadn't since she'd showed him how to become a vampire. Valentia hadn't explained about the dark magic and the curse of eternity that came with the many gifts she offered. But living forever sounded good to a gladiator who had existed on the sword's edge for five long years. Killing a man to achieve eternal life had seemed no different than what he already did for a living. Just like becoming a gladiator, becoming a vampire was something he had no choice in, and a little bit of resentment at his maker had niggled at him for a long time.

He could almost hear Valentine telling him to stop being such a wimp while he circled the block looking for a parking space near her high-rise condo building. He supposed he should stop thinking about her if he wanted his visit to come as a surprise. He didn't know what was going on, whether she'd stolen the puppies herself or why. It was best to approach her quietly and cautiously. He sat perfectly still in his car once he finally found a place to park and didn't get out until he was certain his mental shielding was as tight as he could make it.

It was not that far from midnight and there was very little traffic on the streets of this upscale Los Angeles neighborhood. Night-blooming jasmine and pollution scented the air in almost equal parts. He crossed the street and slipped over a wall into the beautifully landscaped garden that surrounded Valentine's building. It was instantly far darker under the palm trees than out on the street.

It grew darker with every step he took until he was surrounded by a black void. Dan realized he'd fallen into a magical trap, but by then it was too late to avoid it. Instead he stood completely still and let his extra senses roam. It didn't take long before he detected life inside the blackness with him.

Maybe it was a trap, but he had no choice but to go toward the light of a living being.

Six

THE MAGIC DIDN'T FEEL LIKE VALENTINE'S. Not that Tess had ever personally encountered the Ancient Mother's personal energy, but she was certain it wouldn't feel like this if she did. The flow and pulse of the guarding magic didn't have an ancient feel to it for one thing. For another, she'd didn't think she'd be able to detect any spell Valentine cast as quickly as she had this one. And it didn't matter that she'd detected it quickly, she was still stuck in the darkness.

Tess was in a hurry and the inconvenience of the trap did not help her mood. She growled deep in her throat, not something she normally did in human form, but the sound came out anyway.

The last thing she expected afterward was to hear a man say, "Calm down, cub."

The voice was behind her, but where exactly was harder to determine. She was almost dizzy from whirling before she made out another shape in the thick darkness.

"Who the hell—" she began.

"Hello, werewolf," he said. "Fancy meeting you here."

Her sharp ears detected the remnants of a dozen lifes' worth of accents in his deep voice. She could make out no scent in the magical dark, but it was easy enough to guess what he was. "Hello, vampire," she replied.

"Not exactly vampire," he answered. "Although I used to be one."

That revelation was meant to scare her, and it sort of worked. He was letting her know he was one of the vampires who ate vampires—and who knew what else?

"What do you call yourself these days?" she asked. "Enforcer? Hunter? Abomination?" Bravado might not be a good idea, but she just couldn't help herself.

"Dan," he said. "You?"

Oh, shit! What the hell was Dan Conover doing here? What did he want with her? "Tess," she told him. "What are—?"

"I thought at first that you were part of the trap, but it's more likely that you're as stupid as I was about Valentine's security."

"I don't think Valentine had anything to do with—"

"Geoff Sterling, I bet. He's the apprentice living with—"

"Yes," she cut him off. "Do you make a habit of not letting people finish sentences?"

"I don't spend much time around people. I'm not around one now," he added.

His conversational tone really pissed her off.

Then the black bulk of him was looming over her. The darkness made it worse. "Did you take the pups, Tess?"

Though there were none there, she could almost feel hot breath and claws brushing her throat. She was werewolf, she didn't scare easily. This—monster—could certainly do it to her. And why the hell did that turn her on?

Tess made herself concentrate. "I'm here to see Valentine about that." She wasn't sure if it was smart to blurt that out, but it was hard not to respond to such an obvious alpha.

"Me, too," he said, and became all mild-mannered. At least he stopped aiming the threat of danger at her. "Let's get out of here and get on with it," he suggested. "You are a witch as well as a werewolf, aren't you?"

"It's going to take me a while to break a spell this strong," she said. "Though I expect that once the sun comes up—"

"I may have all night," he cut her off. "But I'm not planning on hanging around come daylight."

"Then what—?"

"We combine our brains."

She knew what he meant, and what he suggested was even more annoying than his constant interruptions. It was also dangerous—in a very personal way. They could get into each other's heads, under each other's skins. It could make things—complicated. Especially if there was anything even vaguely compatible in their personali—

He recognized her hesitation. "I promise not to peek, if you promise, too."

He seemed to already be halfway into her head. Damn the vampires and their greater telepathic abilities.

"We're wasting time here, weregirl."

She growled—he really brought that out in her—but she had to agree.

"Fine—fangboy."

He chuckled.

Tess took a deep breath and closed her eyes. Which was stupid considering they were already in complete blackness.

The energy that surged through her was pure orgasmic rush. She didn't know how long she was lost inside pure pleasure inside pure dark.

This is nice. The voice of the vampire eventually floated through the bliss. *But . . .*

Shut up and let me concentrate, she snarled back, embarrassed at her reaction to this monster's—

Do you want me to show you how—?

I'm the witch here, fangboy.

He poured more energy into her. *Show me.*

She concentrated, wrapped her power around his, discovered she wasn't giving enough to control all the energy. Every barrier she had came down. They blended, but somehow she wasn't lost. She longed to linger within this pulsing, shining vortex but she didn't lose hold of what needed to be done. Reluctant as she was to leave these new, exciting sensations unexplored, she took their mixed energy and pushed—pouring light against the dark, conjuring counterspell against the spell that held them.

The perfectly normal night returned with a lurch that twisted her stomach even as it brought reality back into focus. The dark now had many textures, and there was plenty of light—streetlights and car lights and apartment lights and even the faint glow of starlight high above all the night lights of Los Angeles. Scent returned with vision, as acute as ever. Tess realized she'd missed this extra sense even more than she had the presence of light.

"I hate magic," she muttered. It was a supernatural allergy, really. One that most people had little or no reaction to. She wondered what it would be like to be like most people.

"But you use your allergy well," the vampire behind her said. "And you really don't want to be like everybody else."

"I suppose not, but—" She whirled around to face him and snarled. "You'd better get out of my head now."

He stared at her in shock. His mouth even hung open for a moment.

Tess stared back, absorbing her own surprise that the vampire's scent was—delicious. Where'd he get those sexy pheromones, she wondered. "What?" she demanded as his gaze continued to roam hungrily over her.

"Syrilla?" he questioned. There was the roughness of desire in his voice.

Oh, that.

"My name is Tess Sirella," she growled. She pulled her hair away from her face, revealing the werewolf widow's peak and letting him get a good look at her sharp features.

"You look very much like her."

"Yeah, I'm descended from the old bitch."

He showed fang at her tone. "She was dear to me."

"And bitch isn't an insult among my kind, Conover," she reminded him.

"True." He smiled, and actually had the audacity to pat her on the cheek, only laughing when she snarled. He turned and walked away.

She caught up with him as he reached the entrance of the building. He held a cell phone to his ear.

"Still only getting her voicemail." He flipped the phone closed and put it back in his jacket pocket. "And I've never known anyone who could block telepathic contact as efficiently as Valentine." He looked at her. "What shall we do now?"

"I didn't know we were together," she replied.

"Fortunately I know where she keeps her spare key."

She watched as Conover moved to the brick wall, made the shadows around him darken, and began to climb the side of the building.

"Damn flashy vampire," she complained as she watched. Her plan had been to first lay a web of watching spells around Valentine's place the way she had around Conover's. She found the vampire's direct method far more tempting.

Tess stepped up to the brick wall, slipped off her shoes, and extended all of her claws. "You're a bad influence on my family, Conover," she said as she began to climb.

I know, he thought back.

"I hope you haven't ruined your manicure," he said when she joined him on Valentine's terrace.

She looked past him at the sliding glass doors, then flexed her fingers. "As sharp as these may be, they don't cut glass. Do you have any diamonds on you?"

He chuckled as he removed something from under the base of a potted plant.

"That really is a key?" she asked as he straightened. "Does Valentine let you use this place as a safe house?" She knew a lot about strigoi society.

"No, the old girl just locks herself out sometimes."

The "old girl" was about a thousand years older than Conover, and he was no spring chicken. He certainly didn't look any the worse for wear, though. He was a beefy guy, but all muscle and no fat and taller than you'd expect someone born in the Roman era to be. She shouldn't find him attractive—it was a species thing—but he looked good to her. And he certainly didn't smell bad. Tess took a deep breath, and nearly swayed from the rush of lust.

"Those are the same pheromones that seduced my great-granny," she said.

"No," he answered. "I was a mortal when that affair happened." He unlocked the glass door and gestured for her to enter before him. "Don't worry, there's nobody home," he said when she hesitated. "Surely a nosy witch can tell that much."

Tess growled. "It's hard to tell anything about Valentine."

"True," he said as she walked inside past him.

He followed her into the spacious living room. Big place, she noticed, but sparsely furnished. Frankly, she'd expected the décor to be gothic, full of a lifetime's worth of mementoes and walls lined with bulging bookcases. The only thing on any wall was a huge flat-screen television. There was a couch, a coffee table, and a couple of chairs facing the television in the center of the room. The kitchen was on her left, a hallway led off the other side of the room. She felt the vampire come up too close behind her and stopped seeing the room.

Awareness of him surrounded her. His slow heartbeat thundered in her ears. His scent was overwhelming. His body heat rose, his warmth flooding through her. Tess wanted to run.

The fear that flashed up from her gut was all wrong. She was Tess Sirella, damn it, as scary as any vampire!

She forced herself to turn, shifting form.

When she faced him she saw that the vampire wasn't a vampire at all.

SEVEN

Oh, shit. How could she have forgotten Conover was more than a garden variety strigoi?

Frankly, what she now faced looked more like a werewolf than she did. Only a lot bigger and a lot meaner.

These monsters called themselves Hunters. Many vampires called them Abominations, at least out of earshot. The Strigoi Council who ruled vampires named them Enforcers of the Laws of the Blood. Vampires consumed humans; the Hunters consumed vampires who broke the rules of the Council.

"I'm not of your kind," she managed to say though her throat was dry with terror. "I'm not subject to your Laws."

Though she probably knew more about his kind than he did. Knowledge didn't keep Tess from shaking.

A huge paw circled her throat. Claws delicately nicked the sides of her neck.

What are you doing here? His thought drilled into her mind. *Where are the pups?*

"Oh, crap, I don't have your damn puppies," she snarled. Maybe Conover frightened her, but that didn't stop her from being a werewolf.

Werewolves kill hellhounds, he reminded her.

"I haven't yet."

Tess winced as the claws drew blood. That *yet* had definitely been a mistake.

Words rushed from her. "I'm not interested in killing your pups. It's my duty to keep them from killing." She grabbed his arm as the vise around her throat grew tighter. His muscles were pure steel. "You have no idea how they can be used," she choked out. "The magic—"

He tossed her across the room. She landed sprawled on the vast expanse of sofa. Before she could spring up, Conover had changed back to his human form. But he still moved as fast as a vampire.

She snapped at his wrist when he held her down, but had only the satisfaction of tasting his blood. Mortal teeth were practically useless! And it was a trap anyway, because he used his own blood to quickly trace symbols on her chest while he muttered a swift incantation. The magic took hold, leaving her unable to change no matter how much she wanted to.

"I never heard you were a wizard," she said.

"I've been dealing with your kind for a long time," he answered. "I've learned a few tricks along the way."

His hands moved over her in ways that had nothing to do with magic, not in the technical way at least. Her body's response to this alpha handling shorted out her brain, so that it took her a few minutes to ask, "Why did you take off my clothes?"

His knowing chuckle was as much answer as she needed.

"Okay, stupid question. You're not looking for concealed weapons—"

"Hidden charms or spells are weapons, however . . ." After a thorough examination that had him tumbling her around like a doll, he eventually put her on her back and concluded, "No visible body painting or tattoos."

She was panting. Damned animal instincts! "You could have just asked."

Fingers delved between her splayed thighs. "I like to be thorough. You aren't minding a bit," he added when he found how wet and ready she was. He played with her swollen clit for a while, bringing her to a quick, hard orgasm with his thumb. "Life's hard being a virgin witch, isn't it?" he asked after her climax passed.

"How did you—"

"No woman is that delightfully tight inside in this day and age unless—"

"Let's not talk about my—"

"Vow of chastity to increase your magical power, my furry little vestal?"

"If I was furry at the moment, I'd rip your throat out."

"I know. And I wouldn't blame you for trying." He leaned back, though a hand on her chest easily held her down. "Fulfilling your vows is an admirable thing, and I shouldn't tease you about it." He stroked her breasts as he talked. She was all too aware of how her nipples tightened and strained to his touch.

"Excuse me, but would you mind stopping—?"

"How do you manage to stay sane when you're in season?" he wondered.

She didn't know if he was using magic, or if she answered because she couldn't help but respond to his genuine curiosity. "A vibrator and a lot of chocolate."

He nodded. "That's better than most men at any time. But enough girl talk . . ."

He said a word that sent sharp pain through her head and left Tess's ears ringing. But she knew he'd released her from the enchantment that had left her in human form.

"Why?" she asked.

"I don't want you to feel under any compulsions when you answer my questions."

Where are they?

His telepathy did not help her headache, but she opened her mind to him. *I don't know. I'm here to find out.*

He probed and he prowled inside her. He hurt her. She didn't try to fight him. Eventually Conover let her mind go free. Something of his dominance remained inside her though. It was a male to female sort of dominance every member of her kind sought. Damn Conover and his Hunter-self to hell!

It was only then that she noticed how close he held her naked body.

Then the nausea hit and all that mattered was throwing up.

Eight

Dan snatched up the retching werewolf and carried her into the bathroom. He wasn't in the habit of abusing the females of any species, but he was in too much of a hurry to find the pups to question her gently. He was gentle now, knowing that she'd done them no harm. She still held information he intended to find out, but for now he saw to her needs.

He held her head so that she could barf into the toilet bowl and wiped her face with a wet towel when she was done. While she lay collapsed like a sweaty wet noodle on the floor, he adjusted the controls in the shower until the temperature was just right. He lifted her again and eased her under the warm spray.

While waiting for the water to revive her, Dan went in search of clothes to replace the ones he'd ripped and shredded between climbing the walls and turning into a Hunter. Some things it was just better to do naked.

He found a closet full of expensive black clothing in the bedroom occupied by Valentine's apprentice, Geoff. He shook his head at the sight. Why was it vampires wore so much black? Especially the younger ones. The color had never appealed to him. For one thing it showed every speck and fiber. His pets shed a great deal, and not all hellhounds were black.

He found a shirt and slacks that fit well enough to replace his jeans and plaid shirt, then went back to see how the girl was doing.

By the time he returned, she'd dried off and wrapped herself in a white robe. Her wet hair was pulled severely back from her angular face. He stopped in the doorway, stunned and staring. Pain and longing shot through him. He shouldn't be so attracted to a creature so absolutely different from his own kind—but his body didn't seem to be aware that lust between their species didn't happen.

"What the hell's the matter with you?" she demanded.

They'd already established that she was a descendent of Syrilla's, but . . .

"Are you sure werewolves aren't immortal?" he asked.

"We could be," she said. "If we used the same sort of dark magic your kind is addicted to."

Her comment reminded him of other things she'd said, and bits of knowledge he'd picked up inside her mind. The problem with telepathy wasn't in picking up thoughts, but in putting them into context. He'd dug out the specific items he'd been looking for—she hadn't taken the pups, she'd never killed a hellhound, she was looking for them herself, and like him sensed that Valentine was somehow involved. She was, in fact, as much a guardian of the animals as he was. He didn't know why. He didn't know how.

He took her hand, meaning to pull her back into the living room, but he dropped it as soon as their skin touched and an electric charge of attraction passed between them.

"Stop that!" she demanded.

"I'm not doing it on purpose!"

"You were earlier."

"That was only to distract you so I could get into your head."

"Sex as a weapon? That is just so—strigoi."

"It is, isn't it?"

"You don't have to sound so pleased about it."

"Don't whine when you're not in wolf form," he told her, and enjoyed the energy rush as temper flared in her eyes and through all her senses. He turned and walked toward the living room, wondering if she'd jump him from behind. Instead she followed him. He was almost disappointed at her ability to control her wild nature.

"Why do you think Valentine is involved?" he asked after they'd settled on opposite ends of the couch.

"Would you believe me if I told you I sensed her shadow in a dream?"

"I've been known to believe odder things," he answered.

"Someone used ancient magic in an ancient language to distract me. Valentine is one of the few who know the old tongues and the most powerful spells."

"You're Nabatean, from the Roman-era city of Petra, now

in Jordan," she said. "Your native language evolved into modern Arabic."

"The written form did, not the spoken. And I didn't say what ancient language was used in the spell."

"Oh, please. Don't go all mysterious. Could anything else have trapped you?"

Dan shrugged and shook his head. "I don't suppose you speak Nabatean?"

"No. My turn to ask a question. Why would Valentine help a demon steal the puppies?"

"She wouldn't." Dan stood. "What demon? Strigoi don't deal with demons. Valentine certainly wouldn't. If she's in her right mind at the moment," he added in a low mutter.

She smiled at his reaction. "I know that vampires and demons have a formal treaty never to interfere with each other, but do you really think you can trust demons?"

Dan wasn't sure that demons really were demons, not in the way mortals defined them. Of course, mortals had the information about every supernatural species mixed up, if not outright wrong. The strigoi's knowledge of demonkind wasn't much better, even after thousands of years of co-existence with the strange creatures.

"It's not my job to trust demons," he told the werewolf. "My duty is to make sure that the Law against interfering with them is enforced. And I don't believe Valentine would break the—"

"Valentine doesn't give a damn about the Laws of the Blood, remember? She's never acknowledged your Strigoi Council and there's not a single Enforcer who could stop her from doing anything she wants. She's the loose cannon, the wild card, and the mother of all Enforcers. You look shocked, Hunter. Didn't you know about Valentine's brood?"

Valentine—Valentia back then—had made him into a vampire, but—

"She didn't make me what I am."

"I know. The way it works is that vampires turn their mortal companions into vampires. Only members of the Hunter bloodline can turn vampires into Hunters. It was a Hunter named Olympias who turned you into a monster that preys on vampires. But the Hunter line started somewhere, and Valentine is the first of your line, the beginning. She keeps the knowledge of what she is and how she came to be secret, but my pack of werewolf witches—"

"Know more about the strigoi than we know about ourselves," he finished for her.

"We make it our business to find out all we can about every type of supernatural being. Syrilla's pack protects werewolves the way you Hunters protect strigoi. My assignment is to make sure the hellhounds don't fall into the wrong hands. Demon hands are the wrong hands, and demons have been trying to get hold of Syrilla's pups since the beginning."

"I was there at the beginning," he reminded her. "No demons tried to harm the first pups. But a great many of your kind died in the attempt to destroy them."

"A great many werewolves did die at your hands," she acknowledged. "That's why the werewolf community eventually came to the conclusion that my pack would be totally responsible for dealing with the hellhound problem. Not that we ever mentioned this to you strigoi."

"Vampires can be negotiated with, you know. Werewolves are too damn secretive."

She shrugged. "It's a fault, I admit. Probably even a genetic one."

"But you are going to work past this fault and tell me everything now, aren't you?"

"Maybe if we'd simply put you on your guard about why demons created the hellhounds, me and my ancestors wouldn't have had to live in your shadow all these generations."

He'd always known they were out there, waiting to strike. Or so he'd thought. He shook his head. "I've guarded against your kind because of a promise I made to one of your pack, when your pack could have been helping me care for their cousins?"

Tess winced. "Please! Hellhounds aren't sentient. They are no more kin to us than arctic wolves, or Great Danes."

It pleased him that werewolves still underestimated the hellhounds' capacity even after all this time. "They're smart," he said.

"For dogs, maybe."

"Hellhounds," he corrected.

She sprang to her feet. "Exactly! They are straight from hell. Really. That's the whole point and always has been."

He stared at her for a long time. Finally, he said, "I take it there was something Syrilla didn't tell me."

Tess shook her head. "She didn't know. The poor bitch was under a spell when she mated with your war dog, otherwise she never would have done"—she grimaced—"the dirty deed with a dumb mutt."

"Hardly a mutt. I paid a fortune for the animal because of his pure lineage. His ancestry was far more grand than mine."

"But he was still a dog! No werewolf in her right mind could possibly . . . do that . . . with one of those . . ." She shuddered. "It makes me sick to think about it and it's been two thousand years. It's a wonder my whole pack wasn't wiped out to erase the shame of it. It's bad enough we've been tied to the hellhounds' fate ever since."

"You were explaining about spells and demons," Dan reminded.

"Hellhounds were created through demon magic," she answered. "They were brought into the world to eat souls and build power to be used in demonic ceremonies."

He didn't disregard this information out of hand. It was clear the werewolf witch believed it. "What sort of ceremonies?"

"How would I know? The demons have never gotten a chance to get their claws on a hellhound. You've protected them. My pack's guarded them."

"I don't always protect them. I train them and make sure they go to good homes."

"That's just it—we think it's the pups the demons want. We think that they can't use hellhound magic once you've tamed them and trained them to obey strigoi. The demons need to train the pups themselves for whatever it is they want. They've never gotten the chance—until now."

He was on his feet. "Your pack might have told me all this at some point over the centuries!"

Her eyes blazed with anger and she opened her mouth a few times as if to protest before saying, "Yeah. That probably would have been a good idea."

Dan was glad that at least this pack member was able to look past the centuries of mayhem vampires and werewolves had committed on each other over the hellhounds.

"I can forgive and forget if you can. And even work with you if necessary."

She balked at this. "If? What do you mean 'if necessary'? Who got you out of the trap earlier? Who—?"

He'd grabbed the furious woman's shoulders. "No offense intended," he said.

Then the robe slipped off her shoulders and his hands were touching warm, soft flesh and Dan forgot what he'd meant to say next. Two thousand years were gone in an instant. The hot mouth he pressed against his was the same. The wild intensity that flared between them was the same. The small, high breasts he cupped responded the same.

But Tess wasn't Syrilla.

For one thing, he was far more attracted to this werewolf female than he'd ever been to her ancestor when he was a mortal man—and that was saying quite a lot.

For another, he liked Tess far better than he had Syrilla—and that was also saying quite a lot.

"I can't," she said breathlessly after they'd fallen together onto the couch.

He had her naked beneath him once again. Her thighs were wrapped around his hips. He held her ass cupped in one hand. She had a wonderful little ass.

"I made vows—and you're—strigoi and—oh, Goddess!"

She bit his shoulder in response to an intimate caress. It was a love bite, not an objection to anything he was doing.

He laughed in her ear, and bit back.

The taste of her blood was wholly different from any human he'd ever tasted. It was like being introduced to hot peppers and fresh ginger after a lifetime of bland, invalid fare. Everything that was lust and life came to him through her. He'd never tasted anyone like her and he had no intention of stopping.

He wasn't going to drain her dry. But he was going to fuck her brains out.

Dan picked Tess up and carried her to the bedroom.

Nine

What was so great about being a virgin anyway?

This fire burning between them was the real magic. This was life. This was real. This was *important*.

Tess threw her head back and draped her arms around Conover's neck, vaguely aware he was carrying her and not caring where they were going.

He put her down on a wide expanse that was silky soft and cool. She stretched out on the luxurious bed and would have purred if she wasn't a werewolf. The room was dark but werewolf eyes and vampire eyes met and they saw each other clearly. The recognition of like to like that passed between them shook her to the core, but not at the wrongness of their two species blending both body and soul. It was the rightness that shattered but didn't break her.

She cupped his face in her hands and drew his mouth down to hers. She'd never shared a kiss so intense, so intimate.

She'd never shared a proper kiss at all, she realized. At least she'd never initiated one.

This is so going to get me in trouble, she thought.

Me, too, he answered.

There was no repentance in either of their minds, and no hesitation.

This is a first, he thought, *a vampire mating with a werewolf.*

"Well—" Tess began, then decided to let it go. They were in Valentine's bed, but this wasn't the time for conversation about the Ancient Mother. "This is about Tess and Dan," she said.

"It's about who, not what, we are," he agreed.

She ran her hands over the thick, hard muscles of his back and cupped his rounded buttocks. Her foot stroked up the length of his calf. "Let's make it about sex," she told him.

Her fingers reached around to curl around his cock. She groaned as she stroked his penis and testicles, but he soon positioned himself between her thighs.

When he entered her the thrust was so hard she couldn't stop the scream.

"Hey! I'm new to this!" she reminded him.

"Sorry!"

He made up for it by settling into a slow, gentle rhythm that sent amazing bursts of pleasure through her and made time and place disappear.

Tess eventually came down from the series of steadily building orgasms. She tossed her head from side to side and tried to catch her breath. She tried to focus. It would be so easy to stay inside the shared ecstasy forever.

She moaned and grabbed the vampire's hair. "Come!" she begged him. "Now! You've only got until dawn you know."

Dan laughed, flashing fang. And his mouth came down on her breast. There was a quick sharp pain that took her back into the ecstasy that she rode down into the dark.

†ЕП

HE WAS CLOSER TO THE OLD BITCH NOW. KRAAS
knew the time would soon be ripe to confront her. Did Valentine suspect an evil presence just beyond her reach? Had fear invaded her dreams yet? Did the shadow of ripping fangs make her throat ache? He held his master's enemy's true death in his arms and stroked the velvety head while the pup whimpered. The energy released when a demon creature killed Valentine would increase his master's power a thousandfold. Kraas's reward would be equally immense.

"You're hungry, I know. You're getting heavy from all your kills, you know." He rubbed the fat little puppy belly. "You're growing into such a big, fine boy."

He continued to murmur to the pup as he moved silently through the backyards of the sleeping neighborhood. He listened all the while for heartbeats.

The houses were large but most of them held no more than two or three people. The pup needed more than that to eat his fill.

"You're a growing boy. I miss the days when families slept six to a bed with servants huddling around besides. I'm almost ashamed to bring my master into this world. He'll whip the mortals into shape with you and me at his side to share the kills. Ah," Kraas said as they stopped behind the center house of a cul-de-sac. He closed his eyes and listened carefully, counting as he discerned individual heartbeats within the dark house. Eight, he decided. Eight mortals sleeping peacefully. A good night's feast for the youngster.

Kraas remembered to check around the outside of the building for any of the alarm systems mortalkind thought protected them. The house proved to be free of any warning device, and, of course, no spells warded the place from magical entry.

He returned to the back and used a diamond-sharp claw to scrape a hole at the handle of a sliding glass door. Once he had the door a little way open, he let the hellhound pup down inside the house's kitchen.

"Run free," he urged. The pup was already determinedly crossing the room, already on the scent. "Find your prey," Kraas said. "Feast."

ELEVEN

"A MOTEL IN THE MIDDLE OF NOWHERE—HOW charming," Valentine said as Yevgeny turned off the empty road into a gravel parking lot. For all of her sarcasm she was glad to finally be arriving somewhere with four walls and a roof. Though she'd managed to fight off the phobia on the drive west of Las Vegas, she had not enjoyed the wide desert vista or the vastness of the starry sky overhead. She regretted the bravado of letting Yevgeny drive her Cadillac with the top down.

"You shouldn't fear the world," Yevgeny said. "It's the world's job to fear you."

"Oh, shut up."

He chuckled. "I thought it was a very good line. You can use it in your next script if you like."

She sighed. "Everybody thinks he's a writer."

This reminded her of how she'd met Yevgeny at a studio reception for Soviet diplomats back during the Cold War. He'd been an undercover KGB officer. She was a scriptwriter as well as a vampire. She'd been obsessed with him instantly. She looked at him now and he was just as big and blond and impressive as ever. An echo of the old longing stirred.

"Damn it, Yevgeny."

His fingers cupped the back of her neck, the touch so familiar the reality of it was painful. His fingers were not so warm as they used to be, but the contact still sent heat through her.

"There's no Law against vampires being lovers," he said.

"Euwww!" She meant to flinch away but found that she hadn't moved. His touch felt too good. "It's not done," she reminded both of them. "You were my companion—that's incest."

"You didn't turn me into a vampire, someone else did. How can it be incest if you aren't my maker?"

It would be easy to argue this, even easier to give in without an argument. But she and Yevgeny were over, done with. There was too much history, too much bad blood to even start a discussion. She didn't want to know where the discussion might lead.

Besides, there was Haven, her runaway groom. Even if she had sent Geoff Sterling to fetch the man back instead of going herself, she still had a claim on Haven.

She rubbed her temples and stared straight ahead, out into the empty night across a road that didn't go anywhere. "Get your hand off of me, Yevgeny. So I can remember what the hell I'm doing here."

She heard the car door open and felt the air grow colder as he moved away. Valentine jumped in surprise when he appeared beside her. He opened the car door and took her hand to help her out. Always the gentleman. Haven was no gentleman.

"Time to check on the puppy," he said when she was standing beside him.

Her confusion blew away at this reminder of why he needed her here. "Thank the Goddess you picked an isolated spot," she said. "If you aren't the only guest at this fine establishment you soon will be—not that the place is likely to still be standing when we're done."

He laughed. "I rented all the rooms and sent the owner away. We have plenty of privacy to hold puppy school."

She shook her head at his humor and started forward. "Come on, let's wake up the monster while the night is still young."

"The puppy's just a little troublesome," he said as he caught up to her. "You don't have to be so dramatic."

"If it was only a little troublesome you wouldn't have come to me for help."

"I asked for help because I remembered you telling me that you were there with Corvei when he trained the first of the breed. You've at least had some experience—"

"Oh, yes, I was there. We had no idea what evil had been brought into the world. We had a lot to learn before the first ones were tamed." It was her turn to laugh. "We vampires have evil at our core but we can choose how to use it. Hellhounds are creatures born to destroy. They grow stronger with every kill."

"Spoken like a true cat person," he said. "They've been kept as pets for ages."

Valentine shook her head. "I'm not talking about a tendency to chew up the furniture and piss on the carpet. They are monsters who have to be convinced that they're dogs." Valentine waited until she was sure Yevgeny had absorbed her words. "Come on," she said. "Let me show you how it's done."

†WELVE

Wнеп †ess woke she кпеw †нат i† was some-
time after dawn. Not because of the light, since no vampire's
bedroom had windows. She knew it was daytime because
Dan was no longer there. Oh, his body was nestled beside her
all right, with his arm thrown across her stomach, but his skin
was cool, his muscles stony. He wasn't exactly dead, she knew
his consciousness was somewhere inside the frozen shell, but
he couldn't move between dawn and sunset. The price paid
for eternal life was a dangerous half-life.

As a werewolf, she did not approve of the strigoi's type of
magic. But she liked Dan Conover. She smiled as she lay on
her back next to him and turned her head to look at his head
on the pillow beside her. Her body was still reacting to the
time they'd spent making love. Not sex, damn it, but love.

Yes, she more than liked him. She'd consider herself a slut
for having fallen into bed with him so quickly if there hadn't
been the telepathic contact beforehand. And if she hadn't
been spying on him her entire adult life. It wasn't as if she
didn't know him, even if she was mostly a stranger to him.

Did he think of her as one of his companions? she wondered, since she'd tasted his blood as he tasted hers. She gave
a snort of laughter. Dan had a major surprise in store for him
if he thought he could treat a werewolf like a human he'd
sexually enslaved with a few drops of his sacred blood.

"Sacred my ass," she muttered.

Speaking of asses, he certainly had a nice one.

"Maybe I can make you my sex slave, Daniel, my
dear—nah, what fun would that be for either of us?"

Lifemate?

The thought struck her like a lightning bolt.

"Is that possible? For a werewolf to mate outside her own
species?"

She took a deep breath, tasting all the different scents

swirling around the bed. Dan's essence was different asleep than awake; he smelled more like a vampire now. She should have found this unpleasant, off, like meat beginning to spoil. But she was as much drawn to Dan's scent as she had been when his sex pheromones had assaulted her senses the night before. There was more to him than the vampire part of his nature. The Hunter wasn't as prominent while he slept, but the trace of it reminded her why she'd been attracted to him from the moment they met.

Still lying on her back, Tess shrugged. She was attracted to this particular vampire because he was one of the Hunter bloodline. And it all went back to Valentine, didn't it?

In order to achieve the change that turned her and her descendants into beings strong enough to easily kill their own kind, the magic Valentine used involved the sacrifice and consumption of the strongest werewolf of that long-ago time. And it must have been a willing sacrifice or the magic of the act wouldn't still be working today.

So, Dan was a sort of cousin, and being attracted to him wasn't really a perversion. And it wasn't really important right now was it? She remembered she had a job to do.

"Personal life? Ha!"

Tess grudgingly got out of bed, got herself together, and settled down in the kitchen with her iPhone and a fresh cup of coffee.

She wasn't surprised to find two voicemail messages from her mother. Even though it wasn't possible, Tess suspected her mom somehow knew exactly what she'd been up to with Dan Conover. She knew she was being paranoid, but she ignored the messages anyway. She checked for relevant news online instead. And, bingo!

Eight Dead in Unknown Animal Attack in Nevada Home

Appalled as she was, Tess read the news story beneath the headline with growing excitement. It had to be the hellhound pup. It had to be!

She had to go after it. She cursed herself for following her hunch about Valentine when she should have followed the lead from the first murders. Now even more mortals were dead and it was those devil critters' fault. The more the pups killed, the stronger the demon handler became.

She quickly pulled up a map of Nevada to find out where Henderson was located.

It's near Las Vegas. Good. That gives me a place to start.

With a decisive nod, she put away the iPhone and stood, ready to leave immediately. Then she glanced down the hall toward the bedroom.

"Stupid vampires have stupid biology," she complained. "Why do you have to sleep all day when I could use your help?"

Tess immediately reconsidered her instant reaction of thinking she and Dan were on the same side. What had a night of passion really changed?

Hell, losing her virginity might have cost her the ability to use magic. At least she was still a werewolf. She still had her mission to deal with the hellhounds.

For a moment she actually considered leaving him a note to tell him where she'd gone.

But Dan would be determined to stop her if it was necessary to destroy the nasty little whelps.

He wasn't going to let any involvement with her stop him from trying to protect his little darlings.

A couple of orgasms couldn't overcome thousands of years of werewolf/vampire rivalry over the hellhounds.

Maybe the smart thing to do would be to rip Dan Conover's heart out of his chest while he was helpless. Could she do it with claws and teeth or would she need a knife? Was there a blade sharp enough in Valentine's kitchen to help with the job?

Tess actually started to open a drawer before revulsion hit her so hard she ended up puking in the sink. She couldn't kill Dan! At least not outright murder him, no matter how practical a solution this might be.

"Damn."

She rinsed her mouth and splashed water on her face, cursing her own weakness all the while. Well, if she couldn't kill him now, she'd do it later if she had to. Right now the important thing was to get to Nevada.

Thirteen

Dan knew Tess was gone long before the sun set and he could do anything about it. He'd felt her leave and ached for her even though his consciousness had been out searching far beyond the place where his helpless body rested. Awareness of the werewolf woman seemed to have sunk into his blood and bones.

He opened his eyes on the thought, *I'll find her when I want her.* His body responded that it wanted her right now, but at his age he was well able to ignore a sexual urge—even if it was the strongest attraction he could ever remember having.

He got out of bed, stretched and scratched, and went into the bathroom. His cellular phone rang as he went back into the bedroom. He almost crushed the small machine in his rush to pick it up.

"Tess?"

"Who?" Olympias's voice came out of the small speaker.

"Good evening, darling," Dan answered quickly. "How's Baby doing?"

"You could ask how I'm doing first, you insane dog nut."

"How are you?"

"Your dog is driving me crazy."

"Why? What's she doing?" Missing her puppies, he knew, but he wasn't ready to tell the strigoi leader that he had a problem. She wouldn't want to be bothered unless the world was in imminent danger of coming to an end.

"She's growling and whining and doesn't want me to touch the puppy. She snaps at Bitch and howled like a banshee all day—I didn't know until today that psychic animals could get into my dreams."

"Sorry, Olympias. She's missing me, that's all. She's acting out because I haven't left her alone in a long time," Dan said confidently. "She's sulking. Don't let her get away with it."

"And what do you suggest I do about it?"

"You could put on some *InuYasha* anime DVDs," Dan suggested. "And pet her while she's watching. It'll help you bond."

"You want me to watch cartoons with your hellhound. I see."

Dan ignored Olympias's sarcasm and skepticism. "Maybe you can help me with something else. Do you know where Valentine is?"

"You want to spend your vacation with Valentine? Please tell me that you don't have anything better to do."

"Not exactly spend time with her," he answered. "I remembered that there was a spell she promised to teach me back in 1750 and I thought I'd remind her of it now that I have some free time. She's not at her apartment. Do you know where she is?"

He tried to sound innocently curious, but he had never been a great actor. Olympias remained suspiciously silent for a long time. He carefully didn't press her.

"Las Vegas," Olympias grudgingly answered at last. "She called me from there a couple of days ago . . . She said something incoherent to do with dragons and saving the world. I was going to head there to check it out when you diverted me to baby-sit."

No doubt Olympias was happy for the diversion; she and Valentine had never gotten along. Olympias had been a queen in mortal life and was used to having her will obeyed. Valentine was ever the wild card, one who could not be made to obey. It was always impossible to tell if Valentine was about to topple the universe, save it, or ignore it.

"Why don't I check out what Valentine's up to for you," he offered. "It's the least I can do in return for taking care of Baby."

Another long silence. They were strigoi—they were telepaths who could have felt out each other's thoughts and intentions but the age of electronic communication had brought an etiquette about long-distance mind-reading into play among friends. And frequently it was safer not to snoop.

"Whatever she's up to—don't get involved in it," Olympias finally ordered. She sighed. "Whatever you're up to—I don't want to know."

"Fair enough," he answered.

"Where do you keep the DVDs?" she asked.

Dan told her. Then he headed for Las Vegas.

Fourteen

"Mommy, I don't want to wake up. Don't make me go back in there."

Valentine slapped Yevgeny on the shoulder. She poked him in the side with her foot. "Shut up, you miserable wimp. And stop being such a trunk hog."

They'd spent the day curled around each other in the trunk of her Cadillac. She'd never be able to forget how much room the big man took up in a bed, but she hadn't considered how that would translate to the limited space in her car when they decided the hole the pup made in the motel roof would let in too much daylight. And possibly made the already rickety building unstable.

They'd had no qualms about leaving the little demon magically asleep amid the wreckage she'd made.

The trunk lid popped and Valentine shoved Yevgeny out. He landed on the ground with a grunt. She followed him out into the cool night air and gave him a hand up.

"You healed yet?" she asked.

"I need coffee," he responded. "I should have remembered to bring some," he added before she could. He began to rub her shoulders. "How are you doing, Valentine?"

"My body's fine, but my head still hurts. Telepathy can take a lot out of a girl. Tonight you are doing all the head work."

"Think strong alpha of the pack thoughts at her." He repeated her instructions of the night before.

She nodded. "Plus, it wouldn't hurt to give her some of your blood."

He glanced at his stained, ragged shirt sleeve. "She took plenty of my blood last night."

"That was an attack. You need to get her submissive and then share a few drops with her. It's a bonding thing—like with a companion but without the sex."

He frowned. "The point is to train Bela to bond with Sebastian."

"Bela? You've given it a name? See, you're getting attached."

"I'm not."

"Besides, I'm not so sure this Sebastian kid will be able to handle a hellhound even if he is a *dhamphir*. Maybe someday, but right now he's still just a child," she continued. "Only the strongest magically and telepathically of the strigoi have ever been able to keep the creatures. There are good reasons Dan doesn't give them to just anybody. Now, if I was a good little vampire drone I'd encourage you to give your little Bela to the kid. Then the hellhound could kill the *dhamphir* and we wouldn't have to worry about him killing vampires when he grows up."

"Then, why—?"

"I know his parents," she reminded Yevgeny. "Besides, I can't kill a kid any more than you could."

"Your plan is to wait until he grows up?"

"Something like that." She tugged him toward the building. "Come on, let's go teach Bela to fetch."

Fifteen

Kraas saw in energy. The ebb and flow of energy constantly streamed across his skin, through his body. The energy of mortal lives was the easiest to read. It was as common as dirt and as dull. Since he'd taken the hellhound, energy had burned constantly around him. He'd been able to concentrate on the mortals they hunted because he must. He protected his precious one, he found it prey and helped it hunt, but all the while he was dazzled by the dog's pure, evil fire.

"Such a nice puppy," he said, looking down at the animal trotting beside him. It looked up at him with hellfire glowing from its eyes.

It had grown so much that its head now reached Kraas's thigh. Huge fangs sprang out of its wide muzzle. It didn't look a thing like any of its weakling kin the vampires kept shackled from achieving their true beings.

They'd been walking for a long time, but Kraas only now realized that he was following the hellhound's lead, lost in the emanations of its power. They were going west, the hound padding along into the desert with swift determination. Why?

Prey, of course. There could be nothing else on the hellhound's mind.

Kraas smiled. "You've started to hunt on your own. Good boy! What is it you're after, eh?"

Kraas had to move away from the animal's side before he could send his senses out in search of the prey's energy.

There was another hellhound out there, wasn't there? Just barely within Kraas's range of awareness. Even fainter, almost covered by the hound's vitality, there was a hint of vampire. Kraas recognized the vampire's energy signature and threw back his head in laughter.

"It's the child vampire that fancies himself a sorcerer! The one whose spell I rode to fetch you away from Corvei. So, he's out in the desert with your sister. Perhaps she's dining on his guts. Shall we go look? Shall we kill them?"

But the hellhound was already loping far ahead. All Kraas could do was run to keep up.

"FANCY meeting you here," Tess grumbled when Dan came up beside her in the deep shadow of a tree. The thrill of delight was something she tried not to show.

It didn't work. His hand caressed the back of her neck and down her spine. "I missed you, too, sweetheart."

"When vampires say 'sweetheart' they can sometimes be taken literally," she reminded him.

"I would never eat your heart," he answered. "You're not a vampire."

She'd have preferred a promise that he'd never harm her, but why should he give her something she'd never give him? Tess turned to look at him. They were standing in the backyard of a house surrounded by yellow police tape. Mortal investigators prowled the premises, but no one noticed them.

"What are you doing here?" she asked Dan. "Surely you didn't follow me to proclaim your undead-dying love?" She kind of hoped he had.

He held her close and kissed her. After he'd sent a major whoosh of excitement through her, he let her go and said, "I found out that Valentine was in Vegas, but it turned out that she'd already left town. Then I caught the news about the mortal deaths and decided to check out what happened. What happened?" he inquired.

Typical strigoi, letting a sexual partner do all the work.

"One of your puppies did this," she told him.

He looked surprised. "One?"

She tapped her nose. "Does this lie? I haven't been able to sniff around much yet, but so far I've picked up traces of one hound and one demon."

"Valentine?"

Tess shook her head. "She's not involved with this pup."

"But a demon is?" He scratched his head, ruffling his thick hair. "Why did both of us make assumptions about Valentine if she's not involved?" He looked at the defiled suburban house. "There are no coincidences where magic is concerned."

"I've been thinking about that, and my guess is that I associated the spell used to kidnap the pups with something she'd use."

He nodded slowly. "Maybe not something she used, but magic she taught someone else. Let's ask the demon about it when we catch up to him."

He smiled in a dangerous way that showed a lot of teeth. Tess found this very sexy.

Since she knew there was no way she could evade Dan's being in on the hunt, she didn't argue about his coming along. But there was something she had to make clear.

"The hellhound has killed at least twelve people. It's found its true nature and you can't fix it. It can't be allowed to live."

He stared at her angrily, but she wouldn't flinch or look away. She couldn't back down. It was Dan who turned his back on her.

While he glared into the night, Tess concentrated on sniffing out a trail among all the scents assaulting her senses.

Finally she heard Dan say, "If it's necessary."

She knew he wasn't talking to her, or that she could get anymore agreement than that out of him.

"Whatever," she muttered under her breath.

He turned back to her. For a moment his features were hard as a statue's. Then he sighed and focused on her. "Do you have anything?"

Tess pointed. "They went that way. I'm going to transform and head after them."

He put his hand on her arm. "Don't be so old-fashioned. Come on."

He led her to a car parked a street over. She couldn't help but stare at the low-slung auto's gleaming red surface where it sat under a streetlamp.

"Wow."

After a moment's reverent silence, he said, "Go ahead. I've heard it before."

She glanced from the Ferrari to Dan Conover. "The dead really do travel fast."

He went around to the driver's door. "Get in," he told her. "And tell me where to point your nose."

Sixteen

He's not only getting the hang of it, he's getting to like it, Valentine thought as she sat on the edge of the ruined bed and watched Yevgeny and Bela.

The pair were on the floor in the middle of the room, and neither of them was currently bleeding. He had the dog on her back, one hand on her belly and the other touching her head. His big blond Russian eyes were closed, his features stern—except for the occasional hint of a tiny smile. He and Bela the hellhound were deep in telepathic conversation. And getting along quite nicely for the moment.

Yevgeny had finally gotten the idea that the most important part of training a hellhound was conducted from the inside of its bright and stubborn little head.

Valentine nodded in satisfaction that Yevgeny had once again mastered a skill from her.

"Always my smartest pupil. Always the quickest study. Sex. Languages. Magic. This." She sighed. "I miss you," she told him, knowing he couldn't hear her. She gave an ironic shrug. "Regret. The spice of life."

A moment later, Yevgeny let Bela up and backed away on hands and knees. The pup was instantly up and coming at him. But Yevgeny shifted shape as she came, going from human form to the fanged and clawed shape vampires called the mask. He drew his lips back and growled. The hellhound dropped to her belly and whimpered.

Yevgeny stroked her submissive head. "Good girl." He turned his head to give Valentine a triumphant, fanged smiled.

She gasped. Damn he made a gorgeous vampire!

Tess's head jerked to the right as the car passed through a crossroad.

"Stop the car!" Tess shouted.

Dan responded immediately and Tess jumped out to taste the air more thoroughly. Dan joined her in the middle of the crossroads. Stars wheeled above and the roads stretched out across the empty landscape.

"Do you smell that?" she asked him.

"I sense it," he answered. "Strigoi and hellhound."

"Nearby." She turned in a slow circle and pointed. "Demon and hellhound that way." She glanced at the vampire. "Choose."

He didn't answer, but gestured her back to the car.

"What's the matter?" Yevgeny asked. He morphed back to his human semblance. "Are you all right?"

Valentine blinked, focused on his concerned face. *You're prettier showing your true nature,* she thought.

Yevgeny must have caught her thought because he looked startled, but the dog came up behind him and he immediately returned his attention to Bela.

Valentine got up and went to stand by a broken window. She breathed in the cool desert breeze and rubbed her arms. More than air circulated around the deserted motel.

"Something wicked this way comes," she murmured. "Among other things." And stood back to see what would happen next.

Seventeen

When Dan kicked the door open he was transformed into full Hunter's mask. Tess came through the window an instant after him in her wolf shape.

The strigoi male jumped to his feet, holding the brindle pup in his arms. "She's mine!" he declared. "Back off, Conover."

"And your little dog, too," a voice drawled from the shadows.

Tess snarled at the other vampire.

Dan stalked toward the blond vampire. He wasn't sure whether he was going to kill the thief or snatch the pup first. But he hesitated when the pup lifted its head and growled at him.

Still in the corner, Valentine said, "They've bonded." He glanced her way. She shrugged. "What can you do? It's true love."

"Bonded?" the blond vampire shouted. "No, we haven't! Bela's for Sebastian."

"Think again, Yevgeny," she answered. "Do you really think you can walk away from her now? Look at how he's holding her," she said to Dan. "Look at how she's protecting him."

Tess morphed back into her human shape and adjusted the bits of leather wrapped around her to modestly cover herself. She looked like an amazon character in a role-playing game.

Dan came back to his own human form and took a long, hard look at Yevgeny. The younger vampire stared back just long enough to show he wasn't afraid of a fight, then looked away before it became necessary for Dan to prove his dominance.

Smart boy, Dan thought. "Who the hell are you? What are you doing with my dog?" He jerked a thumb at Valentine. "And her? Did you help him steal Baby's puppies?" he asked Valentine.

"Why's the other one with a demon?" Tess put in.

"What other puppy?" Yevgeny asked. "I only took Bela—and I didn't steal her. I left gold for her."

"Oh, shit," Tess said. "It was the spell he used. I bet I know what happened."

All gazes turned to the werewolf witch.

"Go on, Tess," Dan said.

"Demons have waited a long time to get their claws on a hellhound but they couldn't get to them on their own. They're experts at exploiting other beings' use of magic, but not much good at working spells on their own. They more or less need hosts they can attach themselves to so they can manipulate the host's use of energy."

"Welcome to Witch School 101," Valentine said.

"Don't be mean," Yevgeny told her. "Go on," he urged Tess. "Tell me how I screwed up and involved a demon in this mess."

Tess smiled at the big blond. Dan didn't like it. Valentine sniggered.

"My bet is that a demon followed you and stole the other puppy while the spell still held Dan."

"You let a demon into my house?" Dan shouted.

"I didn't mean to," Yevgeny said. "I needed the pup and was following tradition to get her."

"I've left plenty of bodies lying around to discourage that tradition."

He was not happy with what Yevgeny had done, but as he watched the pup lick the younger vampire's chin and the vampire rub the pup's head without seeming to notice, he knew he wasn't going to kill Yevgeny. He'd let him get away with the theft—for the hellhound's sake.

"How did you get involved in this?" he asked Valentine.

"Innocent bystander," she answered.

"I asked for her help training it," Yevgeny said. "And she taught me all the magic I know."

"You poor dear," Tess sneered.

"But where are the demon and my other pup?" Dan asked.

"Here," Valentine answered.

She pointed toward the window just as a huge black body came crashing through it.

Eighteen

"Damn!" Tess said at the sight of the purely malevolent hellhound. It reeked of insatiable hate and hunger. She knew death on four paws when she saw it.

She stopped thinking and morphed, missing some of the action as her perspective and vision changed from human to wolf.

The demon entered to add to the chaos in the crowded room within the instant it took her to change. The creature screamed hatred as he raced toward Valentine. The ancient vampire's attention was on the attacking hellhound.

Tess sprang onto the demon's bare back before the creature reached its prey. She sank her teeth through greenish skin, tasted metallic blood, crunched through bones. It still tried to crawl forward even after she'd severed its spinal cord. Tess used all her strength to hold the demon's body down. She gnawed at the thing until it finally stopped moving.

Roars, shouts, and the crash of bodies drew Tess's attention away from the corpse. Worry killed any desire to feast on fresh meat. She spun, ready to help Dan.

Valentine watched Yevgeny whirl around, using the bulk of his body to protect the animal in his arms. The heavy black beast leapt onto his back. Blood arced upward onto the walls and ceiling. Yevgeny cried in pain.

Terror raced through Valentine.

"Yevgeny!"

The demon appeared before her and blocked her view. The werewolf brought the demon down. This brief struggle kept Valentine from getting to the others, but to immortals a moment was a long time. Actions that would have appeared to happen at light speed to a mortal seemed in slow motion to her.

She shouted to Dan for help, but it wasn't Dan Conover she saw when she looked his way. "Corvei," she breathed.

When the werewolf tried to spring forward, Valentine grabbed her and buried her fingers deeply into thick fur.

"Calm down, Tess," she urged when the werewolf struggled and snapped at her. "I'm saving your life. You can't go to him like this. Corvei specialized in beast hunts in the arena. You need to change shape before he goes after the wolf as well as the hound."

Dan Conover could change into two types of vampire shape but he faced the hellhound in human form. As an Enforcer, he always carried a silver knife, but he didn't have the weapon in his hands now. He was a man going up against a monster, but as a mortal he hadn't been an ordinary man.

Corvei's eyes were cold, narrowed with concentration. His face was expressionless. The ability to kill blazed from his smallest movement. It was a gladiator against a wild beast, facing off in the center of the room.

"He's about to kill one of his own children," Valentine told Tess. "He can't do this any other way."

THE red eyes that tried to stare Dan down were full of intelligence. He wouldn't let himself care. He didn't feel compassion for the madness he saw in those eyes either. He never looked away as he circled slowly, assessing how to attack.

The beast circled as well, its eyes locked on his. Hot drool dripped from fangs too large for its muzzle. Its growl was a continuous diesel-engine rumble in its deep chest. Its steely claws gouged the concrete floor. Dangerous and beautiful, it studied him.

But it didn't have patience. It didn't have experience. It couldn't wait.

"You're still a puppy," Dan said when the hellhound sprang toward him.

He grabbed its front legs while it was still in the air and swung it around. Its huge head swung back and forth, seeking flesh. It bit into his forearm, but Dan didn't let go even as the beast worried at the wound. Vampire flesh was tougher than mortal. Dan bled, but his arm wasn't bit in two the way a man's would have been.

He smashed the beast on its back onto the concrete. He followed it down, planting his knees on its exposed abdomen. It snapped for his throat, raked claws across him. Dan ignored pain and the creature's piteous howling. He extended his own hard claws.

He killed the hellhound the same way he would have another vampire. By opening its chest and ripping out its beating heart. The heart was still beating when Dan stood with it clenched tightly in his hand.

With his own howl of pain, Dan threw the ruined pup's dark heart as hard as he could through the gaping window.

He dropped his arm and looked around for his next kill. He started toward Yevgeny. The other vampire lay still on the floor. The uncorrupted puppy was licking his face.

Tess's arms came around him before he could take another step. She pressed her human form against him, flooding him with her warmth and life. She brought back his sanity with her touch. He grabbed her and held on as hard as he could. He mourned this loss as he had mourned all the lives he'd taken as a gladiator, strigoi, and Enforcer. Tess was a light beyond the pain. Tess beckoned him with the promise of life to hold on to.

"Let go of the hellhounds," she whispered to him. "Now you have a werewolf to call your own."

VALENTINE dropped down beside where Yevgeny lay in a widening pool of blood. She had to push Bela aside to ease his head into her lap.

The skin was blue around his pale lips, his heartbeat faint and slow.

She stroked hair away from his face. "Oh, no, I'm not losing you again."

Bela was sniffing at Yevgeny's shoulder. Valentine held her wrist out to the little hellhound. "Here."

It obligingly bit her.

She thrust her bloody wrist into Yevgeny's mouth and let life pour into him. "This is the second time in a week," she muttered at sharing her blood like this. "I am such a slut."

Within moments, Yevgeny was suckling from her as if he

would never stop. She closed her eyes and let the pleasure of the sharing take her.

When she couldn't take it anymore, she commanded, "Stop!"

His tongue slid delicately across her wrist. A thought teased her, *Are you sure?*

He sat up and they helped each other stand, but continued holding hands. He smiled down at her. "Why did you do that?" he asked.

"You were dying."

"I'm a vampire now," he reminded her. "I'm already dead."

She opened her mouth, closed it. "Right," she said. "I knew that."

"Oh, yes, you knew what you were doing. Don't play the ditzy dame with me."

He pulled her close. They both stank of the heady perfume of blood. Her need for Yevgeny was stronger than ever. Any moment now she was going to sink her fangs deep into his delightful flesh. And he was going to do the same to her.

Fancy that.

"What about your bond with Haven?" he asked as he began to caress her.

"Haven?" she asked, and laughed beneath their kiss. "Let his girlfriend have Haven."

Russian Roulette

✝

ERIN McCARTHY

One

Alistair Kirk embraced the darkness of the night. British born and raised, he had been used to cloudy overcast days, and early in life had despised the bright, burning heat of the summer sun. Ironic then, that as a vampire he found himself living in New Orleans, where the sun could sear your skin to a crisp, throbbing burn in twenty minutes.

But it was also a city that at night still moved and breathed, people flowing in and out of the French Quarter at all hours of the night, together, alone, shifting through shadows in search of good, clean fun, or not so clean fun. It suited Alistair, the contrast of bright and dark, and he stayed inside during the day, asleep, and hit the streets at night to work, to dine, to socialize.

He wasn't doing any of those on this night. He was doing something that was undoubtedly a big-ass mistake, yet he couldn't *not* do it. Couldn't leave it alone. Jack, Alistair's bandmate, had told him not to get involved, but as Alistair moved silently through the lush back courtyard of the expensive condo building, he knew it was the right thing to do.

There was a woman being held captive inside, and while it wasn't any of his business, he knew about her situation, and couldn't just stand back and do nothing. He was a vampire, not an asshole, and he wasn't into seeing someone else suffer. So he climbed into the house through a second-story back window, by way of the porch roof, trying to make as little noise as possible. It was easy enough to get inside with his vampire strength without breaking a sweat or breathing hard. Gaining entrance wasn't the problem. The real danger was that if the owner of the house caught him breaking and entering, there would be a fight on his hands.

Inside the room, which he already knew was a tastefully decorated guest bedroom, Alistair paused to get his bearings. The house was dark, silent, but he realized immediately he wasn't alone. The room should be empty, but it wasn't, and he was relieved to realize he wouldn't have to penetrate deeper into the house. He sensed the presence of the woman he was looking for, smelled her fear, before he saw her.

When he did, eyes shifting to the left where he knew the bed was, he clenched his fists in fury, disgust. He had no idea who she was, but the woman was strapped down to the bed, blindfolded and gagged, her hands behind her head and shackled to the wall. It was a sight that curled his stomach into knots, made all the more sick and twisted by the surroundings of tasteful, upper-middle class décor. The bed she was secured to was an antique four-poster, piled high with silk pillows, while an impressive art collection splayed salon-style over it. Between the bed and the art was the wall mounting for the shackles.

Alistair stared, revolted by the scene in front of him. There was a goddamn flat-screen TV across from the woman, and a bureau with fresh flowers and bottled water, like a guest might arrive at any moment and their hostess wanted to be ready with first-rate hospitality. It went beyond what he had expected. This was a kidnapper toying with her victim, amusing herself, and he no longer regretted his decision to become involved.

He moved toward the woman, trying to ignore the way her chest rose and fell quickly as she realized how close he was to her, her panic clearly increasing. Alistair assessed the straps holding her down. Those he could snap with no problem. He did that first, disconcerted by the gasping sound of fear that wheezed out from behind the gag stuffed into her mouth. She couldn't see him, had no clue who he was, and it tugged at him at the same time he knew there was no time for explanations. They had to get out immediately, damn it, but he didn't want to scare her any more than she already was.

It was risky, but he whispered in her ear, "It's okay. I'm going to get you out of here."

Her body went still and the only response was the rushing of air from her nostrils. Alistair wasn't sure if she was calming down or if she had gone rigid from fear. He didn't have time to worry about it. First things first. He didn't want to have to drag her with him like dead weight, so he needed to fortify her. Since she was clearly too weak to break her constraints, she must have been denied feedings for several days.

Slicing his wrist with his fangs, he moved his hand over her mouth, than jerked down the gag. Before she could scream or say anything, he clamped his wrist over her, his blood trickling down into her mouth. She drank eagerly, her long legs moving restlessly. While she fed, Alistair looked at her, still blindfolded, and confirmed for himself that he had never met this woman before. He would have remembered if he had, because even under current conditions in the dark he could tell she was gorgeous.

She had long, thick, lustrous hair, a rich deep blonde that didn't come from a bottle, smooth skin, high cheekbones, a straight nose, and amazing plump lips that covered his flesh so covetously he was mildly disturbed. He was attracted to her, and he hadn't expected that. Didn't want it. But her long legs, in tight, low-riding jeans, and her flat, taut belly, exposed from the pull of her tiny T-shirt, were too difficult to ignore.

He jerked his wrist back out of her mouth, ignoring her moan of protest, and stuffed the gag back in. There was no time for talking, and if she screamed, they would have some serious issues to deal with, like the possibility of Cassandra walking in and discovering them. But he did want to remove her blindfold, needing her to walk on her own. Digging his hands into her thick hair, he found the knot of the fabric and tried to untie it, but his fingers were too big, too clumsy, too aware of the clock ticking and how long he had already been in the room. So he gave up on gentle and just yanked it over her head, taking a few hairs with him.

When he saw her eyes, he almost wished he'd left the blindfold in place. They were dark, nearly black, their almond shape adding to the exotic beauty of her breathtaking face. She was beyond beautiful. She was exquisite. And furious. There was unmasked hatred in her eyes, fear intermixed with a violent and fierce anger, a hysterical need to survive. It unnerved him, but hell, had he expected gratitude? She had no idea who he was or what the hell was going on, and God only knew what had already been done to her.

Ignoring the venomous expression on her face, he whispered instructions. "When I release your hands, get up and head for the window. We'll climb down, then go straight to the street."

She gave a brief nod, so Alistair reached up and jerked the shackles right out of the wall, taking big hunks of plaster with it. As paint flecks and dust rained down on the woman's head, she closed her eyes to avoid the debris. Then before he even needed to prod her, she was up and off the bed, running for the window, feet bare, the shackles still dangling from her wrists. Alistair followed, glad her fear hadn't overrode her sense of survival. It had made an impressive noise when he'd yanked her free and they needed to get the hell out.

Darting a glance back toward the door, he didn't sense anyone coming up the stairs, and he leaped out through the window after her. Reaching down, he quickly grabbed her arm when she lost her footing and slipped, dangling over the side of the porch roof, shackles smacking her in the thighs. He felt her shoulder wrench out of its socket, and heard her gasp of pain from behind the gag, but when he let her down carefully, she ignored the injury and just stumbled to her feet, glancing around to get her bearings.

Before he could say a word, she took off running.

In the wrong direction. She was headed toward the back of the property, into the labyrinth of courtyards and back alleys behind the condo complex. Alistair caught up to her easily and touched her arm, intending to redirect her toward the street. But when his hand landed on her flesh, she turned and swung hard, nailing him straight across the face with the length of the shackles, her fists closed for leverage.

Alistair didn't duck in time, and he stumbled from the blow, the pain exploding behind his eyes. Fuck. He hadn't expected that. Shaking his head to clear his blurry vision, he yanked his fangs back out of his tongue where they had become imbedded when his jaw had snapped shut. Not a pleasant feeling. She was already running away from him again while he stood stunned, and even as he swallowed his own blood, he had to admire her tenacity. She was no ordinary fledgling vampire, which was precisely why she'd found herself chained to the wall in Cassandra's town house.

"You're going the wrong way," he told her, reaching out and grabbing her arm again. This time he dodged the blow when she swung at him with her chains. The desperate arch of her arms propelled her sideways when the shackles didn't make impact with anything, and she stumbled from the pull of gravity.

Eyes wild, she caught her balance and faced him. He knew exactly what she was going to do. Try to dart past him.

But he could hear movement from the house, and knew that someone was going to find them if they didn't move. He, for one, didn't want to get into a smackdown with the woman he had been married to for about a minute. Two women throwing things at him was really one too many.

So he took the easy route out. He stepped forward, grabbing her around the thighs, underneath her butt, and hauled her over his shoulder. Even as she stiffened and punched him in the gut, he just ran, regardless of how much he was jostling her around, trying to ignore her fists railing at him over and over. The blows didn't hurt, since he was an aged vampire, while she was young and weak from days without blood. But it was seriously annoying.

He was saving her, damn it. At great risk to himself, he might add. Whatever happened to the grateful and swooning fair maiden?

Apparently she had gotten sick of waiting for her knight and was determined to save her own ass.

He could respect that, even if it was bruising his abs. He'd heal.

But when he cut across the narrow streets of the Quarter, feet pounding on the pavement, and finally paused to catch his breath in the alley that ran parallel to the bar he owned, not only didn't she express any sort of gratitude, she took off running again the second her feet touched the ground. As she did, she was pulling the gag out of her mouth.

He had a feeling a massive scream was on tap.

"Shit." Alistair gave a sigh of exasperation and used his vampire speed to move around in front of her and cut her off.

She collided with him, hard, but he held his ground. Bouncing backward, she spoke for the first time, expression fierce. "Get the hell out of my way."

Alistair lifted an eyebrow. She wasn't American or British. Her accent sounded Russian. "No. You can't go running off by yourself. They'll catch you before the sun rises."

Obviously that didn't impress her because she tried to feint past him and run for the street, but he caught her and pushed her up against the brick wall. They needed to get a few things straight. "Stop it, damn it! I'm trying to help you and you're going to get us both staked if you don't knock it off."

"Let me go." She tried to shove him off of her, but he was stronger.

There was desperation in her eyes, but she worked hard not to show her fear. Up close, her features were even more beautiful than when he'd seen her on the bed. All vampires had smooth, pale, and flawless skin, but this woman had a flush on each cheek, and inky dark eyelashes that covered rich amber eyes, exotic and compelling. It was clear she was a survivor, and he admired that at the same time he acknowledged it made his decision to help her more difficult.

Especially when she kneed him in the nuts.

Alistair should have seen it coming, but he had been too busy taking an inventory of her assets, only to find she had nailed him in his. Even as he doubled over in pain, he had enough sense to reach out and pin her to the wall with one hand on her chest, knowing she would use the opportunity to flee.

As a cold sweat broke out over him from the pain and he sucked in a few breaths, and he wondered why the hell there was any justice in still having his testicles racked when he was a powerful four-hundred-year-old vampire, she tried a different escape tactic. This time, instead of trying to dodge right or left, she went limp and slid down the length of him, breaking free of his grip. Alarmed, Alistair stepped forward and pinned her to the wall with his legs. It was a good strategy, effectively trapping her.

Except her head was now buried in his crotch, her hot breath slamming across the fly of his jeans.

He was a man, she was gorgeous, and his body reacted accordingly.

Bloody hell. What an embarrassing way to cap off his rescue attempt.

He really should have stuck to playing bass guitar and bartending, and left this noble hero crap to someone else.

SASHA Chechikov stared at the vampire in front of her, his knees holding her tightly against the wall, hands clamped onto her head, and contemplated her next move. She was squatting a foot from the ground, her legs cramped, feet bare in the dirty alley. Her wrists were still shackled, she was starving for a drink of blood, and she was well aware that the longer she was out on the street, the greater the danger of being returned to that room where she had been kept for the past four days.

The man was stronger than she was. Tenfold. There was no way she could overpower or outrun him, as she had discovered at least three times in the past ten minutes.

Predictably enough, he had an erection quickly growing in his jeans from the way she had slid down his body and the fact that she was eye level with his zipper. It was a typical male response and she knew how she could distract him. How to use the gift of her beauty.

It would be easy enough to reach out, unzip his pants, and take him into her mouth. She could drive him to distraction with the tip of her tongue, let him lower his defenses as she took him into her over and over. Then when he was exploding, insensate with pleasure, she could pull back, and escape.

It would work. But the thought of actually doing so made her stomach heave in protest. She couldn't. Wouldn't. She'd rather die than be forced to use her body to secure her safety, the way she had with her husband, Gregor. And as of yet, though she would embrace her own death willingly, she wasn't really sure how she could arrange for it now that she was a vampire.

So if death or sex weren't an option, she would have to use a different tactic.

"Be reasonable," he was saying from above her, his voice tight. "I'm here to help you. My name is Alistair Kirk."

The name meant nothing to her, and she considered herself well versed in major vampire players. She had learned the who's who of the vampire world in her torturous year of marriage. There was no reason to trust this man. She trusted no one, and he had no reason to assist her.

Reaching up, she gripped the waistband of his jeans, the chain that ran between her hands pulling taut. It brought her face, nose, mouth, into direct contact with his crotch. His erection.

"What are you doing?" he asked, sounding a little disconcerted for the first time.

"I would like to stand," she said. "If you please." She could play nice. Cooperate. Kill him with kindness, as the expression went.

"Oh. Sorry." With his elbows, he helped her rise, keeping a firm grip on her.

Sasha found herself staring into pale green eyes. He was an attractive man, she had to own that. A stern chin, a regal nose, and even, white teeth that gleamed in the dark. His face was narrow, his hair a rich brown, cut very short.

"We need to move," he said. "Cassandra will be looking for you."

That name meant nothing either, though it had to be the vampire who had been holding Sasha captive. The vampire her childhood friend, Ivan, had willingly turned her over to.

The betrayal stung, and despite the days she'd had to reflect on it, it still had the potential to bring her to tears. To make her feel vulnerable and wretched. So she clamped down on those feelings. Stuffed them away. She was good at that.

"Where are you taking me?" she asked, striving for an even tone. She would pretend to cooperate. Then at the right moment, she would free herself from him.

The thought of having to do so, having to run, yet again, wearied her for a split second. It had been a long year of instability. She had left Russia for the first time in her life to go to Las Vegas at her husband's insistence. Now she had come to New Orleans from Vegas for sanctuary, for respite from the running, and for the company of someone she had trusted, loved. That was not what she had found. Ivan had turned on her, and she was in as grave a danger as ever. Perhaps more. There was no use in feeling sorry for herself. That would create weakness she could ill afford.

Nor was there any use in longing for friendship or love. Those were never to be hers, and she knew that.

"We need to hide you."

That she certainly agreed with. Shifting on the wall to put more distance between his face and hers, she curled her fingers into the belt loops of his jeans. It would create the illusion she was leaning on him, relying on his advice, input. "Where do you think is safe?"

His eyebrow went up. "Just trust me."

She was desperate, not stupid. And her natural instinct

was to tell him to go to hell and suffer every mile along the way, but she needed to remain calm and convince him that she was not going to escape. That she was grateful for his assistance. Not trusting herself to speak without sarcasm, she just nodded.

"And who are you, by the way?" he asked.

She hesitated, unsure why he didn't already know that, and wondering if she should give him a fake name. But then again, why exactly did it matter? If he didn't know who she was, then perhaps his motives for releasing her had nothing to do with her, per se, but his relationship with Cassandra. Vampire politics.

She was so damn sick of it.

Only there was no out. There had never been an out for her.

So she just looked him straight in the eye and said, "I am Sasha Chechikov."

He knew the name. It was obvious in the way his expression changed from curious to enlightened. "Gregor's wife," he said.

Unfortunately, yes, for a torturous twelve months, seven days, and approximately sixteen hours. They had been unable to pinpoint the time of Gregor's murder any closer than that. "Yes."

"The undercover vampire slayer turned vampire after your husband's death."

"Yes." News traveled fast. She had been leading an online slayer's group for two years without her husband having any idea what she was doing. Her goal had been to eliminate those who lived so unnaturally, in particular Gregor. He had been her only personal experience with a vampire for her entire life, and when she had gone to Vegas with him and met others she had learned that he did not represent the whole of his kind. She knew now that there were good and bad vampires, and those who floated in the middle, just like with people. Many did what was simply necessary.

That was her, doing whatever was necessary.

Except for sex. She could not trade her body for security ever again.

"And the slayers want you dead now, right?"

"Of course." That was what slayers did, kill vampires.

And she would be a triumph to kill. If they took down the slayer who had turned to the dark side, it would be a major victory. "But they don't know where I am."

"So Cassandra was willing to turn you over for cash."

"That is my assumption."

"Charming. Though just like her to sell out one of her own for a quick buck."

The look on his face convinced her he knew Cassandra and didn't like her. That was definitely to Sasha's advantage. "How did you know about me?"

But Alistair just took her wrist and dragged her to the back of the alley. "I smell vampire," he whispered.

Heart pounding, Sasha followed him willingly. She could deal with Alistair Kirk. The unknown was infinitely scarier.

They wove their way through garbage cans, the overpowering smell of grease assaulting her nostrils and making her stomach churn. Sasha was so thirsty, her mouth and throat dry and irritated, her fangs throbbing from want. The brief drink Alistair had given her had only taken the edge off of her thirst, and she knew she could easily swallow six pints to replace what she had missed in the past four days.

Alistair pushed open a door in the back alley and led her inside a dimly lit storage room. She could see shelves with boxes lining both walls, and when she kicked a box on the floor that she hadn't seen, she glanced down and saw it was filled with bottles of liquor.

"You okay?" he asked her. "We need to find you some shoes."

"I am fine." And a little unnerved at being led by him, his warm, big hand firmly clasping hers. His solicitousness almost felt genuine, and she had to remind herself to stay on guard. No one cared about her. They never had, and she was the only one who could look after her.

Yet somehow it didn't surprise her when he fumbled around on a shelf in the dark and turned to her with some kind of tool. "Hold your hands out."

She did silently, pulling the chain taut between the wrist shackles.

Alistair cut off the chain at the base of each wrist cuff, catching the chain before it fell to the ground. "I can't get the handcuffs off with these, but this is better. We'll just pretend you have odd taste in jewelry."

Then he smiled at her, and an attractive man turned absolutely gorgeous. Unable to answer, she just drank in the sight of him, eyes perusing his features, inspecting his broad shoulders and muscular arms wielding the metal cutters. She felt . . . flushed, maybe almost even slightly aroused, or at the very least attracted to him, and that was more than shocking. It was appalling.

Sasha frowned, unnerved by her reaction. "Where are we going?"

"We're going to hide you right out in the open for now." He pulled her toward another door. "Follow my lead."

Glancing at the back door, Sasha debated her options. She had no idea where she was. Running didn't seem a wise choice at this point. She would stay calm and play Alistair Kirk's game for now. She followed him into a bar, emerging behind the counter of a smoky, dark room, the walls grim and faded, ceiling low. It was a small square, an isolated back bar behind a narrow front room, with three men sitting at stools.

Not men. Vampires.

She could tell the difference now.

The female bartender was a vampire, too, and she glanced over at them in surprise. "Hey, Al, what are you doing here tonight? It's your night off."

Alistair had waved to the men and done a ritualistic sort of handshake with one of them, who had propped himself up in the corner, his shaggy hair in his eyes.

"What's up, bro?" he said, flicking his hair back.

"I stopped by to show off my girlfriend," Alistair said casually, pulling Sasha close against him. "Isn't she gorgeous?"

Two

†HOUGH ALISTAIR HAD SHOCKED HER, SASHA HAD lived with Gregor long enough to be able to effectively hide her emotions under any circumstances. Even as she fought the urge to yank back out of his too-tight grip, his control over her irritating and panic-inducing, she managed to stay still and smile politely.

"This is Jenny."

Jenny? Did she look like a Jenny?

Obviously not, because all three men looked doubtful, the one who'd spoken earlier even saying, "Jenny? For real?"

She nodded and smiled. "Hi."

"So . . . how long have you two known each other?" He took a pull on his cigarette. "I'm Jack, by the way."

Sasha paused, not knowing what would be an appropriate answer. There was something about the way Jack was staring at her that made her feel he knew they were not a couple.

"Lay off," Alistair said, his tone annoyed. "It's none of your freaking business how long we've known each other, and you're making Jenny uncomfortable."

"What?" Jack held his hand up. "Dude, relax. I was just asking." He smiled at Sasha. "Did I make you uncomfortable?"

She nodded. If she pretended to be shy and awkward, she would not have to speak. Though she thought Alistair's reaction was too strong for the innocuous remark Jack had made. He was not playing it entirely cool.

"For real? Shit, sorry." Jack shrugged, looking more amused than repentant.

The whole situation was making her uncomfortable. The room was small and there were four—five if you counted Alistair's—sets of eyes on her. It put her in fight or flight mode, neither of which was the safest or smartest action for her to take. Yet she no longer knew how to make casual conversation, especially since she had spent the previous six months in Las Vegas pretending not to speak English, so her husband would not know she, in fact, could, most proficiently.

"It is all right." Though she was definitely questioning why Alistair had brought her into the bar. Exposing her to the view of others struck her as incredibly dangerous.

She questioned it even more when she realized there were two men in the front section of the bar. Vampires. Moving toward them.

Alistair squeezed her hand and turned her so her back was pressed against the bar, and she was no longer facing the room. Instantly she stiffened, even though she told herself he had done it to shield her. But she still didn't trust him, and she couldn't stand a man pinning her, invading her space, taking away her breath and dominating her.

She was about to step to the side away from him when he hissed in her ear, "Play along. Those are Cassandra's bodyguards."

And then he shifted his mouth and kissed her.

Sasha froze, his lips warm on hers, his arms around her back, threading their way into her hair.

"Relax," he murmured, pulling back. "They're watching us."

It was a valid point, and a good cover, yet she felt smothered, panicked, memories of her husband surrounding her, holding her, his breath fetid and stale, eyes cruel. She knew the damage it had done to her, having sex with Gregor and pretending that she wanted him so that he didn't beat her, rape her. It had been a disgusting, humiliating trade-off, and she knew that she had completely lost her sexuality.

Or so she'd thought. Alistair wasn't Gregor, and his touch was gentle, his grip in her hair soothing, stroking. It was a pleasant kiss. His lips didn't crush and take, but danced lightly across her skin, caressing her mouth, kissing the corners, the center, her chin, her nose. It flustered her, threw her off balance, and made her suddenly want to cry.

She was so tired. So lonely. The idea of resting her head against someone, of feeling the genuine touch of a man who cared about her was so appealing, she felt the ache in every inch of her body. It was a throb, the desire to relax and let down her guard nearly overwhelming.

Which made her feel weak, and powerless.

As she found herself tentatively kissing him back to both preserve their cover and to just see what it would feel like, the sweep of his tongue teasing along her lips, Sasha hated Alistair Kirk for making her want what she couldn't have.

And she was going to make him pay for it.

ALISTAIR had been a little worried his stroke of genius plan to hide Sasha with an impromptu make-out session was going to be shot to hell if she didn't relax and stop standing so damn stiffly. She had looked and felt like she was afraid of catching a communicable disease from him instead of embracing a lover. It had been mildly insulting, frankly, but he told himself to get over it and not take it personally. She'd been chained to a wall not an hour earlier.

It must be tough to play the horny bar wench under those circumstances. Yet he was still relieved, and okay, turned on, when she finally loosened up and kissed him back. The girl had skill. She was doing amazing things with her lips and tongue, matching him stroke for stroke.

If it felt a little rehearsed, a little controlled, like she was an actress playing a part, well, hell, he was willing to over-look that for the moment. She *was* acting, pretending to be his girlfriend to save both their asses. Didn't mean he couldn't enjoy the moment.

He liked the way her hair felt, soft and thick, and the way her thin body pressed against his. She had stunning long legs, and he had a sudden image of them wrapped around him, naked. Taking the kiss deeper, he knew he was going further than he should, knew he was getting well and truly aroused, knew that he wanted to lift her up onto that bar and kiss her from head to toe. Her lips were amazing, full and smooth, kissing him with confidence and a show of experience.

Sasha was only a few inches shorter, and when he opened his eyes briefly to see if the whole thing was making her as crazy turned on as it was him, he was unnerved to see hers were locked on him, a cold question in them.

That would be a no.

She didn't look turned on at all. She looked angry.

Yet her lips were still kissing him.

It was incredibly disturbing, and Alistair pulled back, breaking contact immediately. Looking over her shoulder, he scanned the room for Cassandra's bodyguards, but all he saw was Jack and a few other musician friends grinning from ear to ear.

"Nice," Jack said. "I give it an eight."

Jack had to know this was the vampire being sold to slayers, since he and Jack were roommates and Alistair had never mentioned any new girlfriend to him. Yet Jack was clearly willing to stay quiet about it, even if he hadn't agreed with Alistair about getting involved. His friend was keeping his cover for him, and he appreciated it.

"Thanks," Alistair said, striving for casual, dropping his hands from her hair. "I find Jenny inspiring." He leaned forward and murmured in a low voice. "Two minutes, then we'll leave."

He forced himself to face his friends and ignored the question in her eyes. "What are you guys up to?"

Sam shrugged, his shock of reddish-brown hair flopping with the movement. "Just getting a drink after work. Listening to Jack whine about his chick problems."

Alistair leaned against the bar, like he was settling in to talk, because that's normally what he would do. He owned the bar, affectionately known as The Coffin, though the sign outside read The Corner. The crowd every night was a good fifty percent vampire, Bourbon Street musicians who came in after their last set to drink and hang out, and they liked The Coffin nickname. It amused them. "What's up with you and Cheryl, Jack?"

"Broke up."

Rolling his eyes, Alistair reached for Sasha's hand, because that's what he would do if she were really his girlfriend. He didn't dare look at her. He was afraid he'd see nothing but blind fury on her face and he didn't think he could keep up the farce with those dark eyes shooting daggers into him. "By the way, Jenny, baby, this is Jack, Sam, and Carp. This lovely bartender next to us is Raven."

"It is a pleasure to meet each of you," Sasha said, her voice even, cultured, formal.

Alistair wondered what exactly Sasha Chechikov's story was. He knew she'd been married to the ever weird and always

cruel Gregor Chechikov, and rumor had it she was no griev-
ing widow. When she was still mortal, even before his death,
she'd been a slayer in Vegas. So how had she wound up in
New Orleans chained to Cassandra's wall?

All he'd known is what Jack had told him—a vampire was
being sold to slayers so they could kill her, and that it was
Cassandra doing the deal.

Maybe he should have asked more questions, but having
lost someone important himself to slayers, he had just acted,
appalled at the idea of a vampire turning another of their kind
over for a certain, torturous death.

"So, Jenny, where are you from?" Sam asked conversa-
tionally.

Alistair didn't wait for Sasha to reply. He reached out and
nudged Jack's arm off of the bar. "You're always breaking up
with Cheryl. How long will this last? 'Til tomorrow night?"

"No way, man. This is for good this time. It's finished.
Finito."

It was a diversionary tactic that worked. Alistair had avoided
Sasha having to answer Sam's casual question.

Yet after Jack finished speaking, Sasha turned to Sam and
said, "I am from New York."

Annoyed that she had spoken when he had obviously
turned the conversation so she didn't have to, Alistair
squeezed her hand. She squeezed back. Hard. So hard it cut
off the circulation to his fingers. He increased his own pressure, until they were engaged in some sort of hand combat
behind the counter. It was ludicrous. Yet he would win and he
wanted her to know that.

But when he glanced at her, he realized the blood had
leeched from her face.

Instinctively, he knew that displaying a show of strength,
of dominance, to Sasha was a mistake. She had been captive.
Married to Gregor.

He immediately released her hand and leaned forward to
kiss her on the cheek. "Ready to go home?" he asked, for the
benefit of the room as a whole.

"Sure, just trot her out, start a conversation, then blow us
off. Whatever, you know," Sam said, rolling his eyes good-
naturedly.

"Good, glad you understand," he said. "I'll see you all

tomorrow. It's my turn to play." He spent more time oversee-ing his bar than playing bass in the band these days, but he usually got in one or two nights a week. It kept him from get-ting bored.

"Sure." Jack gave him a pointed look. "Have a good night."

Be careful, was the silent message.

"Yep. Thanks."

There was a chorus of waves and good-byes, and after re-assuring himself yet again that Cassandra's muscle was not in his bar, he led Sasha back through the door they'd entered from. The minute the door swung shut behind them, she yanked her hand from his.

"That was foolish to take me in there." She crossed her arms over her chest. "And do not touch me ever again."

There was that total gratitude again. Not. Alistair sud-denly wanted to start the night over. This was a disaster. He was not only at risk for having his own butt sold to slayers for a profit for interfering, he had managed to rescue a woman who he was attracted to, yet who would probably be the first to hand him over for certain death. The desire to have sex with women who wanted him dead was a pattern he needed to break.

Damn Jack for mentioning vampire gossip in the first place. This was definitely all Jack's fault. He should have known not to bring up Cassandra and vamps being sold to slayers in front of Alistair. He was perfectly willing to admit he was not rational on either of those two subjects.

Now he was stuck with one very sexy and pissed off woman.

"It was either face-off with those bodyguards in my bar, surrounded by my friends, who would cover my back, or face them in the alley, alone, just you and me. Which would you have rather done?"

She didn't say anything, just frowned.

"I thought so," he couldn't help but say. "And the end re-sult is good, right? They didn't even notice us, or if they did, they chose to leave it alone. They're gone, you're not being hauled back to Cassandra's house of horrors, and I don't have a piece of wood in my chest. All's well that ends well."

"And you will let me leave now?" she asked, rubbing the flesh of her right wrist under the metal hand clamp.

He could. But she'd wind up dead. He knew that beyond a shadow of a doubt. She didn't know New Orleans. She had no friends. No shoes. Shackles on her wrists. Most likely no money, and no access to bagged blood. He could see it playing out. She'd steal shoes or money or both. Accidentally kill a mortal by overbleeding him in her desperate hunger. She'd get arrested or shot by mortal police. Then Cassandra would find her, easily, and carry out her original plan of shipping Sasha to the slayers for money.

Alistair wanted to say to hell with her. But that wasn't him. It never had been, and it never would be. It didn't really matter if she fought him tooth and nail and never expressed an ounce of gratitude. She didn't deserve to die, and he couldn't let it happen.

"No. I can't let you leave."

She didn't exactly look surprised.

"Because I don't want to hear three days from now that you're dead."

It was the truth, but Sasha just narrowed her eyes. "As if you have any reason to care whether I live or die."

Life would probably be easier if he didn't, but Alistair had been stuck with a little thing called a conscience for as long as he could remember. He shrugged. "No reason. But I do. And I've involved myself now. If I'm going to get myself killed over you, I'd like to at least go to my eternal damnation knowing you lived. It would really piss me off if you died, too, despite my best efforts."

For a second he thought Sasha was going to smile, the corners of her mouth edging up, but she appeared to will her lips into submission and forced them back down into a frown. "What is your plan of action now that we are here?"

He didn't really have one, exactly, but he could wing it. "We need to hide you."

"So you have said. Then you pushed me out into a public bar."

It almost sounded like she doubted his brilliance and strategizing. Which considering that they were standing in the storage room of his bar and he had no idea what to do long-term, she was probably right. At least he had thought through what to do for the night—he'd known going over to Cassandra's he would have to hide the woman he brought back, and there were really only a couple of places he felt he could confidently hide Sasha. "You have two choices. We can go upstairs to my apartment over the bar." Jack would be there later but he could count on his friend to keep his mouth shut.

"No," she said quickly. "I will not."

"Or we can hide you in the cemetery. I have a tomb—"

"No! Absolutely not." Sasha was pale and her chest was rising and falling rapidly.

Alistair rubbed his jaw. The tomb was really the best option. They could hide Sasha for a few days, then get her on a flight to the East Coast, hell, even Europe. No one would look for her in the cemetery in the meantime. "You got a better idea? Do you know anyone in town you can stay with?"

Biting her lip, she shook her head. "No. But I cannot stay in a tomb. It is out of the question." Her chin came up defiantly, her eyes daring him to argue.

He wasn't going to. He had no desire to stand there for the next hour and give her survival pointers. If she didn't want to, he wasn't going to force it. He would just have to keep her hidden, then get her out of town somehow. *Somehow* being the operative word.

"Fine. We'll go upstairs then." He waited for her response. He was done dragging her around. If they were going upstairs, she was walking.

She nodded. "I suppose there is no other choice."

Good to see she could be rational.

The main stairs to his apartment were reached from a doorway on Conti Street next to the bar, but Alistair didn't want to parade Sasha back through the front rooms and onto the street. The steps in the storeroom led up to a narrow back hallway and stairs to the third floor. The only access to his apartment from this hall was through an odd window that overlooked the staircase, but they could climb in through that.

"After you," he said to Sasha, gesturing to the dark staircase on the other side of the metal shelving that held cocktail napkins and bottles of alcohol.

She looked at the stairs, then back at him. Her face was guarded. "I will follow you."

The chick had issues, no doubt about it.

But Alistair tried to be patient, putting himself in her shoes—not that she was wearing any—in an attempt to understand her fear and paranoia. A woman who had been tied up like that, sought after by slayers and vampires alike, was going to have power and control issues. It was completely understandable, even if it made him question yet again why he had put himself in the role of white knight. He hadn't spent a lot of time being a humanitarian. Not since his wife had died two hundred years earlier.

Her attitude was annoying, testing what little patience he had left.

"Whatever." Going up the stairs two at a time, he was fully prepared for Sasha to turn tail and run out the door to the alley while his back was to her.

He would almost be relieved if she did.

Almost.

THREE

SASHA HAD THOUGHT ABOUT RUNNING, BUT DE-
cided she needed blood, shoes, and a shower first.

She was willing to forgo the shower if the bathroom door
didn't lock, because she didn't trust Alistair, but to her amazement, he actually left her alone in his apartment. He did lock
the front door after he left, but he told her he was going down
to the bar to talk to Jack and that he would be back in fifteen
minutes.

Being alone was both a relief and a strange disappointment. The quiet pressed in on her, but acutely aware of how
little time she had, she sprang into action.

Sasha fed first, going straight to the refrigerator Alistair had
pointed out and downing three bags of blood. She despised the
smell, so she drank it quickly, poking around the kitchen until
she found a wastebasket she could toss the empty bags in. For
being several hundred years old, Alistair had a rather adoles-
cent apartment. Mötley Crüe featured heavily into the décor,
from framed prints to guitars to concert T-shirts. There was
even a collection of band shot glasses on the ledge above the
dish rack.

Yet for some reason, Sasha found the small apartment comfortable. After Gregor's ostentatious wealth, this was very
real, very normal.

Aware of her time constraints, Sasha took a quick two-
minute shower, washing the grime and fear-inspired sweat off
of her skin. Her feet had been scratched and sliced from running barefoot, but once she scrubbed off the dirt and blood, it
was obvious they had healed already.

Alistair had said the bigger bedroom was his, the other
belonging to his friend Jack. After putting her jeans back on,
Sasha left her filthy T-shirt in the bathroom, folded neatly on
the countertop, and walked quickly to Alistair's room. A search
of his bureau revealed a vast sea of black T-shirts. He'd never

miss one. She pulled one over her head, and removed a pair of socks from the drawer below and put those on as well. In his closet, she found black Chucks that were only slightly big on her feet. She was tall, with large feet, and his shoes felt good, stable, since she was used to wearing high heels. Gregor had liked her in heels.

Walking around his room, Sasha admired her feet in the funky gym shoes. She liked them on her, enjoyed the spring they gave to her step, and the feeling that she could run fast and hard if necessary. The T-shirt she'd chosen at random had a leering skull on it. A far cry from her usual designer clothing. Her husband had likened her to a runway model and had dressed her in kind.

Not that she was going to think about Gregor. Or Ivan. She was free. Finally. This was her opportunity to go away, to start over, to change her name, and become someone else. Someone she could like, someone she could start to respect again, someone who had her own identity.

All she needed was a few supplies first.

Rooting around Alistair's closet, she found an olive green messenger bag that she could toss a few bags of blood in. She snagged his comb from the bathroom and a toothbrush that hadn't been opened yet from the drawer.

Sasha was stealing money from the jar sitting on Alistair's dresser stuffed with ones and fives, when she heard the front door opening.

Cramming the cash in the pocket of the bag, she dropped the whole thing between the bed and the window, flicking a pillow over it, and moved forward to face him, willing her heart to stop pounding so rapidly.

She was not afraid.

She'd faced worse and survived.

She could handle Alistair Kirk.

AFTER leaving Sasha alone to shower and feed, again half hoping, half afraid she would take off, Alistair went back to the bar.

"Where's your girl?" Sam asked. He hadn't moved an inch on his stool while Alistair had been gone, though his gin had disappeared.

"Upstairs taking a shower. She's had a long night."

"Where'd you find her?" Sam said. It was a casual question, but they'd been friends for years and Alistair heard the curiosity in his voice.

Since Raven had moved into the front room, Alistair was honest with his friends. He'd need their support if Sasha stuck around for a few days. "Met her at Cassandra's."

Jack made a sound of disapproval, but didn't say anything. Sam raised an eyebrow.

"What's her story?"

"Not sure. But she wasn't a willing houseguest."

"What are you going to do with her?" Jack asked.

"I'm going to have her lie low and hide her until I can ship her out of town."

Jack shook his head. "That isn't going to work. You already had her out here in front of people. Cassandra's guards saw her, I'm almost positive."

Sam nodded. "Jack's right. And Cassandra is looking for any excuse to tie your nuts in a knot."

The thought of his ex-wife knowing he had Sasha made him smile. "That's true. So what do you think I should do? I'm not tossing her back to the wolves."

"You've got to be bold. Shove her ass out here every night. Tell everyone she's your girlfriend. Keep her surrounded by your friends. Never leave her alone. They won't pull anything if we're all protecting her."

Alistair mulled that over, pouring himself a beer from the tap. "You have a point. But I don't want to drag all of you into this."

Jack shrugged. "Why the fuck not? We'd drag your ass into it if we were the ones guarding some hot Russian chick. And you'd do it for us."

That was true. He would.

"You're right. Alright." He drained the beer in one long swallow. "Let me go talk to her. It might take some convincing to get her to go along with the plan."

"She stubborn?" Jack asked.

"That's an understatement." Alistair rubbed his chin, remembering the feelings of his fangs sinking into his tongue when she'd nailed him with her shackles. Speaking of which. "Hey, anyone got any metal cutters?"

"Yeah, right here in my shorts." Sam rolled his eyes. "Give me a break. Go to fucking Home Depot, man."

He'd pencil that in for tomorrow night. After he found Sasha some shoes and convinced her that the smartest thing she could do would be to stick with him. That he'd get her to safety.

Unlike Abby, who had died under his protection.

Wнеп he entered his apartment, calling out a greeting so Sasha would know it was him, Alistair was feeling tired and bitter. He had spent way too much time thinking about both of his wives in one night, and neither left him with happy, fuzzy feelings. He still missed Abby, and still felt the sting of guilt for her death. Whenever he thought of Cassandra, he wanted the ability to reverse time and never meet her, let alone marry her, and if that weren't possible, he wanted to stab needles in his ears so he would never have to hear her grating, bitchy voice again.

Neither was a practical option, and that made him cranky as hell.

But the sight of Sasha made him forget both of the women in his past.

Sasha was wearing his T-shirt. And his shoes. The ones he liked to wear when he was playing bass because they went with the artistically torn jeans and the chain that hung from his front pocket to the back. They looked cute on her. She looked cute. Shy. Her hair hung wet over her cheeks, her hands tucked in the front pockets of her jeans, her eyes blinking up at him from under those luscious lashes.

"I guess you managed a shower, despite the shackles."

She nodded. "I tried to dry them off, but they will probably rust. It does not matter I guess. I will get them off eventually."

"Tomorrow. I'll go get something to cut them off with."

There was a slight hesitation, so brief he might have imagined it, then she nodded. "Thank you."

Alistair was suspicious, only not sure why. Maybe it was because she had clearly gone through his drawers and yet was not bothering to acknowledge or apologize for it, or maybe it was because she was standing still, right next to his bed, and that seemed the last place she would want to be lingering. Maybe there was no reason to be suspicious whatsoever, yet he was, so he moved closer to her. She flinched slightly, but held her ground.

When he moved around her and casually took off his watch and tossed it on his dresser, he said, "Do my shoes fit?"

"Yes, thank you."

"Sure." It was as he was pushing shut the drawer she'd left open an inch that he realized his jar of tips was empty. She'd stolen his money.

Not surprising, but offensive nonetheless. He wanted to confront her on principle, but he didn't care about the money. It had been only fifty bucks at most, and he suddenly felt downright sorry for her. She had nothing, no one in the world. She had his shoes and his tip money, and that was it.

"You want to leave, don't you?" he asked, turning around to face her.

"What do you mean?" She stared at him, expression guarded.

"Look, I'm not going to keep you here. If you want to leave, you're free to go. I think you'd be safer with me, but I'm not Cassandra. I don't keep hostages." Not even if it was in someone's best interest.

"You would let me leave? Just walk out the door?"

"Yes. With the T-shirt, the shoes, and the money. I think you'd be smart to stick with me for a few days, but it's your choice." Alistair was continually impressed by Sasha's ability to control her emotions. She didn't even flinch when he mentioned the money.

Instead, she simply turned, moved behind the bed, and picked up his messenger bag off the floor. She put it over her shoulder as he wondered what else she'd stolen from him and stuffed into that bag. Not that he really cared. He had very little of value, and he definitely admired her survival skills.

"Thank you," she said, as she moved toward him, her long legs lithe in her tight jeans. She walked like a model, one foot moving in front of the other, creating that unnatural, yet very sensual roll of her hips. "For all of your assistance."

Alistair shifted to let her pass. "You're welcome."

Her arm brushed his chest as she stared at him, wary, and

she slid past him, the tension between them thick. He was attracted to her, intensely, and he knew she returned the feeling, but she didn't trust him. Alistair could hear the rapid beating of her heart and the pulse of the vein in her neck, and he hungered for her blood, for her body. He wanted to take Sasha down onto the hardwood floor and taste her everywhere, her mouth, her flesh, her inner thighs, to push himself inside her while her blood flowed over his tongue and down his throat.

"Are you sure you don't want to stay?" he asked, aware that his voice was a little rough, and that he was staring at her full mouth.

She actually leaned slightly toward him, her tongue darting out to wet her lips. Her small breasts rose and fell beneath his T-shirt, but she shook her head. "I cannot."

It was what he expected, but it was still damn disappointing. "Okay. Be careful."

With a nod, she said, "I will."

Then she was gone.

Alistair stared at the door of his apartment for a second after she left, then sat down and tried to watch TV. The screen blurred in front of him and he debated going back downstairs. Maybe company would distract him. Or alcohol.

Standing up, he paced back and forth, going for a bag of blood in the kitchen, than changing his mind. That wasn't what he wanted.

This night certainly hadn't gone as expected. He had thought saving someone from Cassandra would be satisfying, yet he only felt restless and agitated.

Sasha would be fine. She was tough. She obviously wanted to be on her own, and he needed to respect that. He couldn't make someone else accept his help.

A scream, short and high-pitched, cut through his thoughts, and Alistair froze. It had come from the alley.

Throwing the remote control at his couch, he ran.

SASHA was almost down the alley and to the street when she sensed them. Her vampire skills were modest at best, given that she'd only been turned two months earlier, but even she could smell them. At least two vampires, with bad breath and a desperate need for a shower.

She couldn't see them though and she scanned the shadows left and right quickly, moving slowly, silently. Maybe she was only smelling the garbage that clung to the ground, plastered up against the brick walls of Alistair's bar. There was only the sound of her own breathing and voices out on the street, random revelers, still partying the few steps away on Bourbon Street. Maybe it was only her imagination, and the sudden feeling of loneliness that had swept over her when she had turned and walked out of Alistair's apartment and down the stairs.

Gripping the strap of the messenger bag, she took a small step forward, still scanning and listening. She was so close to the street, so close to freedom. But their scent wafted over her again, floating in front of her nose, a noxious cloud.

She never even saw them before she was on the ground.

Instinct had her reaching up, scratching and clawing at whoever it was, and she knew she'd made contact when she heard a curse. Her vision was blurred because he was shaking her, knocking her down onto the ground, the hard blows rattling her brain and robbing her of her breath. It was a man, big and strong and dressed in black, and Sasha had no intention of lying underneath and just accepting whatever he intended to do to her. She'd fight him until the death if she had to.

She opened her mouth to scream but he slapped her so hard the pain exploded in her head, stunning her. The hard asphalt and gravel beneath her ground into her cheek, her shoulder, her arm, and she tried to roll away from him, but he was strong. Kicking up, she nailed him in the gut, which momentarily released his pressure on her chest. She could see the legs of his companion right next to her and knew even if she escaped the first, there was still the second, upright and ready to subdue her.

Their orders were likely to bring her back alive. She was worth money to her captor. But Sasha would rather die.

So she drove the palm of her hand straight up into his chin and felt the satisfaction of hearing and feeling his head smack up and his immediate roar of pain. Driving her knee into his groin, she shoved him off of her, rolling in the opposite direction of the second vampire. Arms were on her immediately, but she kicked backward, hitting a kneecap. The second one was instantly in front of her, looking amused, big, and brawny, a wooden stake twirling in his hand like a baton, a silent threat. Clasping her hands together, Sasha swung as he stepped forward, and struck him straight across the nose with the metal of her wrist cuffs.

His nose burst open, blood gushing down the front of him, the scent strong and ripe.

"Bitch," he said, his voice low and angry as he gripped his nose, trying to stem the bleeding. "Hold her," he told his companion.

Sasha gave one short sharp shriek as she fought the arms gripping her, but there was no escaping. He held her easily as his friend came toward her, eyes gleaming with malicious intent in the dark. She shuddered and shrank back, trying to maneuver away from the vampire in front of her, but he grabbed her head and held her still, his thumbs crushing her temples, her pulse pounding beneath his flesh. It was tempting to close her eyes, but she wanted him to know that she was not afraid. Wanted him to see the darkness of her eyes as he bit her. Let him know that Sasha was not going to quiver or beg or break down.

His brown eyes widened in surprise as they locked gazes, before he was the one to look away first. Chicken-shit bastard. A small triumph in her death, but she would take it.

The pressure was sharp, the invasion repulsive, as he sank his fangs into her neck, and her stomach roiled in disgust. She fought him as he sucked and pulled her life's blood out of her, kicking and shoving and squirming, as the ringing in her ears grew louder and the weight of her limbs grew heavier. She fought even as the dizziness swept over her and her thoughts scattered, confused and disjointed, her mind trying to cling to consciousness.

"Hey, that's enough," she heard the one holding her say, his voice echoing in her pain-wracked skull. "We're supposed to bring her back alive."

The pressure, the pull subsided. "I'm just getting her weak enough so that she won't fight me when I stick my dick in her."

"Uh, I don't know if that's such a good idea, man . . ."

Sasha didn't think it was a good idea either. She reached out with the last of her strength and grabbed the wooden stake held loosely in the man's hand, and drove it straight into her chest. Even as she gasped with shock at the pain and pressure, she smiled in satisfaction. If he was going to rape her, it would have to be over her dead body.

And at that point she would no longer care.

FOUR

Alistair was in the alley in less than a minute, and what he saw infuriated him. Two guys had Sasha down on the ground, her legs flailing beneath the one as he bent over her. Not sure if the guy was biting her or touching her or both, Alistair saw red. It was just all so wrong, and there was no way he was going to let it end like this. He was running toward them, when he saw the bigger man step back away from her body.

Revealing a wooden stake in her chest.

Holy shit.

The mother fucker had staked her.

Alistair hit the guy on the run with the full force of his body, knocking the guy backward onto his ass. Then he turned, hit the other guy in the face to momentarily distract him, and reached down and grabbed a hold of the stake sticking out of Sasha's chest. He was moving quickly, but he could see she was pale and waxy, her breathing short and labored. At least she was breathing. Pulling hard, he removed the wood from her flesh, trying to ignore the moan of pain she gave, and the sick sucking sound of blood and tissue clinging to the stake.

Without hesitation, he spun around and drove the stake into the chest of the man who was moving toward him, fists up, face angry.

There was a howl of pain and shock, then the guy was down on the ground, writhing.

That left the second one to contend with.

Having been a seventeenth-century soldier, Alistair was comfortable with hand-to-hand combat. He went in without hesitation, landing a blow on the guy's face, than shoving him hard to put him off balance. His opponent came by with a wide swing that he easily dodged. It was clear these guys were used to using brute force and intimidation more than skill or intelligence.

Alistair was quicker on his feet and had better reflexes. None of the guy's punches made contact with him, and he was able to get in a half dozen on the kidneys and face. But he needed to take him out or at least encourage him to leave. Not wanting to waste any more time, he used his superior speed and went behind the guy. With a quick twist, he broke his neck, sending the guy crumpling to the ground in pain. The first one was dead, so Alistair retrieved the stake from his chest and impaled the second bodyguard, a sharp in and out with the stake.

He tossed the bloody piece of wood into the Dumpster and wiped his forehead, breathing hard and sweating. The bodies would disappear into dust by morning. Leaving them in the alley until then didn't sit well with him, but he couldn't risk getting caught moving the bodies, and Sasha needed blood immediately. Alistair decided not to worry about it, and reached down and lifted up Sasha.

She looked on the verge of death herself. The T-shirt she wore was wet with blood and she hung limp in his arms, unconscious, the messenger bag still over her shoulder, hitting him in the thigh.

Damn it, he shouldn't have let her leave.

Angry that he had, Alistair carried her up the back stairs and through the window to his apartment. He laid her on his couch. Immediately, he got six bags of blood out of the fridge, the last of his personal stash. Fortunately, his bar kept a large supply to serve to vampires in mixed drinks. Once he was sure Sasha was okay, he'd go down and grab some more. Poking a hole in the bag with his fang, he dribbled it over her mouth and fed her slowly. At first she didn't swallow, and he had to open and close her mouth manually, but then she started to drink voluntarily. He propped a bag against her mouth and let it dribble in as she sucked.

Lifting up her shirt to inspect her wound, Alistair recoiled. It was a raw and gaping mess, her thin and narrow chest just torn open from the impact of the stake. It didn't look to be healing either. Her bra was ripped, and the satin was sticking to the thick blood and bits of exposed tissue. He thought it would be a good idea to remove the bra before her body started restoring itself, given the way it was clinging to her.

Feeling a little nauseated and disgusted with himself for being such a wuss, Alistair tugged off the shirt, taking care with her head and the bag of blood she was feeding from, slowly and with obvious pain, her eyes still closed. He lifted her hair up and out of the way. The bottom of her dark blonde hair was saturated with her blood, and for a man who had spent four hundred years drinking the stuff, he was amazed at how thoroughly grossed out he was. But there was something about Sasha that was so strong and yet so vulnerable, so sharp and raw and fierce, that he was shaken by how close to death she was.

Tossing the shirt onto the floor, he unhooked her bra by sliding his hand under her back. Normally, it would have been a hell of a turn on, but under the circumstances, he wasn't feeling the slightest bit sexual. When he pulled the straps down her arms and went to pull the bra off her chest, it actually stuck in the wound.

"Bloody hell." He winced. That was some seriously nasty shit.

But then it was on the floor next to the shirt and he let out a sigh of relief. He hadn't even realized he'd been grinding his teeth until the deed was done. Switching the empty bag on Sasha's lips to a fresh one, Alistair went for a sheet to cover her up. He'd never noticed how crappy his linens were until he pulled a sorry, dingy white sheet out of the closet. His laundry skills sucked, but it was unlikely she would care at the moment.

When he was unfolding it to settle over her, Alistair noticed all the bruises and scratches on her arms and shoulders. And the vicious bite mark on her neck—stark, throbbing red against her pale skin.

Cassandra's bodyguards had almost killed Sasha. It didn't make any sense why they would do that.

But he knew that it was going to raise some flak when his ex-wife realized her goons were missing. Not that she'd trace it back to Alistair, but there would be questions in the vampire community.

He'd childishly wanted to take a jab at his ex, and damn if

this wasn't a big old poke in the eye. A confrontation was in their future.

But as he smoothed the sheet over Sasha's damaged body, he knew it would be worth it for having saved her.

SASHA was not sure if she was alive. Her body certainly felt real, the pain and pressure in her chest uncomfortable in its hot throb. But her mind felt hazy, disconnected, and her eyelids did not seem to want to open. She didn't think she was in the alley. The ground beneath her was flexible, and her face was no longer in the gravel, but on something that smelled faintly like cologne.

A hand touched her hair, startling her, and she smacked at it, the fear, the anger back. If she wasn't dead, she wanted to be left alone. Why couldn't she ever just be left alone?

"Shh, hey, it's okay. It's me, it's Alistair."

Sasha forced her eyes open, certain she was at least alive, but uncertain if she were in imminent danger or not.

Alistair was staring down at her with concern in his green eyes. He had a bag of blood in his hand, with a straw stuck into the side of it, aimed at her mouth.

She was on his couch, she realized with relief, a sheet over her. A quick glance under it revealed she was naked from the waist up, her chest covered in blood, her wound gaping and visible, but showing signs of healing. "What happened?" she asked, though she knew.

The bodyguard had been about to rape her, while she lay there helpless and weak from lack of blood. So she had staked herself.

And Alistair had saved her from death.

"I found you in the alley. You're going to be fine. You just need blood and lots of sleep."

He held the straw up to her mouth and she took a sip, sitting up slightly. The movement caused a sharp pain in her chest and she lay back, exhausted and nauseous. She wondered how close to death she had been. "The two men?"

"Don't worry about them. They're not coming back."

"You killed them?" Looking up at him, she searched his face, curious what his reaction would be.

But he didn't even flinch. He just nodded, his eyes cool, satisfied. "Yes."

"Thank you," she said, and meant it. She owed him her life. She wasn't sure why he was helping her, or if she could actually trust him, but he had, in fact, saved her life and regardless of his agenda, she did owe him for that.

"You're welcome." Alistair looked like he wanted to say more, but he didn't. He just stared down at her, his jaw stern, his mouth turned down in a frown.

"What?" she asked him, shifting a little on the couch and moving her arms out from under the sheet to rest on her stomach. The dizziness was clearing, and when Alistair handed her the blood to drink, she did so readily.

"Nothing. I'm just wondering why those guys were willing to kill you. The value to Cassandra exists only if you're alive, so she can sell you off to slayers. So why would they be so quick to stake you?"

Sasha's first instinct was to lie or to simply not answer at all. But she felt that she owed Alistair the truth for risking his own life. And she had questions in return for him, so she shrugged. "They didn't stake me. I did it myself."

"What? Why the hell would you do that?" He looked appalled. "Why would you want to kill yourself?"

As if he could possibly understand. Sasha knew she sounded defensive, defiant, but she didn't care. "I have no death wish. I want to live, just as much as the next vampire. But I chose the stake over what he intended to do to me."

It took him a second to process her words, but then his frown turned grim, and his fists closed when he realized what she meant. "They were going to rape you."

She nodded. "And I made the decision to die rather than endure that ag—"

Sasha cut herself off. She didn't want to reveal her past, to share her private pain.

But Alistair had caught what she had intended to say. "Oh, God," he said. "I'm so sorry."

The genuine sympathy in his words made her uncomfortable. She didn't know how to process or respond to compassion. No one had shown it to her in a long time. So she just sipped her drink and watched him. She knew how to watch, how to wait, how to gauge a man's emotion and reactions. It was what she'd spent her entire adult life doing.

"I'm glad I killed them then," he added, his voice quiet but filled with conviction. "Fucking disgusting cowards."

As so many were. Sasha sighed, weary. She wanted to close her eyes and sleep, but that was not a good idea. She needed to think, to plan. She needed to create a life for herself, in another city, where no one knew her, and she needed to leave before someone else came for her.

"I would like to take a shower before I leave."

"What the hell are you talking about? You can't leave tonight."

"Why not?"

"You're hurt. You need to recover. And soon enough, Cassandra will notice her muscle never came home, and then more men will be out looking for you. It's not safe for you to leave."

Sasha knew that. But she did not see what other choice she had. So she changed the subject. "How do you know Cassandra? Why are you involved in my situation?"

Maybe he would tell the truth, maybe he would not. But she was too curious not to ask.

Alistair was clearly caught off guard. He opened his mouth, then closed it again. Then he bit his fingernail and gave her a grimace. "She is my ex-wife."

That was an unexpected response. Sasha raised an eyebrow. "Really? How long were you married?"

"Two weeks of actually living together. Two more months before the vampire court cleared the paperwork and made the divorce official. It was one of those brief moments of insanity that I recovered quickly from. At first, I appreciated her cleverness, and I admit, I fell for the package, but living together it was obvious almost immediately that she was greedy and selfish, and just plain cruel. So I cut my losses and got the hell out."

"You are embarrassed by your mistake, are you not?" She could see that it bothered him. "Yet so many do the same. I think you are too hard on yourself."

He gave her a slight smile. "I should have known better. At my age, I should have been able to slice through the lust and see that Cassandra's core was rotten."

"We do unwise things when we are lonely." She should know. Loneliness had led her to New Orleans, had pulled her to Ivan, who had betrayed her.

"That is very true. Is that why you married Gregor?"

If only she had married him by choice. Then she would have no one to blame but herself, and perhaps she could move on. But she knew her marriage had damaged her irreparably. "No. I married Gregor because he asked me and you do not say no to him."

"So you weren't attracted to him?"

She did not even hesitate, or attempt to lie. "No. I despised him."

"Why would he want to be married to you then?"

"I have no idea. But as a mortal, I was easier to control than a vampire wife would have been. I also suspect I was a political strategy. And perhaps, most important of all, a personal toy for his own amusement. I grew up in his household and he was fond of me." Sasha heard the distaste, the venom, the bitterness in her voice, and wondered why she had just said that out loud. It had to be the result of the loss of blood, the weakness she was feeling. It was dulling her rationale and making her vulnerable. "Not that it matters," she added, to soften the emotion she had revealed. "He is gone now."

She hoped Alistair would drop it, but he didn't. Pulling the coffee table over closer to the couch, he sat on it, hands on his knees. It was a casual pose, nonthreatening.

"Why was a mortal child growing up in a vampire's house?" he asked.

Now Sasha did close her eyes. She did not want to do this. Or maybe she did. Maybe she was dropping hints and pieces of information to Alistair because she never talked about any of this. She tried to pretend it did not exist, and kept her inner thoughts, her secrets, solely to herself. It kept her completely isolated from others, and for once, just once, she wanted to share. Because while it would make her feel better to vent, it would forever alter Alistair's opinion of her. He would be disgusted by the life she had led, and he would willingly let her go, and that was as it should be.

She was destined to remain alone.

"My mother was Gregor's blood slave. We moved in to his

house when I was five years old. He kept several women, and I was raised communally, so to speak, with my friend Ivan, who was two years older, and whose mother was Gregor's favorite."

Alistair was staring at her, his expression incredulous. "I know there are plenty of blood slaves running around, but why the hell would any woman bring her child into that? Just for the pleasure she gets from being fed on? That's crazy."

Sasha shrugged. "I do not think my mother saw any harm from it. I was cared for, educated, and had friends to play with."

"And you grew up, and he wanted you." Alistair's words were flat, repulsed.

"Yes. As I said, he had a fondness for me. Gregor never fed from me. I was never a blood slave." It was important that she point that out. She wanted him to know that her will had never been weak. "But I still had no choice but to marry him. I had no money, no experience of the world outside of the estate we lived on. I was under lock and key. My only access to the outside was on the Internet, which is how I learned English. If I could have escaped, I would have."

"I don't doubt that." Alistair gave her a slight smile. "You're pretty damn tenacious."

It felt like a compliment, and that pleased her. "When we moved to Las Vegas, I saw it as an opportunity to escape. Such a busy, crowded city, with so much glitz and costuming . . . but I never had time to implement a plan. Gregor was killed first."

And she had shed not one tear.

"Then I miscalculated with a vampire who was addicted to drug blood. I used him for access to vampire events, then I pushed him too hard. He turned me, and took pleasure in doing so, knowing it was truly my worst nightmare."

Alistair reached out and pulled her hand into his. Sasha's first instinct was to yank it away. She didn't want anyone holding her, controlling her. Touch had always been manipulative in her life, and someone always wanted something from her.

But the man in front of her, his knee poking through the hole in his faded jeans, wasn't sly or cunning or possessive.

He was honest and concerned and he was trying to comfort her. He had saved her life and he felt sympathy for what she had suffered in her marriage.

She could see it on his face, yet it was almost too difficult to comprehend. No one cared about her, no one. Not even in passing.

It confused her, annoyed her at the same time she wanted to believe it, enjoy it. She was trying really hard to look at him and hate him, but all she felt was a foreign softness in her heart, and a desire to lie on his couch, close her eyes, and sleep under his watch.

So she left her hand in his, even let him stroke the back of her wrist with his thumb. But she did ask, "Why are you involved, Alistair? How did you know about me?"

"Cassandra isn't always discreet. One of her flaws is that she likes to brag. So word went around that she had a vampire in her custody who she was selling to slayers. My friend Jack, who you met downstairs, told me. Jack is the kind of guy that everyone likes and people talk to, so he hears a lot of gossip. If Cassandra is involved he usually tells me." Alistair gave a sheepish smile. "I think it's his way of reminding me what a bitch Cassandra is, in case I'm ever insane enough to think I want to get back together with her. But trust me, there's no danger of that."

"So you intervened in order to anger your ex-wife?" She could understand that, even if it wasn't noble, and she was willing to accept whatever had gotten her out of that prison masquerading as a guest room.

"While ticking Cassandra off has its own appeal, that's not really why I did it. I did it because I was disgusted by the idea that a vampire would turn on one of our own. She knew that turning you over meant death, a bad death. The slayers might have enjoyed torturing you, or experimenting with how quickly a vampire heals . . . they might have injured you over and over just for curiosity or a thrill before finally killing you. I couldn't just sit back knowing exactly where you were. People don't want to get involved, but how could I live with myself, you know?"

Sasha had no idea how many men lived with themselves. She also knew that Alistair was right. The slayers would have taken a certain sick satisfaction in torturing her, because she had been a slayer herself before she had been turned. She hadn't made friends in the group either, because she had been living with Gregor at the time, and was emotionally on the edge. She had been a little intense, and the slayers on the whole had not liked her.

They would enjoy killing her.

But it still boggled her mind that Alistair would risk his life to help her.

"How old are you?" she asked him, curious.

"Three hundred and fifty-eight last February."

"And you are British?"

He nodded.

Sasha turned her head to study him more closely, her injury making her wince in pain when she shifted. "You were married before Cassandra, yes?" He was the marrying kind, she could see that.

"Three times total. First as a mortal, and once as a vampire long before Cassandra."

"And how did your vampire wife die?" she asked quietly, already knowing the answer.

It was confirmed when he pulled his hand out of hers, his lips pursing. But he did answer after a moment of silence. "Slayers. It was over two hundred years ago, though."

"I am sorry. Time dulls pain, but it does not go away."

"No, it doesn't." Alistair's green eyes bore into her. "What happened to your mother, Sasha?"

The words stuck in her throat, but Sasha swallowed hard. He had shared, she owed him the truth, even though it was painful and shameful to admit. "When Gregor tired of my mother, and would no longer feed off of her, or share her bed, she killed herself by swallowing half a bottle of tranquilizers." Leaving her teenage daughter alone and at the mercy of a madman.

He nodded, like she had confirmed his suspicion. "I'm sorry."

"As am I."

"You know, for two people who are immortal, we have seen an amazing amount of death, haven't we?"

Alistair's words caught her off guard as she stared up at him, lying on her side under his sheet, and she sucked in a breath when she realized there were tears in her eyes.

Unexplainable, unstoppable tears.

Perhaps seeing death, knowing extreme isolation was why she struggled to find any joy in life.

For the first time in seven long, isolated years, she didn't fight, and let herself cry.

Five

Oh, shit, he'd made her cry.

It was so unexpected, he just stared at her for a second. One minute she had been looking up at him, grave, but in control. The next, her eyes had gone wide, and silent tears were streaming down her cheeks. Her lip quivered but she didn't make a sound, nor did she attempt to wipe the moisture from her face.

He had come to think of her as such a tough chick, totally unflappable, but after he got over his initial shock, he was relieved to see her releasing some of that tension, that emotion. She'd been keeping years' worth of pain and emotion bottled up, and it was time to let some of it go.

"Hey," he said, reaching over and swiping a stray tear off her chin. "It's okay. It's all going to be okay. You're free and no one is going to hurt you."

She gave a watery smile. "No one can hurt me any longer, Alistair, because I no longer have a heart."

So that was part of her fear. That she'd gotten so hard, so jaded, she couldn't be normal again. "If you didn't have a heart, you wouldn't be crying right now."

Making a face, Sasha ran the tip of her finger across the sheet, still ignoring the wet streaks on her cheeks. "What a strange twist of fate that I am here, with you. This night has been more than you bargained for, I imagine."

In a lot of ways. He had never expected to be attracted to the woman he rescued. And he'd never expected to feel an indescribable and undeniable sensation that his attraction went beyond the physical. Sasha had pricked the emotional wall he surrounded himself with, and he really, really wanted to lean over and kiss her.

Knowing that would result in her biting his lip, kneeing him in the nuts, or thrusting the palm of her hand up into his chin, he refrained. For the moment.

"I didn't exactly know what I was getting into, but I'm glad I could help you." He indulged himself and reached out to touch the tip of her long hair. It still had her dried blood in it. "I'm glad I met you."

Instead of smiling back at him, she looked slapped. Her face went white and she closed her eyes briefly. When they reopened they were shiny with fresh tears. "Can I take a shower?" she asked in a tight voice.

So she wasn't going to acknowledge what he'd said, or what was between them. Alistair took it as a good sign that she didn't just flat-out cut him down. She was fragile and he could be patient. "Is your wound closed yet?"

She peeked under the sheet and made a face. "Not quite."

"Then you really should wait. Why don't you sleep? Tomorrow night you'll feel a lot better. Are you thirsty?"

"No." Sasha finally wiped her tears from her cheeks and took a deep breath. Settling back against the couch pillow, she closed her eyes and murmured, "Sorry I stole your money."

That made him smile. "No problem. I understand." He did. She was trying to survive. That's what her whole life had been about. Even with her eyes closed, she didn't relax, didn't loosen her shoulders, or lessen her grip on the sheet she held tightly to cover her bare chest.

Sasha was wounded, in more ways than one, and Alistair knew he was in big trouble.

Not from bodyguards with more brawn than brain who might be arriving to recapture Sasha, but from the woman herself.

No doubt about it, he was attracted to her. And that attraction was getting bigger by the second.

WHEN Sasha emerged from the bathroom the next night, her body healed and scrubbed clean, her hair still damp, but mostly blown dry, Alistair was sitting on his kitchen counter, bare feet dangling in front of the lower cabinets, his scruffy jeans worn at the knees. His short hair was sticking up in an amusing cowlick and his eyes were bleary, like he had a hard time waking up each night. He wasn't wearing a shirt, and Sasha was startled to realize that she was assessing his body, greedily scanning his biceps and the planes of his chest, curiously eyeing the tuft of hair that poked up from the waist of his jeans.

He was a very handsome man, she had to admit, with a lean and muscular body, and the power of his masculinity was actually sexy to her. Instead of scaring her with his height and strength, it intrigued. Maybe it was because Alistair's brand of male hardness was complemented by his casual, almost sheepish demeanor. He didn't seem to take himself too seriously, and that was reflected now as he sat there looking like he was still half asleep, a bowl resting in his hands that he kept lifting up, tipping, and slurping from.

"What are you eating?" she asked incredulously. Granted, she was only a fledgling, but she had not been able to eat anything since her turning, and if she could swallow it and make it stay down, she would desperately love a piece of chocolate.

"Blood," he said.

She could see the crimson stain on his lips now that he'd lowered the bowl. Sasha raised an eyebrow. He drank blood from a bowl like a six-year-old with the milk left after cereal?

Alistair shrugged. "I grew up on porridge. I like a bowl at the start of my night. It's a comfort thing."

Sasha caught herself before she smiled. He had the potential to be adorable, but she certainly did not want him to know that.

"I see," she said, smoothing his shirt over her stomach. "I borrowed another one of your T-shirts, I hope you don't mind." This time she had perused his T-shirt drawer selection a little more carefully and she had picked a black one—black seemed to be a theme with him—that said The Impalers, with a bloody stake in the corner of the "m." It seemed a humorous irony and a gesture of defiance.

"I don't mind. Nice choice." He grinned. "That's my old band, The Impalers, and I'm kind of fond of that shirt, so can you try not to get staked while wearing it?"

"I'll try, but I cannot promise anything," she said gravely, glad that he was enjoying her little gruesome joke.

"That's all I can ask for." He took another sip from his blood bowl. "There are bags in the fridge if you need to feed."

"Thanks." Sasha moved across the kitchen, wondering if

he would comment on the fact that she was wearing his shoes again, too. And his necklace. She had seen it laying on his dresser and she had impulsively picked it up and put it on. The skull and crossbones on a thick silver chain had appealed to her, maybe because it wasn't a choice for a fashionista, which is what Gregor had molded her into. She had been dressed in designer labels for years, the more expensive the better, and at one political fund-raiser, Sasha had been wearing almost a million dollars in diamonds.

Alistair's masculine and inexpensive necklace felt wonderful around her neck. A symbol of her freedom.

"So what are the plans?" she asked, as she pulled open the refrigerator. It had been implied the night before that she would be staying with him, for a few days anyway, but she wasn't sure what Alistair intended. She grabbed a bag of blood and closed the door again.

"Well, Cassandra will be looking for you, and as we learned last night, you being alone leaves you vulnerable to attack. Jack suggested that the best way to deal is to be bold about it. If we put you in public, yet surrounded by me and my friends, no one will dare to hurt you or abduct you. They won't be able to, because they won't be able to get to you."

"I think I see the logic in that." Even if the idea of everyone knowing where she was scared her. "Where will I be?"

"The bar." Alistair set his bowl down and hopped off the counter. "You're my newest bartender, and as everyone learned last night, my new girlfriend."

Sasha punctured the blood bag, then pulled it back down off her lips. "I do not know anything about being a bartender." Or being a girlfriend, for that matter.

"You'll learn. And everyone will groan and bitch and put up with it, because they'll know it's a charity job for my new girlfriend. And those who know the truth will understand. And protect you when I can't."

Not sure what to say, Sasha just took a sip of blood and let it swish around her teeth and tongue. She was learning to like the taste. "Can you trust your friends?"

He shot her a look, like he was offended, but he just said mildly, "Yes. With my life. And yours."

She nodded. "Okay." It was her impulse to not believe him, to completely distrust, to call a plan that didn't originate from her as unreliable and fraught with danger, but she had to learn to accept that her desire to control everything in her life came from her past. There were going to be times when she had to deal with other's opinions or suggestions if she didn't want to spend the rest of her life completely alone.

Which she didn't.

Yes, she wanted her freedom. She wanted to change her name, cut her hair, start over with a new, nondesigner wardrobe.

But she didn't want to be alone for eternity.

And while she didn't exactly trust Alistair, he had given her no reason to distrust him either.

So if he thought she could handle being a bartender, she was damn well going to prove him right.

"When do I start?" she asked.

Alistair grinned. "Now, Jenny. But first, let's cut off those wrist irons."

SASHA was a quick study. Not that Alistair was really surprised. She was definitely a tenacious female, so he should have expected that she would pick up on bartending by the sheer force of her will.

The back bar wasn't busy, and most nights it was filled with about a half dozen vampires at a time. They were all friends and all simple, straightforward drinkers. They mostly wanted blood and alcohol, hold the ice. No one who came in to his bar would have the balls to request any sort of blender drink, and most drinks ordered had no more than three ingredients, so it was just a matter of showing Sasha around the taps and glasses.

Yet he still felt a ridiculous amount of pride when, within an hour, she had learned how to use the register to open and close tabs and she was well on her way to memorizing what each guy drank regularly. Alistair tried to hang back and let her get her groove, which left him far too much time to just watch her, sitting on a stool in the corner. He definitely liked to see her behind his bar, her long legs carrying her back and forth, his Chucks squeaking on the floor as she pivoted in them. She had quick fingers, elegant and smooth as they slid glasses across the bar. Her lip curled down in a frown of concentration when she took and filled orders, but when she handed them over, she always smiled and made eye contact.

The guys seemed to accept her, even if he caught a few curious glances. They were conducting their usual ribald, nonsensical conversations so that meant they were at least comfortable with her presence.

Sam took his glass from Sasha and saluted her. "Here's to sex, blood, and rock 'n' roll."

It almost sounded like a test to Alistair, Sam's way of seeing if Sasha fit in with them. Alistair was annoyed, and was about to answer Sam himself, but Sasha spoke up first.

"Cheers to that," she said mildly.

Sam smiled, a flirty grin. "So where did Al find you? And can I steal you away from him?"

Sasha gave a breezy smile in return. "Sorry, but there is really no chance of that."

He would have to agree with that. No one was taking her from him. She could walk away on her own if she wanted, though he wouldn't like it, but no one was stealing her. Physically or emotionally, damn it. He wanted Sasha for himself.

The admission had him reaching out for her as he spoke. "Get your own girl, Sam."

"I'm trying, man, but no luck. Thought it might be easier to just snag yours."

"Not going to happen, my friend." Knowing Sam was joking, Alistair still took Sasha's hand and tugged her back toward him.

She tilted her head in question, but she came willingly. He pulled her onto his lap on the stool. Sasha stiffened, so he whispered in her ear, "You're my girlfriend, Jenny, remember?"

Looking at him over her shoulder, she said, "None of your friends really believe that."

"The only one who knows the truth is Jack, so it's better to play along. Especially when you never know who is in the front room of the bar watching."

Their heads were close together, her full mouth deliciously close to his. She shifted on his lap, her small and firm ass resting nicely on his thighs.

"That sounds like a justification for your behavior," she said.

"What do you mean?" he asked, even though he knew exactly what she meant.

"You just want me to sit on your lap, do you not?"

No shit. And he wasn't at all surprised she had him figured out. Sasha was smart and very observant.

"Well, there's no denying I want you on my lap." Alistair slid his hands around her waist to emphasize his point. "But I want you safe first and foremost. If I can have both, that just makes me all the happier."

"It is false and manipulative," she said.

She had a rich, sensual voice, and it did pleasant things to his body. Like made it harden in strategic places.

"It's not manipulative or false because I'm being totally honest with you. I'm not denying I want you on my lap but telling you straight-up, yes, I want you right here—with me, on me, close to me, your body against mine."

Her eyes widened. "I do not want this."

"Are you sure about that?" Alistair tipped his head, shifted in closer, moving his lips until they were almost touching hers. She didn't back away. He kissed her, softly, quickly, and retreated.

They stared at each other, Sasha looking angry, uncertain, aroused. Or maybe the latter was wishful thinking on his part. Alistair didn't want to push, didn't want to risk sending her running. He was patient. He could take this slow. She could sit on his lap all damn night as far as he was concerned, and they'd get past any reticence eventually.

Of course, they only had a few nights, then Sasha would probably leave New Orleans forever. Maybe he should go for it, push a little bit, show her that not all men were like her dead husband.

Jack's obnoxious voice interrupted his musings. "You call that a kiss? Come on, really lay one on her."

Nice. Especially since Jack knew who Sasha really was.

"Do not do it," Sasha said in a low voice, her eyes flashing.

"Never even crossed my mind," he told her, which was true. He knew enough about her to know that attempting a make-out session with her because of drunken vampire peer pressure was a huge mistake.

He knew that.

If he was going to plant a serious one on her it was going to be in private where she would be more relaxed, and hopefully receptive. Not in front of a half dozen drunk vampires.

What he didn't anticipate was that she would lean forward and kiss him in front of a half dozen drunk vampires.

But she did, reaching out and sliding her hand across the back of his hair, her lush lips covering his in a sexy, aggressive kiss. Alistair was so shocked, it took him a full five seconds to get on board with it. Then he kissed her back, knowing somewhere in the back of his brain that this was odd and maybe he should question why she was suddenly the aggressor when she had never trusted him nor particularly liked him. Then he decided her motive was less important than her actions, and he was definitely enjoying that. The kiss was raw compared to the one the night before—less skill and more exuberance.

Alistair gripped her waist tighter, shifting her on his lap so that she was closer, her shoulder pressed into his chest, her breast barely brushing him, her ass coming perilously close to his erection. It was a hot, open-mouthed kiss that had him fighting for control, resisting the urge to grab her and grind and bite the curve of her shoulder just below his mouth. But this was hers, she had started it, and she needed to direct it.

After a nice, long, erection-inducing minute, she broke the kiss off and pulled back.

They stared at each other, breathing hard, as a round of applause came from the room. Alistair turned and tried to glare his friends into silence, but the four guys sitting there just grinned back at him, unapologetic.

"Not bad," Sam said. "Though if it was me, you can bet your sweet ass she'd have gone for a crotch grab. Women can't resist me."

Sam was notoriously incapable of securing any female interest at all, and normally Alistair found it amusing that Sam could laugh at himself. Tonight, he wasn't interested in the usual round of jokes and comments of questionable taste. He just wanted to be alone with Sasha and ask what the hell that had been all about. She had already turned to face the front so that her expression was no longer visible, and a second later she popped up off of his lap and moved to refill Jack's drink.

Damn his friend for being such a lush, because Alistair's lap felt empty without Sasha on it.

As she bent over to grab a bottle of rum, Alistair stared at the curve of her backside in her jeans and wondered why he had thought plunking her down in his bar was such a good idea.

He should have kept her upstairs in his apartment and let her kiss him until they both ran out of spit.

Alistair shifted on his stool. His jeans were too tight.

And it had been far too long since he'd had sex.

He reached under the counter for a bottle of blood. All of his had gone south.

Six

SASHA PUSHED HER HAIR BACK OFF HER FACE and tried not to be aware of Alistair staring at her, but it was impossible. The room itself was small, and behind the bar there was barely enough room for the two of them. To get drinks and use the cash register, she was constantly moving around him, brushing against him, and having to stick her behind in his face when she bent to get glasses.

What had possessed her to kiss him?

Maybe it had been the knowledge that he wouldn't kiss her. It was written all over his face, in his quiet compassion and understanding of who she was, that he would not take such an opportunity and abuse it. He would never push.

And she had been amazed to discover that it actually frustrated her, because while she never wanted to be pushed or dominated by a man again, she did want to kiss Alistair. She was attracted to him. He awakened feelings in her she had never thought she'd experience again. Desire and longing. The need for sexual satisfaction.

So she had wanted to test it, to see what it would feel like to kiss him, to have her body pressed up against his with no pressure, no baggage between them. To just be curious and aroused and see how far she could take that before she shut down emotionally and physically.

Interestingly, the shutdown hadn't happened. She had gotten excited, into the kiss. She had actually enjoyed herself, and the way it felt to have his fingers pressing against her waist, and his mouth moving with hers. Even when she had shifted and felt the hardness of his erection, it had not alarmed or disturbed her. She had actually felt a completely foreign urge to reach down and stroke it, to see if she could make him moan.

Now as she took money from Jack for his tab, she could feel the heat on her cheeks. She wanted to have sex with

Alistair, and that had the potential to really complicate her need to leave town quickly. But she was so intrigued, so damn relieved, to know that she was still *normal*. That she was still a woman who could feel desire, that her body understood the difference between normal, healthy sex and what she had endured with Gregor.

At least she thought her body understood that.

But she really wanted to find out, reassure herself perhaps she wasn't destined to a lifetime alone after all.

At the sound of female laughter she glanced up. Three vampires dressed in jeans and tank tops came into the back room, their faces lit up with smiles, purses over their shoulders, their steps confident and sassy.

Sasha tucked her hair behind her ear and found herself slouching a little. Women didn't like her. They never had. No matter how hard she had tried to make friends in her teens and early twenties as Gregor started taking her to parties and social events, she had always received blatant belligerence or false fawning for her efforts. So as a defense mechanism, she had gotten into the habit of standing tall and straight, assuming a haughty air in her designer clothes, the untouchable girlfriend, and later wife, of Gregor Chechikov.

And women had left her alone.

But she did not want to play that icy role here, in front of Alistair. She did not have the stomach for it anymore. So she would try to stay innocuous instead.

It didn't work.

After an initial round of greetings with the guys, the woman with dark hair cut short and angled approached the bar. "Hey, can I get a Jägerbomb?"

Sasha nodded, then glanced over at Alistair. She hadn't made that drink yet.

"It's Jägermeister and Red Bull," he told her, standing up and grabbing a Red Bull out of the cooler.

"Ohmigod, you don't know what a Jägerbomb is?" the woman asked. "Girl, you don't know what you're missing." She leaned over the bar and smiled. "I'm Janelle. You must be new."

"Yes, I am . . . Jenny." Sasha had a hard time identifying herself by a name as carefree as Jenny, but perhaps she should enjoy introducing herself as simply another New Orleans bartender, without all of her burdensome background. There could be something really liberating about that. "It is nice to meet you."

Alistair made the drink and put it on the counter. "What's up, Janelle?"

"We're having a girls' night out. I haven't been out in three whole weeks, and we are seriously ready to party. So don't be boring or we'll have to leave and find better guys to hang with."

"I'm always boring," he said, leaning on the counter. "You should know that by now."

Janelle laughed. "True. Guess I'll have to flirt with Jack instead."

As the girl turned and moved away with her drink, Sasha frowned at Alistair. "Boring? Why would you say that?" He didn't seem boring at all to her. He was solid, sexy, strong. Sasha reached for the tap. She was thirsty.

Alistair shrugged. "I am pretty boring. I work, I sleep, I feed, I watch movies, I play my guitar. Not an exciting life for a vampire."

No politics. No maneuvering. No crime.

Just an honest night's work and living life with people whose company you enjoyed.

It sounded blissful to Sasha. "An exciting life is overrated. As is wealth."

Alistair gave her a small smile. "I suppose you're right." He put his hand on the small of her back and rubbed it a little. "You're doing great, by the way. You're a very fast learner."

"Thank you." It felt so odd to have him touching her, yet it was not a bad feeling. It was comforting, and that scared her a little. What did she really know about Alistair Kirk?

Another of the women approached her and asked for a beer. "I'm Kelly, by the way," she said with a warm smile. "Jack says your Alistair's girlfriend. I'm married to Harry."

Sasha had no idea who Harry was, and she was starting to lose track of the people she had met over the last two nights. But Kelly seemed genuinely friendly, so Sasha smiled back. "It's so nice to meet you."

"You should go out with me and Janelle some night. Tami can't get out that much because she watches her mortal step-child, but Janelle and I like to hit Bourbon every Saturday night."

"Thanks. I would like that." Sasha wondered why she agreed to something she knew she would never do since she was leaving town in a few days, but Kelly looked so sincere, like she actually wanted Sasha to go out with them. It was such an unexpected behavior from a woman, that Sasha found herself desperately wanting to see what it would be like to spend an evening doing nothing but talking and laughing and dancing with friends.

The only friend she'd ever had was Ivan.

She wanted girlfriends. She wanted to belong.

She suddenly wanted to weep for all that she had lost, for all that she would never have.

And whenever she wanted to give in to weakness and cry, she dug in and faced it down. So she added, "How late are you staying out tonight? Maybe I can go out with you after my shift ends."

"That would be cool. When does your shift end? We're staying out all night."

She turned to Alistair. "When does my shift end?"

His eyes were dark and he did not look pleased with her. "Can I speak to you for a minute in private?"

"Uh-oh." Kelly took the beer Sasha had gotten for her, and said, "Alistair was hoping for sex tonight, I think, not you running off with the girls."

Janelle leaned over and yelled, "Let her go with us, Al! We'll bring her home drunk and horny, promise."

Sasha almost laughed, but the look on Alistair's face stopped her. He was grimacing.

"Wonderful," he said. "I knew I could count on you, Janelle."

"I've got your back," Janelle said, than turned to nudge Jack off his stool so she could sit down.

Alistair took Sasha's hand and started walking, not tugging or pulling her, but encouraging her to follow. He pushed the back door open with his free hand and turned to face her.

Sasha stood tall, ready to face him down. He was going to be bossy and controlling, telling her what she could and couldn't do, and she wasn't going to take it. If she was going to have any sort of relationship with Alistair—not that she wanted one exactly, but they needed to co-exist for a few days—she was going to establish firmly right now that she was not going to be pushed around. So just let him try to tell her what to do.

"Sweetheart, it's dangerous for you to go out alone with the girls."

That wasn't what she had expected him to say, and she just blinked at him for a second. He had called her sweetheart. He looked worried about her safety.

"Because of Cassandra?" she asked, most of her anger dissipating.

"Yes. The whole point of keeping you in the bar is to keep you protected by me and my friends. If you're out running around on Bourbon with Kelly, Janelle, and Tami, you're vulnerable. Not that they can't take care of themselves, because those are some smart women, but the four of you up against Cassandra's bodyguards isn't a fair fight."

"I see." She did. And she knew he was probably right.

"But I'm not going to forbid you to go because I have no right to do that. If you really want to go, just please be careful, okay?" He touched her cheek. "I don't want anything to happen to you."

It could be a con. It could be a manipulation to get her to stay. It could be anything but what it sounded like, but for whatever reason Sasha believed him. She wanted to believe him, that Alistair was a nice enough guy that it would bother him if she was killed unnecessarily by vampires, or tortured by slayers. It probably didn't even matter who she was, he would feel the same for anyone under his protection, but it pleased her. Made her stop, consider, understand the truth of what he was saying.

Her survival instinct was too honed to throw caution to the wind just for a few hours of dancing.

So with regret, she just said, "Okay," and went back into the bar.

Catching Kelly's eye, she smiled at her ruefully. "I guess I really shouldn't go. Thank you so much for inviting me though, and I hope we can do it another night."

There were raised eyebrows all around the room, but none of the men said a word. The women, on the other hand, didn't hesitate to give their opinion.

Kelly looked at Alistair in reprimand. "That's so mean to do that to your new girlfriend in front of us."

"Do what?" he asked, sticking his hands out.

"Your jackass thing."

"I didn't do anything!"

"Oh, whatever," Kelly said in disgusted dismissal. She smiled at Sasha. "We can make definite plans for next weekend."

Janelle said, "And maybe if you take Alistair upstairs for a quickie right now, you can still go out tonight."

"Mind your own business," Alistair said, sounding mildly irritated as he dumped out a full ashtray into the trash.

But Sasha could see what the counter hid from the others in the room. Alistair's erection had reappeared. Which really pleased her. And she knew that she wanted to have sex with him, that she had something to prove to herself, that she needed to know if she could let the past go.

So she said, "That's a great idea, Janelle. Alistair, let's go upstairs."

There was general laughter and a whistle or two from the room, but Alistair's head just snapped up and he stared at her, hand and ashtray suspended over the waste bin. Sasha slid in alongside of him, her hip touching his. "That is a good idea, yes?"

He stared hard at her. "We can't leave the bar with no bartender."

"What time does the bar close?"

"It doesn't. But at four, the new bartender comes on."

"It is three already." She ran her finger down his chest.

His breathing tempo increased. "Yeah, so?"

Sasha smiled, a slow, hopefully seductive smile. "It will still be a good idea at four."

Then she turned and left him to contemplate that.

ALISTAIR didn't know what game Sasha was playing, but it was torturing him. Part of him just didn't believe that she wanted to have sex with him simply for the sake of physical satisfaction, yet he couldn't figure out how else it would benefit her. If it was meant to be a ploy, a ruse of some kind, he couldn't determine any motivation for it. He had already told her he wasn't going to hold her captive. She was free to leave at any time. And he was perfectly willing to protect her without any sexual favors in return. That was not the kind of guy he was.

So why was she suddenly purring like a Russian sex kitten?

But she was, and he was debating if he was strong enough to turn her down. It seemed wrong to sleep with her if he suspected she was conning him, but on the other hand, this was Sasha, and she was *hot*. He didn't want to regret passing up an opportunity to touch her naked body, to sink his fangs into her flesh, and to roll her on top of him.

Damn it. He wanted everyone in the bar to go away and take their laughter with them. He couldn't joke around with Sam and Jack when he was this wound up.

Maybe Sasha was just taking her role as Jenny, his girlfriend, seriously. The question was, how far did her role-playing extend?

Because he had the serious need to shag her.

Which made him a sick bastard.

But if she was willing, he was pretty okay with whatever label applied.

Double-damn it. Alistair watched her pulling a beer from the tap. No, he couldn't take advantage of her. Could he?

The clock on the wall read three fifty-three. Bernie, his mortal bartender, hadn't shown up yet.

"I'm heading out," Jack said, standing up and fumbling to stick his cell phone in his pocket.

Great. Just what Alistair wanted. Jack snoring upstairs while Alistair was trying to determine if Sasha was interested in getting naked or not. That sounded completely unsexy. Maybe it was time to get his own apartment. Immediately. In the next ten minutes.

"Alright, good night, man. See you upstairs." Alistair tried to play it cool, even as Sasha glanced over at him, her dark eyes curious. He suspected she had just remembered Jack was his roommate.

"I'm actually going over to Ashley's."

"Who's Ashley?" Alistair asked, then decided he didn't care. Jack was going to be out of the apartment, and that was what mattered.

"Shot girl." And with that Jack was gone with a wave.

Sasha tucked her hair behind her ear and smiled at Alistair, staring up at him from under those long, sexy eyelashes. She knew they were going to be alone.

Alistair's body was taut with tension and if Bernie didn't show up in the next two seconds, he was not going to be responsible for his actions.

Bernie came out of the back room. "Hey, what's up?"

About freakin' time. "Nothing, we're out of here. Have a great day." He took Sasha's hand and hauled ass out of there. This was going to happen, good idea or not. It *had* to happen.

Only when Alistair got upstairs did he realize that for the first time in three hundred years, he was nervous about being with a woman. He had seen Sasha chained to a wall. Had seen her lying on the ground, staked, bleeding to death. Had been witness to the ferocity in her eyes as she had fought for her survival. Alistair knew she didn't entirely trust him, in the same way he wasn't convinced he understood her motives. It made him hesitate.

He did know he liked her, admired her, respected her tenacity.

And he wanted to have sex with her.

But now they were just sort of standing in his living room staring at each other. Her arms were crossed, the universal symbol for "leave me the fuck alone."

It was a delicate thing, whether or not he should make a move. If he did, and she wasn't ready, then he ran the risk of being categorized with her ex-husband, who had clearly dominated and brutalized her. If he didn't, and she wanted him to, he ran the risk of hurting her feelings and ruining any chance of ever being given another opportunity to take it physical.

He needed some kind of sign from her before he was going to do anything, because this was delicate shit.

So Alistair moved closer to her. "Ever thought about being a bartender for real? You're a natural."

She shrugged. "I never thought about being anything, do you know what I mean? But I did enjoy the work tonight. And I like your friends."

Do you like me? he wanted to ask, but he wasn't that far gone. Yet.

He also wanted to ask her to stay beyond a few days, to stay with him or in her own place, work at the bar, settle into New Orleans, and his life, and see where they could take it, but knew that would sound wrong, too demanding, too much too soon. It would make her run.

"They like you, too."

"Do you think so?" she asked.

Her voice sounded so wistful, so uncertain, that Alistair reached out and cupped her cheek, sliding his fingers over her smooth porcelain skin. "Hey. Yes, I do. They know you're smart and witty."

"Women don't usually like me," she said, her eyes meeting his only briefly before dropping back down to stare at his chest. Sasha still had her arms crossed, but she bit her thumbnail.

"They were probably jealous and intimidated." Hell, she intimidated him sometimes.

"I haven't had many friends. Gregor kept me isolated."

"Then this is a good thing, for you to be able to just hang out, be part of the group."

"Yeah. It is." She gave a brief smile up at him. "But it is hard as well. I do not know how to act. I am socially unskilled."

"If you've had friends, then you know how to act. Just be yourself, talk, have fun. It's all good."

"My best friend growing up, Ivan, became a blood slave. He is the one who turned me over to Cassandra."

Wow. That was shitty. Alistair couldn't imagine being betrayed by someone you loved and trusted. She spoke defiantly, but Alistair could hear the hurt in her voice, see the pain in her eyes.

"Oh, babe, I'm so sorry. But you know when someone is addicted to how a vampire can make them feel, it's no different than being a drug addict. They're not themselves."

"I know."

"But it still sucks." Damn, he wished he could take away all that she had suffered. It tore at him, the way she had never really known love or friendship.

"Yes, it does."

Alistair gently uncrossed her arms, and pulled her into his. "But now you're free. You can do whatever you want with the rest of your life."

She held back slightly, keeping a few inches between their bodies, but she seemed relaxed. "That is true, and I have thought of almost nothing but that. It's tantalizing. Once back in Russia I had a friendship, and what I thought was love, with a young man in America that I met online. I daydreamed about leaving Gregor, marrying Kyle, living a middle-class life in California. He was killed before I could ever implement any plan to leave. But it would have never happened anyway. I was naïve. I am not destined for the role of suburban housewife."

"What are you destined for?" Alistair studied her expression. She looked more prosaic than sad, but he still couldn't entirely wrap his mind around all that she had experienced.

"I am not entirely certain, but for now, I want to be Jenny, the vampire bartender who wears these funny black sneakers and a skull necklace." She smiled at him, and placed her hands on his shoulders. "Now tell me about you, Alistair Kirk. Why do you sound American if you are British, and who did you lose to slayers?"

He hadn't anticipated her directness. But she had shared personal pain with him, he could give her the same back. But first he'd take the easy question. "I sound American because I have been here since 1769. I've lost the majority of my accent over the years. And my wife was killed by slayers before I left England." It didn't hurt as much to talk about it anymore, but he still always felt a pang of guilt and regret. "I met her thirty years earlier when she fell into the Thames and drowned. I pulled her out, but this was before we understood modern resuscitation techniques, and she died. So I turned her. We loved each other. Slayers killed her."

End of story, such as it was. Alistair struggled not to look away from Sasha. "It was not a pretty ending for her, and I was in London when they attacked her. I didn't find out for three days."

"I am sorry, Alistair." She rubbed her fingers over his shoulders. "It was not very long to be together, was it?"

It wasn't the response he expected and he was caught off guard. "No. No, it wasn't. But it was a long time ago."

And he didn't want to talk about it anymore, so he kissed her. Their lips were close and all he had to do was lean forward, take. He intended it to be a light caress, but almost immediately she opened her mouth. Not accidentally, but intentionally, as an invitation, and he didn't need to be asked twice.

Alistair slid his tongue inside her and buried his hands in her hair.

She was such a beautiful woman, so strong, yet fragile at the same time. He was very aware of that responsibility, of the fact that she had not known a normal relationship with a man in her life. He couldn't just take what he wanted and walk away, and he didn't want that anyway. But it was going to be up to her to decide the direction they were going to take, and he was going to have to be paying close attention to her signals.

It was daunting, but damn, she was worth it.

He would just take it nice and slow.

Sasha grabbed his jeans and undid the button and zipper.

Alistair froze when her hand landed on his unit with amazingly accurate aim. "Umm . . ."

So much for slow.

"What is wrong?" she asked, as she worked him over from head to shaft with her lithe fingers.

"Are you sure you want to do this?" It seemed out of character for her, and he wondered if she was nervous. He grabbed her wrist to pause her delicious movements for a second, because he couldn't think when she was doing that.

"Don't you want to?" She looked disappointed, which made him happy.

He almost laughed at the absurdity of that question. "Of course I do. But we don't need to rush if you're not ready for that. I can enjoy the hike up just as much as the view from the top." The last thing he wanted was to rush through and have her regret it later.

"I am not sure what you mean." Sasha used her free hand to grip the back of his head and kiss him again.

It was a nice kiss, skilled and full of soft sweeps of her moist tongue over his, all while her fingers stroked him. Alistair's body was enjoying the hell out of it, even as his head hesitated. Something seemed wrong, and he couldn't put his finger on what it was.

Stepping back slightly, she pulled her T-shirt over her head, and then, standing in just jeans, she licked her fingers so that when she returned to touching him, her hand slid slickly up and down his erection. Alistair closed his eyes at the immediate wave of pleasure that rocked him. Damn it, she was good at that.

But he wanted to touch her, too, so he brushed his thumb over her bare nipple. Her bra had been destroyed in the staking, and he was glad there was no barrier between his fingers and her breasts. Yet Sasha shifted away, like his touch irritated her. Trying to be respectful and attuned to her body, Alistair let her move out of his reach and focused again on kissing her.

There was nothing outwardly wrong. They were kissing, she was touching him below the belt, but Alistair couldn't relax. There was tension, there was something off . . . He wasn't able to read her and it was frustrating the hell out of him. Moving his hands over her bare waist, reveling in the feel of her soft, smooth skin, Alistair tried to undo the snap on her jeans, but again, she moved away.

Sasha unzipped her jeans herself, her tongue sliding across her bottom lip, and pushed her pants to the floor. Stepping out of the jeans, she was in nothing but a tiny pair of black panties, her body long and lean, those eight-mile-long legs amazing to behold. He wanted to touch her, to lick her, to pull those panties aside and slide his tongue into her moisture.

But when he reached for her, she gracefully dropped to her knees in front of him and took him into her mouth, the movement fluid, easy.

Even as he gritted his teeth to hold back a moan, he was putting his hands on her head to stop her. Holy shit, he suddenly knew what was going on, and it wasn't a good thing.

"Sasha."

She didn't respond, nor did she stop.

Alistair tried to step away but she held him in place. So he tipped her head back so she would have to look up at him. The sight of her eyes wide and questioning, her mouth still wrapped around his cock, almost undid him, but he took a deep breath and used his superior strength to step back.

"We don't have to do this," he said. It was obvious to him that she was trying to rush through it, get it over with.

"Why do you say that?" she asked, her lips shiny, long hair tumbling over her bare breasts. Still on her knees, she was mere inches from his erection. "Are you not enjoying it?"

"Yes, I am. But it's not doing anything for you, is it?" he asked carefully. "This isn't giving you pleasure."

Her face suddenly crumpled. "I want it to," she whispered. "I think I can, with you. I like the way you kiss me."

Alistair wished Gregor Chechikov wasn't dead so he could kill him himself. Man, he had messed with Sasha's head, and now Alistair felt helpless to know how to fix it. "Then why won't you let me touch you? I can help you like it if you'll let me . . . do things to you."

But Sasha just frowned. "What things?"

And suddenly Alistair understood the complete and whole truth. Sasha's sex life had been that of her administering pleasure to her husband. That was why she was so good at it, yet she had never been given the same pleasure in return.

It made him so angry he wanted to throw big things and watch them break.

But what he really needed to do was to make this right for her.

"Come on," he said, reaching down and taking her hand in his, so she could stand. "Let's go to my bedroom. I'll show you what things I mean."

Seven

Sasha did not understand what she was doing wrong, but Alistair seemed frustrated with her. Maybe she should take his clothes off of him, because now that she was virtually naked, and they had started this, she wanted to finish it. She wanted to get her first time with someone other than Gregor over with, so she could relax the second time.

She realized that was probably not the best approach to take, but she was in this far and just needed to brazen through it. It was going to take time to be completely sexually normal, and she liked Alistair. She enjoyed the way he kissed her, and she appreciated the fact that when he looked at her with desire, she felt pride rather than disgust or vulnerability. It was progress.

Which was why they just needed to get this over with, so the second time around she could make even more progress.

But Alistair was pulling her down the hall, his hand in hers as he bent over to scoop up her discarded clothes. He wanted to go to the bedroom. She could do that. What she was unsure about were these "things" he was talking about. What exactly did he want to do to her?

Maybe he liked kinky sex or role-playing, which she didn't think she would like at all. She did not want to hear buzzing while she was trying to be aroused, nor did she want to dress like a French maid. She had played a part her whole marriage, she did not want to do that now, when she was trying to actually discover herself.

"Relax," he said, stopping in front of his bed and turning to her. "We're not going to do anything weird. I just want to take it slow, take some time to savor it, okay? And tell me if you don't like something and I'll stop." Then he gave a smile, a devilish, seductive smile that kicked her heart rate up a notch. "And tell me if you *do* like something, so I make sure I don't stop."

"Okay." Sasha took a deep breath and tried to will herself to relax. She was not a person used to relaxation, so it came difficult to her.

Alistair laced his fingers through hers and kissed her shoulder, her cheek, nuzzling against her. She was stiff and resisting, she knew it, could feel it, and she tried to let go of the tension, but it was too ingrained, too familiar.

"You're already naked," he murmured. "That's the hard part. Now comes the fun part."

That remained to be seen, but she was trying.

But as Alistair did nothing but kiss her, over and over, she did relax. She liked the way he held her shoulders, enough pressure to know he was there, that he wanted her, but not grabbing or gripping or shoving. He really was a nice man, and she was very, very attracted to him.

When he urged her back to the bed, she went, her nerves spiking a little again, but Alistair was there immediately, stroking her hair, brushing his lips across her mouth, her neck.

"You are very beautiful," he murmured as he kissed her collarbone.

Sasha had heard those words so many times, they meant so very little. In fact, they were negative reminders of how Gregor had reduced her value to that of a pretty face. Yet she knew Alistair meant it as a compliment, so she said, "Thank you."

"Sure. But that's not what I like about you," he said, his hand sliding over her abdomen, her ribs, her hip bones, while his lips brushed her shoulder.

"It's not?" she asked, glancing at him. All she could see was his dark hair bent over her.

"No. What I like about you is that you're smart and fierce and caring and loyal. The beauty is just a bonus."

"Oh." Sasha had no better answer than that. She was pleased and baffled by his words and she needed to let that sink in.

Except she lost the ability to think when Alistair bit her shoulder and warm, tingling pleasure reverberated throughout her body. She hadn't been bit since her turning, and she was stunned at how good it felt, at the hot rush between her thighs, and the need to grab on to Alistair's shoulders and arch herself toward him.

A moan of disappointment ripped out of her when he pulled back, but before she had time to protest the loss, he covered her breast with his mouth and sucked. She had thought that she wasn't aroused by nipple stimulation, given that it had never brought her pleasure before, but it was different with him. His teeth, his tongue, his biting and licking and sucking had her gripping the bed sheet and moving her legs restlessly.

It felt good. Really good. Eye-rolling good, and she was in awe, her teeth sinking into her bottom lip as she wrapped her arms around his back and felt the movement of his muscles as he tasted her.

Then without warning, his fingers were inside her panties and stroking a teasing, taunting, delicious rhythm around her clitoris that had her moaning out loud. He was hitting a certain spot just so, and she ached with desire as he gently bit her nipple and squeezed her clitoris at the same time.

He was going to put his finger inside her, she knew that, and Sasha felt a momentary panic. She had always used a lubricant so her ex-husband wouldn't comment on her lack of moisture, and she was mortified that Alistair would find her dry, and think it had anything to do with him. It was her problem, her baggage that she couldn't get . . .

Alistair's finger slipped easily inside of her, her body slick and welcoming. She was so startled she let out a cry. "Oh!" She was wet, well and truly wet, ready to accept his finger, wanting his finger, wanting all of him. Instinctively, in response to the pleasure, to that realization, she dropped her knees apart, and now it was Alistair's turn to groan.

"You feel so good," he said.

He felt pretty good himself, and she would have told him that, except he moved lower down her body, raising goose bumps all over her skin, his finger slipping out of her. She didn't want him to stop, but wasn't sure she could make herself request that he continue when it became a moot point. Alistair replaced his finger with his mouth and Sasha almost levitated off the bed. She was shocked and appalled and overcome with the most delicious, pulsing ecstasy that her mind went completely blank, and she grabbed on to his head for support.

He was doing things with his tongue that she couldn't

decipher or visualize, but each and every touch set off throbbing waves of pleasure that she never wanted to stop. Somewhere in the back of her mind she was vaguely aware that she was moaning, loudly, a rhythmic sort of guttural cry that was nothing like any sound she had ever made before. But then again, no man had ever actually given her oral sex, and certainly no man had ever made her feel what Alistair was making her feel.

The orgasm came out of nowhere, steamrolling her and sending her hips bucking off the bed. Alistair held her legs, gripping tightly so that his mouth wouldn't leave her as she rode out the shudders. She dropped her legs back down onto the mattress and tried to catch her breath.

Alistair's clothes came off in a blink and he was over her, his erection nudging against her. He looked down at her, eyes dark with arousal, but arms steady, body and mind in control. "Is this okay? Should I keep going?"

She nodded, not trusting herself to speak. He should be entitled to pleasure, too, after what he had just done to her, for her.

Still poised over her, Alistair leaned down and kissed her, his tongue teasing hers. His taste was different, tangier, and Sasha realized that it was because of what he had been doing, to her, and she was shocked and aroused all at the same time. What he had done had been so sexy that she spread her legs even farther for him, her body aching anew, her breasts brushing his bare chest and enflaming his desire.

When Alistair pushed into her, she snapped her head back and closed her eyes, overwhelmed that it felt good, so very, very good. There was no discomfort, no feeling of pressure, no shame, only beautiful, glorious pleasure as their bodies blended.

ALISTAIR bit his lip and fought for control as he watched surprise cross Sasha's face, followed by pleasure. It was beautiful to see her arousal, her desire, to know that he was giving her something no man ever had, that he was helping her to heal and enjoy sexual experiences.

Not to mention that it just felt so fucking good to be inside her tight body, her hot warmth pulsing around his cock.

When her eyes went wide and she stopped breathing as another orgasm swept over her, Alistair gave up. Thrusting harder as her muscles contracted around him, he went over the edge with her, and allowed himself a tight moan of triumph.

Damn, but she was amazing, and he was in so much trouble.

At the moment he didn't care.

And he still didn't care when several heartbeats later he withdrew and pulled her up alongside of him, and she came willingly, snuggling up against his chest.

"Why don't you stay for a while?" Alistair asked when his breathing and heart rate had returned to normal, trying to sound casual, knowing he probably didn't.

"In New Orleans?"

Sasha's arms were wrapped around him, which he chose to take as a sign of trust and her high comfort level with him. "Yes, in New Orleans. With me. You're safe here."

She just chewed her lip and didn't respond.

Alistair knew that he had to let her leave if she wanted to, but he really didn't like the idea. So he was prepared to lay it all on the line. "I like you a lot, Sasha. I want to be with you, see where we can take this." He kissed her forehead, then her nose. "Don't leave. Please."

When she blinked hard, he realized she was struggling to control tears, and her emotions. He wasn't sure if that was a good thing or a bad thing.

She swallowed hard. "I would like to stay."

"But?" He heard it hanging there, unspoken, and he hated it.

Sasha turned and blinked at him. "But what?"

"But why can't you stay?"

"I can. I just said I would like to."

Alistair gripped her harder, not sure he was actually processing this right. "You mean you're actually intending to stay?"

"Yes. Don't you want me to?"

"Yes." He grinned. "But I thought you'd tell me to forget it."

She didn't smile back. "I am trying, Alistair. I want to try to have a new life, but you have to understand that my life hasn't been normal."

"Babe, I'm a four-hundred-year-old vampire. My life hasn't been normal either. We'll just take it one night at a time and enjoy getting to know each other, enjoy the chemistry and the caring between us. Is that cool with you?"

Now she released her bottom lip from the torture of her teeth and gave him a long, searching look. "That's very, very cool."

Alistair kissed her luscious mouth and erased any remaining distance between them. "Just a warning . . . I'm going to fall in love with you, you know. It's already happening."

"Maybe you can stop it," she said, her fingers playing in his hair, the corner of her mouth tilting up.

"Nope. I can't. It's definitely going to happen." He knew it and he liked it.

"I can't stop it either. If every day is like tonight, I am going to fall in love with you as well."

"What was tonight like?" So he could repeat it for eternity.

"It was safe, honest, sensual . . . it was us being friends, partners."

"Perfect description." And he had an erection just thinking about how awesome it was that she had come into his life. "Now have I mentioned vampire endurance?"

"What do you mean?"

He nudged her. "What do you think? Can I show you some more things?"

"I think I would definitely like that."

Eight

Sasha crawled out of bed and stood for a minute, looking down at Alistair. He was a very cute, sexy man, and he liked her. He really, really liked her. And she believed that sentiment was genuine.

It awed and amazed her that they had stumbled into each other's lives and how wonderful it felt to be with him, how easy their connection was.

Falling in love wasn't going to be hard. Maybe not wise, but definitely easy.

Moving quietly, not wanting to wake him up, she dug around in his dresser and closet until she found sweatpants, a T-shirt, and socks and pulled them on. As a fledgling, she needed to feed more often than Alistair, and she had woken up after all of their exhausting pleasure with her stomach burning from hunger. She knew there was no blood left in the refrigerator, but there was plenty down in the bar. She would just slip down and grab some bags to restock the apartment.

Not sure if Bernie, the mortal day bartender, knew what they were, but she would just try to be casual about it. A glance at the clock on Alistair's nightstand showed it was nine P.M., so hopefully Bernie would be long gone anyway. She and Alistair had both slept through the entire day after wearing each other out. Sasha smiled at the memory, her body deliciously sore.

She found her shoes in the living room and glanced down at herself in amusement. It was a ridiculous outfit, the pants huge on her, the T-shirt bulky and faded, the shoes so low her thick white socks were showing. It was horrible, appalling, and it was completely and totally liberating, representing her right to choices. Bad fashion was hers if she wanted it.

And so was love. A normal life.

When she got downstairs, she took a deep breath and pushed open the door to the bar, hoping it wouldn't be crowded.

Raven was back behind the counter, and she smiled over at her. "Hey, what's up?"

"Hi. I just wanted a drink."

"Sure, grab whatever. Is Alistair coming down tonight?"

"I'm not sure."

"Okay." Raven pulled her cell phone out of the pocket of her black denim miniskirt. "Excuse me, I need to make a call."

"Sure." Sasha bent over and rooted around in the refrigerator. The bar wasn't busy yet, though there was a heavy smell of fried foods lingering, like someone had just ordered mozzarella sticks or tater tots. It didn't do good things for her desperate hunger and she was feeling nauseous and a little dizzy.

When she stood up, a generous splash of blood poured into a glass, she blinked when she saw who was standing in front of her on the other side of the bar. "Ivan?"

"Hi, Sasha," he said, voice quiet, expression contrite, eyes filled with regret.

"What are you doing here?" she asked tightly, gripping her glass. His betrayal still hurt, and it always would. She had loved him as her dearest friend, and he had sacrificed her for his own pleasure.

"I came to say I'm sorry . . ." Ivan ran his hand through his hair and scratched in a burst of nervous energy.

It wasn't much in the way of an apology, but it was something. Knowing he was contrite was balm to her wounded feelings, and she opened her mouth to tell him that she forgave him, but never wanted to see him again.

The arms grabbing her from behind before she could speak caught her completely off guard and she dropped her glass of blood. The crash as it hit the floor was loud and fracturing, liquid splashing all over her pants and feet as she instinctively jerked forward to break the grip on her.

But Raven was stronger than she was, especially since Sasha hadn't fed, and she struggled to free herself in vain, looking to Ivan for help that she knew he would never deliver. He was too weak, too far gone.

Which was apparent when he shrugged. "I really am sorry, Sasha . . . I don't want to do this to you, but I don't have a choice. You understand, don't you? You know we're friends, that I've always cared about you, but that I had to do this. I had to."

"Go to hell," she told him, truly meaning it. Any affection she had ever felt for him was gone, because he was no longer the person she had known.

"I'll take her now, Raven, thank you so much." A blonde had breezed into the back of the bar wearing a business skirt and jacket in an offensive teal color. Obviously bad fashion was this woman's right, too.

Obviously it was Cassandra, the woman Alistair had married. She was beautiful, there was no denying it, but Sasha could see the coldness on her face. In Sasha's initial kidnapping, she had never met Cassandra, and she could have done without the honor now, or ever. But she refused to show any emotion. She even stopped struggling with Raven. Cassandra couldn't have the satisfaction of seeing her frustration, her disappointment in Ivan.

Standing straight and proud, Sasha stared at Cassandra as she approached the bar. The blonde came to a sudden halt right in front of her, and her eyes went wide. "You slept with Alistair, didn't you?"

Sasha didn't answer and Cassandra's eyes filled with tears. "That bastard. I can smell him all over you."

Tempted to sniff herself, somehow pleased at the idea of having his scent on her, Sasha still didn't say a word.

"I should kill you," she said, voice laced with jealousy, fury. "Right here. In his bar."

Sasha didn't flinch. "Try it. You might succeed, but I will take you down with me." She was tired of the threats, tired of the politics, tired of the fear. She had the beginnings of a new life poised in her hands, and she would be damned if she would let a blonde in a bad suit take that away from her.

They stared each other down, and Cassandra looked away first.

"Raven, let her go. This was a mistake, it was all a mistake." Cassandra swiped at her moist eyes, clearly agitated by her emotions. "And to think that I loved him . . . it's all so damn stupid."

A different woman might have taken the moment to rub it in Cassandra's face that she had lost Alistair, but Sasha felt no urge to do so. She would not stoop to this woman's level, and she would never let go of her understanding of what was wrong and right. Taking pleasure in another's pain was something Sasha would never comprehend, and she had suffered too much herself to wish the same on anyone else.

Raven let her go and despite her moral high ground, Sasha did take a certain satisfaction in turning to her and saying, "You're fired."

"You don't own this bar!"

"Do you think the owner will allow you to work here after you were ready to turn his girlfriend over to a slayer broker?"

Raven scowled and pulled her purse out of the cubby under the counter. "Fine."

Cassandra was already leaving, her high heels pounding an angry rhythm on the floor. Ivan was still standing there and Sasha just looked at him, not bothering to hide her disdain. "You need to leave."

But instead of complying, he leaned toward her and said, "Sasha, bite me. Take my blood."

She recoiled. God, he was serious. He had an excited gleam in his eye and he was sticking his neck out toward her, his head tilted.

"No," she said, disgusted.

"Please. It's my way of apologizing . . . I can belong to you, now that you're a vampire. We always did get along well. This will only make that better." Ivan moved down the counter and behind the bar to stand beside her.

He was going to touch her and she felt panic crawling up her throat. It wasn't logical since she was stronger than him and he didn't want to hurt her. He wasn't a threat. But the thought of what he did want was paralyzing in its repulsiveness.

The door to the storage room opened and Alistair stepped into the room. "Jenny?" he said carefully, looking at her, at Ivan, assessing the situation. "Is everything okay?"

"It's fine," she told him, never taking her eyes off of Ivan. "He's leaving. And Raven is going with him."

"Sasha . . ." Ivan pleaded with her. "Please."

Whatever had remained of her anger drained away. Sasha sighed. "Go home, Ivan. I can't help you."

Raven grabbed him by the arm. "Come on, we're leaving."

Sasha stood and watched them both walk away, heading to

the front of the bar, Ivan shooting her one last needy glance over his shoulder.

Alistair moved in next to her and put his hand on the small of her back. "What was all that? You okay? And why is Raven leaving?"

"She tried to turn me over to Cassandra. And that was Ivan, the friend who betrayed me."

"What? You should have let me know, I would have knocked him on his ass." Alistair made a move like he was going to go after Ivan, so Sasha grabbed his arm.

"No, you don't need to do that. I'm fine. Cassandra is not going to bother me anymore and neither is Ivan." She was convinced of that. There had been a humiliation in Cassandra's eyes, and Sasha was sure if their paths crossed again, it would be purely by accident. Cassandra would never intentionally kill the woman Alistair was sleeping with, because she harbored hope of getting back together with him.

Sasha knew that would never happen, but she was willing to let Cassandra consider it a possibility if it meant she left them the hell alone.

Alistair grinned. "What did you do to them?"

"Nothing. I just told them to leave."

He wrapped his arms around her and pulled her up against his chest. "You're a tough chick, you know that? I love that you can take care of yourself." He kissed her. "Though I'm hoping that sometimes you'll let me take care of you, too."

Sasha closed her eyes and leaned in to him, basking in the warmth of his affection, the security of his strength. She felt something akin to hope and happiness for the first time in what seemed like an eternity.

"I'd like that, Alistair. I really would."

DOUBLE
THE BITE

✝

CHRIS MARIE GREEN

AUTHOR'S NOTE

The events of this novella take place within the scope of the Vampire Babylon (www.vampirebabylon.com) world. If any of you wondered why Ginny and Geneva, the vampire "daughters" of Sorin, never came back Underground, this should answer your questions.

Happy hunting . . .

ONE

THE WOMAN MOVED LIKE RED LIGHT EASING OVER a midnight street as she slipped onto the dance floor.

Ben Tyree watched her from his dark corner, hidden from the slow, throbbing disco music. He was biding his time, having traveled too many miles for answers regarding the death of his older, better brother.

As a deputy back home, he knew his way around an investigation. But here, the NYPD seemed so wrapped in red tape that Ben had ventured out on his own. The cops were cooperating by sharing what they already knew, yet Ben hadn't accepted the lack of progress.

"Severe blood loss," the young detective who wore glasses, a plaid tie, and an officious attitude had said. "That's all we really know about the cause of death right now. No clear indication of drug use, no signs of violence or attack like stab or gunshot wounds . . ."

So Ben had done his own tracking, starting with his brother Nolan's hotel concierge, a whey-faced man who'd jokingly mentioned Studio 54 to Nolan after he'd asked about city hot spots. The employee had known the obvious family man wouldn't get in, but Nolan had taken him seriously.

It didn't sound like his brother at all, but Ben had still followed up, even though the cops had already covered this ground.

And his tenacity paid off when he found something they hadn't.

While working his way from the back of the club's waiting mob to the front, Ben had encountered two women dressed as disciples of the Marquis de Sade by way of the Bee Gees. They'd told him that a woman named "Ginny"—early twenties, dark-haired, looked like Elizabeth Taylor back when she was fresh and young—had been seen with "the dead guy" outside this club the night before last.

Consequently, Ben hadn't expected to get in to Studio 54 since it was known for its selectivity, so he'd resigned himself to staking out the crowds gathered around the entrance for this "Ginny." But a slight guy with wiry hair had been handpicking customers, and Ben somehow caught his eye and was ushered past the velvet ropes as women in feathers and glitter and men in butterfly-collar shirts begged the same admission.

Now, under the pulsing lights and the synthesizer-driven chug of music, Ben honed in on the woman who just might hold more answers—the lady who really did look like a young Liz Taylor, swaying so gracefully to the music.

Her short hair curled to just below the ears, a white flower poised in its black curls. Thick lashes surrounded eyes that seemed to flash blue against pale skin. Crimson lipstick shaped a lush mouth.

He couldn't take his eyes off of her. Then again, neither could the other dancers—male and female—who'd gone still to watch her, enthralled.

Every one of Ben's cells hammered downward until they gathered in his gut, stretching, then twisting until they overcame him, tearing him apart with each undulation she made.

A flame, he thought while she smoothed her hands up her red dress, lifting her face to the catwalks lingering over the floor.

A lure that shouldn't be tempting him.

He tore his gaze away, gathering his guts by reminding himself of why he was here and where he was.

A Sodom wrapped around Gomorrah. A cavernous former theater from the 1920s that had been turned into a radio/TV stage, then morphed into this pit. A place with bared bodies writhing under a piece of artwork that symbolized debauchery—a man in the moon, complete with a cocaine spoon lifted to its nose.

Life in the goddamn city, he thought. And his brother had died in its embrace.

As Ben quelled his emotions—he'd already allowed himself grief, but now a desire for vengeance overtook it—the music escalated to a more urgent beat, pumping in time to the lights.

In spite of himself, Ben's gaze was pulled back to the woman's allure.

She would be the key. He just knew it.

Fingers buried in her hair, she had stopped dancing, closing her eyes as if craving the slow churn of the previous song. She allowed her hands to trail down the sides of her long, pale neck, over the clasp of her halter, then her collarbone. Her sliding touch was a sensual fade, like one last long note in the song still humming through her.

She brushed the swell of her breasts, and his belly clenched. But then he forced himself to think about Nolan and the pictures that the cops had shared.

The sightless eyes of a man who'd died in the throes of . . .

What? Ben had been wondering just what the hell it was that defined Nolan's gaze in those photos. It had compelled him, haunted him.

Fascinated him.

Ben had seen a few corpses in his own small-town Texas job, but he'd never witnessed *this*, and he found himself wondering just what Nolan had discovered in death that had eluded him in life.

What could've possibly given him such a look of ecstasy . . . ?

When the images faded from his mind's eye, the woman was gone.

Shit.

He thought of the .45 in his ankle holster. Ready for anything.

Emerging out of his shaded corner, he scanned the club, past the mirrored bar by the dance floor, past the stage, past—

He sucked in a breath when he met a pair of bright blue eyes.

Fight-ready, he immediately went into defense mode, his heartbeat trumping the music and banging in his ears, his chest.

But . . . he couldn't move. God, he was captured by the blue gaze, which had somehow turned a pure, fathomless silver in the endless second it'd taken him to recover.

A strange peace filtered through him, and he thought, *This is what Nolan saw while he died.*

Suddenly, he knew that he shouldn't be so on guard. Not around her.

Not around Ginny.

As he stared and stared, he felt the vague sensation of fingers riffling through his mind, quickly and efficiently exploring.

Then, as soon as it had started, it was over.

He was still looking into her eyes, but they were blue again. Music blasted, as if turned way up, even though Ben instinctively knew that it was the same volume as before.

The woman in red didn't speak over the drumming rhythms, only crooked her finger at him, inviting him to follow her.

He probably should have thought twice about obeying, but he didn't. *Couldn't.* His body seemed to be doing all the thinking for him as he followed her to a staircase, where they climbed to a balcony dominated by old theater seats.

And the chairs weren't empty, either. No, all around, there were bodies—half-dressed, undressed, exposing sleek limbs and grinding hips.

A twinge of warning told Ben to leave, to let the NYPD do their own work, but abandonment wasn't natural to him. Besides, Ginny had taken his hand, leading him past a woman who was snorting cocaine while she straddled another female. The second one was strumming the first one between the legs, a naughty smile on her face as she checked out the new arrivals.

Then they moved on, past a woman wearing nothing but gold paint while she laved the penis of a man who was casually drinking a martini.

Eventually, they found a relatively quiet area of their own, and Ginny turned to Ben.

God, she was so beautiful that looking at her almost seemed blasphemous. But he did it anyway.

And his cock went hot and hard, as if he had no control.

She gestured to a seat, but he refused. Nonetheless, she folded herself into a chair, crossing one long leg over the other.

"From the way you were watching me," she said, "I thought we might enjoy a little privacy."

Privacy would be great for this interview he needed to conduct with her; if it panned out, he'd let the NYPD in on the lead.

Or maybe privacy would be Ben's downfall.

He steadied himself, and she must have misconstrued his hesitation.

"There are other places we can go if that makes you more comfortable," she said. "Haven't you heard about the upper area—the real 'Upstairs'? Private, secret rooms. I know the owners of Studio, so—"

Ben tried to clear his head. What the hell was going on with him?

"I'm not here for any other reason than to talk," he managed.

"Really?" It wasn't so much a question as an amused statement.

"Really. I've got some business to take care of and you're on my checklist, Ginny."

A lift of her brow was validation that he'd found the right woman.

As she cocked her head, inspecting him with cool negligence, he strengthened himself with thoughts of his older brother: Nolan laughing at a family barbecue, then gone the next morning on a business trip to New York. The phone call his wife had received yesterday, announcing Nolan's death in a condemned building in the Bronx.

Ire all but pummeled Ben as it batted away the grief. *Got to find out what happened.*

Then, a crazier thought.

Got to know what Nolan saw before he died with that fulfilled look in his eyes . . .

"You know my name," Ginny said. She grinned. Sultry, languorous.

Ben stepped forward, knowing the interview had begun. Over the balcony's stench of sex and sweat, he caught the lovely scent of the magnolia in her hair.

Or maybe that was the smell of her skin . . . ?

His cock strained against his fly, blood thrusting through his veins and tearing him apart as he struggled for composure.

"Two nights ago," he said tightly, "people saw you outside this club with my brother, Nolan. Seven hours later, he was found dead. I thought you could offer some insight about what happened between then and there."

Something seemed to roll over her, like the moon losing its light, and Ben knew that he hadn't wasted his time tracking her down. This Ginny knew what he was talking about.

But before he could start in again, a voice sounded from behind him.

"You going to tell him, Ginny?" a second woman asked, and she sounded exactly like her. Like Ginny.

When Ben turned around to see who she was, he realized that it *was* Ginny.

Or at least her double.

Two

Ginny straightened in her theater seat as her twin sister, Geneva, claimed Ben Tyree's attention.

Having been inside his mind, reading it like files left willy-nilly over a desk, she knew his name. Truly, she knew everything superficial about him, including the fact that he had what might be romantically called a "cowboy code"—a vision of the universe in black-and-white. A quaint sense of justice that Ginny hadn't seen since the early '50s, back when she'd been a human and swept up in post-war patriotism.

Back in the days when everything had been much simpler . . .

She switched her gaze to the man, a moral compass who fascinated her. When she'd first seen him in the darkness near the dance floor, watching her with such longing, she'd gotten interested. Then, after she'd infiltrated his head, it'd gone to another level . . . one she didn't quite understand since she'd never encountered the feeling before.

Serenity . . .

But, being the creature she was, she didn't know what to do with this abstract niggling. So she'd reverted to habit, bringing him to the balcony, intent on getting her fill of his hard, hot body with mere sex. Foreplay. Afterward, she could get her blood from someone less dangerous—someone who wasn't involved with Nolan Tyree.

Someone who'd be an easier meal for the night.

And in spite of Geneva showing up, Ginny was still going to have him. She could feel her lateral incisors elongating, evidence of her arousal.

Still, she held back, savoring the foreplay as he turned away from her sister to face Ginny again, confusion marking his features.

She took her time in scanning him. Under his white T-shirt, his shoulders were broad, his chest wide, his arms muscled.

His dark green eyes were splintered with white shards that she could easily discern with her heightened vision. A past-the-hour-of-five shadow manifested itself as stubble on his face, hiding a cleft in his chin. He wore his brown hair short-clipped, just like his patience with the lack of leads in his brother's case.

By peering into his mind, she had seen he was a searcher. A perfect victim looking for more than the crumbs life had already offered him. As saddened as he was by his brother's death, Ben Tyree was enchanted by what Nolan had found when he'd passed on.

And, deep inside, he yearned for it, too.

Now, Ginny noted how Ben composed himself in the aftermath of seeing Geneva, her twin, his body going wary. Searchers could be dangerous to vampires. Searchers tended to dig deeper into matters than was good for them.

Thing was, Ginny thought, a man like Ben Tyree could be taken care of with a snap of her fingers. If she wished, none of the creatures in Studio tonight would let him out the doors, because even though her kind ran free in the club, they couldn't afford to have talk of vampires filtering into the city.

Here, in Studio, they fit effortlessly among the beautiful and the odd, among every guest who tried to top the hedonism with more and more excess. There were regular humans who even flocked here to *act* like vampires in the higher rooms or the basement, where the VIPs gathered.

Besides, come morning, no one ever recalled the details of with whom they'd been or why their necks were tender with the bites some vampires, like her, could heal and conceal.

Ginny finally stood from her chair. She'd sensed her twin's growing hunger for a taste of Ben Tyree, and Geneva was bound to be growing less cautious by the moment.

With the speed of a fractured second, Ginny mind-spoke to her twin. It was their special mode of communication. Long ago, when they were young, they would talk in a twin language based on high school Latin classes, and they'd always had a strange consciousness of what the other was feeling or doing. Those talents had only improved as vampires, taking the form of their own intensified awareness. Otherwise, Awareness for their breed was limited to communication between an individual and their maker.

Their creator happened to be named Sorin, a vampire who still dwelled Underground in Los Angeles.

Ginny squashed his name to the back of her head, burying it.

This is Ben, she thought to her sister. *He's the brother of Nolan, from the other night.*

Her twin blinked, then smiled. *I remember Nolan.*

At the name, Ginny felt her sister's cravings escalate.

A tweak of what a human might call trepidation invaded her. Isolation. A facsimile of emotion.

Ginny tried to identify where it'd come from. How strange.

I sure would like a bite, Geneva tacitly added. *So strong, so gorgeous—*

No.

Geneva paused, and Ginny knew what was running through her sister's mind, even though Geneva was attempting to conceal it. She was feeling possessive, as she often did.

Then Ginny mentally assuaged her twin, not wanting her to be angry.

We have an entire club to choose from, she said. *You know this prey is dangerous to us. Just let me get rid of him.*

So you can have him to yourself?

Ginny ignored that, shutting off their awareness and concentrating on Ben again.

It was so much better than battling with Geneva. They'd been at odds with each other too much lately.

Their silent exchange had only taken less than a second and, as Geneva walked past Ben to stand next to Ginny, it was obvious he was still absorbing the new situation.

"Twins," he muttered so low that she barely picked it up with her sharp hearing. "Well, I'll be."

He folded his arms over his expansive chest, looking at Geneva, but saving a longer, more interested gaze for Ginny.

Her veins beat with him, expanding with brutal force. How? After all, she never felt this way unless she was drinking the hot blood of prey, sucking it inside of her.

Her sex even primed itself: a throbbing between her legs, the stiffness of her clit.

"You're in the wrong place for cop work," Geneva said, slipping an arm around Ginny's waist and resting her head on her sister's shoulder. "You've stepped into a different world here."

Ginny held her twin close, her body calming.

Ben's jaw clenched. "Justice applies everywhere."

Such a temptation, Ginny thought. Such a man.

Should she risk revealing herself by going into his mind again? She was drawn to what was inside of him—the virtue, the protective male. Generally, she wouldn't have even chanced a mind-reading outside the chaos of Studio—reading could be unwise in the open when they were Above. And, unlike the privacy of twin awareness, it made a vampire like her or Geneva susceptible to detection outside.

Sorin had raised them to be careful, saying that there were other powerful creatures Above who would bring an end to their kind if they had the opportunity. Although she was a little less cautious these days, she'd never really shaken the lessons, even if she and her sister had deserted the Underground years ago out of personal need.

"Justice?" Ginny asked, taking up where Ben had left off. "You say that word as if it exists."

"It does," he said. "It *will*. And I think the both of you need to enlighten me about what happened to Nolan before I lose what little patience I have."

Her sister sighed. She was thinking about how naïve humans were.

Ben stepped closer to them, having no clue what he was dealing with. A pang of sympathy—or whatever was invading her—pressed against Ginny's chest. He'd lost a brother, after all, and she'd felt the pain inside of him.

Maybe that's what was happening with these "emotions"— she was experiencing the residual effects of being inside a mourning human.

Thing was, the sensation was a thousand times stronger than she could've ever imagined.

"Let's get started," Ben said, voice lower, grittier.

Her twin spoke up. "Do you really want to know everything? Sincerely?"

Ginny started to mentally chastise her sister for toying with him. There were easier meals out there tonight.

But Geneva had already blocked her out, and the rudely

halted twin awareness made Ginny feel as if she'd slammed into a wall.

Then, too far into her own game, Geneva zoomed over to Ben, vampire-quick, coming face-to-face with him.

He reared back, eyes wide.

But Geneva was already talking. "Do you know about the pleasure house? It used to be in the Bronx, but it's been moved because of what happened to Nolan. It's close by now—West Fortieth. Have you looked into *that*, Lone Ranger?"

From that point on, everything happened in a flash.

Preservation won out over secrecy, and Ginny darted over to Geneva, latching on to her sister's identical haltered dress, then hauling her away from Ben Tyree.

Why would you tell him? she thought to Geneva, whose awareness was open again. *What's going on with you?*

Her twin bared her teeth, her eyes going silver as she flashed a hint of fang.

In that one lightning instant, Ginny saw hatred, jealousy. Possession.

And she knew what was happening with Geneva.

Ginny tightened her grip on the dress, ready to assume her own full vampire form if it meant stopping an attack that would only introduce bigger problems.

Sex? Okay. Bloodletting?

Not tonight. Not with him.

Pausing, her twin shrugged, then switched back to the blue-eyed, quasi-human demeanor they normally wore.

Just remember, her sister thought, *you're mine and I'm yours. Always.*

Letting go, Ginny backed away.

Her twin was wrong. They belonged to Sorin. And he had taken them separately to emphasize that.

There were some things she had never shared with Geneva, and this was one of them. Ginny only knew of *her* first bite with their maker: painful and quick, like a disappointing virgin sexual encounter where the male lost control and spilled everything . . .

Meanwhile, Ben was so human-slow that he was only now reaching for something near his boot.

"Don't," Ginny said, suspecting what he might have there. "Guns or knives aren't any use."

He was panting, his face a mask of shock. "What do you mean, God damn it?"

The profanity jerked at Ginny, and she felt dirty. Unclean.

But Geneva was laughing, thoroughly amused with him.

Twin awareness zinged through Ginny, telling her that Geneva's hunger had flared to an even higher level.

But before Ginny could react, her twin zipped over to Ben again, catching his gaze and stunning him with her silvered eye contact.

Playing her games.

After she'd frozen him in her hypnotic thrall, Geneva snuggled up to his neck. She was further proving a point to Ginny, and this man was the example.

Eyes hazy, Ben Tyree didn't move a muscle.

"There's a private room upstairs just waiting for us," Geneva whispered to him in a voice that they used to soothe a willing victim—always willing—right before a bite.

Temptation clouded his gaze while Geneva opened her mouth to show her fangs to her sister.

To show Ginny how far she would go to keep her twin in check.

THREE

HER EYES, BEN THOUGHT. ALL THE ANSWERS ARE IN the silver . . .

During this mind-scrambling haze, while he felt the twin nestling against his neck, he knew he should just shove her away. These females weren't human, not with the eyes and the quickness and the . . . fangs.

But he didn't do any such thing. He knew what was in the silver now. Paradise. And he wanted to stay.

The second woman—or . . . God . . . were they vampires?—coasted her fingers over his chest. Like a drugged man who needed a visual anchor before he lost himself, he somehow wrested out of her gaze and locked on to Ginny, who was standing a few feet away in their corner of the balcony.

She seemed so cool, just like that magnolia in her hair, even as she clenched her hands by her sides. "Stop this, Geneva."

But her sister ignored the comment, dragging his T-shirt out of his jeans, the cotton sliding against his belly.

"Just imagine," Geneva said to him, "what could happen in a secret room. Men dream of that kind of scenario with two beautiful women."

Women? Just women?

The reminder goaded Ben to come to his senses and strain against his mental bonds. But it did no good. Not with Geneva talking a magic rope around his limbs, keeping him still.

"Can you feel our lips on your body?" she asked, her fingers traveling his stomach, circling as if readying for an attack. "Can you picture the kind of kisses you've probably only dreamed about in your boring, normal life? Nasty, wicked, thrilling kisses that even your wildest dreams couldn't conjure up?"

Across from him, Ginny's eyes had come to shine silver, as if she were getting excited by the descriptions.

As if she were imagining what she would do to him, too.

In spite of the danger, his cock pulsed with the blood rushing to it. His thoughts strayed—no, maybe they were *led*—to an image of Ginny on the dance floor, her dress as red as buried sin. In his fantasy, she spotted him watching her, then smiled.

Performing for him and only him, she swayed, writhing her hips while her hands traced down over her breasts, her waist. Then, slowly, erotically, she lifted her skirt, skimming one hand beneath it.

Ben's temperature rose, fevered. He'd had his share of partners, but he'd always protected them from any baser urges that drove a man during his darkest fantasies. But now, this Ginny seemed to be inviting him to take part in every carnal question he'd ever entertained.

His fantasy continued with Ginny stroking herself, the other dream-inspired dancers gyrating around her, oblivious. He was the only one who seemed to notice as she worked herself into a trembling groan of ecstasy . . .

Then, outside of his fantasy, he heard that same groan cut the air.

The sound jarred him, and he realized that he was still staring into Ginny's silver-mist eyes.

Sweet heaven, he'd *seen* the dream there, just as if he was connected to her thoughts . . .

The breath came quick from her red, parted lips, and he definitely knew that she'd witnessed the sexy images, too. His erection beat in time to the frenzied rhythm of his pulse.

Laughter vibrated against his neck, causing him to remember that the twin, Geneva, was still rubbing up against him.

"Why, Ginny," her sister said, her hand starting to dip into the waistline of his jeans as if intending to release his erection, "I guess you're ready and willing for a private room, too."

Ginny's voice lowered, lethal and pointed. "Just get your hands off of him."

"Why? Because he's all yours?"

The change in Geneva's voice released Ben of his malaise, and he realized that she'd been controlling him through her words as well as her eyes.

Vampires . . .

He extricated himself from her clutches, reaching for his .45.

But Geneva was clearly a step ahead of him.

With a graceful sweep of one pale arm, she swatted him aside. He ripped through the air, crashing into a wall, then down into a cluster of chairs.

As bits of plaster sifted over him, Ben's body screeched, his sight getting fuzzy.

Then, just before going dark, he caught Ginny springing toward her twin, her face a blaze of gorgeous, terrible rage.

FOUR

GINNY ZOOMED TOWARD GENEVA, CLAMPING HER hand around her twin's throat and pinning her to the wall.

The balcony cleared, most of the screaming patrons too stoned and frightened to realize that more than your average, garden-variety fight was going on.

"Is this the reaction you want?" she asked her sister as she held her in place by the neck. "Are you happy now?"

Her twin smiled as she flashed fang. She was still entertained, genuinely having no clue that she'd crossed a line tonight.

Or was it Ginny who had crossed some line?

She loosened her hold, allowing her twin to slide down the wall. Still, she kept a hold of Geneva's throat, just as a reminder of who had been humanly born first, even though Sorin had balanced the scales and initiated Geneva before Ginny.

"Riled up over a truffle," her twin said, using their shared slang for a blood meal. "I only wanted a little fun."

She flitted a glare to the seats, where Ben had crashed.

Unable to help herself, Ginny glanced at him, too, finding him slumped and out cold. If she'd possessed a heart, it surely would've cracked at that moment.

Such a big man, she thought, running a covetous gaze over his body, hearing his heartbeat thudding until it consumed her. No doubt he could knock heads in his own world. He would be the type of guy she would've longed for in her own mortal life: a stalwart soldier in uniform, a firefighter, a small-town cop—which is what she'd seen him as when she'd looked into his mind earlier.

All good men that she didn't deserve.

Ginny let go of her sister's throat. As her rage ebbed, music crept back into her consciousness: the primal cadence of a chanting song that she blocked out with preternatural ease.

"You need to stop with these games," Ginny said. "They're wearing on me, Gen."

"We've always liked games."

"Not the ones we play nowadays."

When she turned to Geneva, her twin seemed . . . panicked. If that was the word. There was a definite sense of unease about her, the fear of losing the one thing that she had carried with her into this vampire life.

They didn't have souls anymore, so a twin was the closest to it. But what happened when the other half changed? What happened when they no longer fit together so well?

Her sister's awareness sought entrance, and Ginny listened to her twin, unable to help it. She had always loved Geneva out of habit, and *that* would never change.

Stay with me . . . Geneva thought.

"Don't," Ginny said, touching her sister's cheek. "Don't think that this is the beginning of some end. You know that you're always going to be a part of me, and no truffle will come between us."

The words left a strange aftertaste.

"No matter how he looked at you?" Geneva frowned. "Or how you looked at him?"

"I don't look at him any differently than any other guy who's come up to the balcony with me."

Her twin raised a slim, dark eyebrow.

"It's true," Ginny reiterated.

I can tell when you're lying, Geneva thought.

Lying? Ginny made it a point to avoid glancing at Ben Tyree again.

There. See? She would prove that he was a truffle. Basic lust. Nothing more.

Nothing to do with what she'd seen in his mind: the beautiful soul who wanted to understand what had happened to his beloved brother.

Geneva spoke out loud again. "I haven't seen you so wound up since we decided to leave Sorin."

"Drop the subject, Gen."

Wrong thing to do—ordering her sister around like that. Naturally, her twin stood straighter, pursuing the matter.

"Let's just get out of here and go back to L.A.," she said. "You can't tell me you're not sick of this place."

"Forget it."

Geneva tightened her jaw and pushed away from the wall, bringing herself inches away from Ginny.

"Sorin's expecting us to come back Underground. We've been away for a decade now, more than enough time to have 'explored the Old World,' like you told him we wanted to do. I miss Hollywood."

"And I don't. Let him wonder what happened to us. Let him think we went missing."

Ginny turned away, as if to end the discussion, but her sister wasn't about to let her go that easily.

"Do you think I haven't noticed how we've avoided going anywhere near L.A. so Sorin can't detect us with our maker-child Awareness? Do you really think I'm that dumb or distracted by our travels, Ginny?"

"No." She thought of the other night. "I don't underestimate you in the least. I never have and never will."

Her twin inserted her hand into Ginny's, entwining fingers and minds.

I know you think that Sorin was a poison to us, that he came between us by making us compete for him. All you wanted to do with this sabbatical was search for a way for us to reconnect, and I think we have, Ginny. We're strong enough to go back to him and stick together, through thick and thin.

Besides, she added, cuddling up to Ginny's arm, *I want to see our children, too.*

The vampires they had created back in L.A. Groupies, they had come to call them. Lower beings whose blood had become weaker through the exchange that had turned them. In fact, each generation was weaker, reflected even in the way Geneva's and Ginny's powers weren't as great as those of Sorin's.

Whenever Ginny thought of her progeny, it was with vague interest. She and her sister had only been seeking a "new experience" by initiating movie fanatics into the Underground, and from that, the Groupies had been born. The bites hadn't meant much, not as much as they should have.

Ginny cupped her twin's head, and the two stood together. From the dance floor, the music swelled in its tribal beat. But over the song, Ginny's vampire hearing picked up Ben Tyree's heartbeat again, his breathing, his muddled dreams of saving a brother who was beyond that now.

Her body rhythms matched his and, for the first time in years, she felt true, unexplainable contentment.

He stirred, and Ginny looked into her twin's eyes, which had gone back to a faux-human blue by now.

"I'll take care of this cop and his knight act," Ginny said. "I have the feeling he'll be hounding us about the pleasure house, so I'll do the cleanup."

"And I'll help—"

"No. You've done enough already."

Stung, her sister blinked at Ginny's adamancy.

"Just pick an easy meal on your way to the door before security comes to throw us out, and then go home." Ginny sighed. "We don't need any more trouble."

"All right." Geneva started to leave the balcony, then turned around again, searching their awareness as she asked, "And that'll be all with this Ben Tyree?"

Lately, Ginny had learned to lie and shield without Geneva even seeming to realize it. She'd learned how to restrain her twin with promises.

There was no other choice if she wanted to preserve them both.

"Yes, that'll be all, Gen."

Then, satisfied with the vow, her sister nodded, exiting the balcony and leaving Ginny alone with the truffle.

FIVE

WHEN BEN CAME TO, HE WAS ON HIS ASS IN AN AL-
ley, propped against a brick wall as moonlight scratched over
him. In the near distance, he heard the sounds of street traffic,
constant and low.

As he pushed to a seated position, he found that his mouth
was dry; his limbs felt as if they'd been yanked off and
jammed back into their sockets.

What the . . . ?

But then he remembered: Studio 54. The women in red.

The vampires.

He shook his head, as if to force all the gears back into
working order. Had someone slipped him LSD? Was he on
some kind of trip?

Rising to his feet, he ignored the aches, then took his revolver out of its ankle holster, made sure the safety was on,
and stuffed it in his waistband. He pulled his T-shirt over it,
then crossed his arms over his stomach, adapting a don't-
mess-with-me hunch.

He headed for the traffic and, soon enough, came to the
heart of Times Square, wondering how the hell he'd gotten
from the club to here without remembering.

Not that it mattered right now. All he could focus on was
something one of the women—Geneva—had said.

Do you know about the pleasure house?

West Fortieth. He was going to find it tonight.

Garbage lined the streets, which were showcased by the
jaundiced hue of store lights spilling from windows. He passed
peep shows and porno theaters, staying alert for any threats
while getting his bearings and heading downtown.

At the same time, he avoided pimps and streetwalkers,
hustlers and transients. But he did stop for a stocky, shawl-
covered woman preaching the end of the world. Quietly, he

accepted a plastic crucifix, declining her offer of a Bible, too, then secured the holy item in his back jeans' pocket.

If he wasn't on a drug trip, then he might need the crucifix, plastic or not. After all, hadn't Ginny told him that guns would be useless?

Freakin' *vampires*.

Ben nodded his appreciation to the woman and moved on, his disbelief turning into a heavy sense of horror. What could Nolan, the perfect son, husband, and father, possibly have to do with creatures of the night?

That is, if Ben wasn't dreaming them.

He passed another alley, but then stopped cold at the shiver that made the hairs on the back of his neck stand on end.

A whisper racing past him. A voice?

Looking around, he took out his .45 and the crucifix.

As he inched into the pale-shadow alley, he heard it again— a definite voice vibrating over his skin.

"How're you feeling?" it asked, tearing past him like an edged wind.

Adrenaline spiking, he targeted around the narrow bricked space: the blank windows, the fire escapes.

When he came to someone crouched on one of the platforms, he aimed.

He thought he heard a low sound of distress as that someone spun away from him.

"It's Ginny," the form said, voice garbled. "Put that thing away. I'm not going to hurt you."

That thing. Based on what had happened earlier, he guessed she was referring to the crucifix.

He kept aiming both weapons. Did the holy item repel her, like in those old Dracula movies?

"Sorry for being uncooperative," he said, "but I don't know if you're the bad twin or . . . Well, the badder one. I'm not really up for getting thrown against a wall this time."

"I came to your defense back at the club, so put your weapons away, okay? I got us both out of Studio before security came, so maybe you want to back off?"

"I was alone in an alley when I woke up. Not a sign of endearment, if you ask me."

"I've been with you the entire time, Ben." She sounded

agonized. "I needed to get us away and that alley happened to be one of the cleaner ones in the area for you to rest in."

She stood and grabbed on to a ladder, still keeping her face averted, her scarlet dress flowing around her. With her shift in position, something white—the magnolia—tumbled out of her hair and executed a pale freefall to the ground.

A red angel, he thought. How could this woman be the monster he remembered?

Ben realized that he'd lowered his weapons ever so slightly, his heartbeat jiggering in his neck veins, his sight going hazy with a renewed fascination for her. He hadn't felt this way with the other twin, and he sensed the vamp in front of him really was Ginny.

All the same, he'd keep his eye on her.

"How long have I been out of it?" he asked.

"An hour, maybe less. But you're basically healthy."

"How do you know?"

"I healed superficial injuries, but you're probably still sore." Her voice wasn't as choked now. Was she regaining strength or something? "And I didn't find any brain damage from the crash."

The riffling he'd felt in his brain when he first met her . . . A vampire could go into a person's head. How about that?

God, how could he be thinking so reasonably during such an unreasonable situation?

A slight wind tossed the loose curls of Ginny's dark hair. He was secure about her identity by now.

"I had a feeling you'd be up and about," she said, "looking for that pleasure house my sister mentioned. You're a tenacious one."

Pretty sure that she wasn't going to attack, he secured his .45 in his waistband. But the crucifix? That went in his back pocket again—within easy reach.

As if sensing the repellent was gone, Ginny turned toward him, and it was all he could do to steel himself from the thrill of looking at her in the shy moonlight.

"You guessed right," he said. "If that pleasure house has anything to do with Nolan, then I need to find it."

"Don't you think its clients might not be too happy if you strolled in the door uninvited?"

He almost pointed out that he had weapons, and those

generally did a lot of talking. But would a revolver make a difference? Would a plastic crucifix?

Hell, maybe he should call Detective Plaid-Tie from the NYPD for some backup. Wouldn't that be a hoot? No doubt the department would love a good vampire story from a hayseed deputy. It would amuse them for months.

"I'll do what I have to," he said, "because I get the feeling this pleasure house probably disappears at dawn."

"This is ridiculous, risking your life."

"So says the vampire who probably knows how Nolan got into that pleasure house and what went on in there."

Ginny cocked her head, considering him. "I didn't kill Nolan if that's what you've been thinking."

Ben's blood boiled at the thought of his brother, dead. Gone.

"Then who did?" he asked, voice jagged.

"It's . . . more complicated than an explanation in an alley would cover. Besides, I'm not the killing type."

"You're a *vampire*. From every tale I've heard told, you all do things like drink blood and . . . Oh, yeah, *kill*."

She shook her head. "It's not easy to cover the tracks of a death these days. That's why a smart vampire takes willing victims and leaves them alive, preferably ones who are too wasted to remember exactly what happened. Besides, the laced blood gives a good buzz. Most of us don't *have* to kill for our pleasure."

There was something about the tone of her voice that put Ben on alert.

"Is that supposed to explain everything to me?" He leveled a glare at her. "As far as I can tell, you were the last one seen with Nolan. People fingered a 'Ginny,' and you fit the description."

"Yes, I do."

Again with her tone. Ben had interrogated too many people to miss the subtleties of someone skirting the absolute truth.

Tired of her games, he thought about taking out the crucifix again, just to see if it would persuade her any. But then she leaned forward on the escape, alighting from it, her skirt billowing like red wings before she gently landed on light feet.

Fluid. Ben's gut tightened with heat as he remembered how she had danced in his fantasy.

Naughty kisses, he thought. How would it feel to have her covering his skin with them?

His darker urges emerged, silvered by what he'd seen in Nolan's death gaze. Had his brother been bitten to ecstasy by a vampire?

And what would it feel like?

Stunned, Ben headed toward the street. He *had* to be on drugs.

Ginny caught up in a flash, facing off with him. "So you're going to go from building to building on West Fortieth until you find the pleasure house?"

"Yup."

"A gun would only make most vampires laugh and a crucifix would only buy you time with them. You actually believe what my sister told you about where the place is, or if it even exists?"

"It's a lead. More than I had yesterday."

"And what makes you think your brother wasn't just mugged and murdered in the Bronx?"

"Severe blood loss. Vampires. Math."

"Okay, then why would your wonderful Nolan be in a den of iniquity, of all places?"

She'd hit one of the nails holding him together. "I don't think he *would* go there on his own, but then again, I wouldn't have ever believed that my brother would think about going to Studio 54, either. He was happily married with kids. He wasn't like that."

She paused. "And how much do you really know about Nolan, Ben?"

"I know enough." He swallowed. Damn, his mouth was dry. "Nolan was a community icon. Graduated as a valedictorian from high school, then magna cum laude at Harvard. Came back home to found a computing hardware company, and his business has driven our town's economy ever since."

Ginny was watching him closely. If she had gone into his head, she would already know all this. Was she merely goading him and feeding off his emotions now? *Did* vampires drink more than blood?

"He was the brains and you were always the brawn," Ginny said pensively. "While he was being lauded, you were quietly saving the world in his shadow. Isn't that right?"

Her words cut surgically, deeply, but he remained expressionless. He wouldn't allow her the pleasure.

"I never minded. He was my brother. I loved him."

"That's what we tell ourselves."

Nearby, the steam from a subway grate hissed, scathing his nerves. "What do you mean?"

A melancholy smile settled over her mouth. "I know what it's like to be connected to a sibling. If something happened to Geneva and I didn't have all the answers, I'd search, too." She paused, a shadow seeming to pass over her before she recovered. "Besides, I saw what you're made of. Earlier, in your head."

"I knew it. I don't want you in there again, damn it."

She flinched at that last part, and he wondered if it was because of vampire aversion to holiness. It would make sense in light of the fact that she wouldn't look at a crucifix, either.

Ginny moved closer—enough so he could smell the magnolia remaining on her, even though the flower was gone. Desire gnarled within him, like an old branch twisted by bad nature.

"You're a stand-up guy," she said softly. "And to see you taken from this world so young would be unthinkable. Because that's what's going to happen when you stumble into the pleasure house—if you find it."

"A vampire philosopher. I didn't know you creatures had it in you."

She tilted her head, as if reading him again, although he didn't feel her in his brain this time. Plus, her eyes were true blue, and he suspected all the weird magic happened when they were silver.

"You're headed for big trouble," she said.

"Well, then escort me to this pleasure house and keep me from perishing at the hands of whoever runs it." He was being half-sarcastic. "And answer my questions like a good vamp."

Much to his shock, she actually seemed to consider what he said, folding her hands in front of her. Her red lips pouted in thought, still cryptic, still the stuff of sinful fantasy.

Blocking out what those lips might do to him in a private room, Ben avoided their crimson trap.

But then his thoughts turned silver, like the sometime-color of her eyes, like the fantasies contained within them, and excitement took him over.

Nolan's gaze . . . The answers they were *all* looking for in this life. They were within Ben's reach, weren't they?

With a bite . . . ?

She interrupted. "I see you're not going to quit, even if I beg you to."

He shook his head, turning toward the alley exit, mostly so he wouldn't be affected anymore.

She sighed. "If I did take you to this place, under my protection, just to satisfy your curiosity, will you stop?"

Was he hearing her correctly? "If that's where I get my answers, then yes."

"Would you go to the police then? Because I'm telling you now, they won't believe you. They never do in this city."

He'd suspected that, and he'd already decided that he would do anything the police wouldn't.

Besides, what was stopping him from lying to her to get what he needed?

"I'd keep my mouth shut, Ginny."

She blew out a bigger sigh. "I can't believe it hasn't occurred to you that I'm actually leading you into a trap."

But Ben *had* considered that, and it didn't scare him. Not with what he'd seen in Nolan's final photos.

"The nightclub, and then after, would've both been good opportunities for you to attack me," Ben said, ignoring his true thoughts. "Why would you wait until now?"

Ginny started walking out of the alley, but then she held up a finger and said one last thing. "As long as you promise to go home and stay quiet after I show you the house, I'll take you."

"Then let's get on with it."

And with one last veiled glance, she guided him into the night.

Into a world that he'd never even suspected in his human innocence.

Six

THEY HEADED TOWARD FORTIETH, SEEKING THE condemned apartment building where the pleasure house had been relocated after Nolan's death.

Ginny had meant what she said earlier, about what a tragedy it would be if Ben should die during this crusade of his, so she had decided to be his protector. But it wasn't as benevolent as it sounded.

She had a plan that would satisfy Ben Tyree's thirst for knowledge while keeping him innocent of what had really happened. The truth would scar him, and she refused to be the one who stained his soul by allowing him to know the details of that night.

After all, he loved his brother, just as much as Ginny could recall loving Geneva. And for some reason, tonight she knew just how much discovering the truth about someone you adored could hurt.

So she would alter history, soften the story, give him the closure he longed for.

Then she would cover everyone's tracks, just as she'd been doing all too often recently.

On the way, she kept Ben in the corner of her sharp gaze, drinking him in, an addiction. A growing need.

They got closer to their destination, dodging skulking cats and trash while their footfalls echoed against the sad-eyed buildings. Every once in a while, a cry in the night would ghost her hearing, and she ignored what the blackened windows hid. She had that secure luxury as a vampire.

Meanwhile, she sensed Ben's keening nerves, and she yearned to soothe him.

"Not everyone gets into Studio," she said quietly, using her voice to put him at ease. "But you did. I guess Steve Rubell liked you."

"Who?"

"The little man out front choosing who got in tonight. He mixes celebrities with lovely nobodies for the right party salad."

"I don't do many parties."

"But you're a looker. It got you through the door."

"Got you through, too."

He fixed his gaze straight ahead, as one-track-minded as Ginny had ever seen. Stalwart. A crusader.

"Gen and I cheat to get in," Ginny said. "We give 'the look' and they unhook that rope for us. They'll do it again the next time we want to go there, too, even though there's a dent in the balcony wall, compliments of Geneva."

"You get in because of your vampiric sway," he said. "Or maybe it's because you and your sister resemble Liz Taylor when she was young and so stunning."

"She hangs out at Studio sometimes. Not with us though."

Ben casually graced her with a glance. It abraded her skin, making her feel alive with its heat.

"There's a big difference between you and today's Liz," he finally said, locking his gaze forward again. "You look like she did back when she was in movies like *A Place in the Sun*."

"Yeah, that was back in the Fifties." A wistful smile tugged at Ginny's lips.

His mouth shaped into a question, but then he seemed to remember that she was capable of being forever young—but that would only last until her demise or the death of her maker, which would turn her mortal again.

"Gen and I used to run in the same circles as people like Liz," Ginny added, "although you could say it was definitely a lower circle."

"But she aged and you haven't. Did anyone ever take you for the real thing in those days?"

The real thing. Ginny recalled something Geneva had said after recently seeing the lady herself across Studio. *I'd rather always be a copy of Liz in her glory days than to get old as the real thing.*

Ginny had agreed. It'd never occurred to her to do otherwise until . . .

She didn't think about that.

"We tended to take advantage of the resemblance," she

said instead. "We would hustle movie producers for roles by catering to a certain Taylor-made fantasy, if they wanted. And they usually *did* want."

"And nowadays?"

Ginny shrugged. "Geneva still talks about getting into films. That's one reason we gravitated toward Studio—there're connections galore there. But she never gets around to doing much about it now. As for me? Well, if I never saw Hollywood again, that'd be fine."

Sorin was there, and it might as well have been jail.

Ben was trying to even out his breathing, but his stomping pulse told her he needed more soothing.

"Gen and I were turned into vampires in nineteen-fifty-four," she said with her adjusted voice. "But we were humanly born over twenty years before that in a cramped Chicago apartment. Geneva and I shared everything there—a room, a bed, even clothing. We were the perfect candidates for seeking out the promises and riches of silver-screen stardom. Not that we ever ascended like we thought we would."

"You get everything you want as a vamp though. Doesn't that make up for it?"

"It did." At first.

They'd turned a corner onto a street where homeless people sat bundled against walls and the trees seemed dead, even in late spring.

Ginny soothed Ben again, even though she knew he was a seasoned cop who dealt with violent domestic calls and even dead bodies. He'd seen blood spattered on the walls of a small house, a mouth gaped in a frozen scream, dogs barking in a field, where an open grave belched bare bones.

They were all open cases. The school teacher found slain in her home. The postman who never showed up for his route because he was found in his van around the corner from the post office. The mass grave in a field with victims who were still being identified.

None of it ever ended for Ben, she thought, analyzing what she'd seen in his mind. The gloomy, dead eyes that were so empty and devoid of meaning.

Except for what he'd seen in Nolan's pictures.

"Are we almost there?" Ben asked.

"Just a block more."

They stopped talking, giving in to the dead-of-night atmosphere. His heartbeat spiked, his breath coming faster.

She echoed him, knowing that she shouldn't be absorbing him like this. But tonight had been full of mistakes, the worst being Geneva's loose-lipped prey games with Ben.

Before he had awakened, Ginny had thought hard about what to do with him. Besides this solution, she'd thought of a mind wipe. With it, she could make certain that he would never recall tonight.

But she'd been taught not to steal parts of a person that could never be replaced, such as a memory. Not unless it was absolutely necessary. Also, from only one attempt at doing it about a year ago, a wipe took so much energy that she would be drained for the next twenty-four hours.

Yet there was a third option. She could always exchange blood with Ben Tyree, turning him into one of her kind.

Not a choice at all.

So why did the notion still linger?

Was it because Ben carried such pain within him, and she wished she could put an end to it?

As they drew up to a condemned brick building with black paint and boards covering its windows, she reached out to stop Ben by grabbing his shirt.

"This is it," she said.

"Doesn't look so pleasurable to me."

Brave fool. "Are you sure about this?"

After a pause, he nodded. "As sure as anything."

His wild pulse jabbed her eardrums and, automatically, her gaze strayed to his neck, where his veins stood out in relief against his skin.

Her mouth watered. Blood. Hot . . . *his*. What flavor would he carry?

What would it feel like to have his goodness fill her up?

She released his shirt.

Ben remained impassive, even though his heartbeat betrayed him.

"I looked up to Nolan," he said softly. "I went to his baseball games and then his *kids'* games years afterward. Maybe it looks like Nolan strayed a little on this trip, since he was seen with you or Geneva outside the club and then ended up here, but I'm willing to bet he was baited."

He gave Ginny a hard look, as if fighting a personal battle. Was he telling himself not to go in?

Or was he still too curious?

A scream from behind the walls pierced her sensitive hearing, and she closed her eyes. Ben wouldn't have been able to catch the sound, but she certainly did.

When she opened her eyes again, he was looking at the doorway, which was edged with flaking paint and snags of rust.

She went forward, guiding him, ready to do what was needed.

But then a thrust of awareness came to her from Geneva, who had to be nearby.

Where are you—?

Ginny blocked her twin out, and the choice to do so hacked into her. It was almost as if she'd amputated some part of herself, a part she already missed.

Later, she thought. She would apologize to her sister after Ginny wiped her hands of Ben and went home.

He moved ahead of her, reaching out to open the door, but finding it locked. However, with a twist of her wrist, she easily opened it, then rested a hand on his arm as the door opened to darkness.

Seven

.

Ben couldn't even see two feet in front of him as Ginny led him inside by taking his hand.

Obviously, her sight could cut through the pitch, and all he could do was trust her, concentrate on the softness of her skin and hope that it wouldn't be the last sensation he experienced before going lights out himself.

Was this the biggest error of his life?

Or was he getting closer to the best choice he'd ever made?

He felt her beginning to climb something—stairs—and he lifted his foot to find one step, then another, as she pulled him along.

A sharp wailing sounded from an upper floor, and adrenaline sawed through him.

Screams, he thought, his breath coming quicker. Wasn't this supposed to be a pleasure house?

Suddenly, his brother's death gaze took on new meaning.

And how much do you really know about Nolan? Ginny had asked.

Ben told himself that he knew his brother very well, that he was still the guy he'd idolized while growing up.

They climbed to another floor, the stench of metal—no, *blood*—attacking him. He pulled back from Ginny, burying his nose in the crook of his arm.

He knew the smell. How could he ever forget those bodies back in Holstead County? Especially those from his open cases?

Coughing, Ben cursed himself. *Nolan, what did you do? What am I doing?*

He forged on, continuing to follow a cool Ginny.

They came to the top of the staircase, and she brought him to a halt. Still dark, but there were no screams now.

He suspected more would be coming though, especially since one was strangled in his throat, dying to get out.

Her voice was a whisper. "Here we are."

"So start talking, Ginny."

She let go of his hand. "I met your brother in front of Studio, and he caught my fancy with that . . . Well, something close to that same innocence you have."

She sounded odd, and he couldn't put his finger on the reason.

"He was with his business buddies," she continued, "doing his best to impress them."

"Tabu-Cal, Incorporated," Ben whispered, recalling this meaningless detail about the account Nolan had been trying to secure. But it was so real, where as everything else didn't feel anywhere near it.

Ginny continued, her whisper gentle and harsh at the same time. "Geneva stayed with the group and I took Nolan to the velvet ropes since he wanted to talk his way into the club for him and all his pals. They wanted to see the celebrities, he said."

Ben felt numb, removed, as she guided him around a corner. His eyes adjusted to the darkness enough to see dim lines making a rectangle in the wall before them.

A door hiding the answers.

"But," she added, "they wouldn't let Nolan in, and certainly not his less attractive buddies. And I didn't feel like vouching for all those obnoxious businessmen, so I . . ." Her hesitation was so subtle he barely even noticed it. ". . . told him about this pleasure house, which was in the Bronx before it moved. I wasn't interested in coming here that night, but a vampire from a different clan liked Nolan, and she put him under her sway and took him here."

So his brother *had* been lured. He hadn't come here on his own like a businessman who changed colors away from home.

Vindication, Ben thought, feeling as if Nolan's honor had been preserved. Now all he had to do was catch a killer.

As he clung to that, Ginny took his hand again and guided him toward the door.

A tiny voice inside Ben whispered for him to run down the stairs and out the door, straight back to Texas. But that's not what he wanted at all . . .

She pushed open the door, and it groaned on its hinges, drilling through his gut.

He moved across the threshold, into a stark room lit by weak flashlight beams angling across the floor like wires set up to trip any trespassers. In their crisscrosses, he saw bodies strewn about: slumped against the walls, napping on the floor, entwined in corners.

One person with long stringy hair—a man?—leaned against the wall, hand to his neck, softly laughing and crying while begging no one in particular, "Please, please . . . again?"

From a corner, a perverse sucking noise drew Ben's attention.

As his gaze clarified, he saw that a male was leisurely feasting at a heavy-lidded redhead's neck, their bodies moving in tandem, like sinuous sex.

Next to them, a black, naked woman leaned against the wall, arms overhead as a man and woman licked rivulets of blood from her breasts.

None of them even seemed to realize Ben and Ginny had entered.

He found that he'd gone back to holding Ginny's hand, clutching it, as a matter of fact, but he let go just as soon as he processed the wrongness of touching her.

One of *them*.

"Sometimes," she said, after a pause that he would've described as despondent in any other situation, "these vampires meet their human partners in other areas of town. This is a safe place for them to gather. It's as liberating as Studio."

From down the hall, Ben thought he heard the snick of leather on flesh, then a joyful scream.

"And sometimes," Ginny added, "vampires find a victim who's looking for a certain release, and no club wants that on their hands."

"Nolan wouldn't have wanted any release."

"His death didn't pain him, Ben," she said. "He left this world happy."

"You don't know that."

Ginny didn't say a word.

His temper took control, because he knew he was wrong. He'd seen Nolan's death pictures.

"Who are these people, the victims?" he asked.

"Not victims, more like willing thrill-seekers, just like

Nolan. He didn't talk about it out loud, Ben, but he had a wild side. You all do to some extent, and that's why he was easily lured here. He didn't actively seek it, but he didn't resist, either."

Rage seared through him. "So he was sucked dry just because a vamp needed a meal? Are you sure it wasn't you, Ginny? Or Geneva?"

She stayed stoic. "I told you I'm not a killer. And don't even think about Geneva."

He turned on her, quaking. But Ginny stood her ground, only the slight softening of her gaze letting him know that she felt something.

"Ben . . ."

He closed his eyes, as if that could keep all of this out. But then a British-inflected female voice in back of them broke into his fury.

"Hey, Gins. Heard you from down the hall."

Both Ben and Ginny found a tall woman leaning against the doorframe as if she were posing in a high-fashion magazine. The eerie flashlight beams underscored the bone structure of a model, the stoned cat eyes and plump lips.

"Who'd you bring tonight?" she added, clearly indicating Ben. "A new toy?"

"He's a friend," Ginny said levelly. "We can't stay for long, and he's under my watch, Amelie."

"Pity." The model ran her fingers over her face in sensual indifference.

On the other side of the room, a scream speared the air, and Ben's heart caught in his throat as he spun around to see one of the vampires impaling the naked woman with his fangs. He slurped at her neck, and she held to him, her face a mask of feverish ecstasy as they moved together, groin to groin. The second vampire merely watched, licking her fingers.

A bite. Was the vamp turning this victim into one of them?

The rogue part of Ben that had fantasized about Ginny back at the club kept watching, wondering how a bite might feel . . .

Then he remembered Nolan.

"So what does this all mean?" he asked Ginny, voice garbled. "Who killed my brother?"

Her eyes widened, as if warning him to shut up. The model froze in surprise, then started laughing. Everyone else in the room was too distracted to respond.

"A brother," Amelie said. "You brought one of their brothers here, Gins? Kinky scamp."

"Shut up, Amelie, and move to another location before daybreak. Outside, they've caught word of where you're doing business."

But the model merely shrugged. "I don't have the energy to relocate again."

"That's because your latest truffle was probably on too much dope and it's affected you."

The departing Amelie flicked a wrist on her way into the hall, as if she didn't care and wanted to go back to her blood.

That left the room in near-silence, except for the sucking, the moans.

Ben shut the laconic sounds out. Which one of these creatures was responsible for Nolan's death if it wasn't Ginny? Or Geneva?

"Who did it?" he asked her again, his voice low and threatening. "Which one, Ginny?"

His vampire guide looked as if she didn't know what else to say as the flashlights whipped shadowed lines over her face.

"Who?" he asked, gripping her shoulders.

She withstood his reaction. Hell, a vampire could throw him across a room, so why should she be afraid?

"The creature that attacked Nolan was taken care of after Nolan died," she said, looking away. "She was a rookie and didn't know the ropes, but that's no excuse for what happened. Nolan didn't ask for release, and she had no business—"

"This vampire's been exterminated?" Somehow, not even that seemed good enough.

Ginny swallowed. "Yes. But the vampires in the house heard cops around the area, and they only had time to heal Nolan's injuries and to hide his bites. They were so busy going after the culprit, seeing that justice was done in our own way, that they didn't get back in time to remove your brother's body."

And there it was.

A story that Ben couldn't tell anyone because they would

think he was crazy. A punishment he couldn't bring about because the culprit had already been brought to justice.

Nolan had been vindicated.

So why did it feel as if there was still so much Ben had to solve?

Especially within himself.

Eight

THE LIES DIDN'T SIT SO WELL WITH GINNY AS SHE led a silent Ben out of the pleasure house.

The sounds of lust and stimulation faded in her ears while they headed back to Times Square, where they were able to catch a cab to his modest hotel near Madison Square Garden. She wasn't about to let him out of her sight—not in this city, not in the post-midnight darkness. And Ben didn't question her continued presence. He merely stared out his window on his half of the cab.

Without entering his mind, she found herself wondering if he was truly satisfied with what she'd given him. She itched to know for certain, but she wasn't about to read him out here in the open.

Had she done the right thing by coloring the truth about Nolan? She'd added enough reality to her story—only hinting that his brother wasn't as perfect and faithful as he'd seemed—so that this small-town cop wouldn't get suspicious about a truth that seemed even more terrible now she had been inside Ben.

Had he touched her in some way? How?

Everything seemed so scattered now, even her justifications. She'd told herself that Ben loved Nolan so much that the real truth would damage him; that if a protector like him discovered anything more about his beloved brother's true nature, he would feel compelled to keep it a secret from his family because he wouldn't want to break their hearts, too, and he would suffer under that burden for the rest of his life. This way, he wouldn't know about the part Nolan had truly played in his own death, and Ben could at least think there was some closure.

He could believe that he knew the truth already, and that might go a long way in keeping him physically and emotionally safe . . .

By the time the cab left them off in front of The Mather Hotel, Ginny could feel the darkness lifting; it would give way to sunrise within a couple of hours.

But she could also sense her twin's anxiety in the sputter of awareness she'd been shielding herself from.

Ultimately, she and Ben came to stand in a small court-yard off the sidewalk, near the hotel's tattered, green-and-white entrance awning. Beyond that, weak light from the small but neat lobby filtered over the pavement, and she remained across a line that separated light from shadow.

Ben, of course, kept to the light, as if he were unable to leave it. The idea gripped the heart of her, where emptiness had hollowed her out these past couple of decades.

Where, Ginny now realized, she'd craved something to solidify her ever since she and Geneva had started drifting apart.

She spoke for the first time since they'd left the pleasure house. "I suppose you'll be going home."

He stared at the ground, his body still tensed. "I wish I could be sure that Nolan's murderer was set to rights."

She couldn't blame him for that. She'd already experienced his grief-turned-rage, empathizing with him. "You would have liked to bear witness, just like a cop who takes down a criminal and then watches the execution?"

"I just . . ." he said, voice ragged, "I just want some guarantee that it won't ever happen to anyone else's brother."

Ginny struggled to stay calm under the other lie she had told: The vampire who had led Nolan to death hadn't been exterminated at all.

There were good reasons for that, too, even though deceiving Ben was gnawing at her.

"Hey." She reached out to touch him, then thought better of it. "Why punish yourself like this? There's nothing you can do now."

"It doesn't seem like enough. As you said, I can't report this to the NYPD. They'd laugh me out of the city with a boogeyman story like this." A muscle in his cheek jerked. "I've never been so . . ."

As he searched for words, she supplied one. "Helpless?"

His terse nod confirmed that. She sensed that he didn't want to say it out loud. Not a strong man like Ben Tyree.

She stepped closer, into the light. His skin ... how it would taste, how his blood might fill up all her emptiness ...

Juices flooded her mouth. Overwhelmed, she touched his hand.

Zzzzzzeeetch—

It was as if she'd been shocked from brain to belly, one long, fast swipe of electric interference. An ache twisted between her legs, wringing her out until she grew damp there.

Instinctively, she disconnected, an after-sizzle still tracing her skin. She had touched him before but ...

What had just happened?

She looked into his eyes, just as she had back at Studio when he'd joined her in that dance-floor fantasy, when she'd imagined what it would be like to seduce him.

His gaze returned her own carnal yearning and, in a silver-bolted flash, they were connected again, in each other's heads.

In this new fantasy, he stood in front of her, pausing, then ripping off her dress in a show of dominant passion. He was taking his frustration and anger out in a very physical way, and she liked it, inviting him to go on.

His fantasy-self took her up on that, cupping the back of her head with his rough hand, kissing her deeply, savaging her with lips and tongue, his hand slipping between her thighs to stroke her to pure agony. She saw ... felt ... his fingers thrusting inside her, making her cry out, working her into wet, frenzied submission ...

Yet as her cry reached a peak, hanging above the shared fantasy like a glass pane ready to smash over them, something changed.

Something in his eyes.

In her ... soul?

No, not a soul. She'd given it up during her exchange with Sorin, leveraged it in a bargain she hadn't regretted until lately.

As their gazes intensified, the cry remained poised above them ...

Then it broke, showering down and slicing into her skin, revealing an impossible future in every shard:

Her and Ben, flesh to flesh, limbs entangled as they pressed together.

The two of them again, sitting on a hill after dusk, her back to his chest as he traced her cheek with a finger.

Gray-haired Ben leaning over her, his aged hands touching her still-young face . . .

As the imaginary shards hit the ground, Ginny shook herself out of the shared fantasy. Her head swam, her hunger screeched.

"What was that all about?" she heard Ben say, words strangled.

"I have no idea."

"I think you do."

He reached for her hand again, as if to validate what had just come between them. But Ginny was too fast, dodging farther into the darkness.

"It happened back at the club, too," he said. "I saw it in your eyes. What kind of mind games are you playing?"

She didn't know herself. She'd never lost control with her powers, so there was no explanation for what he did to her. Unless . . .

Did every contact with this particular human infuse her with a sense of his humanity?

She wasn't sure if that were possible, seeing as she hadn't stuck around L.A. to see her breed of vampires evolve. But she had never known this to happen with Sorin, who had cut off contact with humans after taking up with the twins. Sure, he had said he possessed emotions for Ginny and Geneva—his only children—but he'd only used the concept of love to control, and that's all. And since the sisters didn't have any siblings—only progeny whose blood and powers grew weaker with every generation—there was no basis for comparison.

"Okay, so the games continue. Is that it?" Ben went back to the angry man who was aching for an outlet to relieve his sorrows. "Maybe you didn't have your meal yet tonight and that's how you get your victims ready. Is that how it works?"

"No. I mean, yes, Gen and I use our eyes and our voices, our *sway*, but . . ."

"But what?" He angled his head so that his neck was more exposed—a cruel taunt. "I'm not as good as Nolan?"

His agony at always being the second-best brother, at losing the one he'd always looked up to, weighed on her. But her hunger overwhelmed even that. It pistoned through her, threatening to take over if she allowed it to.

"You don't mean that," she said.

"Maybe I do." His eyes were wild. "Maybe I want what my brother found. You said he wasn't in any pain. But that's all I've seen so far in life, and I want to believe you."

The rest went unsaid: *And this is one thing I can finally share with Nolan. One thing that I've been searching for in the eyes of all those victims I've never been able to help . . .*

Her hearing picked up two voices coming down the dark street, and she retreated even farther back into the courtyard. Soon, a couple rounded a corner and drunkenly stumbled toward the lobby.

Even after the interruption, her body was still primed, her cravings at a famished peak.

Ben was asking for a bite, she thought. He was angry yet willing, and she was so starved.

As the night went quiet again, the sounds of the city only a background hum, Ben's voice broke in. He had calmed down a little, his shoulders losing their taut line as he rescinded the offer of his neck.

"Do creatures like you turn every victim into a vampire?" he asked quietly.

He was curious about the bite, of course. His rage was cooling into stone-cold logic now, and that was even more dangerous than fury.

"No," she said. "There needs to be a blood exchange, and having a son or daughter is a big responsibility."

She risked a look at him, finding an expression of such naked vulnerability on his tough-man face that it melted her.

"There's always been a purpose to my bites," she added. "Once, I created a family for my community, but I never . . . felt it. I've actually never felt it."

"What do you mean—*felt* it?"

How could she explain this to a human? "I mean that biting has always been a means to an end for me, whether it's a meal to appease hunger or a way of carrying out my maker's commands. Back when Geneva and I were new, a bite was more of a duty that we performed. Our brood needed citizens, so we turned the willing ones. There wasn't any emotional link beyond that."

She thought of the Groupies: fans of the Elite vampires who had given their mortality to serve the higher beings in the Underground. The Elite were, more or less, celebrities who gave their souls to reinvent their careers. Meeting them had been so exciting at first to her and Geneva. They'd thought to establish business connections Underground, just as they had as hopeful human starlets. But the Elites were so self-involved that they only saw the twins as underlings.

"So you've never experienced a true bite?" Ben asked. "Not even from the vampire who turned *you*?"

Ginny's arousal diminished, just like that. The loss pained her.

"My maker seduced me and my sister into this life," she said. "The first time we met, we went to his hotel and stayed up all night taking turns with him. He was so handsome, charismatic, commanding."

Ginny glanced at Ben, thinking of how Sorin didn't hold a candle to this human.

"We kept seeing him, week after week," she added, "and he would make us jealous of each other, telling us in private how he loved each of us better. And every time, he caused just a bit more distance between me and Geneva. I didn't realize what was going on until well after it'd been happening. He was puppeteering us for his amusement. Then he decided to show us what he truly was—a vampire—and he initiated us separately, driving even more of a wedge between me and my sister by insinuating that he'd given more blood—more power—during the exchange to one of us. But afterward, he would always say he treasured us equally."

She paused. "All his games confused Geneva, so I got her away from him. She was always more sensitive in life, and that carried over to this existence, just as human qualities do with our vampire line. Sorin fed off of that. So, for me, bites didn't even start out as a close experience. It was sexual and stimulating, yes, but never . . . loving. Never."

Ben seemed to let that all sink in, then asked, "And after you left this community of yours? A bite was still a means to an end?"

"No one but Geneva has ever mattered much to me."

Until now, she thought.

Ginny caught a whiff of him again, and she was back to

wanting him, needing him. His scent had gotten stronger because of that fantasy they'd shared; he'd been turned on.

She wanted to touch herself, to ease the stiffness, the erotic anguish.

His pulse beat in her ears, and she felt the rhythm of her own blood melding with his.

Ben seemed to catch himself, his hand going to a defensive arc by his side. "About this community you came from . . . ?"

At the return of Ben the cop, alarm rattled her. Secrecy about the Underground itself was profoundly built in to her, even if she'd left Sorin and the rest of them out of a need to protect her and Geneva.

"I don't have anything else to tell you," Ginny said. "You've got what you need from me."

Frustration seemed to push him forward, until he was in the darkness with her, inches away. Close enough so that the aroma of him filled her like nothing else she'd ever found.

Musk, flesh. Man.

"Tell me," he said. "What did Nolan see when he died? Did a bite do that to him?"

Dizzy . . . so dizzy with him standing right here . . .

Maybe it was to shut him up, maybe it was because she couldn't fight her urges anymore. But in a heartbeat, she was against him, her mouth on his, testing.

At first, he stiffened, but then he groaned, parting his lips, and deepened the kiss.

Soft, exploratory, knee-weakening.

Ginny grasped at his shirt before her knees could give way. Such a human reaction, she thought before her mind turned off altogether.

They sipped at each other, sweet and seeking, and all of Ginny's shields crumbled like walls crashing to dust around her feet. She'd never felt so open, vulnerable . . . almost free.

A blurb of static seemed to rip through her, but she thought it was because of the way Ben had pulled back, then taken her face in his palms to look into her eyes.

Was he trying to conjure another shared fantasy?

Before Ginny could decide, she sensed another presence nearby.

And she knew who it was without a doubt.

She stepped away from Ben to face a woman in a red dress

who'd just entered the courtyard, her faux-human form tensed out of both frustration and a hunger that had become almost unbearable to tolerate.

"Hello, Geneva," Ginny whispered to her twin.

Πίπε

"Daybreak is almost two hours away," Geneva said, arms crossed in front of her chest as she glared.

"I was just about to leave," Ginny said.

Behind her, she could sense Ben going wary again, no doubt recalling how her twin had slammed him against a wall.

"Oh, you were *leaving*, is that it, Ginny?" Geneva said. "All I see is the reason you were shutting me out all night."

Her tone was bruised, and Ginny almost apologized. They'd always stuck together, from Monaco to Belize to Miami to New York. Always.

"Ben, here, won't be pursuing his investigation now that I told him all the details," Ginny said.

Then she added more in their twin awareness.

I covered our tracks, Gen, so I'll be able to feed with you soon. I can tell you haven't eaten tonight, even though I asked you to find an easy truffle at Studio.

Her sister's arms loosened a little. *I was waiting for you. You know I don't like to eat alone.*

The reminder sapped Ginny. It felt so at odds with the way Ben had just filled her up.

Even so, she knew she needed to pay attention to her twin now, because Ginny had always been responsible for Geneva. What her sister did affected her in equal measure.

Ben broke into their consciousness as he laid a hand on the weapon in his back pocket—the crucifix.

Quickly, Ginny used her awareness again. *I lied to him about what really went down. It hasn't been easy, so don't blow this, Gen. Just keep your trap shut.*

Luckily, her sister complied, flicking a careless glance at Ben in response. Then she addressed Ginny. "He thinks he can fight us."

Definitely time to leave.

In the end, it didn't matter what Ginny saw in Ben Tyree, what she'd felt as a result of connecting in such an inexplicable way. She would go on with her existence and he would continue his.

Gathering all her willpower, she faced him, and what she found on his face as he stared at her twin made Ginny cringe.

A look of utter disgust or . . .

She couldn't define it. She didn't want to, because it was everything she'd come to witness about her own decay.

Did Ben look at Ginny like this when she wasn't aware of it? Did he think of her as just a vampire, like the one who had killed Nolan?

She hadn't felt that when they'd kissed. No, she'd only experienced joy, easiness, something pure.

Ginny hastened to leave before he could turn that same repulsed glare on her.

But her twin had other ideas.

He knows too much, Geneva thought, still returning Ben's stare. He would be able to withstand it as long as she didn't use her sway.

And who's going to believe him if he talks? Ginny asked. *The cops around here have dealt with vampire activity, but they don't buy it. And I warned Amelie to move the group to another location.*

She stopped short of saying that maybe she and Geneva should move on, too, but she didn't want to hear more pleading about going back to L.A.

I have a bad feeling about this, Geneva thought, even as Ginny tugged on her sister's arm to guide her away. *I'm going to do a mind wipe.*

"No, Gen," she said out loud, so horrified that she'd blurted it out. She didn't want anything about him erased.

But her sister was already tensing, preparing to spring at Ben.

His honed cop instincts must've kicked in, because he'd already gone into motion, extracting the crucifix from his back pocket.

Undiluted pain struck both Ginny and Geneva, linking them in terror.

Decay . . . loneliness . . . so empty . . .

The thoughts pulled them in to a black hole and, in an effort to resist, they pooled their energy.

It drained them, but they couldn't stand to see such beauty in the crucifix, such a reminder of what they would never embrace again.

"What an idiot I was," Ben said, his footsteps headed for the courtyard exit. "I thought you really hadn't set a trap for me, but I seem to have walked into it now, right, Ginny?"

Holding up their hands to protect their gazes, she and Geneva battled until their bodies went limp. It took so much energy to fight the holy item, yet the more time they had to harden themselves to the sight, the more they recovered.

Second by second, their fangs elongated, their eyes going an ethereal silver.

"I'm not dumb enough to think I can take the both of you," Ben continued. "Not unless I had a stake to put through your hearts."

Was there a betrayed edge to his voice?

The squeal of tires from a side street distracted all of them and, before the twins could react, they sensed Ben leaving the courtyard. Their hearing picked up the sound of a key jamming into the lock of the lobby door as he barged inside.

At the absence of the crucifix, utter relief swept over the sisters, and they collected themselves, transforming to their more human forms.

But Ginny's relief turned to a sick sadness.

He was gone.

The fact haunted her as darkness crept that much closer to sunrise, when the twins would be able to withstand the day, but their powers would be weak.

The sisters walked out of the courtyard, regaining their equilibrium. Ginny glanced up at a third-story window and caught a lamp bringing the thin curtains to light.

Geneva's voice came softly, yet ruthlessly. "You still want him."

There was no point in hiding it anymore. "Yes."

But at her twin's puzzled gaze, Ginny couldn't help softening the blow. "It was a passing thing, Gen."

She held out her arms to her sister, and Geneva came into her embrace, resting her head on Ginny's shoulder.

"We left the Underground to be together," her twin said. "We said we'd never let anyone come between us again."

"I know."

The old vow sank within her, as if burrowing. Her sister turned her head so that her mouth rested against Ginny's neck.

"You know that he really is trouble," she said. "Don't you?"

Yes, he was, but not in the way Geneva was talking about.

Ben Tyree had sent Ginny reeling and, thanks to him, she could clearly see now how far she and her sister had strayed from all their human parents' careful, moral lessons. How far Geneva was still falling.

Ginny cupped her sister's head, bringing her closer out of pure desperation to cling to what she'd once loved about her twin, just as Ben clung to Nolan.

"You told me you'd take care of him," Geneva said. "You should do it before dawn if you care about us, Ginny. He can't leave New York with such a clear memory of us."

Ginny wanted to remind her sister that she'd been the one to bring him into the whole vampire/pleasure house knowledge ring in the first place. For someone who was so careless, her twin was sure adamant about covering their tracks now.

But Ginny suspected why that was: Geneva wanted Ben gone in every way.

Deep down, she knew her sister was right, but only if Ginny wanted to continue existence as she knew it.

As if there *was* any choice. She was a vampire. She couldn't ever go back to the way she'd been as a human—not even with the false emotion she'd acquired tonight.

"I'll take care of it," Ginny said, kissing her sister on the forehead and then letting go.

And she would. She'd spent the night playing a game with herself, and she'd lost.

After telling her twin to go back to Studio, where she needed to finally find that quick, easy meal and then go home, Ginny went to the hotel lobby's entrance, where she waited, her body heavy with the inevitable.

Not long after, a businessman with a prostitute in tow

passed her on his way inside. Quite effortlessly, Ginny convinced him that a threesome was much better than two, and she was on her way, invited into this dwelling and intent on finding Ben's room.

Ten

Ben stared out his hotel window at the empty, streetlamp-flushed sidewalks below, hoping he would see her one last time.

He hated himself for it, too.

But she was gone, and his body, so burnt by the adrenaline that had been coursing through it for the last few hours, finally gave out.

He walked to his bed, taking out his revolver and crucifix, then sitting, shucking off his work boots, socks, and ankle holster. Hunched over, he rested his head in his hands while his fingers dug into his hair.

None of it seemed real: Nolan, the pleasure house . . .

Ginny.

A vampire—one who had turned fearful when he'd shoved that crucifix at her. She and Geneva had barred their faces with their hands, but he'd seen a flash of their fangs in a slant of light.

Why the hell had he trusted her in the first place? Where had his judgment gone?

Worst of all, why couldn't he shake off this craving for her?

Damn it, his lips were even still buzzed with the taste of her: mysterious, intoxicating Ginny.

She'd gotten into his blood, a simmering that made his pulse work double-time. With her, he wasn't the shadow brother anymore. He wasn't the quieter Tyree kid who faded into the background, forgotten too early.

He'd even had what Nolan possessed for such a short time, and it was the indefinable, yet purely conclusive, answer to everything.

So what did that make Ben? Some kind of freak?

Is that what Nolan had ultimately become, too?

Less bothered by this question than he should've been, Ben heard a knock on his door.

At this time of night?

He grasped his .45 and the crucifix, then moved to the entryway, glancing out the peephole.

Outside, a bellboy stood in the wan hallway light, holding a manila envelope.

"What is it?" Ben asked.

The young man fixed big, brown, bloodshot eyes on the hole. "I'm sorry to bother you now, sir."

His speech was a little slurred, and Ben figured he'd taken a few tokes on the graveyard shift. Kids.

"I've got an urgent delivery," the bellboy added. "The woman who dropped it off said it was some kind of information that you'd want about a Nolan?"

Ben's veins contracted. Ginny? Was there something she hadn't told him about his brother?

But why would she do this after what had happened outside with her fangs and his crucifix?

The kid held out the envelope. "Will you allow the whole package inside the room, sir?"

Maybe Ben should've noticed the odd way the kid had phrased it. But he was so driven by the urge to get that envelope in his hands that he said, "Yes."

He took care to hide the .45 in his right hand behind the door. Then, with the crucifix still in his grip, he cracked the door open, leaving the chain still hooked.

As the kid slipped the thick envelope through, the door flew open, busting the chain, and sending Ben against the wall. He dropped the crucifix but managed to recover enough to aim his .45 at the streak of motion that had entered his room.

Where Ginny had already taken a spot next to the shabby beige curtains.

The door smacked closed, and Ben's blood raced.

Nonchalantly, she nodded toward the envelope he had dropped.

"It's filled with newspaper," she said, "so don't bother going through it."

His mind flailed to catch up. *She* was part of the package and he'd invited all of it in. Damn her.

"You messed with that kid's mind," Ben said, still aiming,

although he didn't know why. God, she'd told him that his gun wouldn't make a difference, but did he believe her? And what about the crucifix? Could he get to it before she made a move on him? "I'll bet you persuaded him to bring you up here and fool me into getting you inside my room."

Ginny ran her fingers over the curtain, as if finding the humble hotel room lacking. "He was off duty, popping a pill in a service hallway, halfway to blottoville, so he was easy to persuade. I guarantee I'll just be a weird dream to him."

Ben quelled a tremor that dragged through him. "You're here to finish what your sister wanted to start."

She stopped her curtain inspection, glancing at him. "I'm here to smooth your mind out. That's all, Ben."

He left the door, inching closer to the crucifix, which had slid into the bathroom. What were his chances of beating her with the draw of that holy item?

"Smooth me out?" he asked.

Ginny cocked her head at him, and he thought her gaze held some regret. But he was sure vampires didn't have the capacity for it.

Or maybe they did . . .

"Geneva talked too much earlier tonight," she said, tracking him. "And even if you have your answers, people like you never stop when they think there's more. I realize now that we can't have that."

"Why didn't you think about that before?"

"Because I . . ." She frowned.

His pulse skipped. Shouldn't she have attacked him by now? Why hadn't she?

Hope invaded him. It seemed as if, maybe, just maybe, her heart wasn't in this head-clearing task.

"You what?" he asked.

There was an emerging shimmer in her eyes. A hint of silver fantasy in the deep-blue depths. He lowered his weapon, unable to resist because it was all he truly wanted.

"I can't let you go," she said.

He wasn't sure if she meant that she couldn't allow him out of this room with the information he had about vampires or if she really *couldn't let him go*.

His sight went fuzzy as her eyes silvered even more.

She left the curtains and came toward him, one hand reaching out, even as her voice shook.

"I promise it'll be painless, Ben." She was talking about what she had to do to his mind. "I can even make you forget about Nolan altogether if you want."

Ben's rage spiked through the silver haze. "I don't want."

She halted, dropping her hand to her side. "Why would you wish to remember?"

"Because . . ." Ben blinked, but the hypnotic force of her stayed strong. ". . . even with all this pain, I would never let go of him. I'd like to hope that what's good about him is good in me, too."

"Yes," she said, softly. "I know what you mean."

The groan of a car's high-gear engine from the otherwise quiet street came between them, but it didn't destroy their silver connection.

"The thing is," she said, "sometimes what's bad about them can be a part of us, too."

She seemed more human than ever right now. Ben probably should've even been wondering if this was a creature trick. But why did that matter when he was all too willing to give in to it?

He set down his revolver on the floor, and she closed her eyes, as if not wanting to see what would come next. For a second, her silver faded from him, and he died a little.

But then she opened her gaze again, and their re-established connection shook him to the core.

And then it happened—the shared fantasy world he'd been hoping for.

In her eyes, he saw Ginny, suddenly naked and breathtaking, standing before him. He pulled her in, his own bare, sweat-slicked skin against hers, his cock hard and pulsating as it slid between her thighs, their breath harsh as she wrapped a long leg around him . . .

At the same time, outside of the fantasy, he felt her hands on his real body. Her fingers feathered over his throat, down to his chest, then his stomach. In primal rhythm, his muscles jumped beneath her touch, seizing until his penis stirred against his fly.

She paused in her exploration, her compelling gaze still

locked to his, and his body frantically pumped blood to his cock.

Then, she touched him, tracing his growing erection.

In and out of the fantasy, he felt her shudder, as if in near climax.

As if unable to hold back.

Eleven

No matter what Ginny had promised her twin about wiping Ben's mind, she couldn't do it.

Not with his scent tearing her apart. Not with the ridge of his penis beneath her fingertips.

He was a part of her, and it was beyond any experience she'd ever had as a vampire or human. She'd only linked with Sorin and Geneva, and somewhere along the way, she'd started to leave both of them behind.

She slipped her fingers lower, cupping his balls, and Ben moaned. At his instinctive sign of pleasure, she lost another grain of control.

Her fangs threatened, but she held back. Desperately.

See if he really wants it, she thought. *See if he's ready.*

She rubbed his cock to greater hardness as their gazes swirled together, her sex hot and pounding for him.

Then, as Ben's hands came up to grip her arms, their shared thoughts undulated until they coalesced into a vision that reflected real time, their clothing still on, their foreplay just starting.

A mirror where she could see every stroke, every caress, just as if she were a voyeur.

Turned on by the ability to watch, she undid his jeans, then worked his cock out, his length veined and thick. At the sight of it, she grew hungrier than ever before.

She wrapped her fingers around him, and he hitched in a hard breath as she reveled in his girth. Her mouth watered while she smoothed her grip up, down, up again.

Pausing at his tip, she circled with her thumb, exploring the slit there, the hint of beading come.

"Ginny," he said under his breath, and she held on to the way he said it, as if he was *inviting* her inside of him this time.

She couldn't move, because it was happening—she could

leave her own world to go somewhere foreign, scary, but beautiful as she peered in from the outside.

Ben's soul.

But then, as if sensing her hesitation to come in, he took over, roughly sketching his hands up her arms, her neck, then down her waist until he cupped her ass and brought her flush against his arousal.

Wincing, Ginny automatically lifted her leg so she could feel his cock nudging her sex. She ground into him, assuaging the stiffness of her clit, slipping and sliding with the juices drenching her. She clung to his shirt, hearing the weave of it tearing bit by bit.

Throughout it all, their gazes stayed locked, as if they couldn't bear to glance away from the mirror they'd created.

She kept straining against him, and he ripped off her halter, then eased one hand to her bare back while he used his other to palm a breast.

Seeing how Ben hungered for her, seeing how she responded to it in their mirror, she arched against him, keeping eye contact.

In his gaze, she saw that he was doing the same thing—getting hotter as he watched every sinuous move. He shaped her breast, kneading it.

Ginny grappled with his T-shirt, tearing it clean off in her excitement. Their hips continued rocking, driving her insane.

He made a sound low in his throat, animal and brutal, and her sensitive hearing thundered with it. Her body even rose up to the challenge of that growl as her fangs elongated.

Bu-bump-bu-bump . . .

The hammer of his heart took her over, beating as if it were her own, then traveling down to her sex, where she swelled to the point of nearly exploding.

She wanted to feel his skin against hers, and she surged forward, forcing them both to fall back against the dresser and lose eye contact. At the lack of it, her vision went dark for only the slightest moment before it lit up again, their lovemaking now etched into her mind with the same mirror-fantasy movements.

He was engrained in her now, even without the eye contact.

Overcome by the realization, she latched her mouth to his throat, just so she could feel his pulse with her lips.

Bubump-bubump . . .

Oh, to be inside him . . .

She opened her mouth against him, scratching him with her fangs, then, too late, fearing his reaction.

But . . . he seemed enticed, on the edge of that paradise he was searching for.

Wanting to give it to him, she slid down his hard body while taking his jeans with her, licking his inner thighs, making him buck and groan. He threaded a hand through her loose curls.

"You want it?" she found herself asking. "Not an exchange. Never an exchange. But—"

"A bite," he said through his teeth.

"Yes." She turned her head so that his penis skimmed her cheek. In their engrained fantasy-mirror, she got off at the ecstatic look on her face, got off on how he shivered at her touch.

Then she pressed her lips to his length. "A simple bite," she said, kissing, tasting. "Nothing else."

Because a full exchange would mean separating from Geneva, and Ginny wasn't sure she could do that, even if the idea had entered her mind.

His grip tightened in her hair, and she smiled against him.

"Are you afraid, Ben?" she whispered.

A gruff laugh answered that. "I'm beyond afraid."

She could see in their mirror that he wasn't joking. His honesty took her aback, but it made her burn for him even more.

Pushing his thighs apart, she positioned herself to take his length into her mouth. He kept his hand on her head, his grip loosening, and she could mirror-see him watching her go to work.

She deliberately swirled her tongue around him, up to his tip, kissing him softly there. Then she made a show of running her tongue over her lips to taste the fluid that had already seeped from him. His gaze was fevered.

She raised his erection again, dipping underneath to touch her tongue to his seam, tracing upward. He whispered a curse.

In punishment for that, she allowed her fangs to brush him, and he groaned in excitement as well as surprise.

"Your curses don't sit well with me," she said.

"Then put a stop to them."

With more strength than she would've given a human credit for, he yanked her upward, then tore her dress away from her body until it hung in rags. He did the same to her panties, too.

As she stood before him in only wisps of cloth and her pumps, she saw the lust . . . the utter starvation . . . on his face.

Bu-bump, bu-bump . . .

His heart was picking up speed again, tugging her toward him with every beat. She followed the pulsing command, climbing up to straddle him. His tip sought the wet folds of her, and she teased him, bracing her hands on his shoulders.

Bubump, bubump . . .

"One taste," she said, anticipation creeping through her with devouring heat. "Just one taste of you, Ben."

"Yes." His hand tightened in her hair as he brought her to his neck.

Bubumpbubump—

Breathing him in, she opened her mouth, then reared back, impaling herself on his cock while striking forward and sinking her teeth into a vein.

He grunted and dug his fingernails into her back.

Her first true bite.

It was too much—a rush of sensation barreling into her, within her, ripping every cell to shreds.

At the same time, she sucked at him, churning her hips with each sip.

Bubububububu

His heart—his body—was priming to explode, and she wanted to ride him until he did. He tasted sweet and thick in her mouth, his blood easing down her throat and into her with red, delicious bangs that she knew he was feeling, too.

She was in his mind, his heart, and soul.

They moved together, flew together, caught the air as it took them up and up. Still, all the while she strained against something holding her back—

Ben groaned and thrust into her with such force that she tore away from whatever she'd been bonded to—the something outside this room that had kept her prisoner. Geneva.

Finally separated . . .

At a hovering peak, she grabbed Ben's hand and he held on to it as everything about them entwined, making it hard to see where he began and she ended.

Then they fell, long, soft, and hard as they hit the ground.

Withdrawing from his neck, she clawed for breath, realizing that he had climaxed at the same time, his eyes unfocused, his pupils dilated. She stroked his face, his pierced neck, and they stared at each other for what felt like hours.

She knew why he had come into her existence tonight. Finally knew.

With a light touch, she pressed her fingers to his bite wound, healing it, even though the effort drained her and it took much more time than a higher Underground vampire would've needed.

And as their bodies calmed, the mirror faded, their mind-connection dimming.

"I'm going to come back to you," she whispered, leading him to the bed, "but while you wait for me, sleep, Ben."

He lay down and smiled, caressing her cheek, his eyes containing the look all humans found at the end of Ginny's and Geneva's bites.

Absolute peace and completion.

As he finally closed his eyes, she stood, unable to take her gaze off of him. His eyelashes fanned against rough skin, his lips slightly tipped in slumber.

She dressed in one of Ben's shirts, which was long enough so that she could belt it at the waist and pretend it was a dress. Then she left his room to go back to the apartment she shared with her sister, knowing she'd been severed from her twin already.

TWELVE

GINNY TRAVERSED THE PREDAWN STREETS SO QUICKLY
that anyone she passed—a transient huddled against a store-
front, a baker going to work, a doorman at his post— probably
only felt a chopping breeze as she whisked by.

Not long afterward, she came to a halt in front of her
building on the west side of Central Park. Composed of gray
stone and fleur-de-lis molding, its faded elegance paled against
the turning night.

She and Geneva could afford the place because of a
benefactor—a former Broadway producer Geneva had chosen
because she'd believed he could get them parts in a show. But
his glory days had already passed, even if his vaults were still
bulging with riches, so the roles had never materialized. However, he'd showered them with a lot of money, under the table
and unofficially.

Needless to say, he had died very happy, yet also very
naturally five months ago, leaving the sisters in posh straits.

On her way inside the building, Ginny nodded to the doorman, who was well-trained enough to not give her shirtdress
a second glance. He didn't even comment on her quickened
breathing as she tried to shed the contented air of a vampire
who'd just experienced the most mind-blowing bite of her
life.

Ben, she thought, addicted, maybe even obsessed because
of this morning afterglow.

But after getting into the elevator, with its marbled floor
and golden railing, Ginny's spirits sank. How was she going
to tell her twin about Ben?

She opened her awareness, then realized her sister had
shut her down.

Strange. Ginny would've expected Geneva to be eagerly
awaiting her return.

After alighting from the elevator, she walked down the

hall to their apartment, opening the door quietly so as not to disturb her twin. Maybe Geneva was already at rest.

But that wasn't the case at all.

At the sight that greeted her in the foyer, Ginny stumbled back against the wall.

The black-shrouded windows kept out the near-breaking dawn, but Ginny could still discern the body her twin was feasting on, her face buried in the stomach of a young man wearing a polyester dress shirt and pants.

At Ginny's gasp, her sister raised her head. Blood dripped from her mouth, her fangs grisly, her eyes a metallic silver that cut through the dark. She was breathing like a beast, smiling mindlessly.

No wonder her twin's awareness had been dark—Geneva had entered her own little world.

"I'm eating," her twin said. "Just like you told me to."

Ginny just stared, seeing the last vestiges of the sister she'd loved disappearing forever. She'd tried so hard to stop it. So hard.

"You killed him." Her voice barely made it out of her throat. "Geneva, didn't we decide it wouldn't happen again?"

"Maybe you don't like that I left you out of it this time. You weren't here for him to choose you over me."

Sorin's games had warped her twin. "Gen—"

"Or maybe you don't like that I ignored your command and did my own thing." Her sister cocked her head. "How does that feel, Ginny?"

So this was a punishment because of Ben.

Ginny slid down the wall, trying not to look at the desecrated body of Geneva's prey. Things could've ended so much better with her sister. Not like . . . *this*.

But what had she expected from a vampire who had grown bored with her existence and become reckless and arrogant in the pursuit of new pleasures?

"I caught him coming out of Studio, and I brought him back here," her twin said. "He was perfectly willing, so don't worry."

"Perfectly willing to *die*?"

"Yeah." Geneva laughed. "He chased that mental orgasm. He begged me, and I allowed myself to give in also. It's such a ridiculous rule they had Underground, to hold back from the big death."

Ginny scanned the bloody corpse. "You can't keep doing this. Someone's going to miss this man. He's obviously not homeless."

A bead of blood fell from her twin's mouth to the marble floor, splattering. "Well, don't *you* always know best? The humanly older sister, the gentle one, the provider."

"You're going to get caught, and I'm not going to be there to cover for you anymore."

Shocked loss—an instinct rather than emotion—flared in Geneva. Ginny could sense it, even if their awareness was mangled.

"So you're going back to that Ben Tyree." Geneva sniffed. "I can smell him on you. You fed from him, and he . . . he *changed* you."

Ginny slumped, wanting to be honest for once, but not wanting to hurt her twin. "Gen, you and I started to go our own ways a while ago. It's just more official now."

Geneva's eyes showed the betrayal of being left behind. "I'm not going to let you go."

"You have to."

Geneva pushed at the corpse, done with it. "We'll always be connected, no matter how much you resist. Just like the other night, with your new pet's brother."

She licked the blood around her lips, as if tasting the memory of Nolan.

Ginny tried not to remember any of it, but the images were too recent, too fresh.

As if it were happening all over again, she saw the colorful crowd in front of Studio, saw Nolan Tyree and his buddies in their disheveled business suits talking their way to the front so they could get in.

When Ginny had told Ben that *she* was the one who had approached his brother, it'd been to save her lover from knowing that *Nolan* had picked *Geneva* out of the crowd that night. She had been using Ginny's name, just like they'd done for years when they wanted to shake things up, and he had merely been another drunk husband away from home—an easy and nicely attractive truffle looking for a good time.

Since they were outside in the open, the twins had forgone entering Nolan's mind, so Ginny had never seen him the way Ben obviously did: a golden boy. A paragon.

When her twin had brought Nolan to Ginny, he'd lost his friends in the mob. Then they had taken him behind the club, nibbling on his skin, snacking as he indulged in sharp kisses and lots of cocaine.

All the while he'd told them how nice it felt to be away from his wife, how he wished he could find what made all these other party people so happy.

Geneva had told him about a place where that could happen—a pleasure house secretly located in the Bronx where they could get as happy and naughty as they wanted.

And that's where they had headed, even though Ginny didn't like this new place. Some clients killed prey there, and that had always been taboo to the twins. Too risky.

Now, in the midst of memory, Ginny recognized her sister's awareness nudging at hers. Numb, she allowed Geneva in, shivering under an icy joining that no longer felt so natural.

Her twin's awareness frosted Ginny as Geneva commented on the memory in progress.

So I see Ben doesn't know that his brother wanted *to explore the pleasure house, knowing full well what went on inside of it.*

No, he doesn't know, Ginny answered.

And he doesn't know that Nolan got excited by the torture rooms . . . and even asked for that scenario himself.

No. No.

In Ginny's mind, she heard how Nolan had screeched with raw delight as Geneva had restrained him, bitten him, choked him with straps until he had climaxed and asked for more.

Ginny had stayed outside, having no taste for Geneva's new games. It was clear that her sister was revealing a buried side both twins had tried to repress, and now it'd finally been given free reign.

Yet Ginny hadn't gotten involved—not until Nolan had yelled for her to take Geneva's place as his sadist.

And that's when it had all fallen apart.

Geneva had been struck with possessive rage, attacking Ginny with their awareness. Sinking her teeth into Nolan's neck. Sucking him dry until he screamed, "More! More!" while chasing an orgasm to death's door itself.

Caught off guard, Ginny had frozen, trapped outside in the shared awareness as she and Geneva had both convulsed with pounding climaxes, bursting apart, Ginny finally falling to the ground, satiated.

But afterward?

While Geneva had laughed wildly, discovering her Shangri-la, Ginny had stumbled into the house, up the stairs, to the fresh corpse, intent on healing evidence of the injuries and bites.

Covering up like a good vampire should.

So in the end, part of the story she'd told Ben had been true: The cops really had been nosing around the area that night, and the vampires had deserted the place. But a severely weakened Ginny had been concentrating on getting her crazed twin away, and Nolan had been left behind.

As the memory faded, Geneva pulled her awareness out of Ginny with a jarring yank.

"Ginny?"

Reluctantly, she focused on her sister, but the sight of the newest corpse made Ginny turn away.

"Ginny!" Geneva sounded anxious now, no doubt because she'd felt through their cold awareness just how disconnected they truly were. "I'm the one who accepts you for what you are. Ben won't. Especially if he ever found out that you got off on Nolan's death as much as I did."

"Don't even mention him knowing, Geneva, because I won't allow it."

Flinching, her sister's lips parted, her silvered eyes widening as if Ginny had gutted her swiftly and silently.

Then, wiping the blood from her mouth, her twin got to her knees.

"I wonder," she said, voice low, "what your Ben would do if he knew all of it."

"He's never going to."

And she meant it with all her heart . . . or whatever she had gained from Ben. She would protect him until her last breath.

Geneva stood, her arms curved by her sides, her eyes flashing as her temper escalated. "You mean that you *hope* he never finds out."

Without a word, Ginny got to her feet, too, using the wall for balance. For the first time, the stench of the corpse's blood turned her stomach and vised her head.

"I'm going now," she said.

Back to Ben, away from what used to be her sister.

"No, you're not," Geneva said.

Ginny didn't even have time to answer before her twin zoomed across the foyer and grabbed her by the throat.

"*No*"—Geneva banged her into the wall, where marble chips crumbled—"*you're*"—she slammed her into it again—"*not!*"

Ginny's sight scattered into pieces as she gagged, grasping at her sister's hand around her throat.

Strong, much too strong.

Sorin's mocking words came back to her. *One of you is more powerful. I made sure of that with my blood.*

Now they knew which twin it was.

Geneva kept on pummeling, adding insult to injury.

"I'm going to"—slam—"tell Ben"—bam—"everything!"

Feeling no pain now, just a vague thudding as her head banged against the wall again, all Ginny could imagine was Ben's face if he should find out the real truth about Nolan.

He'd look as beaten as she was.

It sent a bolt of fire through her, and she gathered all her strength, yelling while she grabbed Geneva's hands and tore them away from her throat. In one furious move, she had Geneva pinned to the wall.

"Don't do this, Gen," she said, panting. "Don't—"

Geneva narrowed her eyes, and awareness stabbed into Ginny's head. Their connection had warped into a deadly weapon, and it was all Ginny could do to withstand the spear of agony.

But she kept seeing Ben. *Ben.*

Mentally blocking her sister's attack, Ginny struck back with shattering force, harder, faster.

Again . . . again . . .

Geneva's silver eyes rolled back in her head, her mouth gaped in a scream that halted mid-screech.

Confused, Ginny withdrew from her twin's mind.

One of you is more powerful. I made sure of that with my blood.

Maybe that twin hadn't been Geneva at all.

Her sister slumped, a doll in a red dress pooling on the floor. Her eyes, which had now gone blue and dull, gazed up at Ginny.

Then a voice insinuated itself into her awareness.

Ginny?

The pathetic plea ricocheted through every cell, slaying a little piece of Ginny with every lancing contact.

"No," she said, trying to undo the damage, using her hands to heal her sister, using her brain to attempt a mental repair, but it was beyond her powers. A master vampire might be able to undo this, but not her . . .

Ginny, her twin said, through their remaining twin awareness, *I'm so sorry. Stay with me—please?*

Not knowing what to do, Ginny cradled her prone sister. Her tears wet Geneva's dark hair and washed the corpse's blood from her skin.

It took her a few minutes to realize that Geneva's awareness had started to feel warmer, less hateful and separate.

They lay like this for hours, Ginny's aching skull healing as she tried to talk Geneva back into movement. But all her twin could do was repeat Ginny's name, as if she didn't quite realize that her motor skills had been fried and her circumstances went way beyond Ginny leaving her now.

Eventually, Ginny took her twin to a favorite chair near the curtained window. Hours passed and night fell once again, and she opened the curtains so Geneva could at least see the city.

Then, as Ginny stroked her sister's hair back from her blank face, she thought of how Nolan's killer really had been brought to a certain justice, just as Ginny had told Ben.

A lie had ended up becoming the truth.

Her hand fell away from Geneva's head. Ginny had seen her twin choose a path they'd been taught to avoid, but after joining with Ben, she finally felt the pain. But she hadn't *wanted* Ben to experience the same agony, so she had lied to him, protecting him—always protecting somebody—from a truth he deserved to hear.

A pall hovered over the room. A choice.

Should she tell him? Could she ease him into the truth?

Time ticked on as Ginny watched the night, sitting at

Geneva's side, listening to her twin repeating the same pleas over and over.

Ginny? Ginny???

She picked up the telephone, dialing Ben's hotel.

Thirteen

After finally receiving a call from Ginny, Ben wasted no time getting to her apartment. He didn't doubt that he belonged with her; after all, how would he fit in at Holstead, Texas, now?

Besides, Ginny was his air, his blood, an integral part of him after their bite.

He knocked on her door and, soon afterward, it creaked open.

And there she was, heart-stopping in a pale dress.

But her eyes were ringed with a sadness so deep that he reached out to her.

She fell into his arms and held on to him for what seemed like dear life. He embraced her just as forcefully.

Ginny was his home. His world.

"I thought you'd be back at the hotel last night," he said into her hair.

He was trembling in his belly, and he thought he felt her quivering, too.

"I was going to come back," she said into his chest. "I wanted to, believe me, but . . ."

As he framed her face in his hands, he saw the silver shards in her blue eyes. This time, there was no shared fantasy to confuse him, just . . . sorrow.

Yeah, his Ginny could definitely feel sorrow, and he wanted to ease it.

He led her deeper inside the apartment, which was spacious and gothic. At the same time, she told him about the fallout between her and her sister, which had evidently come to a head because of Ginny's attachment to Ben.

But he could tell there was something else she was holding back. He gave her time.

"My sister couldn't stand the thought of existing on her own," Ginny finished. "And, somehow, she made sure I'd stay."

She looked up at him, her eyes going silver, and his veins tightened until they throbbed.

They hadn't seen each other for hours, but it felt like years.

"Ben," she said, her voice and gaze wrapping around him. She led him to a couch and slowly eased him down to it.

If she wanted his blood he'd give it to her. He'd give her anything.

She smoothed his brow with her fingers, whispering affectionate words, lulling him until he felt as if he were floating on water, the moon of her gaze shining down on his humming body.

But when she gently started telling him about Nolan, he slowly sank into an anesthetic nothingness, suspended in darkness.

Yet even under the drowning weight, he still saw Ginny wavering above him, extending a hand to pull him out in the end.

Fourteen

Years and years later . . .

Ginny went to bed, lying down next to Ben.

In the low lamplight of their West Seventy-fourth Street condo, she lavished a gaze on her human lover. Ben had chosen to live in this modest one-bedroom, which was close to her sister and the old apartment yet far enough to bar any twin awareness.

He was sixty-four now, his dark hair sprinkled with gray, his rough face slightly lined with wrinkles around the eyes and mouth. Over the years, he had grown used to her habit of resting during daylight and coming to full energy at dusk. He'd always been a night owl, too, he'd confessed.

But that had been long after the night when she'd told him the truth about Nolan.

He had been buried under it all at first, yet Ginny had persevered, determined to see him through the same pain she'd undergone with Geneva. It had taken him days, nights, to accept what she'd told him—and that she'd first lied about it—but then he'd come back to her.

And she had welcomed her other half—her substitute soul—with open arms, sharing everything else with him, too: the Underground, her and Geneva's vampiric life.

Everything.

As he felt her body press into the mattress, he opened his green eyes. "Is it late?"

"Ten o'clock more or less."

"So you're home for the night."

"You bet."

Every time darkness fell, Ginny visited the silent sister who sat like a mourning statue at the window overlooking Central Park. There, Ginny nurtured her and talked with her via their awareness. She also offered her blood, but her twin rarely needed it, seeing as Ginny had hired a young vampire she'd trained as a caretaker—one who gladly gave his own red for her.

But that didn't mean her twin still didn't plead with Ginny to take her back. However, Ginny had accepted that long ago, because she did her best for Geneva, yet always went home to Ben.

"Don't tell me," he said, grinning at her. "You're here to drink my blood."

"Among other things." She rested a hand on his neck, stroking with her thumb.

Her flesh, still youthful and unblemished, provided contrast to his tanned roughness, making her all hot and wiggly.

She didn't bite him yet though. They had all night.

"Don't you ever wish I was still a young buck?" Ben asked, his eyes going heavy with each of her strokes. "You could've preserved me nearer to my peak, you know."

"I want you like this." She bent to kiss him softly.

She wanted him gloriously human, uncorrupted, and he'd lived up to her dreams, also providing her with blood so she wouldn't have to hunt for it anymore. Commitment to a partner had always been in her nature, even though an official marriage was out of the question because of the mess it could create with the recent fake ID that accounted for her never-changing age.

But that didn't mean she and Ben weren't married all the same.

His hand sketched behind her, up her back, down to her butt. He squeezed, and she moaned, slipping down to his neck, where she kissed him.

Ben, her Ben. She smelled him, reveled in him. Then, with loving deliberation, she primed his vein by nipping at it, rubbing his belly until they'd both gone into their own place, where they could still see each other in those mental mirrors.

As she slid her palm down to his crotch, knowing he was so ready that he wouldn't feel pain, only pleasure, she pierced him. Sucking lazily, she took him in until she was near to bursting.

Up, up, floating, expanding and—

Agony wracked her.

But it wasn't an orgasm.

She broke away from Ben, rolling away, off the bed.

Crashing to the hardwood floor, her vision quaked, convulsions rocking her as she fought an agony so terrible that she wished it would kill her.

"Ginny," she heard Ben cry, his hands on her, grasping, soothing. "Ginny, what's happening?"

She didn't know . . .

Then, as soon as it'd arrived, it left.

As she wrestled for breath, she felt her skin loosen over her bones, her innards shift, her body grow into itself until she huddled into a fetal ball.

"Ginny . . . ?"

She sought him with her gaze, and he hovered in her vision, his face a mask of wonder. Tears flooded his eyes as their mental mirror showed her the truth of her new appearance.

Old, her skin heavily mapped, her hair turned pure white.

"My maker," she said in a tinier, weaker voice. "Gone. Someone must have killed him . . ."

Ben gathered her into his arms, and she reached up a hand to touch his cheek.

Human. She was truly older than he was in human years.

"I'm . . . seventy-six, Ben," she said, not knowing whether to laugh or cry. "Seventy-six. Geneva, too."

"I'll call her caretaker, and we'll go to her."

Ben held Ginny in one arm, cradling her so he could get a better look at her face.

No—what if he decided he didn't want her anymore?

Mortified, she began to cover herself with a hand.

"Don't," he said. "You're more beautiful than ever. Don't you know that?"

As she lowered her hand and allowed her lover to drink her in, Ginny realized that he was right.

He'd made her feel much more beautiful than she had ever hoped to be.

Thicker Than Blood

✝

MELJEAN BROOK

To Kat, for giving me Philly
and a lot more.

One

Less than two weeks ago, Annie Gallagher would have slain another vampire for this.

She'd followed the human to his home, anyway. He'd turned off the lights in his second-story bedroom, but she continued to wait; she wouldn't feed from him until he slept. And so for the second time that night, she stood on a sidewalk and stared across a street at a pair of darkened windows—but this time, she didn't let the ghosts overwhelm her.

Annie blinked and looked away from the house. *Not ghosts.* Even she didn't believe that the spirits of the dead haunted the Earth, let alone a pizzeria in Northeast Philadelphia. And except for her father, all of the people she'd been thinking of were still living.

Not ghosts, but phantoms. Memories strong enough to bring the flavor of tomato sauce and mozzarella to a tongue that could no longer taste anything but blood.

Fighting the restlessness and hunger that began pricking the length of her spine, Annie rolled her shoulders within her heavy jacket and tugged at the neckline of her black tank. The body-hugging fabric didn't tug far, and the movement only made her acutely conscious of the sweat soaking the material.

No air-conditioning unit protruded from the face of the brick row home, but she'd heard one rumble to life moments after he'd gone inside. His house would be blissfully cool. But it probably wasn't yet—and although his psychic scent indicated that he'd finally slipped into sleep, it wasn't deep. At least ten or fifteen more minutes of waiting stretched ahead of her.

Loitering. Suspicious behavior, maybe, but Annie doubted that she would be noticed by any of the neighborhood's residents. This part of Mayfair was blue collar to its core, early to bed and early to rise. Even the weekends didn't see much action after the local bars closed, and it wasn't exactly bumping with traffic on a Thursday night.

Or, considering that it was two-thirty, early Friday morning.

Thursday, Friday . . . *Whatever*, she thought, suddenly impatient with herself. A vampire didn't move to the same circadian rhythms as the rest of the city, so it hardly mattered what day of the week it was when the sun came up—it only mattered when it went down.

Of course, if it hadn't been Thursday, she wouldn't have been standing there now.

Annie closed her eyes. *All right.* So it mattered. Enough that it hadn't been the sight of Tony's Pizza that had stopped her in her tracks when she'd been walking down Frankford Avenue, but the stabbing realization that only a few hours earlier, her mother, her brother, and his family had probably been in the restaurant. Annie's two nieces, and the nephew she'd only seen in pictures—all carrying on the Gallagher tradition: Tony's every Thursday night.

Surely they'd kept going after Annie's transformation and her father's death. Hell, even before she'd been turned, med school and her residency had prevented Annie from joining them half the time, anyway.

But however many dinners she'd missed since then, there had been enough memories to keep her riveted to the spot, staring into the past and letting the present recede into shades of gray. And even as she'd cursed herself for letting such a little thing—such a *bygone* thing—get to her, she hadn't been able to break away until a glint of auburn had burned through the haze of remembrance.

Just another phantom, another bygone. But unlike the first—the jab of pain, the re-opening of an old wound—that flash of color deepened an ache that had been lurking beneath the surface of her skin for six years, leaching into her flesh, her bones.

The man had turned down a side street as she'd pulled her gaze away from Tony's, but even in the shadows that pooled between the streetlights, Annie had seen his rumpled hair was a shade too brown for auburn. The sun would lift out the red like the glow of a fire.

Just like Jack Harrington's . . . although this man couldn't be him.

He'd rubbed at his face as he walked, and she'd heard the sandpapery scrape of his palm over his jaw. *Definitely not Jack,* she'd thought, and the startled gallop of her heart had settled into a steady, relieved beat. Mayfair wasn't Jack's neighborhood—and she doubted he'd ever gone five hours without shaving, and never looked unkempt. Certainly his white shirt wouldn't have been untucked, wrinkled, and clinging damply to his back. Not because of the Bureau's dress code—it was the way Jack had been, on duty and off. He was the poster boy for "eager and fresh-faced," intent on saving the world, and Annie had loved him for it.

But then, she'd been exactly the same.

And she couldn't recall making the decision to follow the human; her feet had simply begun to move.

She'd hung back a block, keeping just out of sight, but she couldn't mistake the scent of alcohol he left in his wake. The odor was too sharp for beer—his drinking had been serious that evening.

Serious, but not heavy. His face had been downturned, as if he'd had to concentrate on the placement of his feet, but he hadn't staggered. A slow, even stride had carried him past the unbroken line of row homes, past the trash cans and recycling bins caged just off the sidewalk, until he'd reached a block where lawns grew in tiny patches and separated the concrete from the front steps of the houses.

He hadn't appeared alert to his surroundings, but he didn't have to be. Unlike some parts of the city Annie had walked through during the past ten days, kids did not roam in packs, laughing and hollering, their weapons bulging in their pockets and outlined in the bottoms of their backpacks.

They'd laughed and hollered at Annie until she'd gotten close. Then, like hyenas suddenly aware of a lioness in their territory, they'd settled back, watching her warily.

Her guns didn't bulge and her blades didn't gleam, but in the sweltering July heat, her long black coat always drew a second, apprehensive glance. So did her pale skin, glistening with perspiration; her light eyes, searching—and probably shining with desperation. As the days passed, it became more difficult to conceal.

Thankfully, the one she'd followed hadn't looked around. Didn't know what waited outside his home.

Five minutes now—and the night would still be young when she finished. There was more than enough time to stop by the clinic and steal a unit of blood. She should; she'd been alternating nights so the packaged blood wouldn't wear her down too quickly. This was supposed to be a packaged blood night.

But she wanted this one. Maybe it was stupid to allow nostalgia to affect her this way—and maybe she just had little defense against her old life when it teased her with ghosts and darkened windows, reminding her of easier, brighter times.

And maybe she was too damn tired.

Not physically tired—she couldn't fight the daysleep that came upon her every morning—just soul weary. She hadn't stopped for a moment since returning to Philadelphia and discovering that every vampire in the city had been slaughtered over the course of a single night—since discovering that the new life she'd made had been destroyed along with them.

Annie shook herself, straightened her shoulders. Nostalgia, exhaustion, whatever. She had good reason not to go back to the clinic: Feeding from a nonliving source would eventually make her weak and stupid.

Weak and stupid wouldn't help her find Cricket.

A twelve-year-old girl alone in the city had more things to worry about than vampires, demons, or any of the other creatures who stalked the night; there was hunger, loneliness, and fear.

And hyenas—or, more frightening, the monsters. Hyenas might laugh and holler, but most of it was for show. The monsters hid behind friendly, quiet faces, and their smiles were widest when the horrors began.

Annie could easily imagine the unspeakable things that happened to young girls alone—they'd been drilled into her from birth.

Worked a new case today, Annie. A little girl—not much older than you. They had a drawer full of pictures. A girl can't ever come back from that, Annie, not all the way.

She was just a little kid, and once she was knocked up, he didn't have much use for her anymore. So you make sure you wait until you've got his ring, Annie; a man who doesn't give you one isn't worth giving anything in return.

A little girl, Annie. Found pieces of her in a bag off of the turnpike.

The stories had always been accompanied by a warning not to trust strangers. Annie had later learned that advice only applied to little girls: She'd grown up, been transformed, and it had been strangers who'd taken her in.

She wasn't going to repay them by leaving Cricket alone in a city of strangers who might not be as kind as those Annie had found.

Steeling herself, Annie focused, opened her senses, and reached into the surrounding houses. One mind after another—and although Annie had grown up only three blocks away, and had probably known many of these people once upon a time, the flavors of their psyches were all unfamiliar.

No Cricket.

Her head throbbed painfully when she finished. Too many minds in too short a time. Annie had walked through most of the city in the past ten days, touching hundreds of thousands of them, extending herself as far as possible. She didn't know if—or when—she would hit the edge, but hunger would probably get her there faster.

Sighing, she rubbed her sweat-slicked forehead, trying to ease the ache. Another probe toward the second floor of the house touched on the man's psyche, soft and heavy with sleep.

She started across the street, then paused. Her hand found the grip of her sword, but she didn't draw the weapon.

Another mind touched hers—dark, searching, and powerful.

Annie threw her psychic shields up full. Probably too late. The barn doors shut, but now someone would know a cow was loose. She waited, her gaze scanning her surroundings, her heartbeat pounding in her ears. No traffic, no one on the sidewalks—and a careful examination of the sky told her that no demons lurked, ready to descend on her from above.

It hadn't seen her, then, but had only felt her psychic presence. There was no telling how far away it had been.

And she had enough reasons to find Cricket and get the hell out of Philly—but whatever she'd sensed had just given her another one.

* * *

An icy blast of air-conditioning welcomed her through the front door. Annie stood for a moment, closing her eyes in relief. The heat didn't pain her, but the sweat and oppressive humidity left her feeling disgusting, uncomfortable.

Carefully, she replaced her lock-pick tools in their velvet pouch and rolled it closed. The cylinder fit neatly into the pocket she'd sewn in the lining of her jacket; from another pocket, she withdrew an instant hot pack. Fabric rustled as she slid off the heavy coat, but nothing clinked. The quiet ticking of a clock, the deep sound of breathing from the upstairs bedroom were no louder than the crinkle of plastic when she squeezed the package in her hand.

It was intended for first-aid kits—the chemical reaction created a temporary heating compress—but Annie held it in her mouth, careful not to pierce the casing with her fangs, and surveyed the room.

He must have just moved in—or was preparing to move out. The sofa faced a blank wall. No TV, no stereo, no coffee table.

Annie piled her jacket and sword on a stack of boxes near the door, but didn't remove the holster that lay against the small of her back. With light steps, she climbed the stairs, testing the surface temperature of her lips and tongue against the back of her hand. Warm. Their touch probably wouldn't shock him awake, but they would cool quickly.

She'd used a sedative on the others, but this one had been drinking; doping him might be dangerous. With luck, the alcohol would deepen his sleep, and he wouldn't think her feeding had been anything but a pleasant—very pleasant—dream.

His room was as sparsely furnished as the rest of the house: a large bed covered by a navy fitted sheet, and a dresser heaped with clothes. Although he'd taken time to fold his laundry, he hadn't put it away. Not a slob, but not obsessively neat, either.

His white shirt lay on the floor, the sleeve trailing beneath the bed. He hadn't made it out of his pants. Annie studied the sprawl of his body, calculating the least disruptive approach, the best location to bite.

He'd landed on his stomach, his arms wrapped around his

pillow and his face buried in the crook of his elbow. The position brought his shoulders up and in toward his neck; it'd be difficult to reach his throat without moving him. The sides of the abdomen and ribs had too many nerve endings. Of all the flesh exposed, his back had the fewest pain receptors.

Her gaze moved down the smooth muscles parallel to his spine, the hollows just above the low waistband of his black trousers. He looked to be of average height, and he wasn't too bulky or too lean—just a man who kept himself fit and strong. Anticipation began to build its ache in her fangs. The bloodlust wasn't upon her yet, but arousal sparked softly within her.

Briefly, she wished she'd warmed her hands. Wished for a connection deeper than her mouth, his blood.

But there wouldn't be. Couldn't be. She wound the damp, heavy mass of her hair into a bun and fastened it with an elastic band. A few red strands escaped, and she tucked them behind her ears, leaving nothing to brush or tickle, so that he'd swat at her in his sleep as he would a mosquito.

She leaned over, bracing her palms alongside his waist. The mattress didn't squeak as she eased her knees onto the bed, straddling his legs without touching him.

Breathing wasn't an option. An exhalation would be cold against his skin, an inhalation would bring his odor to her—and she didn't want to be reminded that this was a stranger. Didn't want harsh reality. She'd imagine a clean, lemon-bright scent, instead.

She'd never asked him if it was his soap or an aftershave.

Jack, she thought, closing her eyes and gently touching her lips to his shoulder.

Harsh reality caught her wrist, rolled beneath her, and shoved the barrel of a pistol against her throat.

Annie froze. *God damn it.* Lowering her guard to indulge in a memory and missing his shift from sleep to consciousness could only be called stupid. Inexcusably, tremendously stupid.

But she could berate herself later; right now, she needed to pretend to be weak.

The last thing she wanted to do was scare him. She'd had her throat shot out before, by a rogue vampire who hadn't wanted to give up feeding from—and killing—humans. It wasn't the pain that worried her; she couldn't afford to lose that much blood.

"Do you have anything in your hands?"

His voice was flat, controlled. No, this man wouldn't spook and pull the trigger. His heartbeat had sped up, but it wasn't racing.

Daring a movement, Annie opened her eyes. A taut pectoral and the brown disk of a nipple obscured her field of vision; if she lowered her lips even an inch, they'd meet the crisp, reddish-brown hair that roughened his chest.

"No," she said.

Without a word, he reached up. Light pressure against her back made her grit her teeth, but she didn't stop him. His fingers unerringly located her weapon, and he eased the revolver from its holster.

"Any more?"

Did he expect her to answer truthfully? "No."

"Right." It only took him a beat to decide a course of action. "Keep your hands flat against the mattress, and slowly back off the bed." The push of his gun against her neck emphasized *slowly*.

Annie could have been across the room in a blink. But feeding from humans to survive was one thing; there wasn't yet a reason to break the other rule she'd lived and killed by for six years: preventing humans from discovering the existence of vampires.

So she edged her knees backward, her face down and her posture nonthreatening. Her compliance hadn't eased his tension; only a marble statue might have matched the rigid cast of his abdomen. A small fold of skin stretched across the upper curve of his navel, and three tiny scars from a laparoscopic appendectomy marred—

Oh, no. Annie stopped moving. Her fingers clenched in the sheet. *Please, no.*

It had been at her parents' dinner table, less than a month before her transformation. When Jack had grabbed at his stomach, pain twisting his features, they'd thought it was a comment on her mother's meatloaf.

Fifteen minutes later, Annie had been in an ambulance, helping the paramedics prep him for surgery.

Aside from a single, impersonal handshake when they'd been introduced, it had been the first time she'd touched his skin. It had been the night he'd told her his name was Jack, not John Harrington the Third, or—as she'd thought of him until that moment—simply Harrington.

It had been the night he'd confessed he'd been messed up over her since that handshake. She'd waited until his morphine drip was off before confessing the same.

"Whatever you're considering doing down there, lady, it's not smart." Cold steel slid from her neck to the underside of her chin, and he nudged it up. "Keep heading on back, and look at the ceiling as you do it."

And she'd heard him speak softly before, but it had never been sharpened by the dangerous tone he was using. She squeezed her eyes shut and averted her face.

Don't recognize me. Don't see what I've become.

Maybe he wouldn't. It had been so many years, and there were a few differences. Her hair color, the makeup. Both were dark now, because roses and cream belonged to the day.

Annie didn't—not anymore.

"You picked me out as an easy mark the second I left Buddy's. I expected you to try something when you followed me," he said. "But to actually come *into* my home, that takes some . . . kind . . . of . . ."

The anger in his voice faded with his words. The pressure of the gun eased.

And his heart was racing now.

She should run. Should tear away, without looking back.

She stayed.

"Who are you? You can't . . . it can't be—" Jack dropped her revolver to the mattress, and his fingers tangled in the hair piled atop her head. "Look at me, damn it."

She did, but only because she wanted to see him, too. To take one glance away with her.

His face was leaner. Time hadn't dulled his features, but honed them—and he could still trip her breath, skip the beat of her heart.

His brows were heavy and low over eyes darkened by confusion and shock.

"Annie? Oh, Jesus love me—*Annie?*" His gaze hungrily

searched hers, hope and disbelief spilling from his psychic
scent in a rich, warm tide. His hand opened, began sliding
from her hair to her cheek.

Her cold cheek.

Annie pulled away. He probably didn't see the movement
she used to collect her gun. He continued to stare as she stood
and forced herself to walk—not run. There was no longer any
need to pretend to be weak.

Jack had always been the only one with whom she had to
pretend to be strong.

two

Jack caught up with her on the stairs. From just behind her, Annie heard him say, "Gallagher told me you were dead."

Her brother, Brian. It shouldn't still hurt, but it did. And she shouldn't answer, but leave him as silently as a ghost. A dream, to doubt in the morning.

But she said quietly, "He told me the same thing."

"That *I* was dead?" Jack's reply contained a strange mixture of outrage and relief.

"No." She allowed a bitter smile to part her lips; from his angle, he couldn't see her fangs. "That I was."

Jack would wonder about the sword, but Annie didn't try to hide it. She looped the cord over her shoulder, anchored the scabbard to her hip. The coat didn't sway when she slung it over her forearm—too many things inside, weighing it down.

She didn't look at him. She couldn't trust herself to keep going if she did.

"I went to your funeral, Annie."

She hardened herself against the thickness in his voice, and reached for the door handle. "Was it nice?"

He slid in front of her, his back against the door. His hard smile was at her eye level. "I don't know. I only got through it with the help of a fifth, so I was too drunk to see much of anything. Gallagher told me I was an embarrassment."

Suddenly stricken, she dropped her gaze to her boots.

"Frankly, I couldn't give a shit about decorum, or the dignity of the Bureau. The only thing I noticed was that the casket was closed, and that your mother didn't attend. I thought it had all been too much for her—first your father's heart attack, then your wreck two days later. It never occurred to me you might not be in there."

She'd never asked her mother what story they'd told, but a

car accident made sense. It would have been convenient. A closed-casket funeral—not because the body was missing, but because it was supposedly too mangled to view.

"Stay, Annie," Jack urged softly. "Stay long enough to tell me—" She could almost hear every question that ran across his tongue—*why the sword, why were you in my room, why do you look like you do, why haven't you contacted me all of these years*—before he finished with, "—to tell me that you're okay."

And there were so many questions that she wanted to ask him. Yet she turned the handle, and only said, "I'm okay," before tugging it open, forcing him to step forward.

But this was Jack, and she couldn't leave like this. Not without knowing— "Are *you* okay?"

A short laugh broke from him. He'd crossed his arms, was shaking his head, his expression torn between amazement and longing. Hers probably looked the same. "I really don't know, Annie."

She met his eyes, the blue so much darker and warmer than her own. Memorized his face, so familiar and so new. Then she left, because it would be far too easy to talk herself into staying, and try to help him figure it out.

По chance in hell was Jack letting her slip away. If Annie wouldn't stay, then he'd go.

He didn't bother to put away his gun or grab a shirt and shoes before heading out the door, certain that if she left his sight for even two seconds, she'd disappear. Maybe one second—she was already halfway across the street.

Jack swore and broke into a run, relieved when she didn't do the same. He might have dogged her heels, just to draw a reaction, but he came up even with her instead.

She didn't slow her loose, sidewalk-eating stride, only glanced at him sidelong with crystalline blue eyes. That look caught him like a teeth-rattling kick to the head, clearing the haze of drink, sleep, and shock—and driving home everything he'd seen but hadn't yet processed.

When her hair had been a light auburn and her lashes blonde, those eyes had been extraordinarily pretty. But contrasted with the black liner, her pale skin, and wine-red hair, they were stunning. And despite all the artifice, she wore it naturally.

Annie apparently had a dark side—and she'd become very comfortable with it.

What had happened to bring it out?

When it had happened was clear: No one randomly pronounced a sister dead and held a funeral for her—particularly not a man like Gallagher. The only person more devoted to his family than Annie's brother had been Annie's father.

Six and a half years before, as Brian Gallagher's new partner and without immediate relations of his own, Jack had been invited into the close-knit circle only by virtue of belonging to a larger family the Gallagher men held almost as sacred: law enforcement. Jack had allowed himself to be talked into a Thanksgiving dinner, suffered through Mrs. Gallagher's version of roasted turkey, and had been trying to escape when Annie had arrived home, worn from a three-day shift in the emergency room.

She'd offered him a handshake, a smile, then dragged herself upstairs to sleep—and Jack had finagled dinner invitations for seven months, braving the terrors of Mrs. Gallagher's kitchen, his reward a few minutes of conversation with Annie. Those minutes had quickly become hours, extending into the living room or over a beer on the patio—until finally, finally, he'd admitted how he felt.

God, how he'd loved her, wanted her.

But there hadn't been much fooling around. Not just because she was his partner's sister—Annie had still lived at home, and her father was a decorated city cop who'd worked himself up to a position behind a desk. Unlike Jack's own father, Captain Gallagher hadn't been a complete asshole, but his style of parenting had been heavy-handed and strict. And Annie hadn't been sheltered—no ER resident in a Philly hospital could be considered sheltered—but she'd never indulged in anything casual.

In any case, Jack had quickly learned he didn't want something casual. Not with Annie. He wanted permanent, forever after, and he'd been willing to be patient.

Only after her funeral had he regretted that decision. Regretted never asking her to marry him, never making love to her. He'd waited for that, too—taking it as far as he could in the few private moments they'd had, but he'd wanted their first time to be better than a hasty grope in an empty hospital room. Even an overnight stay at Jack's downtown apartment was impossible—it meant Annie would have had to face her father the next day, and have a shame placed on her that didn't belong.

But it was obvious that something else had been placed on her. Annie's brother must have blamed her for their father's heart attack; it didn't take an FBI agent to deduce that.

And a damn good thing, Jack thought, considering that he had resigned from the Bureau a week earlier. Brian Gallagher had been part of the reason for that, too.

But whatever her brother had done or said, Jack didn't think Gallagher was the reason for the changes Annie had made in her appearance. He studied the line of her jaw, the proud set of her shoulders and neck. There was defiance there, just under the surface—but that was expected, normal.

The caution and weariness that accompanied it were not.

However often she'd had to stand up against the overbearing force of her father and brother, she'd never feared that they'd hurt her. But something *had* wounded her. Something repeated and long, because Jack couldn't imagine her not bouncing back from a one-time hurt.

Anger kindled, but he tamped it down. Without a target, he might take it out on Annie. Chasing after her might piss her off, but whatever injuries had been done to her, he wouldn't add to them.

And at least she wasn't running. She slanted him another look as they reached the end of the block.

"Your gun is conspicuous, G-Man," she said softly.

G-Man. It was an endearment from her, a teasing one. The tension knotting his gut eased.

"And a sword isn't?" *A sword.* He couldn't begin to imagine why she had one.

Her lips curved, but she looked resigned as she slung her jacket around her shoulders like a cape, hiding the weapon. Jack frowned, suddenly wishing he hadn't mentioned it. No one was on the street to see them, and Annie wasn't just glowing with perspiration, but sweating. Drops gathered at her hairline, glistened over her skin, pooled in the hollow of her throat.

She met his eyes. With a shrug, she let her gaze fall to his bare chest. "Your outfit is likely to draw as much notice as mine."

She must have mistaken the reason for his frown. For Chrissake, compared to the sword, a long jacket in July was hardly a blip on the radar. "But I won't faint from heat exhaustion," he pointed out. "Or dehydration."

"Neither will I. But if you cut your foot, you'll be in trouble."

"Will you stitch me up and kiss it better?"

She began to laugh, then caught herself and turned her head. "Go home, Jack."

There was hunger in her voice. It sparked his own need, and gave him hope. "Will you come with me?"

"No."

"But you came in before."

"I didn't know it was you." She indicated his body with a sweep of her hand, then the neighborhood. "Everything said it wasn't you."

It was true. He looked like warmed-over shit. Self-consciously, he smoothed his palm over his hair, and something softened in her eyes.

"You don't have to—" She broke off, drew in a breath through barely parted lips. "You look good."

"You look incredible." He watched pleasure and regret flash over her features. Her expressions were still so familiar; he could still read her so easily. How many times had he seen other women—a quirk of their eyebrows, a movement, heard a laugh—and been struck by memories of Annie?

Had she done the same?

She'd followed him home. Her clothing suggested a burglary, but a thief would have taken one look at his living room and left to find better pickings. Not crawl onto his bed.

"If you didn't know it was me," he said slowly, "then I must have *reminded* you of me."

She stepped off the curb, and he crossed the street with her. Her lack of response lifted his heart to his throat. She was evading the question, but not lying. She hadn't even offered the glib response or denial that she usually hid behind whenever she was confronted with something she wished wasn't true. And the thing about Annie was—even after she'd shrugged something off—she eventually forced herself to face the truth.

So she'd already confronted this, had already accepted it. She'd thought of him, missed him, and had intended to use someone who looked like him.

Use him for . . . what? Sex? Comfort?

Hell, Jack was ready and willing to offer both—but why would she need to break into a stranger's home for either? "Do you need help, Annie?"

"No, I just—" She stopped in the middle of the sidewalk, her jaw and fists tight. Her struggle was apparent on her face, and he waited. There was her knee-jerk denial. Now she was forcing herself to face the truth—which meant she'd decide whether to let him help or not.

She slowly turned. "There's a girl missing. Ten days now. I've called the local hospitals, shelters—but there are some avenues for information that I can't access. You can."

Not any longer. But he didn't hesitate. "Yes." He might not have access to the Bureau's resources, but he had a hell of a lot of free time on his hands, and more than enough money to look as long as she wanted him to. His own project could be a second priority. "Have you filed a report?"

She shook her head, and wiped the sides of her neck and face with her sleeve. "It's complicated."

"Because you're supposedly dead."

She'd grown up around cops; even with the cosmetic changes she'd made, someone might recognize her.

"No," she said. Grief flattened her lips, her tone. "Because everyone else *is*."

Jack's brows drew together, a dark suspicion rising in his mind. Ten days. Everyone dead. "Everyone, who?"

"Everyone who might recognize her, and that she might go to. Her legal guardians. The people we knew. Everyone." She palmed her forehead, slicked back the tendrils of hair that had escaped the loose bun. Her gaze slid past him, her eyes narrowing slightly. "Probably too hot for him inside, hmm?"

Jack glanced around. Two and a half blocks south, male, late sixties or early seventies. A white wisp of hair, slightly hunched back, a cane. A yellow polo shirt and khaki pants. Jack looked back at Annie, and shrugged. "Probably. At least he has clothes on."

Her smile barely lifted the corners of her mouth. That had changed, too. The night he'd met her, Jack had been certain the sun couldn't have competed with the brightness of her smile. And when she spoke, her upper lip was still, as if she was trying to hide an overbite; she held her lower lip just on the edge of a pout.

It did things to her mouth that were as sexy as hell, but not the least bit familiar.

He recognized the worry pinching her features, though, and he frowned as Annie's hand crept to her sword.

Her gaze was fixed behind him. "Let's go back to your place, Jack."

"All right. But why—"

"He's not sweating," she said quietly. "Even you are."

Even him? But her urgency couldn't be mistaken, and he scrubbed his right palm over the cotton of his pants, wiping away the moisture from it and his gun. When he was certain his grip wouldn't slip, he glanced back again. The old man was striding toward them, his cane hooked over his forearm.

Jack couldn't make out the man's features yet, let alone detect any perspiration. "How can you tell?"

"I can't see it." She touched his elbow, briefly, and a shiver raced up his skin. Her hands were *frigid*. Was her fear so extreme? Taken aback, he looked at her, but she was still staring at the old man. "And his eyes—oh, God. Let's go, Jack."

What had gotten into her? The guy was spry for his age, sure—but there was no indication that he was dangerous. No evidence of weapons. He was simply walking toward them, without hesitation or fear.

Walking toward two strangely dressed, armed people in the middle of the night. Young or old, anyone else would have approached with some caution.

His breath suddenly came sharp and shallow, and he fought the overwhelming instinct to turn and run. Jack backed across the darkened street with her, trying to understand his reaction, his sense that he'd just fallen ass backward into a completely fucked-up situation.

Or was her fear just feeding his?

He shot a glance at Annie. Her skin had been pale before; now she was white, her lips colorless. Her grip shifted on her sword. A SIG semiautomatic pistol was in her left hand, the barrel elongated by a silencer.

"Shut up," she hissed, and Jack blinked. Was she responding to the old man? Jack hadn't heard anything.

The clench of her finger on the trigger and the burst of suppressed air stunned Jack to his core. The old man staggered. A dark hole opened on his forehead, and blood spilled over his face.

"Annie!" He grabbed for her gun, but she stepped away too quickly. "Jesus fuck me, Annie! What the hell are you—"

Jack froze. The old man was still upright and moving. His pace didn't appear to have increased, but he was close enough now that Jack could see he was smiling. The blood was gone.

So was the bullet wound.

Jesus Christ. What the fuck? Jack trained his pistol on his chest, looked harder.

Horror ripped through him, left his skin cold, his gut shaking. The man's eyes were missing—they were just two black holes in his friendly face.

"Listen, Jack," Annie said, walking backward. Jack was forced to turn and jog in an awkward sidestepping gait to keep up with her, but his aim never wavered from the thing coming after them. "Her name's Cricket Snow. She's twelve. When you find her, say that Annie sent you, that you're my sunshine boy. Then she'll trust you."

Those words terrified Jack more than the old man did. His head cleared; his stomach turned to lead. "Don't you dare, Annie," he said hoarsely. "Don't you dare think it's going to happen."

Her steps slowed. "Everything I own is under the name Anne Douglas. My mom can make sure that Cricket gets all of—"

Anger rose up, burned away the fear. "Don't you *dare*," he bit out.

"Go back to your place, Jack, as fast as you can." Her voice wavered, then firmed. "He can't hurt you, but I don't want you to see what he does to me."

Jack stepped in front of her. "He'll have to come through me."

"Oh, Jack," Annie said softly. Her breath was cool against his back, then his arm. She was allowing him to protect her, he realized, but moving just enough that she could still see past him. "It doesn't matter. He can go *around* you."

The old man stopped in the middle of the sidewalk, twirling his cane, his smile broadening. "Cricket Snow," he said in a voice that should have been on television, hawking butterscotch candies or oatmeal. "I've only to tell her that I'm Annie's sunshine boy."

Annie's response was confident. "She knows you can't touch her."

The man's eyes glinted. They weren't missing, Jack could see now. Just a pure, deep black.

Somehow, missing would have been less sinister. More human.

With an inclination of his head, the old man said, "Not without her permission. But if I explain to her what I can do to you, I imagine she'll agree to anything I propose. So I've decided to leave you alive until I come to an understanding with her."

Annie drew in a sharp breath. The man twirled his cane again, and for an instant Jack thought he saw something else there, caught the impression of a huge figure with crimson skin, glowing red eyes, and black feathered wings.

Then it vanished.

Jack blinked, then swept his gaze in a wide arc, searching. Nothing. Annie's voice echoed in his head: *He can go around you.* Jack turned in a full circle. Still nothing.

He glanced at her, his brow furrowing. Annie was hunched over, the back of her jacket poking up from her body as if she'd tried to hide a broom handle beneath it.

She whimpered. Her arm jerked downward; so did the thing beneath her coat. A wet, sucking sound filled the air, and she staggered. The old man's cane clattered to the pavement.

Oh, Christ. Jack shoved his gun into his waistband and fell to his knees in front of her, opening her jacket. The creature had thrown the cane—had *impaled* her with it. Her hands were pressed over her stomach. Blood leaked between her fingers, shockingly red against her pale skin.

Jack raised his frantic gaze to her white face. "Annie—"

"I'm okay," she said through tight lips, then turned and began walking. "But we should get inside."

Astonished, Jack stood and stared after her, then down at the cane. Gore covered the smooth surface, from the flat tip to the U-shaped handle; the blood had smeared where she'd adjusted her grip to pull the length of it from her body.

She'd pulled it from her body. Yet she was steadier on her feet than Jack was.

Holy Christ. What the hell had happened to her in the past six years?

Jack almost shouted it after her retreating form, but stopped himself. Whatever had happened, she obviously needed help—not for him to become another problem.

He ripped his hands through his hair, tried to think over the questions screaming in his head. A flyer for a lost dog was stapled to a streetlight pole. Jack tore it down, then used it to pick up the cane by the bottom, ignoring the blood that soaked through the picture of Fido's cocked head and friendly expression.

So many missing, but no one had been looking for them— just covering up the disappearances. He'd resigned over it. Hell, it had been past time to resign. He'd been chasing ghosts for five years, risking his career, sleep, alienating more friends than he could count—and he hadn't cared, because Annie hadn't been there.

Everyone dead, she'd said. But she wasn't a ghost—and now he thought that all the answers he'd been seeking were in the one person he thought he'd lost.

THREE

"LET ME SEE, ANNIE."

Annie didn't respond, but kept walking through Jack's living room, heading for the hallway and the half-bath tucked beneath the stairs. Talking meant breathing, and breathing meant that she'd smell her blood.

Pain, exhaustion . . . bloodlust. She didn't want to deal with all of them, not at the same time, and definitely not when she was alone with Jack.

Pain and exhaustion were enough.

"Annie." There was steel in Jack's voice. "If you won't accept my help, your mother is only three blocks away. I'm sure she'd want to know that her daughter has a hole through her gut."

Annie stopped, turned to glare. His brows rose, and he returned her stare evenly, then opened his right palm in a gesture that said the ball was in her court, the decision hers. The cane dangled from his left hand, the tip wrapped in fluorescent green paper. Even with her speed, she had barely seen the movement the demon had made when he'd thrown it; it had been *so* fast, and his aim perfect. An inch to the left, and he'd have hit Jack.

How could a vampire defeat something like that, or defend those she loved against it? A lump of despair thickened her throat, and she looked away.

"Annie," Jack said, softly now. "Please."

She swallowed hard, nodded. His steps were light as he crossed the room. Cautious, but not for the right reasons—he probably didn't want to frighten her.

"I'll show you," she said with the last of the air in her lungs. "Just don't touch me."

Her blocks were up, her psychic shields tight, but she couldn't mistake the hurt that flashed across his expression—and she regretted causing it, regretted that it was necessary to protect herself.

She rolled the hem of her shirt up and, when he stumbled back a step, was glad she hadn't let him put his hands on her. A gentle touch would have been sweet, if painful; withdrawal was excruciating and bitter.

His mouth opened, but no sound came out. She looked down at the livid, puckered crater in her abdomen. The wound had closed and was no longer bleeding, but her tank and pants were sticky with it.

Jack pressed his fingers to his jaw, then his chest, as if he was convincing himself that he was there, that this was real. His shock smoothed into a flat, searching speculation. "I've either had too much to drink, or I shouldn't have traded my comic books for Ludlum and McBain when I was fifteen. What was it—gamma radiation? A radioactive spider?"

She inhaled; a wave of need swept through her. "No."

"But it was something."

Her fangs began to ache, and she said through clenched teeth, "Yes, but I can't . . . I can't—"

Oh, damn it. He smelled like lemon, whiskey, and healthy, red-blooded male—and he looked better than any man had a right to look. Like sunshine and home . . . like pulse-pounding, passion-drenched nights.

His gaze rose to her face, the speculation deepening, heating. Deliberately, he stepped closer.

Annie turned, lunged for the bathroom. She forced herself to stop with her hand on the knob. Bloodlust gripped her throat, her tongue, and the words were guttural. "I need clothes."

His voice low, he took another step. "I'll bring some—"

Closer. "Leave them outside the door," she ground out, and slammed through it.

Annie rinsed her top until the water ran clear, then moved on to her pants. The bloodlust slowly receded; hunger remained, though not as sharp or demanding.

But she still needed to feed. And she should probably tell Jack what she was, and that she'd broken into his house intending to suck his blood.

Knowing Jack, he'd offer it to her.

Knowing Jack. Above the sink, her reflection taunted her.

The medicine cabinet was a utilitarian metal rectangle with rusting hinges; the vanity's bright pink tile looked like a stomach-churning Pepto-Bismol accident.

Outdated, ugly. Nothing like the comfortable, homey loft apartment he'd owned in Old City. What the hell was he doing in a place like this? It didn't fit the Jack she'd known.

Annie met her eyes in the mirror, then looked away. There it was again: *the Jack she'd known.*

She'd been feeding off memories for so long . . . . *too* long. And the thought of real intimacy, of feeding from him now was an irresistible lure.

But he was as much a stranger as she was to him—and any connection she felt could easily end up being just another phantom.

Over her head, the stairs creaked as Jack came down from his bedroom. He rapped on the door a moment later.

"I've put a shirt, jeans, and shorts on the hall table." He'd raised his voice, likely thinking she couldn't hear him through the door and over the running water. "I ripped my last bra while I was pretending to be J. Edgar Hoover, but if you need the support I can lend a hand. Or two."

All right, so some things hadn't changed. Annie grinned, turned off the faucet, and tried not to imagine his palms cupping her breasts, his fingers teasing their peaks to aching hardness.

It didn't work. She shifted her weight to distract herself from the fluttering low in her belly, the tightening of her nipples.

That reaction wasn't bloodlust, and it wasn't just memory—though memory helped it along. Jack possessed a magician's touch, sensitive and skilled.

"Thank you, Director Hoover," she finally said.

"Is that a yes?"

"No."

He gave an exaggerated sigh of disappointment, then asked, "Cosmic rays?"

His voice was light, but when she reached out with her mind, his psychic scent was as sharp as her sword. His nonchalance acting as a cover for his burning curiosity—and a deep-seated anger.

Her smile faded, concealing her fangs. A twist of her

hands squeezed a flood of pink water from her pants. "No," she said softly.

THERE was no getting around it, so Annie didn't wait for him to ask. As soon as she stepped into the kitchen, she lifted the hem of the borrowed Eagles jersey to her ribs.

"So," she said, and the forced, cheery note in her voice made her want to cringe, "no need to call my mother."

Jack's gaze rose from the smooth skin at her waist to her face, and Annie closed her eyes against his expression. Half-rebuke, half-concern—and all seeing too much.

With a sigh, she sat at the small dining table. Jack turned back to the counter and the bubbling percolator. Coffee, Annie mused, was very likely the only thing that he made in this kitchen. His cupboards probably held a few boxes of cereal and a carton of Tastykakes. His refrigerator might contain take-out leftovers, and the bacteria count in his milk would put a petri dish at the CDC to shame.

Jack poured, set a steaming mug in front of her, and snagged the nearest chair. He'd put his shirt back on, but he must have been in a hurry: He'd buttoned it crookedly. "It's sweet, just as you like it," he said, and took a sip of his own. "But light would involve chunks. The milk's bad."

Something tightened in Annie's chest. She steadied her breathing.

"It's fine," she managed, wrapping her fingers around the cup. He was close. If he happened to touch her, she wanted her hands to be warm.

God, she wanted to be *touched*.

She met his eyes, hesitated. Where to begin?

Jack did, with a list of names. "Tanya Schiele," he said. Annie blinked, made a sound of disbelief; Jack held her gaze and continued, "And her husband, Daryl. Noah Schmidt and Natalie Ackerson. Lucy Chan, Daniel Fleming, and—" His mouth firmed and he squinted slightly, clearly searching for the name of the third member in the partnership.

"Leon Alvarez," she finished, her voice hoarse.

His nod was slow, but his heartbeat had sped up, his psychic scent a mixture of surprise and acceptance. He'd half-expected her to know them, she realized, but it had still shocked him when she did.

"Twenty-seven that I've been able to—" Something in her expression must have told him. Jack paused, then said carefully, "How many more?"

"Almost one hundred and thirty in all." A sizeable community, though nothing like those in the larger cities, or spread across Europe.

Though it didn't show, the same anger she'd felt from him earlier burned through his psychic scent again, made her head throb. Annie blocked as much as she could.

"All killed by that thing." It wasn't a question.

"Probably more than one," she said softly.

"But you escaped them?"

"I was in New York, on a job." Hired out as an enforcer, tracking down and slaying a rogue vampire. She wasn't ready to throw that at Jack yet. What was coming up would be enough. "And there were rumors flying around, about mass disappearances in D.C. and Berlin and Rome, and something in Seattle that didn't go down. So I stayed in New York an extra two days, keeping my ear to the ground, because in Philly we don't hear much. The community here is—*was*—isolated."

Annie shook her head when he opened his mouth. She'd have to explain that later. "The extra days saved my life. These things, they're called nephilim, and they're a type of demon. And they've been going into cities, and killing everyone . . . like me."

Her gaze never left his face as she watched him take that in. His expression didn't change, but he'd been resting his forearms on the table, mirroring her posture; now he sat back in his chair, tugging at his ear as he thought it over.

"Demons," he finally said.

"Yes."

"Killing people."

"Yes."

Eyes narrowing, he leaned forward again. "Like you."

Unable to hold that steady gaze, Annie looked down at her hands. Freckles still dusted her skin. After a few more years without sun, they'd fade completely.

"Jack—" God, she was floundering. She didn't know whether to start with the past or the present. Overwhelmed, she spread her palms; they were pink from the heat of the cup. "There's *so* much."

Jack studied her face. After a long moment, he nodded. "Start with Cricket. That's her legal name?"

He'd given her a reprieve, then—and the thought of Cricket steadied her. There were priorities, and dealing with her unsettled emotions was not the highest one.

"Yes. Her mother was a *The Young and the Restless* fan." Annie smiled slightly at his blank look. "Never mind. Her mother died about a year after I did, and guardianship passed to Cricket's sister, Christine, and her husband, Stephen."

Judging by the way Jack's voice softened, he didn't miss the hitch in her breath. "But now they're dead, too?"

"Yes."

"And they were also . . . like you?" His eyes were warm, filled with quiet humor.

Gratitude swelled beneath her grief, lightened it. Oh, thank God for Jack. Only he could make a game out of her reluctance to reveal what she was—taking the pressure off of her, as if she'd challenged him to discover the truth.

"Like me," she confirmed, then pushed away from the table. She couldn't sit. "I took those two days in New York, like I said. When I returned ten days ago, I could see that Cricket had been in my apartment, but I didn't think much of it. Not until I went to Christine and Stephen's later that night." She paced to the window above the sink, stared out over the little enclosed backyard.

"Did you find their bodies?"

Something in Jack's voice made her look over her shoulder, lift her psychic blocks. He didn't expect her to say yes . . . and he was right. "No. Stephen's sword was on the living room floor, a chair had been overturned, there was a little blood. Nothing else was disturbed. And when I went looking for Cricket, thinking she'd run to one of our friends' homes to hide, I found the same had happened to them. To everyone. And she hasn't tried to call me, so she must assume that I'm dead, too."

"But you think she'd been hiding at your place."

Annie nodded. "Something scared her off, though. Someone came in or—"

She stopped. God, this was stupid. Just stupid. She had a trained investigator in front of her, and they were sitting here discussing it in his kitchen.

"I could use another pair of eyes," she admitted. "I'm out of ideas. Maybe you'll see something I didn't."

Immediately, Jack rose to his feet. "I thought you'd never ask." His wide grin as he approached had her belly fluttering again, and she lifted her gaze from his mouth to his eyes. "And I'll also be trying to solve another mystery."

She pressed her lips together, torn between anxiety and amusement. "About people like me."

"That, too. But there's something else missing that I'd like to find." He flicked the tip of her chin with his forefinger. The laughter faded from his eyes, his voice. "Tell me, Annie: Where has your smile gone?"

FOUR

IF I SMILED, YOU'D SEE MY FANGS.

Annie had silenced herself before the automatic response escaped. As she waited for Jack to change his clothes, another reply rose in its place, just as honest as the first: There wasn't exactly much to smile about.

But she knew that hadn't been what he'd meant. And the truth was, she hadn't let herself show any strong emotions in years. There had been too much at risk, so she'd closed herself off.

Closed herself off, and lost almost everything to a threat she'd never seen coming.

Almost everything, but not quite. And so she could still smile a little.

Annie gathered her coat, the bag holding her wet clothes, and sword when she heard Jack returning downstairs.

He held her gaze as he crossed the room with that long, easygoing stride. Wearing jeans now, a black T-shirt, and a lightweight jacket—probably carrying a weapon beneath it.

The shadow of his beard was still a surprise, but Annie thought it fit him. For all of his family's money, for all of his grooming to look the part of a spit-shined federal agent, he hadn't appeared refined, but rough and masculine. Whether in jeans or one of his impeccably tailored suits, he'd always looked as if he'd be at home in a fisherman's village or striding across a moor.

And if she licked his jaw on her way down to his neck, it'd be as abrasive as a cat's tongue. She shivered and glanced away.

"You drive," Jack said, pitching his keys at her.

She'd caught them before she realized what he'd done. That hadn't been a slow toss, and her hands had been full. The speed with which she'd looped the scabbard cord over her shoulder and transferred the bag of clothes to her left hand must have seemed instantaneous.

She narrowed her eyes. "Sneaky, G-Man."

He was still chuckling as they reached his SUV. Annie wedged her sword between the front seats for easy access, tossed her jacket into the backseat with an audible thunk. Ignoring Jack's raised eyebrows, she pulled onto the street. In the rearview mirror, his garage door lowered, concealing another stack of boxes.

"Are you moving out?"

"No." With a slight grimace, Jack cranked down the heavy metal pounding from the speakers. His thinking music, he'd once called it, and he used it whenever he was stuck on a case. Emptying his head, and letting intuition make the leaps that logic couldn't. "I haven't unpacked."

"Just moved in, then," Annie murmured, but she was trying to make a leap, too. The music suggested that he'd been preoccupied with something even before she'd shown up—and he was aware people were missing, even if he didn't know the people were vampires. Had the FBI become involved somehow?

"A little over five years ago, shortly after my fiancée gave me back my ring," he said.

Annie's lungs seized up, and her gaze flew to his face. "What?"

"Didn't wait long, did I?" His tone was rueful, but his psychic scent had a layer of frustration over it. And regret. "The road, Annie."

"Yeah." She looked ahead, righted her steering before she broadsided a parked Buick, and forced a carefree note into her voice. "Not a long time, but, you know, whatever. It's not a big deal. When it happens, it happens. Lightning strikes, you get stars in your eyes. Not something you can help."

"Jesus, Annie." She heard the scrub of his hand over his face, but didn't let herself look. "That's not how it was. I—"

"I don't need to hear it." Didn't want to.

"Too fucking bad, because I intend to say it."

Shocked, Annie snatched a glance at him. Had his temper shortened, or had she just never provoked it before?

Before she could decide, Jack continued, "There was a spark. And I wasn't going to wait until she was in an accident, until I was at another funeral. Jenn moved in a week after we began dating. Got a ring within two weeks. We thought about buying a house, and I suggested we look out here in Mayfair, for a place we could fix up together, start a family. Then we ran into your mother, and Jenn figured it out about the same time that I did. Jenn didn't look a thing like you, but she was a nurse, had a big heart, a huge smile. I gave her the loft in Old City, then bought the house we'd been looking at. I never unpacked because I thought I'd move on." His fist had been clenched on his thigh; as he spoke, it slowly relaxed. "There's been a spark here and there, Annie, and God knows I didn't wait for it to burn out—but lightning's only struck me once."

Her heart was in her throat, her fingers tight on the wheel. "Jack—"

"Don't." He shook his head. "Don't say anything yet. Wait until you've had a chance to sit on it." A wry smile lifted the corners of his mouth. "And I'm not half-drunk."

"All right." God. Shame and apology had lurked beneath his speech. For unwittingly using another woman as a replacement, or because he'd been with someone else? "Just don't be sorry, okay? Not on my behalf, anyway."

What would he think when he figured out what she was? What *she'd* done?

She felt him study her face before he said, "So long as you aren't sorry, too."

A glance confirmed that he'd been watching her, his expression grave. "I'll try," she said, then sighed and returned her attention to the road.

To her surprise, despite everything left unsaid, the silence that fell between them was comfortable. But it had always been so with them, hadn't it?

And the silences had never been empty. Like now, there were his hands to think about, his lips to consider, his clean, masculine scent to draw in deep. And in that last, incredible month, their silences had been filled with breathless kisses, the slide of fingers over skin, the heat of his mouth.

Damn it, damn it. The bloodlust flared, and Annie stopped breathing. Not that it helped—Jack's presence couldn't be denied by refusing to smell or look at him. And she couldn't ignore the sharp interest in his psychic scent, the flavors of it; curiosity and male awareness formed a potent, shield-penetrating combination.

Sweat trickled down the back of her neck. The silence was no longer comfortable, but simmering.

"Tell me, Annie," Jack said. He ran his fingers down the leather-wrapped handle of her sword. "What does a person *like you* do?"

"What most people do. Try to hold a job, try to have a life outside of one."

"So you work?" Metal sang as he pulled the blade half out of its scabbard and examined the edge.

"Yes." She couldn't resist adding, "Nights."

"In medicine?" He tugged the sword higher, lifted his brows. "Surgery?"

She suppressed her grin. "No. Although when I can, I volunteer at the Lady of Mercy." Donating time, and as much blood as she could afford to give.

"The urgent care clinic in West Philly?" His eyes narrowed when she nodded. "They've got a remarkable reputation. Normal rate of success and recovery for nonlife-threatening wounds. But for GSWs, stabbings, vehicular accidents—which a clinic usually doesn't even handle—the mortality rates are half that of a well-equipped hospital."

"That's what happens when you've got a bunch of nuns praying next door." Vampire blood couldn't perform miracles, but it accelerated healing, and a transfusion temporarily strengthened the recipient. "How do you know what kind of reputation an inner-city clinic has?"

"It's all part of the job."

She glanced over, caught the sardonic edge of his smile. Yes, she thought. Somehow, the FBI had become aware of the vampire community. They might not know what they were looking at, but they must know it was unusual.

"Investigating miracles, G-Man?"

"Only on a volunteer basis." His gaze fell to her waist as if he could see through the jersey to the healed skin beneath, then he nodded at the blade. "And when you aren't helping the nuns' prayers along, Annie, are you using *this* on demons?"

"No. I wouldn't have a chance against one."

Uneasy with the direction he was taking, she cupped her palm over the butt of the sword handle. Jack didn't offer any resistance; he let go, his fingers dancing lightly over her wrist as she pushed it into its sheath.

A simple touch, and need sizzled, burned, from her fangs to her womb.

Shivering, she pulled her hand away, fisted it against the steering wheel. Her head began aching again; raising her psychic blocks didn't help.

With a frown, Jack lowered the air-conditioning, then shifted toward her. "Annie—"

"I use it on people like me," she interrupted flatly. She hadn't wanted to frighten him, was hoping that when he figured it out, he wouldn't see her as evil, as damned—now she was afraid he'd cast her in the role of a saint. "If they break the community's rules, I hunt them down, then cut through their heart or take their head. And I'm paid well for using that sword, Jack. I'm good at it. Better than I ever was with a scalpel."

Jack was silent for a long minute. "And a bullet wouldn't do the job," he finally said, apparently recalling the shot she'd fired into the demon's forehead.

"A bullet works better on people like me than one of the nephilim. One in my body would slow me down, one in my brain will drop me to the ground. I'd probably look dead for a few minutes. Then I'd get up."

A muscle in his jaw flexed. "You've gotten up."

Remembered pain rose like bile through her voice. "Twice." And the first time had been the worst.

Without a word, Jack slid his hand over her knee, squeezed. A warm touch, one she knew wasn't meant to arouse, but the bloodlust roared through her.

God, there were times she hated it. Hated how it overwhelmed every other emotion, how it took away choice. Unless it had been satisfied, it reduced everything to fucking and feeding.

She battled the hunger, trying to hold on to the comfort he offered—and knowing that the bloodlust meant she wouldn't be able to hold on to him. Not for long.

And he needed to know that the changes in her weren't just surface, weren't just about speed, strength, or hair color.

"That's where it went," she told him. "I'm not the one with the big heart and smile anymore."

"All right, Annie." Another squeeze, and his hand fell away from her knee. She was wrestling with her disappointment when he added, "You're heading for Center City. You live downtown?"

"Yeah. It's convenient."

His laugh was short, disbelieving. "Convenient? What neighborhood?"

She shrugged her shoulders.

"Annie," he said softly.

She clenched her teeth, then admitted, "Old City. About three blocks from your place."

"Jenn's."

"Whatever." She glanced at him, but Jack wasn't watching her as she'd expected. His eyes were closed and he'd tilted his head back against the headrest, looking as if he intended to nap—except for the grin widening his lips.

His position exposed his throat. She swallowed hard.

"Annie."

Her response was a low growl.

His brows rose, but he continued in a matter-of-fact tone, "As soon as I'm not half-drunk, I plan to kiss the hell out of you." Without opening his eyes, without losing his grin, he added, "The road, Annie."

Shit. She straightened the steering wheel, managed, "I'll be moving as soon as I find Cricket. I can't stay in Philly."

"Moving on." He lifted his head, met her gaze. "I've recently decided that it's time to do the same."

FIVE

ANNIE'S BUILDING WAS A NEWER HIGH-RISE, METAL and glass—the kind Jack's father would have called an Old City eyesore and an insult to the city's history. He'd spent considerable rage and money trying to block the construction of any structure that the Founding Fathers wouldn't have built themselves.

But the old man had raged himself into an early grave, and Jack liked the contrast of old stone and modern steel—the city, moving on.

It was going around.

Six years ago, Annie living in a place like this would have surprised him; it was too expensive, and too sleek, cold. But the widening of the doorman's eyes as he took in Annie's jersey and loose, faded jeans told Jack that sporty and casual wasn't her typical look anymore, either.

"It's the security," Annie murmured as they crossed the lobby toward the elevators. Jack frowned, and she glanced at him. "That's why I'm here. They couldn't stop a demon, and they're not so good that I can't sneak a sword in under my jacket—" She gestured with the coat she'd folded over her forearm. "—but because a human probably won't break in while I'm sleeping. And the fireproofing and extinguishing systems are top of the line."

Security reasons, he could believe, particularly after she'd described her job. But was she serious about the last part? That tiny smile was playing around her mouth, and Jack couldn't decide.

He followed her into the elevator and studied the set of her shoulders as she punched the button for the top floor. The doors slid closed, her features reflected in the mirrored panels.

Sweet Jesus, but hers was a face that haunted a man. Beautiful, unforgettable. He could look at her forever and never tire of the soft curve of her lips, the stubborn angle of her jaw, the glacial clarity in her eyes.

Her gaze met his. Awareness snapped between them, bringing his cock to instant, aching hardness. She lowered her lashes, hiding her expression—but he saw the raw need and the way she fought it: her mouth flattening, her fists clenching.

The hairs on his arms rose. His breath quickened.

Not just the clothes, the sword, the smile. Something else had changed within her, and it was hungry. Dangerous enough that Jack could readily accept that those who couldn't—or wouldn't—control it had to be hunted and killed.

It didn't strike him as human, yet it was nothing like the alien horror of the demon, wasn't frightening. There was no room for fear when his instincts were telling him to hunt, capture, hold.

And do whatever it took to keep.

"Annie," he said quietly, and stepped closer. "Don't move."

She didn't, except to look up, watching him in the mirror. Her body was rigid. If he hadn't recognized the hunger within her, he'd have thought it was the petrified stance of a doe or rabbit preventing herself from running, instead of a predator holding herself back.

He lowered his mouth, let it hover above the bare skin of her nape. Was it difficult for her to stand so still, exposed and vulnerable? He listened for the rush of her breath, but heard nothing.

Only his own.

But she shuddered as his palms curved around her waist. Beneath the jersey, her muscles were taut.

"You're still half-drunk, G-Man."

Remembering his promise to kiss her, he laughed softly, felt her shiver when his exhalation skimmed her neck. "Not half. Only about one-quarter now."

"That makes all the difference." But even as she rolled her eyes, she tilted her head to the side, allowing him easier access. His hands slid higher, and he almost groaned. Her nipples were hard.

So was he. Christ, like a stone. And being a quarter drunk probably did make all the difference. If not for the alcohol dulling the edge of his arousal, he might have come just from the perfect weight of her breasts filling his palms, the thundering race of her heart.

Annie. The sweet scent of her shampoo made his head swim. His thumbs flicked; she sagged back against him. He pressed his lips to the soft skin below her ear.

And froze.

His gaze met hers in the mirror. A long second passed, broken by the chime of the elevator, the doors sliding open.

Annie strode out of his embrace without looking back.

SHE'D looked back once before, in the form of a single phone call that had been a good-bye, and it had torn her apart. Six years ago, Jack hadn't known what he'd heard—but he realized it now.

Gallagher had been the one to contact Jack the morning after her father's heart attack. And although Jack had spent the day trying to get a hold of her, Annie hadn't returned his call until after night had fallen.

Her fractured sobs had brought him to his knees, and her refusal to let him come to her had left him feeling lost, useless. He'd thought her repeated apology—*I'm sorry, Jack, I'm so sorry*—had been for shutting him out.

It *had* hurt that she hadn't wanted to lean on him, but he'd fought his resentment, knowing it was out of place in the face of her grief. And a day later, when Gallagher told him she'd been killed in an accident, Jack's only emotion beneath the agony of loss had been the relief that his resentment had remained silent. That the last time he'd spoken to her, it had been words of love and support.

But maybe it would have been easier for Annie if she had walked away with anger at her back. Easier if she'd thought there was nothing to come back for.

Jack had regrets—God knew he had them. He'd second-guessed himself thousands of times: What if he hadn't agreed to give her time, had pushed his way into her grief, had stayed so close that he'd have been driving the car? But never had he imagined that she'd been out there, alive. If he had, nothing on Earth could have prevented him from going to her.

And knowing Annie, nothing on Earth could have prevented her from returning to him.

But demons might have . . . or a being with cold, pale skin, who wouldn't need to breathe during a minute-long elevator ride.

What if her *sorry* hadn't been for shutting him out, but because she'd been forced to leave him behind?

Shaken by the onslaught of memories, by the new, unsettling notion of what Annie might be, Jack joined her at the door to her apartment. Her head was down, and she fumbled through the pockets of her coat, producing a key. Wordlessly, he took it from her trembling fingers, let his hand linger against her cooler one.

His gaze fell to her mouth. If she happened to smile, if he kissed her, what would he find there? He suspected he knew.

But he wasn't sure he'd convinced himself of it yet, couldn't make it feel *real*. And judging by Annie's reaction, she wasn't prepared for him to know, either.

A few hours wouldn't hurt, and would give each of them time to steady.

With effort, Jack forced his contemplation of cold skin and reflections to the back of his mind, and switched gears.

"She had her own key?" he asked. When Annie blinked up at him, he prompted, "Cricket?"

"Yes." And in the space of a word, her expression changed. Gone was the hesitancy; her gaze flattened and cooled. "She has permission to come up even if I'm not available to clear her through. Security has a video of her entering from street level at oh-three hundred hours on the twenty-sixth of June. She exited, running, just after fifteen hundred hours on the twenty-eighth, carrying her backpack—which was holding, I believe, ten thousand dollars cash and two firearms."

His brows rose, but Jack didn't question that as he followed her through the door. Her apartment was spacious. Clean and simple, with low, cushioned furniture and teak cabinetry. "Have all nonresident visitors to the building been accounted for, the times verified with residents?"

Annie nodded. "I knocked on doors."

"Neighbors?"

"There are four penthouses; only three are occupied,

including mine. Northeast corner is a dickhead broker; he's seen nothing. Probably because his head's up his ass." They shared a look. That tiny smile flashed, then she continued, "The Carlsons are in Europe. I've checked theirs and the vacancy. There's no evidence that she's been in either."

"Access to the floor?"

"The elevator, two stairwells, and . . . out there."

Absently tugging at his ear, Jack walked over to the sheet of windows and the glass doors that led out to the wide rooftop balcony—and remembered an impression of glowing eyes, crimson skin.

"It had wings," he said.

Annie slung her coat over the frame of a shoji screen, then stepped behind it. A dragon with jade and gold scales snaked across the folding panels. "Yes. The transformation was quick; I wasn't sure if you'd seen it."

He hadn't been certain, either. "You're assuming that someone came in, spooked her, and she ran. Why couldn't it have been a phone call?"

"Her cell is still at Christine and Stephen's," Annie said as he rounded the screen. A cabinet full of weaponry was open in front of her; she reached up, laid her sheathed sword across two wooden pegs. "I've got nothing listed on my caller ID, and the redial is still my mother's number. Cricket doesn't know about Mom."

Her holster was next. Jack stopped her before she put it away; frowning, he ran his fingers over the shiny, cracked surface of the leather. The opposite side—the side that wouldn't rest against her back—was smooth, supple.

A soft, sad smile touched her mouth. "Dad gave this to me on my fourteenth birthday—my first gun. Back then, he still intended to make a cop of me. I've kept the holster in good condition, but the last ten days . . ." She sighed, hung it on another peg. "I sweat too much."

She wasn't sweating now—but the air-conditioning was cranked so high that Jack was glad he'd worn his jacket. Pushing his hands into his pockets, he studied the cabinet. She'd already replaced the SIG, but there were still several empty pegs.

"The guns and the money came from here?"

"Yes. She could have grabbed them on her way out." She

closed it. No lock, he noted. Dangerous with a kid around . . . unless the kid might need quick access to it, as well.

"You planned for this," he realized. "Not just defense, but escape. And you included her, prepared her."

"Not *this*, exactly. I didn't know about the nephilim until New York." She dug a pouch from her jacket, then passed him in a blur. A second later, she strode from the hallway into the kitchen. "We have to be careful of demons—but as a human, Cricket didn't have to fear any would hurt her. Anyway, they generally leave us alone." A shadow crossed her face. "Generally."

"Then it was a precaution against other people like you." A drinking glass was in the sink, a spoon and bowl. He opened the freezer, saw the chocolate chip ice cream that matched the dried residue at the bottom of the bowl. The fridge was empty. "The dishes were hers?"

"Yes. I haven't taken time to clean."

And hadn't eaten here in ten days. "Don't start now."

She nodded, then crossed her arms and leaned back against the counter. "And you're right: It's because of people like me. The community elders—we called them The Five—could be unreasonable when it came to certain matters, and any act that might expose the community was at the top of their list."

And dead humans would risk exposure. "Hence, your work," Jack guessed, stepping around the center island to glance into the garbage. The contents resembled his own: Tastykake wrappers, an empty cereal box, several clear plastic bags that looked like—

His stomach lurched. Units of blood. Not so much like his, then.

Refusing to let his instinctive revulsion show, he tamped it down and continued on to the pantry. Snack food, but nothing substantial; just items that Annie probably had on hand if Cricket showed up.

But Annie didn't have any blood on hand. And she had a reflection.

Maybe he'd come to the wrong conclusion—and hadn't it been an insane conclusion in the first place? He could have misinterpreted everything: the lack of food, the plastic bags, the rapid healing, her pale and cold skin, her speed, the new pout to her lips.

That was a shitload of evidence to misinterpret.

"Yes," she said slowly, and he turned to find her standing by the trash bin, staring down at the contents. "And due to the nature of my work, I risk exposure—and risked angering The Five—more than most."

Her face was expressionless when she glanced back up, but her gaze hesitated at his neck before she met his eyes, and Jack had to pretend that his heart wasn't pounding, that his knees didn't feel as if a mad scientist had been at them with a quart of novocaine and a blunt hammer.

She'd broken into his house to drink his blood.

Holy Christ. *Welcome to reality, Jack.*

"I also risk those close to me." She spoke calmly, but there was fear in the way she stood so still. No longer the hunter holding herself back, but a woman expecting a blow—and he realized that if he didn't step carefully here, it was Annie who risked being hurt. "And I appreciate you offering to help, but if you are disgusted or scared—"

"Annie, please. Disgusted? *Scared?*" He put a fair amount of sneer into the word. "I'm Special Agent Jack Harrington, FBI."

Her lips twitched, but her gaze remained clear and steady. "If anything you discover about people like me bothers you, I wouldn't think less of you for leaving."

Did it? Maybe it should, but right now the image of her feeding wasn't *bothering* him. No, the memory of how she'd climbed into his bed produced a much different response.

Which meant that he could be sick or perverted—or still completely messed up over her.

"Did you hear those three letters, darling? F—B—I." Jack stalked toward her, put a swagger into it; he'd have flashed his badge if he'd still had one. When her shoulders began shaking, he maneuvered close and pushed his advantage. "That's 'Fucking Balls of Iron' to people like you. You could ram your knee into my dick and it'd just ring like the Liberty Bell."

It began as he'd expected it would, with a snicker that she tried to suppress. Then she grabbed the edges of his jacket and pressed her forehead to the base of his throat, hiding her face, laughing wildly.

Jack grinned in response. God, that was familiar and sweet.

A deep, uncontrollable laugh, the type he knew would continue on, bubbling up again before she could stop it.

But his grin lasted less than a second. Then his heart expanded, filled his chest with unbearable pressure. *Annie, Annie, Annie.* His eyes closed, his arms enfolded her against him.

He was holding her again.

It didn't matter how this miracle had happened. Only that it had. And he wouldn't let her go.

His embrace tightened, but his joy and wonder slid away as her shakes became shudders, her sobs as deep and uncontrollable as her laughter had been.

He waited it out with an aching chest and a thick throat. Jack Harrington, formerly of the FBI—unable to do anything but listen to her cry.

"Annie," he whispered into her hair when it finally subsided, but he didn't have anything to say except her name again. "Annie."

"God, Jack." Her voice was small, muffled against his shirt, and he had to strain to hear. "Ten days, I've been walking through this city. And no one knew. One hundred and thirty of us, gone, murdered, and no one knew. No one grieved, or wondered, as if we'd never been real, as if we never existed. As if we never loved, never had families. All of us, just phantoms."

And he knew who to blame for that. Jack stared over her head, his jaw set.

"And then there you were." She drew back, pushing the moisture from her cheeks with the heels of her hands. No red eyes or nose; if anything, she was paler than before. "Of all people, it was you."

He framed her face with his hands. Cool skin, cold tears against his palms. "We'll find Cricket. And we'll make the rest of it right."

Six

Annie led Jack to the bedroom Cricket had used, grateful of the opportunity to compose herself. How long had that been building up inside her? She didn't know, hadn't expected it, yet she couldn't summon any embarrassment for breaking down.

Even shared, the weight of one hundred and thirty lives was heavy—but it was easier to bear.

And maybe, for the first time since she'd returned from New York, the dreams in her daysleep wouldn't amplify that weight into a mountain.

Her daysleep. *Damn it.*

"Jack."

His expression was distracted as he glanced up from the bureau drawer he'd opened—the one that still contained the change of clothing Cricket had brought. "She as crazy about clothes as some girls?"

"Yeah. Maybe more than some." Cricket didn't have many connections with kids her age; those she did, she worked as hard as she could.

"But she didn't grab these before running." He nodded slowly, stood up. "There's nothing wrong with your eyes, Annie, nothing I can see you missed. All signs point to someone coming in."

That was what she'd hoped *not* to hear. "Someone I can't smell."

"That you can't . . ." He shook his head. "What?"

"You, people like me, even the old guy tonight—we all have a scent. His was human. And waffle-y."

His brows shot up. "He smelled like a waffle?"

"Not exactly. But kind of buttery, syrupy." She averted her face when he began to grin, and tried to tame her own. He'd probably only thought that was funny because he was punch-drunk tired, but God, he turned her insides to jelly.

"My point is, I can tell when someone has been in my house. And demons—the other kind, not like the old guy—don't have a scent."

Jack pulled his hand through his hair, let it fall back to his side. "Shit."

A check of the clock told her only thirty minutes remained until sunrise. Annie was starving, but it'd have to wait until tomorrow.

"I'm going to crash pretty soon, Jack. I'll be out all day. Is there anything you need before then?"

"A picture, if you have one. Names of her friends or classmates— Why are you shaking your head?"

"Come this way." As they walked to her bedroom, Annie explained, "I don't know of anyone she's close to—and she's homeschooled."

"You disapprove?"

Had he picked up on that note in her voice so easily? "Not in theory. And I understand the reasons behind it: Christine's and Stephen's schedules made it impossible to look out for her during the day."

"But?"

"It's no life for a kid. And Cricket has adjusted to our patterns, looks out for herself pretty well, but . . ." She trailed off with a sigh and a lift of her hands. "She doesn't sleep as long as we do, especially in the summer, so she has to occupy herself for stretches of time. She isn't allowed to go out. And even with movies, books, video games—it's got to be lonely."

And Jack, she thought, would know that better than most. She remembered that he'd told her the same of his own childhood: He'd had everything a kid could want, but was still isolated, lonely.

"Yes," he agreed. "What will you do when you find her?"

Her laugh was short and humorless; she didn't like to think beyond finding Cricket. "I have no idea. Probably the same thing. Until she's a little older, I don't know what else to do. I don't even know what *my* situation will be."

His curiosity filled his psychic scent, but he didn't give voice to his question. She didn't want to explain it yet, anyway. Didn't want to tell him she would have to find a vampire to feed from—and do everything demanded by the blood-lust.

She avoided looking at the curtained bed against the far wall of her room. The picture she wanted was on her vanity. After sliding the photo from the frame, she turned and met Jack's eyes.

"This is from last Halloween, at Eastern State Penitentiary's annual scare-fest. She's not wearing makeup or a wig; just the fangs are fake."

She didn't say anything about her own, and knew his gaze skipped over Cricket's brown, curly hair, the cute face shedding the last of its baby fat, to Annie's wide smile.

When he didn't respond, she cleared her throat and added, "We, uh, try to do a lot of those things. Movies, events at all of the historic sites—the prison's her favorite. We'd planned to do the Bastille Day one this weekend. I've been through the penitentiary three times with her, that twilight tour they do—not to mention visiting every supposedly haunted house in the area."

"I've done the same," he said quietly, and pocketed the photo. "She's alone much of the time. What about e-mail, MySpace? Online friends?"

Annie blinked, shook her head. "I don't know. She has a computer in her room. I didn't think to check it."

"We'll pick it up tonight, have a look around their place. After you wake up."

She didn't miss the emphasis he put on the last. Swallowing down the vestiges of panic, she jerked her thumb toward her bathroom. "I have to get ready for bed, then . . ." Ah, screw it. "You must have worked it out by now."

She loved his broad smile, the teasing glint of his eyes—loved them even more for appearing *now*. "I think so."

"And it doesn't frighten you?" she asked, then waved off whatever answer he'd have made. The important thing was, he hadn't already pulled his gun on her. "Never mind. Balls of iron, all of that."

"Yeah." He hesitated for an instant. "About that, Annie."

"What? No ding-dong?" When he grimaced and laughed, she tilted her head at the bathroom door. "Come in and tell me, Jack. And I want to hear how you knew about Tanya, Daryl, and the others—but we don't have much time."

* * *

HE'D resigned from the Bureau.

At her sink, Annie slowly rinsed cleanser from her face, trying to absorb the news.

It was the one thing she'd never expected him to say. In his way, Jack had been as driven as Annie. He'd once told her the FBI had figured into his plans since his teens—the ironic consequence of his father leaving him alone with super-heroes, detectives, and spies for company while the old man tended to business. And although his father had clearly believed Jack would abandon the FBI and take over the reins when he'd made Jack the sole beneficiary in his will, Jack had simply sold off stock and most of his properties to more interested parties, and carried on as he'd begun.

She'd never thought he'd give up his career—and she'd never have asked him to, any more than she'd have asked him to remove his own arm. But if she had . . .

God, what if she had?

Swallowing against the ache in her throat, Annie patted her face dry and sank down onto the gold brocade chaise tucked in the corner. On the sill beside the oversized claw-foot tub, candles sat in hardened pools of wax. Plate-glass windows overlooked the balcony, and a dark slice of the Delaware River showed through two buildings nearer the shore.

The bathroom was extravagant, but this was the one place she allowed herself to slow down, to linger.

And it was where she'd spent so many hours dreaming of what might have been. Remembering Jack's touch, his mouth, the easy perfection of every minute she'd spent with him. Her fingers and imagination had been poor substitutes—and though she'd treasured every friendship she'd had in the past six years, safety had demanded that she maintain a certain distance.

Safety. No, even if she'd known he'd eventually leave the FBI, her choices wouldn't have been different. Jack's dedication to his job wasn't the only reason she hadn't gone to him the night after she'd been transformed. It wasn't the only reason she'd stayed away in the years following.

"It doesn't mean I can't help you find Cricket, Annie."

Startled, she glanced at Jack through wet lashes. He'd braced his shoulders against the linen closet door, crossed his arms over his chest. His stiff tone suggested he'd taken her extended silence as disappointment.

"It's not that. I'm just surprised." She tugged the elastic from her hair, absently ran her fingers through the tangles. "It was voluntary?"

"Yes." Jack crossed the room, sat beside her. "I wasn't asked for my resignation—but by then it was a relief to my superiors. And to Gallagher."

She tried not to gape. The poster boy had become a problem? "Why? What happened?"

"According to your sources, the nephilim happened."

That was too recent. He'd said *by then*. "No, I meant—"

"What led up to it?" At her nod, he agreed, "I'll start at the beginning then. In any case, it's all related."

Her brow furrowed. "To the nephilim?"

"Apparently." He bumped her thigh with his, and a hint of his teasing grin reappeared. "This could take a couple of minutes. We should get comfortable first. Hold on."

She let herself relax when his arm came around her waist, allowed him to turn her until they were both reclining on the chaise, facing each other with the crook of his elbow pillowing her head.

Jack couldn't really be comfortable, not with his jacket on and his weapon under it—but neither his psychic scent nor his expression suggested that he was in a hurry to move.

Neither was Annie. And the bloodlust burned, but even if it consumed her whole, left her weak and starving, she wouldn't ruin this moment.

"Can you light those candles with your mind?"

She blinked; then a laugh shook through her. "I wish. Why?"

"For atmosphere." He paused. "And I saw it at a séance once."

He'd attended a séance? "It was probably a parlor trick." Impatient, she prodded his ribs with her forefinger. "Talk, G-Man."

"Five years ago—the same month Jenn and I separated— Gallagher and I got a line on a guy who'd been forging IDs. And feeling it out, we ran across what initially looked like a racketeering operation."

"Organized crime?"

"Yes. Payouts to a circle of individuals in return for protection." Jack shifted a little, as if settling in, and managed to pull her closer. Always sneaky. "Then one morning the guy washed up in the Delaware with a couple of holes in him—"

"Bullet holes?" And human, if his body hadn't disintegrated in the sun.

"His throat cut open to his spine, and stab wounds to his heart from a dagger or similar blade." Jack's gaze dropped to her mouth. "No unexplained injuries. And that's when an occult specialist out of the San Francisco office showed up. What we had, she said, wasn't mob activity at all, but a Satanic cult. She had files—other cases she'd worked—and comparable evidence to back it up."

"So you let her in on the investigation."

He nodded. "Partly as a courtesy, and partly because it was her area of expertise. Her record spoke for itself. She knew her shit, and neither Gallagher nor I were going to waste a resource like her. Lily Milton."

He spoke the name with the bemused tone of a man wondering, in hindsight, how he hadn't seen the snake coiled beneath a rock until it bit him.

Then his eyes met hers again, and he smiled. "You remind me of her. Especially now."

Annie shot up to her elbow. "What?"

Her eyes narrowed when his smile widened. "You're thinking there was a spark. Nothing like that. I wasn't interested in being interested, and she once said that Boy Scouts like me were the first to stab a woman through the heart."

"And how, exactly, is that like me?" Annie asked in a dangerously low tone, tracing her finger in an X over his chest. His heart was pounding beneath her fingertip, in her ears. "I've got a soft spot for good boys."

Jack made a rough noise and grabbed her hand, held it still. "I thought I did for good girls, but Jesus, Annie, this dark side of yours does it for me, too. I don't have a single soft spot on me right now." He stared at her for a long second; then, with a slight groan, he focused over her head. "I have no doubt that if Agent Milton expended a little effort, she could have any man on his knees and begging. Probably for a riding crop on his ass."

Annie sputtered into laughter. "Well, now—"

"You wouldn't have to expend any effort."

Something inside her melted. As cover, she made a show of glancing around. "The lack of men on their knees and begging for a whip suggests otherwise."

"Maybe it's just me, then."

He looked at her again, his gaze dark with need, and she dropped her head to his shoulder. Her hand flattened over his heart; her breath fluttered over his pulse. The bloodlust raged.

After a moment, he cleared his throat. "As I was saying, you both have a way of moving that suggests power beneath it—and not just physical. I used to watch you in the ER, Annie. It was chaos, but as soon as you stood over a patient, everyone fell into line around you, began controlling it. With Milton, you just wondered who she'd pissed off, keeping her in the field instead of in charge of an office. The difference is, you work with people; you don't bump heads. She's the type who does."

"She bumped yours?"

"No. Gallagher's. She started talking about some of her cases, demons and . . . vampires, like they were real. Only, she did it with this little smile. So I thought she was pulling his leg—and when she saw that it was pissing him off, she pulled it harder."

"Oh," Annie realized quietly. "She knew. And she knew Brian did, too."

"Obvious now, right? And I'll admit she had me half-convinced, enough that I started asking a few different questions, looking at different angles. Not expecting to find anything—except people who *thought* they were connected to some bloodsucking demon god."

"Did you find anything?"

"No. Practically overnight, every single person in that payout circle disappeared. So did everyone linking us to the circle. In her report to our SAIC, Agent Milton gave the opinion that they'd run to another city—that the lack of finesse during our initial inquiries tipped them off to our interest. Furthermore, that the speed of the investigation had been hindered by my pursuing leads of a *fantastical* nature."

The load of bitterness behind the word told Annie that was exactly how Agent Milton had phrased it, but she couldn't focus on the implications of it. Her stomach had condensed into a lump of dread.

Five years ago. *Every single person in that payout circle disappeared.*

Oh, God. Annie knew what had happened to them. She'd been there.

"Annie?"

She swallowed, sat up, and swung her legs to the floor. Lowered her head into her hands. "I'm fine. What happened then?"

"What you'd expect," he said slowly, then rose to his feet. "It leaked out. Mostly just ribbing, but Gallagher . . . Gallagher said he couldn't believe I'd fallen for her line of bullshit." He sighed. "I hadn't, but she was as clever with how she'd worded and presented her report as she had been with everything else. And it wasn't long before I was proving her right."

Hands in pockets, he walked to the window, stood looking out. Annie couldn't; the pale light in the sky pricked at her eyes. Sunrise was minutes away.

There was so much to ask—but time demanded that she jump to the end. "How does this relate to the nephilim?"

"Not the nephilim," Jack said. "The cover-up. One hundred and thirty people disappear at once—jobs, homes suddenly abandoned—but no one notices?" She squinted over at him, saw him shaking his head. "I only caught on to it when one of my property managers called me. I kept a few of my dad's buildings; this was in Kensington. The door left open, signs of a struggle. So I checked with the occupants' references, and found the same thing at their house. And so on. I opened a case file."

His footsteps alerted Annie to his approach before he sank on his heels in front of her. "Within a day, Annie, it was taken out of my hands."

But who—? Oh. "Agent Milton again?"

"Yes. Under a new division of Homeland Security—and with enough power to take over the investigation. And those disappearances I knew about were suddenly being explained: sick relatives, accidents, better jobs or apartments . . ." He trailed off, his eyes unfocused and his anger radiating off him like waves of heat. "One hundred and thirty lives erased. The

Bureau didn't put up any resistance, and Gallagher was happy
to let it go."

The sick ball of dread in her stomach tightened. Annie
scrubbed her palms over her face, wondering if she could ever
explain her response.

Probably not. But it had to be said.

"It was the right thing to do, Jack."

He rocked back a little, his baffled gaze searching her
face. What he saw there hardened his jaw. "You don't mean
my resigning," he said flatly.

"Maybe that, too." She swallowed, got to her feet. He rose,
smooth and quick. "But what Milton did—it was right."

"How, Annie?"

Despite his confusion and anger, his question was controlled; she couldn't do the same. She pushed past him, seeking distance.

He came after her. "How, Annie? You tell me that 'people
like you' are just like everyone else, with jobs and family.
They aren't soldiers. They aren't agents. They haven't signed
over their lives in the name of national security, to be swept
under a goddamn government rug. You cried in my arms because no one knew they'd died. Yet it's *right*? Fuck that."

"And what would you do, Jack?" Her teeth were clenched;
it was little better than a growl. She ripped aside the curtains
surrounding her bed, hating them suddenly. Gaudy. Stupid
and gaudy and *embarrassing* to need a bed with jade satin
curtains. "Expose us? Let everyone know we're here?"

"Who is here?" He flung his hands wide with a hard, disbelieving laugh. "Who is left to expose? Everyone but you is
dead, Annie. You've said these demons can't hurt humans.
Couldn't we have offered some protection? Prevented it? Or at
the very least, if we'd known what was happening, then people like you might have, too—and prepared for it."

She yanked off her boot, threw it across the room. "And
what about protection from people like you?"

"Like me? Humans?"

"Yes," she snapped, and the second boot made a matching
dent in the wall.

His silence was sudden and cold.

Oh, Jesus. Annie turned, faced him. He'd closed himself

off somehow, raised emotional shields. But she could read his expression. Could see the bleakness there.

"I don't—" The words stumbled. She brought her fingers to her lips, as if she could drag them out by force. "I don't mean *you*. Not personally."

"No?" He stalked toward her, his gaze hot upon hers. "Tell me, Annie—why didn't you come to me six years ago? Did you think I'd hurt you?"

She snorted. "What—afraid that you'd pull out a stake? Whatever."

His mouth tightened, but he didn't answer—just kept coming. Wondering if she'd back up? To test the truth of it, to see if she *was* afraid?

She wasn't. Not of him. Not now.

Her hands curled in denial. She closed her eyes when he stopped in front of her, avoiding that intent gaze, trying to suppress the bloodlust it stirred. "Maybe a little," she admitted. "But it was more than that. And everything was . . . confusing."

God, what a weak word for the turmoil she'd gone through. The painful riot of emotion.

Her eyes flew open when she felt his hands at the hem of her shirt. "What are you doing?"

"Taking back what's mine." His voice was rough, but his movement smooth as he tugged the jersey up and over her head. A second later, he was shoving the jeans she'd borrowed over her hips.

Almost naked—and hungry.

Annie crossed her arms over her breasts, excited, terrified. "Bad idea, Jack."

But it was too late to go anywhere. And she didn't want to run from him. Didn't want to fight.

"You, in your panties, on a bed? *Very* good idea, Annie." He picked her up, pushed her back onto the mattress. He tore out of his jacket, let it drop to the floor. "I should have done it six years ago."

He didn't waste time now. His body covered hers, long and hard. Even through his clothes, he was like a furnace against her skin. His palm swept up her side. Annie clenched her teeth against the pleasure of that simple caress, the rampant need.

His lips were hot against her ear. "Maybe if I'd touched you more often, maybe if I'd been inside you, a part of you—if you'd known how I cherished every inch of you, you wouldn't have been afraid."

Her heart twisted. "No, Jack." Annie turned, cushioned his cheeks in her hands, met his eyes. "I knew. I knew."

His mouth flattened. "But it wasn't enough. You didn't come."

"It was everything." Her breath shuddered, and she traced the line of his bottom lip with her thumb. "That's why I didn't come."

A muscle in his jaw worked beneath her palm before he made an obvious effort to relax it. The corners of his mouth tilted up. "Maybe you can explain *that*. Later."

Nodding, she lifted her head. His lips met hers in a kiss of surprising delicacy. It shouldn't have been so soft, not when need and hurt lay sharp and pointed between them. But it was, his mouth gentle as she parted her lips, the touch of his tongue like a whisper across hers, coaxing a moan from her throat.

Bitter coffee, a hint of whiskey. She couldn't taste him, had never regretted the loss of that sense so much. But she could scent them, remembered their flavor, and the decadent slide of his tongue past her fangs sent a delicious shiver under her skin.

Magic hands, magic mouth.

With a groan, he deepened the kiss. Flavor struck, bright and blinding over her tongue.

Annie jerked away, scrambled to the corner of the bed.

"*Go, Jack.*" She wrapped her hands around the bedpost as if she could anchor herself.

It wasn't going to matter. She couldn't resist the bloodlust, couldn't stop once she'd had a taste.

Not unless he resisted, too.

He wouldn't. Jack had risen to his knees; he wasn't running. Crimson dotted the finger he'd touched to his lip, but he didn't look at the blood in horror.

And his arousal hadn't abated. His hair was tousled, his chest heaving. He lowered his hand to his side.

His eyes met hers. "Come, Annie. Take what's yours."

Not like this. But her body didn't heed her mind—only the thirst.

Her leap knocked him onto his back. Her hands tore at his jeans, shoved down to stroke his rigid length. Her womb clenched. He was thick, ready. She'd be filled, quenched, warmed.

His body arched beneath hers on a strangled groan.

Shaking, Annie lowered her mouth to his neck . . . and continued descending, into darkness.

The bloodlust shrieked a denial—but it was relief that carried her through to dreams.

SEVEN

FOR A HEART-STOPPING INSTANT, THE COMBINA-tion of cool skin and dead weight made Jack fear the worst: She'd been taken away from him again.

She'd fallen slack, her face buried in his throat. Her chest wasn't moving; he couldn't feel her breath.

He slid his fingers to her inner wrist. His blood ran cold, killing his arousal. No pulse.

Jesus, no no—

Then it was there, a soft beat against his fingertips. His guts in a knot, he waited. Almost ten seconds later, he felt another.

Swamped by relief, he pressed a kiss to the point of her pulse. She'd said she would crash soon; he hadn't expected it would be so dramatic.

Had the sun risen?

If so, that explained the curtains around the bed. They didn't fit Annie, now or then. But they would be practical—if she ever forgot to close the heavy drapes at the windows, the satin would still block the light.

Nights. She worked nights.

He began shaking with laughter. She'd made a joke of it, and his tired brain hadn't gotten it until she was prone on top of him, in a sleep that felt like death.

Awake from sunset to sunrise. Even with her speed—and any other abilities she had—that didn't give her much time to look for Cricket.

He could extend that for her.

Reluctantly, he rolled her over. No rigor; her body was simply limp. He tucked the sheet around her shoulders, let his fingers tenderly roam her face.

She'd dyed her brows to match her hair, but the makeup around her eyes had been washed away. Her lashes were pale fans above her cheeks. Naked—yet even in sleep, she didn't look vulnerable.

The points of her fangs gleamed behind her parted lips.

The cut on his own lip was stinging now, but it hadn't hurt when he'd scraped it on her teeth. No, it had been more like being Tasered. A hit of pure sexual need, arcing from her mouth to his cock, jolting his arousal to impossible, painful levels.

Jack hoped to God she woke up hungry.

THE early sun glared off the windows of Gallagher's house. Annie's brother pushed through the front door, and Jack slid on his sunglasses—more to hide his exhaustion and blood-shot eyes than to shield them from the light.

He'd stopped at his own house for a blistering shower and three cups of enamel-stripping joe, but the wait outside Gallagher's had been longer than he'd expected, and the edge the caffeine had given him was starting to wear.

So was his patience.

The heat soaked through Jack's T-shirt the instant he climbed out of his Land Rover. Seven-fifteen in the morning, and it was already shaping up to be a steaming bitch of a day. Hopefully, Gallagher would roast in his suit every time he stepped outside, sweating as much as Annie had searching the streets alone.

Gallagher blinked when he noticed Jack, then glanced back toward his house. The windows were empty, but a curtain was falling into place the next home down the row. Annie's mother.

Family meant so damn much to Gallagher that he'd bought a home that shared a wall with his parents'—and made his sister unwelcome in both.

"Running late today, Brian?" Jack's grin must have been on the maniacal side; Gallagher's friendly smile turned wary.

"Marnie and the kids are down the shore, so there aren't as many stops to make before heading in." He came to a halt, studying Jack's face. "What's up with you, Harrington? You're retired; you should be sleeping in, not haunting my yard."

"I'm looking for a favor."

"Ah, fuck me to hell. I knew this day would come." Gallagher's trapped expression was a good-natured, male version of Annie's. "All of those boxes. It'll be damn hot moving them. I'll need beer. A keg."

With a shake of his head, Jack passed him a folder containing latent fingerprints from the cane, Cricket's glass, and Annie's front and balcony doors. "I need you to run these."

Frowning, Gallagher set his briefcase on the concrete walk, flipped open the file. "Whose reference prints?"

"A missing girl, a demon, and—"

"God damn it, Jack!" A tide of red rushed beneath Gallagher's jaw, and he slapped the folder shut. "You might not give two shits about your career, but don't drag me down—"

"And Annie," Jack finished quietly.

Gallagher sucked in a breath. He fumbled through the folder, tugged out the ink impressions Jack had made of her fingers while she'd slept, and studied them as intently as he would a picture.

There was love in that gaze, and regret—and Jack wanted to ram his fist through Gallagher's face.

Never mind that he considered his former partner a friend. Never mind that he thought meatheads who resorted to chest-thumping displays of aggression were assholes. Before him stood a man who'd told Annie that she was dead to her family—a man who'd been cozily sleeping three blocks away while a demon had stabbed a cane through her stomach.

Gallagher had contributed to the pain *his woman* had experienced—and by God, there would be blood.

Jack shoved his hands into his pockets when Mrs. Gallagher came out on the porch, shielding her eyes against the sun. But he couldn't stop himself from stepping closer, nose-to-nose with Gallagher.

"I ought to drop you where you stand." He spoke through gritted teeth. "Six fucking years, you lied to me. Kept me from her."

"Back off, Jack," Gallagher said wearily.

"Left her to go it *alone*."

"Back off!"

The shout echoed through the street. A vein throbbed at Gallagher's temple, but apparently he realized Jack had no intention of backing down. Gallagher retreated a step, shot a glance over his shoulder.

Annie's mother had disappeared inside her house, but obviously intended to return; she'd left the door open.

"Christ." With a heavy exhalation, Gallagher staggered to his own porch, sank down on the top step. The folder dangled from his fingers, his wrists limp between his knees. "You didn't see Annie that night, Harrington. Licking the blood off her hands—her own goddamn blood—and she couldn't stop herself. Because she hadn't fed yet. She told us she hadn't wanted to, because she couldn't control the . . . other."

Gallagher averted his eyes, but Jack barely registered the other man's embarrassment. He wished Gallagher had punched him; it'd have been easier to take than the image of Annie he'd painted. Sickening, pathetic.

Heart-wrenching. She must have been terrified.

"Her *own* blood?" He rasped the question through an aching throat.

But Gallagher only nodded absently, either assuming that Jack already knew what had happened, or too lost in his memories of that night to hear Jack's confusion.

"I said things that I regret, but I don't know if I'd have changed anything. I had two little girls next door, and Marnie with another baby on the way. Dad was dead on the floor, Ma begging him to wake up. And Annie didn't have control." He lifted his gaze to Jack's. "She agreed that leaving was the right thing to do. That telling everyone she'd died was."

The right thing to do. The whole damn Gallagher family had a different definition of that phrase than Jack did.

"And I thought Annie and you hadn't been any more than buddies, hanging out here. You two sure as hell never let on," Gallagher continued. "I didn't know until the funeral."

When Jack had been shit-faced and broke down; he remembered Gallagher's shock and discomfort too well.

With a soft curse, he looked away. The urge to hit something didn't fade, but his anger dissipated into frustration and disappointment.

"I just didn't think that Annie would . . . not with someone she didn't know."

"She knew me," Jack said quietly.

"That's what I'm saying." Gallagher sighed, rubbed his

forehead. "I didn't understand it. Looking back, I could see how it happened with you. Yet by the time the funeral rolled around, she'd been shacked up with Dante for a week and a half. That's not the kind of thing you break to a guy who wept through the hymns."

Every muscle in Jack's body tightened. His stomach hollowed. But a soft step and a pair of light blue eyes prevented him from demanding answers.

Mary Gallagher glanced from her son's face to Jack's, then lifted the bucket she'd carried out. Chunks of ice floated in water.

"As you boys have settled down, I won't be needing this. Will I?" She sent a quelling look toward Jack, and he shook his head, the tension in his body fading.

He didn't know if it was something every mother could do, or just Annie's—but her calm manner and quick humor always put him at ease.

After setting the bucket down, Mrs. Gallagher wiped her hand on the leg of her trim blue pants, patted the blond hair clipped at her nape. "You haven't visited in a while, Jack. A part of me wants to dump ice water over your head for your neglect—the sight of you in a wet T-shirt would make up for a multitude of sins."

Gallagher's groan was almost as loud as Jack's laughter. "Jesus, Ma—"

"Don't curse, Brian," she said mildly, smiling up at Jack. "What brings you here now?"

Jack removed his sunglasses. With Gallagher, he'd wanted the shields. With Annie's mother, it felt rude to wear them. "I had a visitor last night."

Her gaze flicked to the cut on his lip. "What sort of visitor? You look like hell, Jack Harrington."

"Not as bad as the last time he ate your meatloaf, Ma," Gallagher said. "He's here about Annie."

Surprise smoothed her features, then relief. "She called you then. Is the girl still missing?"

Jack didn't correct her assumption; there was no need for them to know Annie had broken in, or why. By the time he'd finished detailing the rest of the evening, ending with Annie giving him Cricket's picture, Mary Gallagher was sitting on the step next to her son, her face pale.

"A demon," she said, horror lingering in her voice. "What can we do?"

Jack met Gallagher's eyes. "That depends on whether Brian will stick his neck out."

Gallagher stood, his face a rigid mask. "Your crazy obsession was never about Annie before, Harrington. Don't question what I'd do for her."

"Good, because I need more than prints. I want everything you can find on Lily Milton." When Gallagher swore, Jack ignored it and pushed on. "Particularly in the past eighteen months, since she left the Bureau."

"For God's sake, Jack. Her division's got more layers of security than the spooks do. I don't even know if I can get past—"

"If you can't, I'll go directly to her." He saw the frustration in Gallagher's expression, knew it matched his own. Milton was the last person he wanted to approach for information. "We don't know anything about what Annie's up against. Even Annie doesn't know much. But I'd bet Milton does."

"And when Milton stabs us in the back?"

Jack spread his palms, shook his head. Gallagher had more to lose than Jack did—and it wasn't the job or the salary that mattered, but the badge behind it.

"You'll be free to vacation with your wife," he finally said. There was simply no reassurance to offer.

"Marnie did mention she and the kids were missing you, Brian." Mrs. Gallagher stood up, patted her son's hand. "Now go on to work, so you can get started. Jack, you look as if you could use something to eat. I planned on hiking to Haegele's this morning . . . oh, dear. Try not to look so relieved."

A chagrined smile tugged at Jack's lips. It remained as Gallagher reversed his sedan onto the street, as Mrs. Gallagher returned with her purse.

He fought with his impatience—felt like an ass for it. He could always use more coffee and sugar, but there was too much to do before his inevitable crash. Catching up with Mrs. Gallagher wasn't at the top of his list.

"And now you look too guilty," she observed as soon as they hit the sidewalk. "You should leave that to old biddies like me. Do you know that for three years after Donald passed, I continued cooking for myself—because I was ashamed at how relieved I was whenever I ate something that I hadn't made. As if being grateful that I didn't have to eat my own cooking anymore meant that I was grateful he was gone."

Jack opened his mouth, but every response stopped in his throat. Jesus, what could a man say to that?

She smiled kindly, then gave his hand a pat, just as she had Gallagher's a few minutes earlier. "Of course, I knew that wasn't true, but it took my heart those three years to catch up with my head. And the guilt still tugs at me now and then."

Jack nodded, as if he understood, and immediately wondered if he should have shaken his head.

But Mrs. Gallagher didn't seem to notice his inadequacy; her gaze was soft and unfocused as she mused, "He was very traditional, Annie's father. And so long as I tended to the kitchen, he never complained about what came out of it."

Jack frowned, recalled the redheaded giant of a man. "He expected Annie to join the force."

The glance she slanted at him was puzzled; then realization slid over her expression. "His children were Gallaghers— and male or female, Gallaghers are cops." She stopped walking, her brows drawing together. "He was a good man, Jack Harrington. Fixed in his ways, strong in his faith and his ideas of how the world ought to be—but still, a good man. I enjoyed cooking, even if the results were terrible; if I hadn't, he wouldn't have expected me to do it. And he loved Annie enough to bend, to support her when she chose medicine."

"Yes," Jack agreed quietly. Unlike his own father.

"He loved her enough. But he wasn't flexible enough." Tears suddenly sheened her eyes, and she began walking again. After a moment, she continued, "As a mother, as a wife, as a woman—the night Annie came home and told us what had happened to her was the worst of my life. Not because of what she'd become, but because Donald couldn't bend that much. He thought he was doing the right thing. The *righteous* thing. And in the space of a few minutes, I went from wishing him dead to trying to save him, but his heart had just . . ."

She lifted her hand, as if to say there were no words, then delicately wiped her cheeks.

And that simply, it came together and ripped a hole in Jack's chest. The row houses wavered like a mirage, and he shoved his sunglasses over his eyes.

He'd contemplated the worst: Annie, losing control, killing her father. He'd wondered if the heart attack had been a lie, just as her accident had been.

But a different picture was forming, of a father who couldn't see a vampire as anything but damned. Who'd used his gun, and tried to destroy the evil he thought his beloved daughter had become. A mother's grief and fury turned against her husband.

Then Annie would have gotten up.

"We Gallaghers know guilt." She looked up at him, her gaze sharp. "Annie knows more than Brian or I possibly could, and deserves none of it."

It was Jack's turn to stop, a muscle in his jaw working. "Do you think I'd add to it?"

"I think that when you came to us six years ago, you were wanting a family almost as much as you wanted Annie. And you were still looking for that family after she'd gone."

He couldn't deny it. He'd jumped straight into a commitment with Jenn, had begun thinking of a home and children. Trying to re-create what he'd had with Annie, what he'd wanted for them.

And he'd failed, not because he'd tried to replace Annie—but because it hadn't *been* Annie. If he'd wanted a life with Jenn or any of the other women, he'd have fought to keep it.

In a low voice, he said, "If that was all I was looking for, Mrs. Gallagher, I'd have had it by now."

She studied him, then resumed their walk. "Have you considered that even though you've found her again, she can no longer give it to you?"

"No, I haven't." Because it didn't matter. He wanted the same thing he always had: a future with Annie.

And he didn't give a damn what form it took.

He drew in a long breath. "I appreciate that you're trying to protect Annie—but she doesn't need protection from me. I'm the least of her worries."

"I doubt she sees you as the 'least' of anything," she said, and her soft smile returned. "Do you know, even though

Annie and I have dinner once a month—well, *I* have dinner—I have no idea where she lives? I didn't know Cricket existed until last week, when Annie asked if I'd spoken with her. And she didn't ask for my help, even then."

There was no reproof or jealousy in her statement, but there was a question. A need to be useful.

This walk hadn't been time wasted after all.

Eight

Even sleeping, Jack was sneaky.

He'd trapped Annie on her back, his bare thigh heavy on hers, his arm wrapped across her chest. There was no way to scoot out without waking him.

Silently, she turned her head, and her heart contracted. Even with his face half-buried in the pillow, she could see his features were lined with exhaustion.

The perfume of her shampoo was thick in the air, the crisp scent of mint toothpaste, a lingering dampness. He'd prepared for bed here, but it hadn't been more than two or three hours ago.

She'd wait a few more minutes then—to let him sleep, and to savor the moment. It was the first time she'd ever woken up with someone next to her.

How wondrous that, of all people, she'd ended up waking next to Jack.

Each of his breaths was deep and even, his lips slightly open. His jaw was clean-shaven. The night before, she'd loved the roughness of it; now, she only felt the slow-burning anticipation of tracing her fingers over his smooth skin.

Had he anticipated it, too? He'd used her shower, her soap, but he'd had to have brought his own razor. Planning ahead . . . intending to be ready when she woke.

Intending to continue what her daysleep had interrupted.

Oh, God. The realization sent the bloodlust tearing through her. She whimpered, her hands fisting in the sheets. Her nipples stiffened, and she fought to keep her body still, to keep from arching and rubbing the taut flesh against his arm, to keep from opening her legs and rolling him beneath her.

He'd be hard after the first bite, and she'd have him inside her seconds after it jolted him awake.

Her hips rolled, once. She squeezed her eyes closed, shutting out the sight of his skin, the brevity of his undershorts, the strong length of his body that, even in sleep, didn't look or feel soft.

No, he'd never been soft. And with the sheets bunched in her fingers, she recalled how hard he'd been six years ago in her brother's backyard, long after everyone else had turned in for the night.

It had been his shirtsleeves in her fists then, her teeth clenched and back arched, her sundress around her waist. She'd had no idea where her panties had gone, and couldn't care. He'd been using his hands, and his tongue, until the stars had spun out of control behind her eyes. And he'd wrapped her legs around him then, rocked, rough denim and slick heat, biting her shoulder, shuddering against her.

She'd carried the bruise for two days, and it had healed within moments of her transformation.

And soon, she'd be drinking from him.

It had to be that way. Packaged blood could ease the hunger in the short-term, but didn't nourish a vampire. The blood had to be living.

It would be Jack's—and when she took it, she'd take him.

Not like this, not like this. Her mind chanted it, but her body and the thirst took up the rhythm, timed it to the pounding of her blood.

Her hips undulated. Her fingers dug into the mattress. *Hold still, Annie.*

"Annie?" The drowsy question sharpened with concern. "What's happening?"

No, Jack. Sleep. She just had to get to her nightstand—

Her eyes flew open as his weight shifted. He leaned over her, his hand cupping her cheek. "Tell me."

"I need—" Blood. To take him inside her. "—to feed."

His gaze lowered to her mouth, and she felt the rise of his cock against her thigh. "Then feed."

"No." She began panting as he bent his head, kissed the hollow of her throat. "Not like this, Jack—"

"Will it kill me?"

She shook her head, then cried out as his lips closed around her nipple. So hot. The bloodlust escalated, lifting her body, seeking more pressure, more pleasure.

Her hands found his shoulders. "Jack, listen, listen, *please*."

His tongue halted its devastating swirl.

"You don't know how it . . ." She stopped, regathered, forced it out as crudely as she could. "We'll fuck."

"Good," he said bluntly.

"Jack—"

"I lost you once, Annie. It taught me not to wait. Not when I want something." His eyes met hers, his face dark with need. "And God knows, I want you. More than I have any other— more than I ever will any other."

Her fingers tightened on his shoulders. "There have been others for me."

"I know," he said, and his voice softened. "I never expected that you'd wait another six years. Do they matter?"

"No." And that was the point. But he didn't know—couldn't understand. She needed to fight back the bloodlust, explain. "That's why—"

Annie's breath hissed through her teeth as he wedged between her thighs. Heated and thick, grinding against her aroused flesh.

Her craving spiked. With a ragged moan, she began to move with him.

"This," he whispered roughly against her ear. "I want this. To hold you, to be inside you."

She wanted, needed that, too, and it was shredding her control. The pounding of his blood filled her senses. "Jack—I can't—"

"I need to fuck you, to make love to you. To hear you, to feel you." He gripped her hips, rolled her over. Turned his head and exposed his throat. "However, whenever. Whatever it takes, Annie."

Whatever it takes.

She moved quickly. Her chest ached and her eyes burned, but she saw his confusion when he ran his fingers over his left triceps, found the injection site. She felt his shock when his gaze fell to the syringe in her hand.

"You'll just sleep," she promised hoarsely.

His anger rent through her psychic shields. Swearing, he struggled to sit up. She caught his shoulders, easily pushed him back against the pillows. His voice was already weakening.

She pressed her cheek to his, drew in his scent. When he slept, she bent her head.

And she fed.

JACK sat on the edge of the bed, his head in his hands.

Christ. He wasn't sure if it was a head or a bucketful of wet sand. Whatever Annie had stuck him with had put him to sleep for another hour, but he was still groggy as hell.

A glass appeared below his face. "This will help."

He glanced up. Her extraordinary eyes were cool, reserved.

His teeth clenched, but he took the orange juice she offered, and wondered how to cross the distance she'd put between them.

A distance he probably deserved. His skin flushed. Jesus, he'd gone after her like a rabid pitbull.

"You prepared well," she said quietly. "You already took the vitamins that were on the counter?"

He nodded, then tested both sides of his neck. The left was sensitive to touch, but there were no open wounds.

Her eyes followed the movement of his hand. Her lashes were dark again, her eyes outlined in smoky gray. "My blood heals it. Heals the bite. I did your lip, too." Her gaze settled on his mouth, then flicked away. "If you're hungry or dizzy, I can bring in that Haegele's box from the kitchen. I have to admit, the pastries even tempted *me*—but I thought you were a Dunkin' Donuts guy."

Her barely there smile was more barely than there.

"I am." A gulp of juice washed away some of the grittiness. "I bought them this morning with your mother."

"You did?" She sat gingerly on the bed, her attention never leaving his face.

Not distant, he realized. Wary. "Yes. She's operating under the assumption that, although you've kept this part of yourself separate from her, you have let me in." His mouth flattened into a bleak line. "Which makes two of us who assumed too much."

Annie stared at him, started to say something, then seemed to think better of it. After another second, she said, "What happened to your balls of iron?"

"What do you think, Annie? You've got them like this."
He made a claw of his hand, then twisted his wrist. "And you
know I turn into a sap when I'm drugged. Or drunk."

"Then I'm almost sorry I went out for your coffee instead
of dropping by a liquor store. Drink that first, though; your
blood sugar has probably bottomed out." She tilted her chin at
his juice, and her lips slowly curved. "And I can't wait until I
get my fangs into you again."

"Hurrah for me. Another nap." He looked away from her
fading smile and drained the glass, ignoring the twinge in his
chest that told him he was being an asshole.

But it ate at him. No matter how he circled around it, the
bare fact was she'd doped him so that they wouldn't have
sex.

Yeah, he'd come on strong. But for Chrissake, a sharp
word or a pinch would have brought him to his senses, and
he'd have remained still and just let her feed. It would've been
torture, but he'd prefer to lie on the bed with his dick on fire
than miss a single moment with her.

Hell, even if the effect of her bite meant that he couldn't
control himself, she was strong enough to hold him down.
She could have stopped any guy with little effort.

So why hadn't she done it that way?

Jack frowned and glanced over, then blinked. He'd been
brooding for three seconds, tops, but Annie wasn't on the
bed. His clothes had been laid out in her place, a clear message that it was time to get ready, to work; she'd already left
the room.

Fast. Strong. Yet she'd had a tranquilizer ready.

He dragged on his jeans, then stood in the cold room, staring at the bed.

Maybe it wasn't the guy she had to worry about. A little
scrape of Jack's lip, and sexual arousal had sizzled through
him like a lightning bolt. It had sent her tearing away from
him. If Annie had felt anything like he had, or if the blood she
drank amplified what he'd experienced—

Oh, Jesus love him.

There'd been others, she'd said. But Gallagher was right—
it didn't make sense that she'd immediately gone to another
man. After waiting twenty-eight years, she wouldn't have
hopped into bed with a stranger.

I'm sorry, Jack. I'm so sorry.

Six years, and he could still hear it so clearly. But she had nothing to apologize for.

Unless that was the reason she hadn't come to him.

JACK was angry.

Even over the anxiety twisting her stomach, Annie could sense it. And though he was trying to bury it, the bitter heat rose and skimmed the turbulent surface of his emotions.

When his footsteps sounded from the bedroom, she glanced out from behind her paneled screen, then continued choosing her weapons. Nothing that he'd been projecting showed in his expression. Five minutes before, she'd felt a spike of painful realization from him—but whatever conclusion he'd come to, he was apparently still working through it.

And knowing Jack, he wouldn't confront her until his head had cleared.

Almost on cue, she heard him pop off the plastic top of his coffee cup, and had to smile at the rip of a sugar packet.

Maybe she'd been right, then, to leave the bedroom when she had. When he'd woken, she'd gone in with the intention of explaining everything. But he'd obviously been feeling miserable—and between his shame, his sense of rejection, and her fear of his reaction, one of them would have said something they'd regret.

They just hadn't had enough time yet to sort through everything.

Her hands trembled slightly as she strapped on her holster. She paused, staring at her shaking fingers, her throat thick.

They wouldn't get much time.

She was beginning to exhibit the effects of alternating living blood with packaged. Soon she'd be tired, slow-witted—and one human couldn't supply all Annie needed.

But two vampires could drink from each other forever.

Her breath hitched. Slowly, she closed the cabinet, leaned her forehead against the door. Her heart raced, a thready beat, a need so deep that it felt like sickness.

Forever. With Jack.

It would be asking *so* much. Six years ago, they'd have been married, no question. But they'd both changed during their time apart, and transformation was more than marriage; it meant a completely different life, sacrificing the day, and concealing their nature.

Would Jack conceal his? He hadn't changed his mind about the cover-up Milton had done—but if he pursued it as a vampire, still thought to expose their kind, a demon might take notice.

A demon had taken notice before, with horrific consequences. Remembered fear shivered beneath Annie's skin.

Maybe it wasn't even *right* to ask him; a vampire lived with risks humans never had to face. When The Five had ruled the community, Annie's position had been too precarious, and she hadn't wanted them to know Jack existed.

Now the nephilim posed a greater threat than The Five ever had. What had changed, that she could consider bringing Jack into her life now?

From the kitchen, she heard Jack's heavy sigh, then his determined approach. Annie rubbed her face, composed herself before he came around the screen.

Cricket, first. And as they searched for her, Annie would let him see what it meant to be a vampire. He'd either choose to be the same, or let her go.

And she'd try to find the strength to move on.

Jack's eyes were solemn when they met Annie's, and he examined her features before his gaze dropped to her hip. "The guns don't surprise me," he said slowly. "You could always talk weapons and procedure with the rest of us."

She shrugged. "Cop family."

"Cops don't carry swords. You're good?"

Her fingers played over the hilt, and she nodded. "The first year, practicing was almost all I did." Reading the question in his eyes, she explained, "The community enforcer—Dante—needed a partner. I showed up at exactly the right time, had a background that fit what he needed. And when he was killed, I took over his job."

He frowned. "Only a year?"

"We move faster and think faster than humans, so we can fit more into a day. So that year was the equivalent of twenty years of training for a human." Although she sensed she hadn't taken the question exactly as he'd meant it, she continued, "I'm not as old as most vampires I hunt down, but most vampires don't train with weapons . . . and they didn't grow up with my dad."

"They just live normal lives."

She knew her smile exposed her fangs. "As normal as possible."

His answering grin broke the tension between them. He held her gaze for a long moment, then glanced at the cabinet again, tugging at his earlobe. Thinking. "You prepared for an emergency with weapons, money. Didn't that plan include where Cricket would hide?"

"Only if she was hiding from vampires. If it was anything else, she was supposed to hole up, open her shields, and wait for us to find her."

His brow furrowed. "Open her what?"

"Her mind. I'd recognize the scent of it. The *feel* of it." There was really no way to explain the psychic senses. Sometimes they registered as a taste, a scent, a touch—but were not exactly like that, either.

Jack was utterly still. "You can read thoughts?"

Annie shook her head. "Only emotions, and we can recognize an individual's distinct flavor. But demons are more powerful psychically—and we don't know how much more. It might be that they can take a location out of our heads. That's why we didn't plan one in advance."

His breathing was unsteady, but he nodded. "And when you went searching for her, you didn't . . . feel her."

"No. Which probably means her shields are up."

"Which means she's not expecting you to look for her."

"Yes," Annie said.

He smiled faintly. "Your mother and I might have changed that. Should we go?"

"Yes, but what—"

"You'll see." Jack snagged her jacket from the top of the screen, his eyes widening. "Jesus. What's in this?"

Annie stuck her arms through the sleeves, then opened it like a flasher.

"Because a woman can never have too many daggers," he said dryly. He stepped closer, running his fingers down the lining. "And pockets filled with . . . ?"

"Everything."

"No wooden stakes," he observed.

"No garlic, holy water, or crucifixes, either." She let the jacket fall closed. "I do have a few shuriken."

"Throwing stars?" He put a hand over his heart. "Quieter than a gun, more distance than a sword—and with a dark/ mysterious/sexy rating of ten. How's your aim?"

She struggled to contain her laughter, gave a cool shrug. "Decent."

"You rock my world, Annie."

Tears sprang to her eyes, and she looked away.

His grin faded. "But you knew that."

Swallowing to clear the lump in her throat, she said, "Not until you said it. For all I knew, everything you felt stemmed from six-year-old memories. Or that you were angry and uncertain because you can't recapture now what you felt for me then." She moved past him. "A person can feel violent without hitting, happy without smiling. I'm walking to the door because we need to go—but that's not what I'm feeling."

"And if it was?" His tone teased, but she caught the intensity behind it. "If I only have your actions to judge by, I might think that you only want me for my blood and for Cricket."

Annie pivoted. Before Jack could blink, she shoved her fingers into his hair and pulled his mouth down to hers.

She couldn't be gentle, not when she poured her longing into it, her heart. It was fierce and passionate, hungrier than the bloodlust at its sharpest.

His kiss was, too. She felt the powerful swell of his emotions, a match for hers. Desperate to touch, tongues seeking, breath mingling. He took what she gave, offered as much.

And together, it became more, pulsing into a low, liquid need.

With a harsh sound, Annie dragged her lips away. She forced her legs to stop quaking.

"So, just blood and Cricket? Whatever, G-Man," she said, and turned.

His breathing was as ragged as hers. "Maybe you're only hot for my body."

"Vampires aren't hot for anything—and you can't goad me into a repeat."

"Damn." He opened the door. "And now I can't wait until you get your fangs into me again."

"Nap or not?" She paused, met his heated gaze with her

apologetic one. "I should have explained, Jack, and I'm sorry I didn't." Her fingers smoothed over his left arm. "I don't plan to use it again."

"Good." He pocketed her keys. "What are you planning instead?"

"To explain," she said.

Nine

It had been hot that night, too. And a holiday weekend, so the ER had been busy.

"Kids with fireworks, idiots drinking too much before lighting up the barbeque or getting in their car—we had it all," Annie told him. Jack was driving this time; she stared out the passenger window, her sword across her lap. "I saw the paramedics wheel this guy in. Obviously DOA. A good portion of his frontal lobe had been sliced away, almost like a textbook cross section. Deep lacerations in his chest and neck—a near decapitation. The attending confirmed death, and then they must have taken the body down."

"To the morgue?" Jack asked quietly, and she heard him swallow when she nodded. "That's where you called me from. One in the morning, before you got a nap in."

And they'd only spoken for a few minutes. She looked down at her hands, opened herself to the flood of memories. "It was quiet down there. God, I was so tired. I'd been on since that night at Brian's—I was thinking of you when I fell asleep. And when I woke up, I was already dying."

"He got up." Jack's voice was hoarse. "The DOA you saw earlier."

"Yes. Woke up hungry, and without enough brains to have control. He hit my jugular, and I was a goner." No chance after that. No chance but a miracle . . . or something else. "That's when the demon showed up to finish the job she'd started on the vampire."

She glanced over at Jack. "You look as shocked as I probably was. She appeared human, except her eyes were red, glowing. And by the time she'd chopped off the vampire's head and got some of his blood on my neck to heal me, I was pretty much dead."

"But a demon—she?—saved you."

"Yes. It pissed her off, too; she bitched about it the entire time." Annie allowed herself a smile. "Saying that being friends with a vampire had made her a witless idiot. Saying that Lucifer would punish her regardless for letting the DOA get away earlier, but that the punishment for a human dying would be worse than turning a human into a vampire. Saying that she'd descended so far that she was doing a Guardian's job. All the while, telling me that I had to drink the vampire's blood, that I had to willingly accept the change for the transformation to work."

"And you did."

"I did, and she dumped me outside one of the community elders' houses. Flew me there."

Jack was silent for a minute, absorbing it all. Finally, he said, "Lucifer?"

"Yes."

"Jesus." He was quiet again. "What's a Guardian?"

"I'm not sure. There are stories about an army of men who are like angels, but I don't know anyone who's actually seen one." She hesitated, then said, "But when I was in New York, I heard them mentioned several times. Tied to rumors about the nephilim who'd been defeated in Seattle, and there's a vampire community in San Francisco that supposedly had help overthrowing a demon."

They stopped at an intersection. Jack glanced over, studied her expression. "You're wondering about them. These Guardians."

"Yeah," she said softly. "I want to know. And when I leave Philly, I'm thinking about heading that way. Cricket would like San Francisco."

"Count me in, then. Chasing down angels won't be any different than what I've been doing."

In the same instant, his answer lightened her heart and weighed it down. "And what is that?"

Jack shook his head. "You haven't finished explaining."

"Oh." Dread gripped her chest, tipped the scale to heavy. "So the demon dropped me off with the elders who headed the community at the time."

"Before The Five?"

"Yes. They took over a year later." Remembering his story from the night before, she met his eyes. "That's something else I need to tell you about. The demon came back."

He shot her a puzzled look. "All right."

"All right." She drew a long breath. "They said the same thing as the demon did—you have to be willing, that resisting the bloodlust can hurt the transformation, and those who do just waste away and die." Her shoulders hunched, and she barely noticed when she began rocking a little in the seat, back and forth. "And I was so hungry. Worse than when I woke up today. The DOA had had enough in him to change me, but I hadn't really fed. But Dante was there, said I could take his blood. And I was thinking how disgusting it was . . . but I wanted to live, so I just told myself to go for it, to throw myself into it."

"I'm glad you did, Annie." Jack's warm hand clasped her knotted fingers, and the echo of his words filled his psychic scent.

"The blood tasted incredible. *Felt* incredible. I was halfway done before I even realized that I was . . . That Dante and I were—" She closed her eyes, forced herself to finish. "Fucking. And it was good. Like it didn't matter what I wanted, who I wanted. So after we'd finished, I was just . . . shattered. And so ashamed."

"Annie." His grip tightened. "Don't."

"It was supposed to be you," she whispered. "We wouldn't have lasted until we married—but marriage was never why I'd waited. I wanted sex to mean something. It was important to me, that intimacy. Dante and I were as intimate as animals."

His other hand cradled her cheek, and she realized dimly that they'd parked. Her eyes burning but dry, she met his stricken gaze.

"And it stayed that way for a year. I was a tool to him, we fed from each other, but there was never anything else. I didn't want that with you."

"I understand that, Annie." Jack's voice was low and careful. "But even with six years apart, we had more between us tonight. It could never be just feeding. If all you did was stick your fangs into my neck and ride me, it still would mean more than that."

"There's an image." She tried for a smile. Failed. With a sigh, she finished, "I've only had sex when the bloodlust was in control. But I held on to you—the memory of what we had.

Now you're here. And I'll be damned if the bloodlust takes over the first time with us. Or the second."

"But it's all right the third time, hmm?" His thumb smoothed the corner of her mouth.

Her breath escaped in a silent laugh. "I do have to eat. But I promise I'll be gentle when I ride you."

"Ah, Annie. You destroy me." Jack dropped his forehead to hers, and she felt the familiar anger lifting through him, a multi-pronged hurt. Felt him battle against it before he said abruptly, "Let's go then. I couldn't find parking, so we've got a three-block walk."

The damp blanket of heat enfolded Annie as soon as she left the SUV. In the apartment above the street, a man yelled for his kid to get him a beer. Almost everyone had a TV or stereo on; some had both. Teenagers lounged on stoops, laughing, flirting, fronting. And over it all was the constant blow and rattle of ancient air conditioners.

Jack joined her on the sidewalk. He'd put on his light-weight blazer again.

"There's no reason for both of us to cook; you can dump the jacket," she said. "I have more than enough weapons."

"Everyone in West Philly has more than enough weapons."

They strode past a group of now-silent, wary-eyed teenagers, and Annie grinned. "They made you, G-Man."

"Or they're wondering how you escaped the Matrix."

"Hey, now. I don't wear vinyl and leather. Not in the summer, anyway," she muttered, tugging at the front of her tank. Sweat was already trickling between her breasts. "You should just tell me what's eating at you, Jack. Or I'm going to start thinking the worst—like you can't forgive me for being with someone else."

"Forgive you?" His brows snapped together as he rounded on her. "Jesus, Annie. The bloodlust slipped you a Mickey. You aren't to blame, and there's sure as hell nothing that needs forgiving."

Emotion clogged Annie's throat, but the hurt in him was still there, buried like shrapnel. She focused on it, precise as a scalpel. "You mean, nothing to forgive the first time."

"No. I mean every time. You feed, or you die, right? And if

you hadn't chosen to live . . ." He dragged his hands through his hair, then dropped them to his sides. His voice flattened. "Did you think I'd blame you? Is that why you didn't come?"

Whatever, she wanted to say. But his pain was at the surface now. This was the root, and it bloomed when she admitted, "I was afraid you might."

His bleak expression ripped at her heart. "Did you think me so small-minded, trust me so little that you thought I'd consider it a betrayal? That I'd judge you? I *loved* you, Annie."

She reached forward, caught his hand. Held it tight. "My dad did, too, and he—"

"Oh, Christ." Jack stilled. The bleakness melted into a well of compassion. "I should have—"

"Listen." He knew that her father had shot her, she realized—but she had to push past those memories. She couldn't dwell on them now. "You didn't have to judge me, Jack. *I judged myself.* I felt I'd betrayed you. If I hadn't, I'd have gone to you first. But I was trying to find the courage, and thought my mom and dad would be behind me, help me. And instead he . . . and I—" She had to stop, but Jack still deserved to know why she hadn't come. "I felt so guilty. For Dad, for Dante . . . for everything."

"You aren't to blame for either."

She smiled at his fierce tone. "I know. It took me a while to see. But at the time . . . there was just too much, all at once."

Annie let go of his hand, allowed silence to fill the space between them. Jack must have been thinking through what she'd told him; slowly, the anger and hurt faded.

They were almost to the house when he narrowed his eyes. "Here's what I don't understand, Annie: Dante."

She sent a cautious glance toward his profile. "What about him?"

"Come on. *Dante?*" His brows lifted.

She bit the inside of her cheek. It wasn't full-blown jealousy, but it was still some kind of male thing. "It wasn't his real name."

"He chose it? Jesus. Did he name himself after the poet or the guy from *Clerks*?"

She stopped, tilted her head. "Which is worse?"

"Did he wear flowing, ruffled shirts?"

"No," she said, grimacing. "But it must have been the poet; Dante was about a hundred years old."

"I bet he wore tights," Jack said. Then the humor dropped from his tone, and he pulled the keys from his pocket. "He had a century of experience, and something was able to kill him?"

"The demon came back," Annie said simply. "I'd actually been on the verge of contacting you—after a year of training, I'd worked through most of my guilt. But then everything changed."

Jack's head whipped around as the door swung open. "You would have called me?"

"Probably just showed up at your—" Her heart stopped. The scent from inside the house was faint, but unmistakable.

Buttery. Syrupy.

Annie drew her sword.

TRYING to provide backup for a woman who could search an entire apartment before he got past the foyer was a fucking joke—and Jack wasn't laughing.

But he was surprised out of his anger when Annie returned to the stifling living room, her sword at her side, her jaw set. Before he could say a word, she lashed out with her boot. An armchair flew across the room, smashed into a sofa.

Jesus, she was incredible. Awed, he glanced from the splintered chair to her face. A warrior woman—a dark, avenging angel.

But it was a damn inconvenient time to become aroused. Jack reined it in and holstered his pistol. "What'd he get?"

"Her computer, her cell phone, and a picture," she bit out. "His stink is all over the place."

"Eau de Demon Eggo," he offered.

Annie choked on a laugh.

His tone mild, he added, "If you ever go through a door like that again, Annie, I'll shoot you myself and save anyone inside the trouble."

She startled, then bared her fangs in an overly pleasant smile. "Whatever."

He'd insulted her, but it wasn't personal. "I'd have shot Gallagher, too. If we're going to do this together, *we'll do this together.* Don't leave me hanging with my dick out, jerking off and wondering where the fuck you are."

"Did you jerk off with my brother, too?"

Christ, how he loved her. "Annie."

She turned her face to the side, hooking her hair behind her ear. "All right. You're right. I'm just used to doing this alone."

"Then get used to a partner. You know how it works."

Even as she nodded, something passed over her expression—hope, yearning. But when she looked at him again, her features were blank, her gaze level.

"Let's do a walk-through then, partner; maybe you'll see something I missed."

He suspected that her sharp eyes hadn't missed anything—but Jack was seeing something new. He tried not to stare as Annie stepped to the side, and she observed the room with the detachment of a stranger.

That was familiar—but not because he'd witnessed it in Annie before. In the ER, she'd worn her heart on her face each time she'd fought for a life.

No, he'd seen it on her father and brother, on the faces of federal agents out in the field. And it probably mirrored his as he took in the living room, the worn, comfortable furniture, the little personal touches that declared it a home.

She was still fighting, he thought—but now, it was to prevent the harm being done, rather than repairing it . . . and exacting retribution from those she couldn't stop.

Annie had become a cop, after all. She had different rules to follow, but the heart of it was the same.

Vampire cop.

It took effort to check his grin.

Annie sent him an odd glance as they walked to the master bedroom. "What?"

Jack shook his head, focused. An array of pictures sat on the bureau, the pattern broken by the missing frame. Cricket, he recognized. The female half of the smiling, fanged couple in wedding clothes must have been her sister, Christine. A candid shot of a very young Cricket and a middle-aged woman faced the bed.

The giant bed—and no curtains, because there were no windows in the room.

His brows rose. "If you're married, why sleep with half an acre between you?" He'd buy a twin bed to share with Annie.

"Some partners sleep apart or in different rooms—especially if they're just together to feed." Annie hung back by the door, her hands in her pockets. "Stephen and Christine didn't. They snuggled."

There was a catch in her voice, and though her expression didn't change, she averted her face.

Jack glanced at the wide expanse of the mattress. Not just a bed, but a dinner table.

After Dante died, where had Annie eaten? "I opened a file on twenty-seven missing people," he said slowly, "and all of them lived with at least one other person. Not one was single, in twenty-seven. But you were."

She looked at him, then at the bed. Her chin lifted, gesturing toward the near side. "That was my spot. I didn't sleep here. I just came over every night, fed. Then they snuggled, and I either hung out with Cricket until they got up, or left for a job."

Stunned, Jack only stared. Annie, a man, and another woman. He should have been turned on, but what she described didn't sound sexy. Just lonely.

He finally found his voice. "Why?"

"They were my friends," she said quietly. "And I saved Cricket. When Dante was killed, and The Five thought it'd be best to rotate me through the community, Stephen and Christine opened their bed, instead. And they loved each other, wanted only each other, so I was like having seconds. But at least that meant the bloodlust, it didn't always—" She shifted on her feet. "Most of the time, it was just feeding."

He fisted his hands, turned away. *Seconds.* What kind of world was it when a woman like Annie was made seconds? "More and more, it sounds to me as if you should have taken your sword to these Five."

Her light laugh rolled through the room. "Oh, I would have, Jack—if there hadn't been five of them, and they hadn't always been together. Even at my best, I'd probably have only taken out three before the last two got me."

He nodded, then strode to the door and captured her face in his hands. "Dark and sexy rating of ten? I missed the mark. You're off the charts, Annie."

She grinned. "Well, there would have been six, but I took off his head . . . right there." She pointed down the hall.

He kissed her, hard and fast, then moved on to the next bedroom. Immediately, he noted the empty desktop—but it was the walls that had him blinking. "This is a twelve-year-old's room?"

Annie pursed her lips, nodding as her gaze traveled across movie posters. There were a few elves and pirates, but most were filled with fangs and blood. "She skipped the Disney phase. We tried, but she has a thing for Dracula. Luckily, she hasn't shown any interest in hardcore gore." A shadow passed over her face. "Probably because she's seen some of it."

"Right there?" He looked toward the hall.

"Yes. And God knows what she saw when the nephilim came in. There was a lot of blood before it ashed."

He frowned. "I thought you said there were only a few drops."

"There were. The sunlight destroyed most of it through the windows in the living room." She hesitated. "If we're living, the sun sets us on fire within seconds, kills us. A dead vampire or blood disintegrates into ash."

He'd already guessed that much. Jack nodded, idly glancing through a few brochures pinned to a corkboard. Haunted houses, theme parks, Eastern State Penitentiary's tours.

Cricket and Annie had planned to attend the Bastille Day celebration; would the girl still go?

Nothing, he thought, would be lost if he went during the day, looked for her. Annie could join him after sundown.

His brows drew together, and he turned to her with a half-smile. "If the sun kills you, Annie—does that mean a sunshine boy is a bad thing or a good thing?"

To his surprise, she didn't return his smile. Uncertainty trembled around her mouth until she firmed it, said, "Cricket wants to become a vampire as soon as she turns eighteen. I've convinced her to wait longer, because when you turn, there's no going back. And as much as you gain, you have to sacrifice, too."

"Like the sun," he realized softly.

Tears shimmered in her eyes, tore at his heart. "Most people choose to transform; they aren't forced into it like I was, and they have time to get ready. So I told her there's no need to rush—especially if she finds something she'd miss more than sunshine."

In two quick steps he went to her, held her tight. "Like a boy," he whispered into her hair.

She nodded against his shoulder, echoed, "Like a boy."

TEN

"Did you ever kiss my brother in a little girl's bedroom?" Annie wondered. In the visor mirror, she saw the lounging teenagers watch them drive away. She'd shown them Cricket's picture, and struck out.

"No. He never fixed his lipstick after I kissed him, either."

"What a strange partnership this must be." Though she kept her voice light, her heart pounded. She'd never been frightened like this. Even that night at the morgue—everything had happened too quickly. Now terror, hope, dread, and love twisted inside her, tightening, tightening.

"An unequal partnership," Jack said. "I have more questions now than when we went in. So tell me: the elders, The Five, the demon, Dante, and headless number six."

She nodded. How long would it be before it clicked for him? Not as long as it had taken her last night, she thought—but the elders' deaths had been the last thing on her mind when Jack said he'd resigned.

"The elders used to collect a tithe from the community," she began. "Money, in exchange for protection, and for contracting services from other communities and from humans: like providing identification for new vampires, or those vampires old enough to need new IDs."

Realization whipped through Jack's psychic scent. "Jesus fuck me."

No time at all, apparently. "One night, they called the community together. And halfway through the meeting, in walks the demon who'd transformed me. She announced that the elders had brought the community to the attention of the human authorities." Annie glanced over at Jack. "She didn't say anything about the human forger who'd been murdered, but thinking about it now, the method was similar to how one of the elders had killed the elder before him, and took his position."

"A vampire killed him." Jack shook his head in disbelief. "And then?"

"The demon changed. One second, she appears human; the next, she's got red skin and wings, horns, and two swords. Dante moved in on her, and—" Annie snapped her fingers. "Like that. I've never seen anything so fast . . . until the old man the other night. So then the elders looked to me."

Jack's pulse was racing. "And?"

"And she laughed and shot me." Annie shivered, touched her brow. "When I got up, the place was like a slaughter-house. All of the elders slain, and a few others who provided services. Christine told me later it had taken her less than fifteen seconds, and that she'd left them with a warning not to risk exposing themselves to humans again."

"And when The Five took control, they took that to heart," he guessed.

"Yes. Six, at first. But they went too far. If they knew of any vampire who still lived with a human, or had close relations with one . . . the Six decided that no human who could expose us should live."

Jack's face was grim. "Like Cricket and her mother."

"Yes." Her breath hissed out between her teeth. "I went to their house with him. I had no fucking idea what he'd planned, and I couldn't stop him in time. But when he went after Cricket, I got him. Then took his head back to The Five, and we struck a deal: I continue as their enforcer, stop any vampire who might bring the demon back, and they don't touch any humans. The damage had been done, anyway—the community quieted down, closed up. Those who had human family mostly moved away."

"You were in New York."

"Yeah, well—" Annie smiled, huffed out a breath. "The Five stopped tithing, and there weren't that many vampires who needed to be hunted down in Philly. So The Five hired me out to other communities, and kept a percentage."

"And instead of showing up at my door, you worked."

"I couldn't risk you."

He looked over. "And now that they're dead?"

"I don't know," she said quietly. "There are still the nephilim, still demons."

"Yes, there are still demons." A frown creased his brow, and he tugged at his ear. "What did she look like, Annie? The one who transformed you."

Annie sat up straight. "You're thinking that it was Agent Milton."

His eyes narrowed. "Obviously you are, too."

"Five ten, one-forty, black hair to her waist. Gorgeous enough to make a dead gay man sit up and beg."

"For a riding crop on his ass."

"Yes." Annie stared at him, felt his rising dread. "What's in your head?"

"It's 'Oh, shit.' We need to call Gallagher."

"Why? What has he—" She gasped, turned in her seat to look behind them. "Oh, fuck fuck, the fucker! Stop the car. I'll be right back."

Jack pulled over, grabbed her wrist before she could open her door. "Annie."

She glanced back. "It's not dangerous. Two seconds."

He nodded. Two seconds later, he ripped his hands through his hair, yelled, "You call sprinting between speeding cars 'not dangerous'?"

"Yeah." She shoved a sheet of bright pink paper in his face. "The demon bastard taped this to the bus stop. 'Found: Annie's Sunshine Boy,' " she read. " 'Looking for a Cricket Girl to Call Home.' And it gives . . ." She trailed off with a frown. "My cell number."

"Your mother was busy," Jack said, his voice even now, though his heart was still thudding. He put the vehicle back into gear. "Can't cook worth a damn, but she's a whiz with a copy machine."

JACK had never seen Annie so nervous. He should have chosen somewhere else to meet Gallagher—maybe a restaurant in Center City, where he and Annie could have arrived first and she'd have had time to prepare. He'd picked Tony's Pizza thinking that she'd be most comfortable in familiar surroundings, but he should have realized her fond memories of the place would only increase her anxiety.

She once regarded it as a symbol of family; now, it might just emphasize how splintered their family had become.

She took his hand in a death grip as they walked through the entrance.

Jack knew she spotted Gallagher and her mother the same instant he did, but instead of approaching their table, he spun her around to face him.

Her features were pinched with tension, and though she met his eyes, he thought her psychic senses were attuned to the table in the corner.

"Listen, Annie," he said fiercely. He saw her focus shift, knew her attention fixed on him. "Blood is supposed to be thicker than water—but we both know that's not always true. I don't know what's going to happen when we sit at that table. I only know that what's between us is thicker than water, thicker than blood, and I swear I will *always* be here for you. And I will love you until I die. Maybe longer."

For the second time in a few hours, her eyes swam with tears—and for the second time, she grabbed his hair and yanked him down to her mouth, kissed him until his brain leaked out his ears.

And when she drew away, the stubborn tilt to her chin was back, confidence glinted in her eyes. Her fingers threaded through his.

"You weren't even drunk," she said as they wound through the tables. The points of her fangs showed with her smile.

"I'm high on love, Annie."

She snorted, and was still laughing when they reached the corner, as she leaned down to kiss her mother's cheek. Gallagher stood when she straightened.

Wariness lurked in the other man's eyes, and Jack was seconds from punching him when Annie's mouth dropped open.

"You're worried that *I'm* going to reject *you*?"

Gallagher appeared baffled for an instant. Then he shrugged. "Not having you around for six years gave me a different perspective. I was an asshole."

"Was?" She rolled her eyes. "Whatever." Her smirk disappeared when Gallagher suddenly pulled her into a hug. Her eyes closed and her hands fisted behind his back.

Jack took the seat across from Mrs. Gallagher, and didn't listen to the quick, private words Annie and her brother spoke. He was halfway through a slice and on his second coffee before Annie sat next to him.

Gallagher folded a slice, popped a circle of pepperoni into his mouth. "You batted a thousand on those prints, Harrington."

Jack paused. "Even the one from the balcony door?"

He nodded, swallowed, and gestured to a folder by his elbow with the point of his pizza. "But get this: He's listed in military records as MIA, presumed dead . . . since 1968."

Jack looked at his greasy fingers. Annie reached, then placed the file between them so they could both see it, flipped to the first sheet. A grainy black-and-white photo depicted a young soldier with a jaunty cap, shaved head.

"Hawkins, Jacob, SP4. Out of Kansas," Annie read.

"A grunt," Gallagher said. "Went missing in Vietnam. And less than ten minutes after his info came up, I get a call from San Francisco."

"Milton," Jack said. He saw the apprehension on Annie's face, knew it matched his own.

"Yeah, but here's the strange thing: She was *nice*. Said that she understood I'd recently lost a sister, and gave me her condolences. So I said, Annie's not dead. Then she was quiet for about a second, before telling me that if I didn't get Annie the fuck out of Philly right away, she would personally bend my dick around backwards and shove it up my ass." He sheepishly glanced to his right. "Sorry, Ma."

"I can hardly be upset if you curse while repeating someone's words, Brian." She delicately patted her lips with her napkin. "I'm more concerned with what she said. Should Annie leave?"

"Not without Cricket." Annie's tone brooked no argument.

Gallagher didn't disagree. He simply picked up another slice, continued, "So she tells me these nephilim are killing vampires because of some prophecy saying that vampire blood will be their downfall."

Annie leaned forward. "How?"

"Your blood will weaken one. You get vampire blood on a weapon, it's like poison to them, slows them down. But not by much—so she said not to try it unless you've got no other choice."

She sat back, her jaw clenched.

Jack looked at Brian. "Did Milton say what they were?"

"Yep. They're demons who possess the bodies of humans who'd died and were bound for Hell. And that they take on the personality of the host—which means you've got one perverted fuck on your hands. One who has a thing for young girls."

Annie turned to the next sheet and paled, pressed a hand to her stomach. "That's him."

Jack studied the photo, felt his flesh crawl with remembered horror. Lawrence Oates. The bastard's sheet stretched back five decades: molestation, rape, child porn. His prison cell had had a revolving door. "You got an address."

"I checked it out," Gallagher said. "It's above an ice-cream shop, the ones where they make the waffle cones. His whole place smelled like them—but he'd cleared it out. Employees below said they hadn't seen him in a day or two."

"I need to be out there," Annie whispered, finally glancing up from the file. "I need to get back out there, be looking for her."

"All right." Jack wiped his hands, stood. "You got anything else, Gallagher?"

"Yeah." He looked from Jack to Annie. "Milton said you can expect a couple of visitors soon. She asked you not to shoot them before they can explain who they are."

Annie shook her head, shoved to her feet. "I'm not promising anything."

ELEVEN

Annie closed her eyes and submerged herself in hot water and bubbles. The throbbing in her head had eased, but her disappointment and fear didn't soak away so easily.

An hour remained until sunrise, and they were no closer to finding Cricket. They'd spent most of the night taping up more flyers, and Jack slowly driving while Annie had riffled through thousands of minds . . . until the pain in her head had prevented her from searching through more.

He'd been the one to force her to stop, told her to rest. That she'd been hurting too much to fight told her he was right.

The bathwater reverberated in a soft, even rhythm: Jack's footsteps. Annie automatically slipped her arms over her breasts, but his jolt of shock and horror had her erupting out of the water, snatching up her weapon.

Jack stood as if frozen. Then he shook his head, laughing quietly. "I forgot you don't need to breathe."

"Oh." Suddenly laughing, too, she settled back into the tub—this time, with her head above the bubbles. With a toss, the dagger was back on the sill with the row of lighted candles. She eyed Jack's T-shirt and jeans. "Are you coming in?"

He said something that might have been "Hell, yes," but it was muffled by his shirt, already over his head. Annie bit her bottom lip, holding back her quiet growl of appreciation as each long, rangy muscle was revealed, as he discarded his jeans in record time.

Her gaze centered low as he approached. She wanted to reach out, stroke him, but she kept her hands beneath the water, soaking up the heat.

She wasn't an icicle, but . . . "I'm not very warm, Jack."

He grinned. "It won't be a problem. Trust me."

She nodded, scooted back. He eased into the water in front of her, and she couldn't resist a nip at his taut ass.

"Already biting," he muttered as he settled between her legs, leaned his back against her chest. "Uh, Annie—although this is very nice, I can't do much in this position. And your knees are gorgeous, but I like to grab soft parts."

"You talk. *I* grab." She kissed the side of his neck, curved her palms over his shoulders, down the planes of his chest. "Our partnership is still unequal—because as hard as I try, I can't figure out why you went to a séance."

She felt his pained groan vibrating against her cheek. Her hands disappeared below the bubbles, her fingers running the ridges and hollows of his abdomen. "C'mon, G-Man. Spill."

"You go any lower, and I will." With a sigh, he tugged on her knees, wrapped her legs around his waist. His erection was hot against her calf. "All right. Milton pissed me off. And I couldn't understand how someone like that had made it as far as she had—but considering my experience, it seemed likely that she'd twisted the truth to suit her needs before. So I looked at her past case files. Flying out to re-interview, going over evidence."

Her hands stilled in surprise. "The FBI approved it?"

"No. It was on my own time. And I found discrepancies. Tiny ones, but when you added them up, you got a different picture than the one she painted. A picture that suggested some freaky shit, but it was still blurry—because in her files, she found a way to explain everything supernatural. But the witnesses I talked to weren't convinced, and it was consistent: visits from people who were dead, tempting them into various sins. People who changed their faces, had glowing red eyes. A few mentions of angels."

"No vampires?"

"Not many. And pretty soon, word had gotten out how I was spending my time—and I was ordered to back off. So I dropped Milton's files, but I was hooked. I started checking out locals, listening for anything that might be worth looking at: the cure rate at the Lady of Mercy, haunted houses, the séances." He paused. "Eventually, Annie, I'd have run into you."

She smiled against his neck, her heart huge in her chest. "You think so?"

"I think of Milton, of you taking Cricket around to the

same places I went, of all the different ways our paths might have crossed. Fate, God, or just dumb luck—I'd have found you again."

Emotion flooded her throat. With her hands braced on the side of the tub, Annie slipped around, straddled him. Heat flushed her skin, water and sweat slicked it.

His gaze fell. Tiny waves lapped at her breasts, bubbles played a peekaboo tease with her nipples. With the pad of his forefinger, he circled the pink tip, cleared a path. "So we're equal now?"

Annie arched into his hand. "Yes."

"You don't mind that, according to most of my colleagues, I've become a certifiable nutcase?"

"I suck blood, Jack."

He laughed, bent forward to sip a drop of water from her neck. A shudder ripped through her, tore at her control.

Her fingers streaked wet trails into his hair. She took his mouth with hers, a long and needy feast. His cock rose hard against her belly.

Then his hands found her, and she was drowning. She'd been overwhelmed with need before, but it had been like a blade, flat and sharp, a single destructive edge. Now it rushed in on a caressing wave, surrounded her with murmurs of love and wonder, with an eager, seeking touch.

As devastating as the bloodlust, but made up of so much more.

She clutched at his shoulders as he drew her nipple into his mouth, as he eased a finger between her slick folds. Her legs trembled, and he deepened the invasion, gently thrusting.

Annie gasped, writhed against his hand. Water slapped the sides of the tub, her ears filled with the desperate sounds she made, Jack's harsh breathing.

Her hands speared down, found him, stroked. His hips jerked beneath her, and he froze, strained to hold still.

Annie rose until the thick head of his cock pushed against her sex. "I can't wait," she panted. "I can't wait."

"Thank you, God." His head fell back against the edge of the tub. "Next time, Annie, I'll get my mouth on you for an hour—"

His words strangled as Annie took him in. Her flesh resisted for an instant, then gave way to the heated pressure of his shaft. Jack sucked in a sharp breath, and she leaned forward, cried out as he sank deeper, filled her.

"Annie . . ."

She rocked, took him in again. The uncertainty clouding his eyes burned through with need, but didn't disappear. With her lips against his, she said softly, "I waited, Jack. So my first time was after my transformation—and I healed."

He held her still when she tried to move. "Every time?"

"It doesn't hurt."

"Jesus, Annie," he breathed, but the uncertainty fell away. His hands anchored her hips, his mouth possessed, his tongue plundered.

Mine.

It was fierce, a claiming. Annie gripped his shoulders, claimed in turn: his body, his heart.

And, when he tensed beneath her, his blood.

BATHED in shadows, the curtains around the bed drawn tight, Annie lay on her side and stroked lazy fingers down his spine, hating the coming day. But he would fall asleep with her, she knew. His fatigue would take him down, as the sun took her.

Jack watched her, and when he spoke, his voice was heavy with exhaustion. "You only drank a little."

Her fingers reached the sheet draped over his hips, started back up. "I just needed it to have an orgasm. Not to feed."

"I'm not complaining. It was one hell of a jolt. And tomorrow?"

Her soft smile faded. "We'll go to the clinic. You can't every day."

"Annie—"

"You can't."

A long breath escaped him. Then he rolled, pulled her to him, chest to chest. He draped his leg over her hip. "We're snuggling."

She wiggled in closer. *"Now* we are."

"So this is what I've missed. Six years of cold hands on my cock— Don't you even think about moving them." He tensed. "Or, all right, move them like that."

She laughed, brought her hands back up to his chest.

"Tease." He said it softly, pressed a kiss to her lips before meeting her eyes. "Maybe it was best that you didn't show up at my door, Annie. I'd never have turned you away—but I don't know if this would have been so easy to accept, either. Not without all of the changes in my life; not without losing you first."

"I don't think a lot of people could accept it," Annie said. "And I couldn't blame them."

Jack held her gaze. "That's why you think the cover-up is right."

"I think many people would have the same reaction as my dad. When I weigh truth—people's right to know—against safety, I just can't put truth ahead of vampires who are simply living their lives. And seeing how meaningless it all is when a community is wiped out, for God knows what reason, only makes me more certain that exposure isn't an answer. But I don't know what is."

The constriction around her heart eased when he nodded, then stared thoughtfully up toward the ceiling.

"But you're right: You *are* different than you were six years ago," she said. "You're angry."

"I'm actually about as happy as I've ever been."

"Not right now. In general. The gloss has burned off—that gleam of idealism. Things touch you more personally now, you feel them more."

She felt the hurt at the edges of his surprise. "I've never been a robot, Annie."

"No, you were passionate, but it was almost all here." She touched his forehead. "Now it's here." Her palm covered his heart. "And it's wonderful, incredible."

He grabbed her hand, kept it against his chest. "Get me drunk quick, Annie—or tell me that you're still in love with me."

"A tiny part of me from six years ago is still in love with you." The words quivered, but she refused to let them break. "But the rest of me is falling again, deeper and harder than I did before. And it's not easy this time, because I know the risks, and I know the hell of not having you. There's fear there now."

"Too much?"

She shook her head. "I love you forever, G-Man."

He pressed his face to her throat, said in a rough voice, "Sunshine boy."

"Whatever."

Twelve

Jack struggled to wake, couldn't think past the heavy fog in his brain. Christ. Annie hadn't needed to drug him this time. And where the hell was that goddamn ringing coming—

He sprang out of bed, tripped through the curtains. The glow of Annie's cell phone in the darkened room led him straight to her vanity, and he snatched it up.

Silence greeted his hello, and his heart thudded.

"Cricket?"

He heard a gasp, a shaky breath. Young. A girl's. "Cricket, you know Annie can't be awake, so you must have called to leave a message. You probably saw a flyer outside, about a sunshine boy. That's me. My name is Jack Harrington, and I knew Annie a long time ago. So you can leave your message with me, and I'll tell her when she wakes up."

For an endless second, there was no reply, and he felt the dreadful certainty that she would disconnect. Then there was another shaky breath.

"She's not killed?"

The wealth of fear in that small voice made his heart ache. "No, sweetheart. She was in New York, and she's been looking for you since she returned. We're at her apartment now. Do you want to come here?"

"No!"

"All right, Cricket, that's fine." Jack quickly backpedaled, reconsidered. She'd been frightened away from here and her own house—neither location would work. Anywhere she might feel trapped could send her into hiding again. "Annie said that she'd promised to take you somewhere this weekend. How about we keep that promise?"

* * *

"You're sure?"

It was the third time since she'd woken that she'd asked him, but Jack apparently didn't take offense.

"I'll be more certain when she shows," he said. "But yes."

"God, I love you." She smashed another kiss to his mouth, then strode past him, yanked on a shirt. "Where'd she call from?"

"Gallagher traced the number to a pay phone—only two blocks from the penitentiary, as it turned out."

Where the Bastille Day celebration was probably in full swing. Everyone dressed as French peasants and aristocrats, reenacting the storming of the prison walls.

Giddy excitement rolled through her. She couldn't stop smiling, laughing. "And I just hang out near the guillotine?"

"And if she determines that it's safe, she'll come out."

"And you?"

His voice hardened. "I'll cover you, and watch for Oates."

Some of her giddiness drained away, and she methodically checked her weapons, strapped them on. "I should have invested in plastic explosives. Get close, slap it on, then blow his head off."

"Another day or two, and I might have— Jesus, Annie! Get down!"

She dropped, rolled, and pointed her pistol in the direction Jack was facing. His gun was out, his aim steady.

Two men stood outside the glass balcony door. The nearest one had his hands up, his brows lifted almost to his shaved hairline in amusement or surprise. Maybe twenty, she thought. The one behind him—darker, leaner, older—had no expression at all.

"It's Jacob Hawkins, Annie," Jack said softly. "The grunt who was MIA."

"Aged well, hasn't he?" Annie muttered, then gestured with her gun, inviting them to slide the door open.

"About as well as a vampire ages," Hawkins said as he stepped through, his voice Midwestern, friendly. "But we don't wrinkle so much in the sun."

"That's funny. Isn't it, Jack?"

"Hilarious," he said, his tone as flat as hers. "You've been here before, and scared her little girl away."

"I did." Hawkins grimaced. "We were looking for survivors

and cleaning up after those the nephilim killed. Unfortunately, I was on her before I noticed her. She has great psychic blocks for a little kid. Almost as good as some Guardians do."

Annie's heart gave a little skip. "That's what you are?"

"Yes." He glanced from Jack to Annie. "And I'd love to explain, but it's more important that we go get your little girl."

"You'd better explain *that*," Jack said, his voice like ice.

Hawkins gestured to his companion. "Alejandro, my silent but deadly friend here, has a better nose than I do. We were at Oates's apartment earlier today—and Alejandro picked up the same scent outside on your balcony."

"Oh, Jesus," Annie breathed in realization. Oates had gotten to Cricket's computer before them. How could he have known to get it, unless he'd been listening or following Jack and Annie? And letting them lead him to Cricket.

"He is not out there now." Alejandro spoke quietly, with a melodic Spanish accent. "But he may have overheard the plans you made over the phone."

Jack shook his head. "I told Cricket to watch out for him, gave her a description."

"But he is intending to use Ms. Gallagher to manipulate her, is he not? And he knows where Ms. Gallagher will be, and when she and the girl will come together."

Jack glanced at her in dismay, and Alejandro continued, "We will accompany you and assist you."

"Not him." Annie gestured to Hawkins. "If Cricket sees you, she'll take off running again."

Hawkins sighed heavily, then turned to Alejandro. "Why do I always have to look like the girls?"

"Shift," Alejandro replied, then looked to Annie. "He will be bait."

A second later, Annie's mirror image stood in Hawkins's place. Even her clothes, her jacket.

"Holy shit." Annie took a quick step back. She stared for a long moment, met Jack's astounded gaze, then glanced at Hawkins again, shaking her head. "It's not going to happen."

Hawkins reverted to his own form, his own clothes. "You're afraid that she'll catch on, and run—"

"Yeah, that about covers it."

"So you'll watch for her from above—from the walls of the penitentiary."

"When Oates moves in," Alejandro said, "so shall I, and distract him from the girl. With luck, I will slay him. A vampire could not."

Whatever. Annie's teeth ground together; she couldn't deny it. She didn't have the speed or the strength needed.

Alejandro's dark gaze met hers. "As humans, both the girl and your man are safe from Guardians and from the nephilim. You are the only one at risk, Ms. Gallagher. We want to decrease that risk."

"Annie," Jack said softly. "We *could* use the help."

Her hand found his. When Jack squeezed, she reluctantly nodded. "All right."

"Then we're off to a beheading," Hawkins said, grinning, and he turned to the balcony. Giant white wings sprouted from his back. "Who wants a ride?"

THE guard tower atop the old stone wall had only been used by tourists since the early 1970s, but it served the same function. Annie could see out over the prison courtyard and the front of the wall with barely a turn of her head.

Annie searched the sea of faces surrounding the silent form standing by the guillotine. Beside her, Jack lowered the binoculars Hawkins had given him.

"We *were* flown here," he said quietly.

A smile lifted the corners of her mouth. "Yes," she answered, equally low—though she doubted anyone was listening. Though occasionally bumped and jostled by the humans visiting the tower, no one paid attention to them. Probably mistook them for security.

"Just checking. Did you get much out of him?"

"No." Alejandro had been silent on the flight over. "Your guy?"

"He never stopped talking," he said, turning to scan the courtyard. "What did you do in the bathroom with him?"

"Traded shirts, so that he'd smell like me. I think he looked at my boobs. Well, *his* boobs, but— Never mind. Then he sprayed water on himself, so he'd appear sweaty."

"They know what they're doing, then."

"I hope." She glanced at Hawkins's familiar profile: her own jaw, her nose, her hair. "So he explained what they are?"

"Something about a big war in Heaven, demons going to Hell. Then a second war that the angels barely won, and only with the help of humans, so the angels passed their powers on to them. If you die the right way, a human can become a Guardian."

There was a right way to die? Annie shook her head, kept searching faces. "And vampires?"

"That first war, some angels didn't take sides. They were cursed. It's their blood that created the first vampires."

"Nosferatu," Annie whispered, and shivered against the chill that ran down her spine. "I've heard of them. They're like the monster version of vampires. I didn't know we came from them."

"Remember that flight that went down last year, London to New York? That was a nosferatu's work."

Annie frowned. "I thought it was a terrorist. They caught her, then she escaped."

"That story was Milton's work." He glanced at her. "Hawkins was in Seattle when the Guardians destroyed the nephilim there—and he trains with Milton in San Francisco, as well. He said that she *was* a demon, but she's not anymore."

Her chest was a tight knot. "Are we stupid to trust them? Stupid to think of heading that direction when we leave Philly?"

"I don't know," he said softly. "But I think there's a lot more to learn. And I'd like to find out."

She swallowed her fear, nodded. Hawkins turned his head slightly, and Annie followed the line of his gaze. Hope rose, then quickly deflated. Just a teenager with hair similar to Cricket's.

"Annie." Jack tugged on her sleeve, never lowering his binoculars. "The courtyard, southwest corner."

Annie looked, then had to force herself not to shout Cricket's name. God, she was quick. She moved smoothly through the jumble of people, and though it was late, though there were mostly just adults now, no one glanced twice at her.

"I can intercept her before she even reaches the guillotine," Annie murmured. "I could get her, leave the Guardians and the nephilim out of it."

She saw that Jack considered it for a moment before shaking his head. "If she screamed, made any kind of commotion, you'd just draw their attent—" His fingers tightened on the lenses. "Annie, look."

Her blood froze. Oates was threading through the crowd ten yards behind Cricket.

"He made her from her picture," Annie realized. "Oh, God. What now?"

Jack squeezed her hand. "Let it play. This isn't any different than what we planned."

But she hadn't known she'd feel so helpless. She tore her gaze from Cricket, stole a glance at Hawkins, and growled through her teeth. "He's not even looking in the right direction. He's expecting her to come from streetside."

Her heart racing with panic, Annie watched Oates quickly close the gap between himself and Cricket. Too quickly.

"Oh, God, Jack." Her fingers flexed. "I can't stand here and do nothing. I can't."

He nodded. "All right, Annie. You slow him down. But listen—if he comes after you, then you run, or you get behind me, or you use any other human as cover. No arguments."

"I don't have any." Annie yanked open her jacket, pulled out her throwing stars. A gun wouldn't slow Oates down. Just her blood. "You get Hawkins's attention, make him turn her way."

"Doing it now," Jack said, but Annie didn't look to see how he would.

She lifted her shirt. Just a slice across her belly, and she'd have the poison she needed.

A hand clamped around her wrist.

Instinct took over. Annie pivoted, jabbed up with her elbow. Was blocked. Her hand slashed up—and she stopped with the razor-edged point of the shuriken against a woman's throat.

Shock ripped through her. Annie knew that woman's face. But the eyes weren't red, weren't glowing.

From beside her, Jack's voice was cold, deadly. "Back off, Milton. Right now."

Milton's gaze didn't waver from Annie's. "Throwing that would have been a good idea . . . if we'd held up our end of the plan," Milton said. Her dark eyes were fearless—and amused. "But about five minutes ago, Alejandro sniffed someone out. So we made a few changes."

"Annie?"

The small, uncertain voice came from behind Milton. Annie pushed the woman aside, stared. "Cricket?"

Cricket's face was pale. Her hands were fisted around her backpack straps. "The angel said you were here—"

Annie flew forward, scooped her up. Clutched her tight. "Oh, sweetie. I missed you. Are you okay?"

Thin arms wound around her neck, hugged her back. "I was so scared."

"I know, sweetie." Her voice broke. "I know."

"Annie," Jack said softly. "Come look at this."

She led Cricket over to him, her wary gaze on Milton.

Milton waved her hand in a dismissive gesture. "Don't mind me. I'm just here for the show." She stepped close to the wall, looked over. "Fireworks." She glanced back at Annie. "I recall that there were fireworks the night we met."

Jack drew Annie in against his side, tucked Cricket between them. "Agent Milton—"

"It's Lilith now. And watch, for one minute. There's Alejandro, letting the nephil in close. If Oates's perversion wasn't so strong, the demon inside would have probably recognized the difference by now."

Annie looked. Oates was only a step behind the shape-shifted Guardian, and twisted pleasure had taken over his face.

"Now, Alejandro, he's got a special little Gift. Of all of the Guardians' powers, it's one of my favorites. *He* doesn't enjoy it so much, of course, but it does come in handy. Particularly when he has a string of explosives to wrap the nephil in."

It was almost too fast. Still in a little girl's form, Alejandro turned. He caught Oates's arm, while his own whipped around. Oates began to transform: growing, black wings sprouting. Then the Guardian's white wings spread wide.

And they both burst into flames. Engulfed, they shot straight up into the air like the launch of a rocket.

Annie's head snapped back as she followed the streak of light into the sky. "Oh, my God," she whispered.

"Get distance from him," Lilith said quietly, staring up. "Get a safe distance, you stupid—"

The explosion split the air, scattering bursts of colored light.

Surprise and appreciation lifted through the crowd, smatterings of applause. No fear—no one had really *seen*.

Annie looked for Hawkins. He was gone. Lilith stepped to the side, spoke urgently into her cell. "Tell me you caught him, Jake, or I'll rip your wings off."

A second later, she lowered her phone. "Burns to heal," she announced. "But that takes almost no time. Now, Harrington, Gallagher—tell me you are coming to San Francisco. I could use you both at Special Investigations; we won't even have to train you as much as we do others."

Jack's arm tightened around Annie's waist, on Cricket's shoulder. "To do what?"

She frowned, as if it should have been obvious. "To save the world, of course." Her gaze shifted to Annie. "And if you need a partner, we'll work something out."

"She has one," Jack said.

Lilith's brows lifted, and she looked pointedly at his mouth. "Not yet."

Thirteen

Annie called Brian for a ride. He showed up with their mother, and Annie and Jack sat in the backseat with Cricket between them.

She'd hidden in the penitentiary, she told them, in a little, unused office that she could slip off to during the last tour of the night, and curl up under the desk.

"I'm sneaky," Cricket announced.

Annie nodded. "Just like Jack."

She stole a shy glance at him, smiled. "And during the day, I went to the theaters. I saw the new Batman thirty times," she said, with something that sounded like pride, and Annie didn't let herself break, though all she could imagine was a squalid, dark little room—and Cricket sleeping, cold and alone, with nightmares of the nephilim for company.

And then spending her days in darkness, too.

Halfway to Annie's building, Cricket went from animated to sound asleep. She didn't stir when Annie carried her from the car, and the girl felt as insubstantial as a feather in her arms.

But maybe it was only Annie's own strength that made it seem so.

"Kids are resilient, Annie," her mother said as they rode up the elevator. "She'll be all right."

Annie closed her eyes. "She'll be alone most of the day."

Making sure the night-light glowed in the corner of the guest room, Annie placed Cricket on the bed. Sat with her, listened to Jack describe the night's events to her mother and brother. And finally stood up when she heard him at the bedroom door.

Love shone in his gaze, and she went to him, let him hold her. She was on the verge of crumpling when Cricket rolled over, said in a voice that had no trace of a little girl, "Are you leaving again, Annie?"

"No." She dashed her tears from her cheeks before she

turned, stalked to the bed. "And if I ever have to go, I'll take you with me."

Cricket sat up. "Swear?"

"Yes," Annie said, and drew one of her daggers. With a quick slice, she opened her own palm. "Give me yours."

Cricket's eyes widened; solemnly, she held out her hand.

The cut was tiny, and Annie threaded their fingers together, palm to palm. "You're my blood now, my family. I might not always be there when you wake up, but I will always look for you if you are lost, I will never turn you away, and I will fight to the death to keep you safe. You're my sunshine girl, Cricket." She felt the weight of Jack's hand on her shoulder, the warmth of his body at her back. "And someday, when he knows you better, loves you like I do, my sunshine boy will swear this, too. And you'll have both of us. All right?"

"Yes." Tears trembled on her lashes, and she looked at her palm. Annie used a tissue to wipe it clean; the wound had already healed.

"You're the bravest girl I know, Cricket," she said, and pressed a kiss to her forehead. "Someone will be here when you wake up. I swear that, too."

In the kitchen, Brian got to his feet when she and Jack returned from Cricket's room. "She's sleeping?"

Annie nodded, not trusting her voice. She didn't know what to do. Simply did not know. Cricket needed a normal life—but there was no way Annie could let her go.

Jack rounded the counter, opened the Haegele's box. After selecting three pastries, he took a bite of the first. "Mrs. Gallagher," he said, "would you be willing to stay overnight, be here tomorrow while we're sleeping?"

"Of course." Her eyes were worried, Annie saw. She kept looking beyond Annie to Cricket's bedroom door. "But, Annie—will that be enough?"

Jack was already working on the second, a bear claw of apples and cinnamon. "What do you mean?"

"You mentioned California, Jack. Are you and Annie considering moving there?"

"Yes," Annie answered while Jack licked sugar from his fingers.

"Well, as much as I enjoy living near my grandchildren, Brian doesn't need me."

He frowned, as if wondering how he'd been brought into this. "Ma—"

"Hush. I'm still young, I've got a big empty house with no one in it, and I'd prefer to be useful. I think Cricket and I could get along fine during the days. Here or in San Francisco."

"And I'm sure we'd love to visit, Annie," Brian put in before she could reply. "My girls are about her age now."

Annie held up her hands. "Give me a second. Jesus." She looked at Jack. "What do you think?"

He polished off the last Danish. "I think it sounds about perfect."

The wonder of it swelled in her chest, and she nodded, fighting tears. "Yes. Absolutely perfect."

Aппiе was in her bedroom, standing at the window with the drapes open when Jack returned from Mayfair. He dropped a duffel bag by her closet, wrapped his arms around her.

"It makes a difference, doesn't it?" he asked. "Knowing the Guardians are out there—that it's not just us against the demons."

Us. Warmth and hope spilled through her. She and Jack would move on, leaving nothing but phantoms behind.

And they'd take the memory of one hundred and thirty lives with them.

"Yes," she said quietly. "And knowing that we can help."

His arms tightened. "Your mom went straight to Cricket's room," he said. "Long night for her."

"For me, they're never long enough." She rested her head against his shoulder. "You smell like Tastykakes."

"I ate a cartonful on the way back. My last meal. Oh, Jesus, Annie—don't cry." He turned her, smoothed his thumbs down her cheeks. "This is what you want, isn't it?"

"Yes. More than anything." Overwhelmed, she closed her eyes. "But do you want it? For yourself."

His hands slid down over her bottom. In a quick move, he hitched her up, her thighs around his waist, his erection hard between her legs.

He began walking toward the bed, and Annie bit back her moan. His voice was rough in her ear. "Doesn't that feel like it's for me?"

"I hope it's for me, too, G-Man."

Jack grinned, tumbling her onto the mattress and following her down. "My dark/sexy rating goes up. I can lick you underwater until you scream. I can toss cars. I can love you forever."

"Oh, Jack." Though she was laughing, tears rushed in. "You won't see the sun again."

"Annie." He turned until she rose over him. Gently, his fingers traced the curve of her smile. "Yes, I will."